Praise for *Murder of Angels*

"I love a book like this that happily blends genres, highlighting the best from each, but delivering them in new configurations. . . . In *Murder of Angels*, the darkness is poetic, the fantasy is gritty, and the real-world sections are rooted in deep and true emotions. Lyrical and earthy, *Murder of Angels* is that rare book that gets everything right."
—Charles de Lint

"[Kiernan's] punk-rock prose and the brutally realistic portrayal of addiction and mental illness make *Angels* fly." —*Entertainment Weekly* (A-)

"Kiernan's best book to date, joining her always-prodigious gift for language with a wrenching, compelling story." —*Locus*

"Kiernan can write like a banshee. . . . [She] paints her pages in feverish, chiaroscuro shades. A bridge to the beyond, built out of exquisite dread." —*Kirkus Reviews*

Praise for *Low Red Moon*

"The story is fast-paced, emotionally wrenching, and thoroughly captivating. . . . Kiernan only grows in versatility, and readers should continue to expect great things from her." —*Locus*

"*Low Red Moon* fully unleashes the hounds of horror, and the read is eerie and breathtaking. . . . The familiar caveat 'not for the faint of heart' is appropriate here—the novel is one of sustained dread punctuated by explosions of unmitigated terror." —*Irish Literary Review*

"Effective evocations of the supernatural . . . a memorable expansion of the author's unique fictional universe." —*Publishers Weekly*

Praise for *Threshold*

"*Threshold* is a bonfire proclaiming Caitlín R. Kiernan's elevated position in the annals of contemporary literature. It is an exceptional novel you mustn't miss. Highly recommended." — *Cemetery Dance*

continued . . .

"A distinctively modern tale that invokes cosmic terrors redolent of past masters H. P. Lovecraft and Algernon Blackwood . . . a finale that veers unexpectedly from a seemingly inevitable display of supernatural fireworks to a subtly disarming denouement only underscores the intelligence behind this carefully crafted tale of awe-inspired nightmare." —*Publishers Weekly*

"[Caitlín R. Kiernan is] the most singular voice to enter the genre since Neil Gaiman popped up in graphic novels and Stephen King made movies live inside books. . . . If you haven't sampled her work yet, you haven't really been reading the future of horror and dark fantasy, only its past." —SF Site

"Kiernan's prose is tough and characterized by nightmarish description. Her brand of horror is subtle, the kind that is hidden in the earth's ancient strata and never stays where it can be clearly seen." —*Booklist*

"*Threshold* confirms Kiernan's reputation as one of dark fiction's premier stylists. Her poetic descriptions ring true and evoke a sense of cosmic dread to rival Lovecraft. Her writing envelops the reader in a fog concealing barely glimpsed horrors that frighten all the more for being just out of sight." —*Gauntlet*

Praise for *Silk*
**Winner of the International Horror Guild Award for Best First Novel
Finalist for the Bram Stoker Award for Best First Novel
Nominated for the British Fantasy Award**

"Caitlín R. Kiernan draws her strength from the most honorable of sources, a passion for the act of writing. Her tightly focused, unsparing, entranced gaze finds significance and beauty in the landscape it surveys." —Peter Straub

"A remarkable novel . . . deeply, wonderfully, magnificently nasty." —Neil Gaiman

"A daring vision and an extraordinary achievement. . . . Caitlín R. Kiernan is an original." —Clive Barker

"Caitlín R. Kiernan writes like a Gothic cathedral on fire. . . . [Her] work is populated with the physically freaky, mentally unstable, sexually marginalized characters who have caused so much consternation in conventional circles—but Caitlín R. Kiernan is headed in an entirely different direction. Her unfolding of strange events evokes not horror, but a far larger sense of awe." —Poppy Z. Brite

DAUGHTER
OF HOUNDS

CAITLÍN R. KIERNAN

A ROC BOOK

ROC
Published by New American Library, a division of
Penguin Group (USA) Inc., 375 Hudson Street,
New York, New York 10014, USA
Penguin Group (Canada), 90 Eglinton Avenue East, Suite 700, Toronto,
Ontario M4P 2Y3, Canada (a division of Pearson Penguin Canada Inc.)
Penguin Books Ltd., 80 Strand, London WC2R 0RL, England
Penguin Ireland, 25 St. Stephen's Green, Dublin 2,
Ireland (a division of Penguin Books Ltd.)
Penguin Group (Australia), 250 Camberwell Road, Camberwell, Victoria 3124,
Australia (a division of Pearson Australia Group Pty. Ltd.)
Penguin Books India Pvt. Ltd., 11 Community Centre, Panchsheel Park,
New Delhi - 110 017, India
Penguin Group (NZ), cnr Airborne and Rosedale Roads, Albany,
Auckland 1310, New Zealand (a division of Pearson New Zealand Ltd.)
Penguin Books (South Africa) (Pty.) Ltd., 24 Sturdee Avenue,
Rosebank, Johannesburg 2196, South Africa

Penguin Books Ltd., Registered Offices:
80 Strand, London WC2R 0RL, England

First published by Roc, an imprint of New American Library,
a division of Penguin Group (USA) Inc.

First Printing, January 2007
10   9   8   7   6   5   4   3   2

 REGISTERED TRADEMARK—MARCA REGISTRADA

LIBRARY OF CONGRESS CATALOGING-IN-PUBLICATION DATA:
Kiernan, Caitlín R.
Daughter of hounds / Caitlín R. Kiernan.
p. cm.
ISBN-13: 978-0-451-46125-4
ISBN-10: 0-451-46125-8
I. Title.
PS3561.I358D38 2007
813'.54—dc22   2006018475

Set in Sabon
Designed by Ginger Legato

Printed in the United States of America

For my agent, Merrilee Heifetz, for whom I will someday
write a *pleasant* book...

...and for Poppy and Chris and the city of New Orleans.
May the days ahead be kinder.

In memory of Elizabeth Tillman Aldridge.
(1970–1995)

AUTHOR'S NOTE

The attentive reader will note several obvious debts that this book owes to the works of Howard Phillips Lovecraft (1890–1937), as well as to Sir Richard F. Burton (1821–1890) and his classic English translation of Antoine Galland's French rendering of the original Arabic *Alf Layla* (*The Thousand and One Nights*, c. 850 CE). Considering the medieval legend that anyone foolish enough to read the whole of *The Thousand and One Nights* would go mad, it seems not unlikely that it may have served, in part, as the inspiration for Lovecraft's Arabic *Necronomicon*.

Never once has a novel come easily to me, but I think it's safe to say that I've never written one during a time of such personal and emotional turmoil as I endured during the two long years spent writing *Daughter of Hounds*. My grateful thanks to everyone who has made these difficult times a little less so, but especially to Kathryn (my own heart's Book of Shadows), Jim Shimkus and Jennifer Lee, Byron White, Jada Walker and Katharine Stewart, Anita W. Nicker (my girl in Barcelona), my mother, William Schafer and Subterranean Press, Nar'eth ni'glecti Mericale (figment, familiar, reluctant goddess, and five-time alter ego), John Morgan (this book's first editor), and Liz Scheier (its second) for all their enthusiasm, insight, and encouragement, the intrepid Travis Burton (who got me into the old train tunnel beneath College Hill), and to my agent, Merrilee Heifetz. A special thank you to Dr. Richard B. and Carol Pollnac for their generous aid and hospitality during the summer of 2004, while I was scouring Rhode Island and Massachusetts for the black keys with which to unlock this story, as well as to the staff of the Robert W. Woodruff Library and the William L. Matheson Reading Room (Emory University) and the Providence Athenaeum. And also to the readers who've stuck with me all these years and, particularly, to everyone who's been brave enough to subscribe to *Sirenia Digest*. Shine on, all of you.

This novel was written on a Macintosh iBook.

All look and likeness caught from earth,
All accident of kin and birth,
Had passed away. There was no trace
Of aught on that illumined face,
Upraised beneath the rifted stone
But of one spirit all her own—
She, she herself, and only she,
Shone through her body visibly.

—SAMUEL TAYLOR COLERIDGE

I lost a world the other day.
Has anybody found?
You'll know it by the row of stars
Around its forehead bound.

—EMILY DICKINSON

PROLOGUE

I

The ghoul lady takes out her white linen handkerchief and uses one corner to dab at her watering left eye. It's an old wound, a relic of her spent and reckless youth, but it still bothers her sometimes, especially when the weather Above is wet. And today the weather Above is very wet, all of Providence caught up in the final, rainy, death-rattle sighs of something that was a hurricane only a few days before. She sits on the wooden stool that's been provided for her and blinks and gazes down her long muzzle at the dozens of faces staring impatiently back at her from the candlelight and shadows trapped beneath the Old North Burial Ground. The restless assembly of her wards, ghoul pups and human changelings seated together on the damp earth, wriggle about and whisper among themselves. She clicks her teeth together once, a sound that might draw blood, and they grow a little quieter. She wishes again that she were back in the warmth of her own dry burrow, deep beneath the basement of the old yellow house on Benefit Street, the familiar weight of College Hill pressing down around her, protecting her ancient, aching bones and her bad eye from this damned inclement weather.

"Myself, I would have postponed this outing," she says, and not for the first time that night, "but Master Shardlace feels most *emphatically* that schedules are made to be kept, so here we are, one and all."

Up front, one of the changelings sneezes.

"Likely as not," says Madam Terpsichore, addressing the child directly, "we shall *all* catch our deaths this evening. But let us not falter an instant in our dedication. At least the program shall not be disrupted." And with that, she shifts her poppy-colored eyes towards the spot where Master Shardlace, lately of the Mystic and Stonington Village warrens, is crouched, half-hidden by the dangling roots of a sycamore tree. He flinches at her glance, and that gives her some small measure of satisfaction. "Wipe your nose," she barks at the child who sneezed, and it does so.

"The question at hand," Madam Terpsichore continues, "that most *urgent* matter of history and propriety and etiquette which has brought us forth from the succor and haven of our dens, which has brought—nay, *dragged*—us each and every one out into this *tempest . . .*" And she pauses here to spare another acid glance for Master Shardlace and his roots. He pretends not to notice. "The question," she says, "is, indeed, a *grave* thing."

A few of the students snicker at the pun while Madam Terpsichore dabs at her eye again. One careless moment more than a century ago and she still bears this scar, the ugly mark of a lost instant's indecision, an insult that she would have done well to let pass. Then tonight her eye would not be throbbing and watering as though it envied the storm Above.

"A wonder we are not all drowned," she says dramatically and shakes her head.

"The *lesson*," Master Shardlace growls softly from his hiding

place, prompting her, risking another glare or something more substantial. "If we could only proceed, we would sooner find ourselves
home and snug again."

"Oh, most *assuredly*," Terpsichore hisses between her long incisors
and eyeteeth, and he looks quickly down at the ground between his
splayed feet and retreats deeper into the tangled veil of sycamore roots.
She wonders, for the hundredth or so time, exactly what he might
have done to deserve his exile and, more important, why ever Master
Danaüs chose to give him safe haven in Providence. And, more important still, what *she* must have done to so displease the dark gods that
she deserves to be weighted with such an officious waste of hide and
bone and sinew. Her bad eye weeps, and she wipes the tears away.

"Yes," she sighs. "The lesson at hand." And the ghoul draws
a deep breath, filling her lungs with air that smells and tastes and
knows of the subtle complexities of mere human death, the turning
of great stone wheels upon the infinite axis of time, the sugar-sweet
reek of loss and forgetfulness and regret, slow rot and embalming
and scurrying black beetles. Above, the storm reminds her that summer has finally given way to autumn, the orangebrowngolden season
of harvest, of reaping, of closing doors and grinning pumpkins, and
if her kind ever had a season in *this* world, it would be autumn. She
makes a tight fist and squeezes until her claws draw claret droplets
of blood; then Madam Terpsichore opens her left hand and holds it
out for all to see.

"We play so desperately at being fearsome things," she says, and
her sooty lips curl back in an expression that is not nearly so kind
as a smile, but still something more charitable than a snarl or a gri-
mace. One of the changelings coughs then, the same girl who sneezed
a few seconds before, a pretty, ginger-haired girl who has chosen for
herself the name of Sparrow Spooner, a name she borrowed from
a tombstone, as has always been the custom of the stolen ones, the
Children of the Cuckoo.

"Take strength, child," Madam Terpsichore tells Sparrow Spooner, and the *ghul* offers her bleeding hand to the girl. "Warm yourself against the cold and the wet and what's to come."

Sparrow Spooner hesitates, glancing anxiously from Madam Terpsichore to the faces of the other students. She can see that some of them are jealous of her, and some are frightened for her, and some are hardly paying any mind at all. A pup named Consequence rolls his yellow eyes, and a boy who hasn't yet taken a name sticks out his tongue at her. She turns back to the ghoul, not pretending that she has a choice, and crawls on her hands and knees until she's kneeling in front of Madam Terpsichore's stool.

"We need the world to think us monsters," the ghoul says to her, "and so monsters we become."

The girl leans forward and begins to lick at the blood oozing from her mistress' leathery, mottled palm.

"We must, all of us, keep apart the night from the day, the world Above from the world Below, the shadows from the sun, and we must keep them apart at any cost," Madam Terpsichore says, watching the others as she gently strokes the child's head with her free hand, her razor claws teasing at Sparrow Spooner's matted ginger hair. "Even *if* we should find our death of cold in the effort."

"There has been a breach," Master Shardlace grumbles from the safety of his place among the sycamore's dangling, dirt-clod roots. "A trespass has occurred, and we are *all*—"

"I am *coming* to that," Madam Terpsichore barks back at him, and he mutters to himself and grows silent again.

Sparrow Spooner stops cleaning her mistress' bleeding left hand and gazes up at Madam Terpsichore. The changeling's lips and chin and the tip of her nose are smeared with sticky crimson, and she absently wipes her mouth on the sleeve of her dingy dress.

"I *know* you, child. You've come a long, long way, through the Trial of Fire and the Trial of Blades. Next Full Hunger Moon, you're up to face the Trial of Serpents, and, if you survive, you'll win your Confirmation."

The changeling only nods her head, not so dull or frightened that she doesn't understand that the time for words has long since come and gone. The ghoul's blood is bitter and salty on her tongue and burns her throat going down to her belly. But it warms her, too, pushing back some of the chill that's worked its way into her soul.

"Do you know the story of Esmeribetheda and the three gray witches?" Madam Terpsichore asks the changeling, and Sparrow Spooner nods her head again. Of course she knows the story, has known it since she was very young, one of the seventy-four "Parables of Division" recorded in the *Red Book of Riyadh* and taught to the Children of the Cuckoo before they are even old enough to read the words for themselves.

"Then you remember the *crime* of Esmeribetheda, don't you?" Madam Terpsichore asks Sparrow Spooner.

"Yes, ma'am," the girl replies and wipes her mouth again. The blood on her face has begun to dry, turning the color of rust.

"Then will you tell us, please?" and she motions towards the students. "Perhaps some of the others have forgotten." For a moment, the chamber beneath the cemetery comes alive with nervous chatter and tittering laughter at Sparrow's predicament. But Madam Terpsichore narrows her eyes and silences them with a look.

"She . . . Esmeribetheda became curious, and she wanted—"

"Stand up, please," Madam Terpsichore says, interrupting her. "Stand up and face the class, not me. I already *know* the story."

"So do they," the changeling complains and earns a scowl and another click of the teeth from her mistress. She apologizes for her impudence and gets to her feet, brushing some of the mud from her dress and bare legs, then turns to face the others.

"Esmeribetheda became curious, and she wanted to know how the children of men and women lived, what it was like to have a mother and father. She wanted to know what she'd lost when the Hounds of Cain had stolen her from her crib."

"And what did she do to learn these things?" Madam Terpsichore asks.

"She was sought out by three human witches, Arabian necromancers determined to locate a route to the world Below that they might learn its secrets and gain greater power in their arts. In the desert, at an altar beneath a dead tree that had once served as a temple to the goddess Han-Uzzai, Al-Uzza, youngest daughter of Allah, she was met by a blue-eyed crow. In truth, though, the crow was one of the witches who had disguised herself, and it promised that Esmeribetheda would be reunited with her parents if she'd show the necromancers a doorway and lead them down to the Hall of . . ." And Sparrow Spooner stops talking and looks over her shoulder at Madam Terpsichore.

"What's wrong, dear?" the ghoul asks her. "Have you forgotten what comes next?"

"No, ma'am," the girl replies. "But they *know* the story. They know *all* of it."

"Yes, but we never, ever suffer from hearing a good tale retold, do we? Especially when it's a story with so much to teach us, so much we should take pains to remember."

Sparrow Spooner licks at her dry lips, tasting the ghoul's blood again. The warmth it left in her stomach has already begun to fade, replaced with something hard and cold that twists and turns like a winding ball of pink worms, something much colder than the late November night.

"Continue, please," Madam Terpsichore says.

"Well, Esmeribetheda was shown images of the life she might have lived. She saw herself in her mother's arms. She saw her brothers and sisters. She saw herself growing into a young woman and marrying a handsome man who gave her children of her own, children she could *keep*. The witches promised her she could have all this back, all that might have been, if she'd show them the road down to the hounds. She agreed that she would, and the crow flew away to tell the other witches."

"She agreed to show them the way?" Madam Terpsichore asks. "Even though she knew perfectly well that it was forbidden for her to reveal those paths to mortal men?"

"Yes," Sparrow Spooner replies, promising herself that whatever's going to happen, she won't cry. She doesn't want the others to see her cry. "She was a very foolish and ungrateful girl. She'd never been able to accept the life she'd been given. On a moonless night, Esmeribetheda led the witches across the sands to a warren doorway. But the hounds knew, and they were waiting for her."

The nameless boy who'd stuck his tongue out at her earlier was now pretending to hang himself, tugging at an imaginary noose before his head lolled to one side in a pantomime of strangulation. The ghoul named Consequence snickered, but Madam Terpsichore seemed not to notice them.

"And what happened next?" she asks Sparrow Spooner.

"The three witches were killed there on the spot and their corpses carried down into the tunnels. Esmeribetheda was led back through the dunes to the dead tree in the desert, and the ghouls hanged her there, and then they set the tree on fire."

"Yes," Madam Terpsichore says, speaking now so softly that only the changeling can hear. "They did. Would you call that justice, child?"

Sparrow glances over at the rootsy place where Master Shardlace is hiding, as though he might decide to help, when she knows damned well that he won't, that she's been brought here tonight instead of some other, later night at his insistence.

"Was it *justice*?" Madam Terpsichore asks again, and now she rises from her place on the stool, standing up straight so that she looms over the girl and her head almost scrapes against the low roof of the chamber.

"Esmeribetheda just . . . she only wanted to go home . . . she only wanted to get back the life that had been taken away from her."

"I *know* the story, child," the ghoul sighs, almost whispering, and presses her muzzle gently against Sparrow Spooner's cheek. "I have asked you a question."

"She wanted to go home," the changeling says. "That's all. She wanted to go home."

"Your life will be spared," Madam Terpsichore says, not unkindly, her wet nose nuzzling the girl's face, her eyes on the other students. "But there must be a punishment, you understand that?"

"Yes, ma'am," the changeling girl says, her legs gone suddenly so weak that she's afraid she might fall. Her mistress' breath, hot as a summer day, smells of lifeless, broken things that have lain a long time beneath the soil.

"She should *die*," Master Shardlace growls.

"No, she will live," Madam Terpsichore tells him, "but she will always remember this night and the folly of her actions. She will learn, tonight, that desire is only another demon that would happily see her strung from the branches of a burning tree."

"And what of the witch?" demands Master Shardlace.

"The witch will die, just as the three died in the story of poor, misguided Esmeribetheda." And Madame Terpsichore grips Sparrow Spooner by the back of the head and forces the girl down onto her knees. From the shadows, there comes the rough sound of stone grating against stone, stone ground against metal, and then a sudden gust of fresh night air threatens to extinguish the candles. All the changelings and ghoul pups turn to see the open door leading up to the cemetery and the world Above and to behold the face of the one who has led Sparrow astray from the path set for her by the Cuckoo.

"You be strong, child," Madame Terpsichore tells Sparrow Spooner, and the girl shuts her eyes.

II

The old hearse, a 1948 Caddy slick and long and blacker than the stormy New England night, subtle as a fucking heart attack, rolls unchallenged through the wild Massachusetts night. In the passenger seat, Soldier drifts between her uneasy dreams and the nagging edges of wakefulness, dozing and waking and dozing again to the metronome rhythm of the windshield wipers. The radio's set to a classic-rock station out of Boston, and she's already told that asshole Sheldon that she'll break his goddamn fingers if he so much as touches the dial. He can listen to that indie-rock college shit on his own dime, not when she's trying to catch a couple hours' shut-eye before a job.

After Providence and their brief meeting with the Bailiff and one of his boys at the Dunkin' Donuts on Thayer Street, the hearse left the city and followed I-95 north all the way up to and across the New Hampshire state line, finally doubling back at Hampton Beach, because that's the way the Bailiff had told them to do it. Just like always, everything worked out ahead of time to the letter and in accordance with the Bailiff's precise instructions, the plans he'd cobbled together from star charts and newspaper astrologers and the obscure intersections of geometry and geography, nothing Soldier even pretended to understand. She listened when he talked and did what she was told.

Past the Hamptons, then on to Salisbury and Newburyport, U.S. 1 traded for State 1A, past sleeping houses and fishing boats tied up secure against the storm, across the bridge spanning the brackish confluence of the Merrimack River and Newburyport Bay.

Other bridges over other lesser waters, over railroad tracks, Rowley to Ipswich, and when Sheldon jabs her in the arm and tells her to wake up, Soldier tells him to fuck off. But she opens her eyes anyway, squinting out at the dark streetlights and the darker windows of the houses along High Street and the raindrops hitting the windshield. Eric and the Animals are coming through the Caddy's speakers, "White Houses," and at least that's one thing about the night that's all right by her.

"We're there?" she croaks, her mouth dry as ashes, and reaches for the pint bottle of George Dickel she stashed beneath the seat before leaving Rhode Island. "Why the fuck is it so dark?"

"Not quite there, but close enough," Sheldon replies. "Time to rise and shine, Sleeping Beauty."

"Fuck you."

"Babe, if I thought there was time—"

"Why is it so *dark*?" she asks him again. "What's up with the streetlights?"

"Power's out. The storm, I expect."

"Jesus, I need a goddamn drink," Soldier says, changing the subject, and her hand has to grope about for only a moment before it closes around the neck of the bottle lying on the floorboard behind the heels of her army-surplus boots.

"The Bailiff wants you sober for this one," Sheldon says and glances anxiously at Soldier as she unscrews the cap.

"The Bailiff doesn't pull the fucking trigger, now, does he? Why don't you shut up and watch the road?"

Old Hill Burying Ground rises up on their left, countless listing rows of slate and granite markers lined up like a dutiful army of stone soldiers gathered together beneath the swaying boughs of oaks and hemlocks, an army of the dead standing guard since sometime in 1634. And Soldier remembers this place, the delivery they made there a year or so back, one of her first rides with Sheldon, and they left a heavy leather satchel sitting outside one of the vine-covered mausoleums. She never found out what was inside the satchel, never asked because she never wanted to know. It isn't her job to know.

She takes a drink of the whiskey, and if it doesn't quite drive away the fog in her head, it's a halfway decent start.

"What time is it?" she asks, and Sheldon shrugs.

"You got a watch, lady," he says. "You tell me."

Instead, she takes another swallow of George Dickel, rubs at her eyes, and watches the night slipping by outside the hearse. She realizes that she's sweating and unzips her shabby bomber jacket, a WWII antique she took off a corpse a couple of years back. The fleece lining is nappy and moth-eaten and worn straight through in a few spots.

"It's almost three thirty," Sheldon sighs, checking his wristwatch when it's clear Soldier isn't going to check for herself. "We made pretty good time, all things considered."

"Yeah? All things considered, looks to me like we're cutting this pretty goddamned close," she replies, tightening the cap on the whiskey bottle. "If we miss Bittern—"

"—then I suppose we're fucked, good and harsh. But we're not *gonna* miss him. Ain't no way that card game's gonna break up until dawn, right? No way, lady, especially not with this blow. Hell, he's probably into Jameson for ten or twelve Gs by now, easy. Ain't no way he's gonna walk with that many Franklins on the line."

"Look, man, all I'm saying is we're cutting it close. It would have been nice if we'd had a little more notice, and that's *all* I'm saying."

Sheldon Vale slows for a traffic light that isn't working, then steers the hearse off High Street onto North Main. On the radio, Eric Burdon's been replaced by the Beatles' "Continuing Story of Bungalow Bill," and he reaches for the knob.

"Don't touch it," Soldier says.

"Oh, come *on*. I've been listening to this crap since Providence, and I fucking hate the Beatles."

"Why don't you just worry about getting us to Bittern and forget about what's on the radio," Soldier tells him and returns the bottle to its spot beneath the seat.

"I should have let you sleep."

"Yeah," she says, "you *should* have let me sleep."

"He gives us as much notice as he can," Sheldon says, and it takes Soldier a second or two to figure out what he means, to remember what she said about the Bailiff.

"You think so? You think that's how it is?"

"Where's the percentage in doing any different?"

"You really think it's all that simple?"

Sheldon snorts and turns left onto State 133 and crosses the swollen, muddy Ipswich River.

"What I *think* is I was driving this route, running for the Bailiff, when you were still shitting your diapers, and maybe old Terpsichore and Danaüs got their plans all laid out for you, all right, but you don't know even *half* as much about operations as you like to let on."

Soldier laughs, then goes back to staring out the window. "That was a mouthful, Sheldon. Were you rehearsing that little speech all the way up from Providence?"

Sheldon frowns and wipes condensation off the inside of the windshield with his bare hand.

"You know that's gonna streak," she says. "And you know how the Bailiff feels about hand prints and streaky windshields."

"Yeah, well, I can't fucking *see*."

Soldier shrugs and folds down the passenger-side sun visor. There's a little mirror mounted there, and she stares for a moment at her reflection, stares at the disheveled woman staring back at her—the puffy, dark half circles beneath her bloodshot eyes, half circles that may as well be bruises, her unkempt, mouse-colored hair that needed a good cutting two or three months ago. There's an angry red welt bisecting the bridge of her nose that'll probably leave a scar, but that's what she gets for picking a fight with one of the ghouls. She sticks her tongue out at herself, then folds the visor up again.

"You look like shit," Sheldon Vale says, "in case you need a second opinion."

"You're a damned helpful cunt, Shelly."

"Shit," he hisses, glancing at the rearview. "I think I missed the turnoff."

"Yep," Soldier says, pointing at a green street sign. "That's the fucking Argilla right there. You missed it. Guess that'll teach you to keep your eyes on where you're going, instead of letting yourself get distracted by my pretty face."

Sheldon curses himself and Jesus and a few of the nameless gods, slows down and turns around in a church parking lot, slinging mud and gravel, and then the hearse's wheels are back on blacktop, rolling along with the rubber-against-wet-asphalt sound that's always reminded Soldier of frying meat. Soon they're on the other side of the river again, retracing the way they've just come, left turns become rights, and there's the cemetery once more.

"What's on your mind, old man?" Soldier asks, because he might be an asshole, and he might have shitty taste in music, but Sheldon Vale can usually be counted on to get you where you're going without a lot of jiggery-pokery and switchbacks.

"You think they're gonna kill that kid?" he asks her and turns off the highway onto a road leading away towards the salt marshes and the sea.

"Don't you think she's kind of got it coming?" Soldier asks him back, and then she has to stop herself from reaching for the bottle again. "I mean, she knew the fucking rules. This isn't some first-year squeaker. She's one moon away from Confirmation. She should have known better."

"She's a kid," Sheldon says, as if maybe Soldier hasn't quite entirely understood that part, and he slows down to check a road sign by the glow of the headlights. "Town Farm Road," he says, reading it aloud. "Man, just *once* I wish someone else would pull this route."

"Kids screw up," Soldier says. "Kids screw up all the time, just like the rest of us. Kids screw up, and it gets them killed, just exactly like the rest of us."

"So you think they're gonna do her?"

"No, I didn't say that. But this is some pretty serious shit, Shelly. If we're real damn lucky, it's not so serious that we can't put it to rest by visiting Mr. Ass-for-brains Joey Bittern and—"

"She's just a kid," Sheldon says again.

"Some rules, nobody gets to break," Soldier says, watching the half-glimpsed houses and marshy fields and the trees that seem to appear out of nowhere rush past the hearse and vanish in the night behind them. "Some rules you don't even bend. And this isn't anything you don't already fucking know."

The Beatles make way for Jefferson Airplane, and Sheldon looks at the radio in disgust, but doesn't reach for the knob.

"Grace Slick is a fat cow," he says.

"Not in 1967 she wasn't."

Sheldon mutters something under his breath and stares straight ahead at the rain-slick road, the yellow dividing line, the stingy bits of the night revealed in the headlights. And Soldier's starting to wish she'd asked for another driver, beginning to wonder if Sheldon's up to this run.

"Someone does something like this," she says, "I don't care if it's just some kid or one of us, Madam Terpsichore or the goddamn Bailiff himself—"

"You've made your point," Sheldon tells her, and then he turns the wheel as the road carries them deeper into the marshes leading away to the Eagle Hill River and the Atlantic.

"You just don't mess around with shit like that," Soldier says, knowing it's time to shut the fuck up about the kid and let him drive, time to start thinking about the shotgun in the back and exactly what she's going to say to Joey Bittern when they reach the old honky-tonk at the end of Town Farm Road.

"I just don't think it's right," Sheldon Vale mumbles so softly that she barely catches the words over the radio and the storm and the whir of the tires on the road.

"Whole lot of crazy shit ain't *right*," she replies, then begins singing along with "Don't You Want Somebody to Love?" while Sheldon drives the hearse, and Soldier tries hard not to think about whatever is or isn't happening to Sparrow Spooner back in Providence.

III

In the night Above, the dying storm hammers cold-rain nails and gusting wind down upon the quaintly ancient and indifferently modern rooftops of sleeping Providence, filling metal spouts and concrete gutters far past overflowing, choking sewers, drumming at windowpanes, and wearing away sidewalks and slate shingles and gravestones bit by infinitesimal bit. Demons never die quietly, and a week ago the storm was a proper demon, sweeping through the Caribbean after her long ocean crossing from Africa, a category five when she finally came ashore at San Juan before moving on to Santo Domingo and then Cuba and Florida. But now she's grown very old, as her kind measures age, and these are her death throes. So she holds tightly to this night, hanging on with the desperate fury of any dying thing, any dying thing that might once have thought itself invincible.

But there's still magick left in her, the wild, incalculable sorcery of all storms, great and small. She wields invisible gale-force tendrils that whip and weave themselves through the groaning limbs and branches of an enormous oak tree that has stood watch at the Old North Burial Ground since a forgotten late-summer day in 1764 when it was planted here by Mercy Tillinghast, widow of Colonel Peter Mawney, planted here that something strong would stand to mark his life and her grief, something to shade the family plot from the wide Rhode Island sky. But now two hundred and forty-six summers have come and gone, and the tree, like the storm, is an old, old creature. The wind does not so much kill it as help it to die, helping it to finally lie down as its roots at last pull free of the soggy ground. It falls across the graves of Colonel Mawney and his wife and their children and grandchildren, shattering headstones and driving broken limbs deep into the earth.

Eighty-five miles north and east of the cemetery, Sheldon Vale comes to the end of Town Farm Road and kills the Caddy's engine, and the changeling named Soldier stares eagerly, anxiously out across the night- and rain-shrouded marshes.

And back in Providence, in the world Below, deep within the labyrinth of catacombs and chambers excavated by the ghouls all those long millennia before the first white men came here, like this storm, from lands far across the sea—down there, the sound of the tree falling is the rumbling grandfather of all thunderclaps. The children assembled before Madam Terpsichore and Master Shardlace (who have been joined now by Master Danaüs and Madam Mnemosyne) look up towards the ceiling of the chamber, and more than a few of them cry out in surprise or fear or a little of both. Madam Terpsichore raises her scarred and shaggy head, waiting to see if the layers of earth overhead will hold. It would be almost ironic, she thinks, if the evening's proceedings were to be interrupted by so simple, so random a thing as a falling tree. They might die here, all of them, *ghul* and pup and changeling brat, victims of a universe with less than no concern for their petty laws and taboos and ideas of justice.

"Be *still*, all of you!" she growls, perking her ears, flaring her nostrils, listening as the rumbling, root-cracking, wood-splintering cacophony quickly subsides, as dust and loosened bits of dirt and stone sift down and settle over her wards. She counts her heartbeats, waiting for the collapse, for a crushing, smothering burial they would all deserve, venturing so near the surface on a night like this. But apparently they're not meant to die tonight, and the ceiling of the chamber holds, braced up by strong pine timbers and brickwork arches. Terpsichore whispers a hurried, grateful prayer and crosses her heart three times.

"Luck favors fools," she sneers and bares her teeth for Master Shardlace, who has finally come slinking out from behind his sycamore roots to grovel before Danaüs and Mnemosyne.

"This is a very serious matter," Master Danaüs grunts, and brushes dust from his fur.

"So is my life, dear sirrah," Madam Terpsichore replies. "So are the lives of my students—"

"A matter to be settled *swiftly*," Danaüs continues, as though he has not heard her or doesn't care, "before further and greater damage is done. Damage we can't undo."

"Yes, *yes*," Shardlace simpers. "That's exactly what I was telling her only a *moment* ago. That's what I was saying, precisely."

Terpsichore turns and snaps her jaws at Shardlace, half wishing for a fight, for a fair and incontestable chance at his bare throat. But Shardlace only whines and withdraws once again.

"Surely," she mutters. "Then let's have ourselves done with it." And Madam Terpsichore yanks away the burlap hood covering the head and shoulders of the mortal man who has been led through the stormy night, across the wide cemetery, and down into the chamber by the pair of changeling couriers who found him hiding at the center of a circle of salt and hen's blood, mumbling the Twenty-Third Psalm, inside his tiny apartment at 7 Thomas Street. The man is bald, and his eyes are the color of clay. When he sees her face, the bald, brown-eyed man doesn't scream, but his lips tremble, and he shuts his eyes tight. Master Danaüs stands on his right and Madam Mnemosyne on his left, and the two changelings who brought him here are waiting near the rear of the chamber, should he try to run.

"*This* is him?" Madam Terpsichore asks, and she barks out a dry laugh. "This pathetic . . . this *man* is the fearsome magician who has so inconvenienced me and mine? Is this a joke, Danaüs? If so, it's a poor jest, indeed. He's no more than a drowned *rat*, near as I can tell."

The man's clothes, a white T-shirt and blue jeans, are soaked through and streaked with mud, and rainwater drips from his long salt-and-pepper beard and off the end of his nose. Sparrow Spooner, still kneeling at her mistress' feet, glances at the bald man and sees that he's lost his left tennis shoe. It's hard to tell what color his sock might be for all the mud.

"Sparrow, is this him?" Madam Terpsichore asks, staring down at the changeling girl. "Is this cringing, sodden rat standing here before me the man with whom you have spoken of our secrets?"

"He said—"

"We'll get to that, child. I simply asked you if this is the man."

"Yes," Sparrow Spooner replies, "that's him." And she immediately goes back to looking at the man's muddy feet.

Madam Terpsichore nods once, then tells the man to open his eyes. When he doesn't, she leans forward and whispers in his ear, "Would you prefer, rat, that we open them *for* you? It would be a pleasure, and thereafter there would be no danger of my having to ever ask you again."

"I've done nothing wrong," the man says unconvincingly, and Madam Terpsichore grins and licks her lips.

"Open your *eyes*, witch."

The bald man breathes in deeply, exhales the musty, mushroom-scented air, and then opens his clay-colored eyes. He stares into the devouring black-hole pupils of the creature that will be his judge and, most likely, his executioner before this stormy night has finished. He struggles against his terror and panic to fashion a still place somewhere deep inside himself, a mental sanctuary that he fills with an arbitrary litany of mathematics and hermetic symbols, a familiar, impromptu order to stand against the suffocating chaos of his fear.

"Is this not what you've worked for, what you *wished* for, Mr. Higginson?" Madam Terpsichore asks the man, leaning so close that her stiff gray whiskers brush painfully against the tip of his nose, and he flinches. "Isn't *this* why you've seduced our poor darling Sparrow into betraying us all?"

"*She* came to *me*," he replies, trying too hard to sound courageous, trying harder still not to shut his eyes again.

"Yes, rat, she did. She came to you; she allowed herself to be *lured* to you, and for that, I promise, she will be punished. But *you* laid the trap, Mr. Higginson."

"I . . . I *know* . . . what you are," the bald man stutters. "I'd seen so much already. The child, she was . . . was only a means of further affirmation."

"You, sirrah rat, know *nothing*!" Madam Terpsichore snarls and places the tip of one clawed index finger lightly against his left temple, pressing only hard enough to draw a thin trickle of blood. "Even now, when you believe that all your careful, exhaustive researches, your divinations and discoveries and unholy dreams have at last been justified, that you have been rewarded with some half-imagined truth; even now you *still* know *nothing*, nothing whatsoever."

"I know that *you're* real," he says, the words slipping recklessly from his lips. "Yes, I know *something* . . . I know about Iscariot and Narcissa Snow, about William Wellcome, and, by the gods, I know a few things about Richard Pickman, too."

"You will *not* dare repeat those names, Mr. Higginson," Madam Mnemosyne admonishes. "Those names are not spoken here, not ever."

"I've even seen one of Pickman's paintings," Elgin Higginson continues undaunted, because he can't imagine he has anything left to lose. Beads of sweat and rainwater roll down his brow and sting his eyes. "Did you really think you'd found them *all*? That you'd *destroyed* them all?"

"*Enough*," Master Danaüs barks and then shoves the bald man so hard that he almost loses his balance and falls. "The child should offer her testimony now. There's nothing more to be gained by listening to this *man*." Mesdames Terpsichore and Mnemosyne nod and murmur their agreement.

"Yes," Madam Terpsichore says. "Sparrow Spooner, who has passed unscathed through her first two trials, who was chosen by the Cuckoo even before her birth and has been among us for all her short life, will speak now, as is her right and duty." And the ghoul looks down at the child kneeling beside her.

"What else do you want me to say?" the girl asks and glances nervously up at the bald man.

"Only what you have already told me and Master Shardlace—how this man, by duplicity and deceitful magicks, drew you forth from the warrens, from whence you were forbidden to leave before your Confirmation, and how he then tricked you into divulging secrets entrusted to you by the Cuckoo."

"But I've *already* told you," Sparrow says, still looking up at the bald man, at the rivulet of blood creeping down the left side of his face. "That's him. He's the one."

"Yes, dear, but you now must tell us in his presence."

"I don't see why," the changeling mutters and turns away. All of them are watching her, waiting—all the other students, her *ghul* masters and mistresses, and the odd bald man from Above who let her walk with him beneath the sun. "There's nothing that I haven't already said. Nothing *important*."

Madam Terpsichore exchanges a quick glance with Master Danaüs and then drops down onto her skinny haunches, her aged knees and anklebones cracking loudly from the sudden exertion. She places a hand beneath the child's chin and gently turns Sparrow Spooner's head until she's gazing into the girl's eyes again.

"Do not forget that your *own* fate will be determined this night," Madam Terpsichore tells the changeling. "The decision has already been made to spare your life, but a penance may yet still be uttered that will make you regret our mercy."

When Sparrow Spooner opens her mouth to reply, the ghoul slaps her so hard that her ears ring, and she bites her tongue. Madam Terpsichore's claws leave five parallel gashes in her pale flesh, ragged crimson wounds that will become scars that the changeling will carry all her life, however short or long that might prove to be.

"Now, do as you've been bidden," Madam Terpsichore tells her, and when the girl begins to sob, the ghoul raises her hand as if to strike her again. "Don't you *dare* cry, Sparrow Spooner. I shall not abide that human weakness in my sight."

"Leave her alone," the bald man says, and he takes a step towards Sparrow Spooner. "If you want to hurt someone, hurt me."

"Don't worry, rat," Madam Mnemosyne replies, pulling him back, showing him almost all of her yellow teeth at once. "We shall do that, momentarily. But there is an order to these things. Do not be impatient for your undoing. It's coming."

"We're *waiting*, child," Master Danaüs says irritably.

His eyes are like fire, Sparrow Spooner thinks. *His eyes are like spoonfuls of fire.*

And then she wipes her nose and does as she's been told, because she's seen enough in the eight years since the Cuckoo delivered her to the warrens dug deep beneath College Hill and Federal Hill, beneath Swan Point and the Old North Burial Ground and St. Francis Cemetery, to know that the ghouls hate the contrivances of human speech too much to waste their breath on idle threats. She faces the bald man named Mr. Higginson, the man who bought her frozen lemonade and taught her seven new words for *green*. The man she showed a particular mausoleum on the west bank of the Seekonk River. The man she drew a crude map for and answered questions she knew she shouldn't. The man she daydreamed might one day become her father.

"I'm sorry," she says to him, and then Sparrow Spooner tells the ghouls everything they want to hear.

IV

At the windy nub end of Town Farm Road, where the asphalt has turned to gravel and mud and potholes, Sheldon Vale and Soldier sit in the hearse, listening to the rain falling hard against the roof of the Caddy. Sheldon lights a Marlboro Red and passes it to Soldier, and she takes a deep drag and keeps her eyes on the place where the uneven edge of the road vanishes into tall brown marsh grass and cattails.

"So, you really think they're gonna kill her?" Sheldon asks.

"Fuck, will you shut up about the kid? Right now, the kid ain't our problem."

"What if they know we're coming? What if—"

"Sheldon, shut up a second and listen to me," and then she takes another pull off the Marlboro and holds the smoke until her head begins to buzz, then exhales through her nostrils. "They don't know

jack shit, okay? I scried this one myself last night. I scried it fucking *twice*, okay, and they don't know bupkes," Soldier says, silently
daring Sheldon to make a crack about her less than stellar magickal
abilities.

"All the obfuscation lines are in place," she continues, "and
they're working like gangbusters. Trust me. Those assholes are sitting in that dive playing fucking New York stud, drinking beer, talking trash, and they *don't* know we're coming."

Sheldon lights another cigarette for himself and sighs. "You know
I get the shakes," he says. "That's all. Give me a minute and they'll
pass. Give me a minute and I'll be right as rain."

"I swear, Sheldon, it's beyond me how you ever made it through
the trials."

"It wasn't a pretty sight, I'll tell you that," he says, and laughs,
then stares out the driver-side window, looking past his reflection at
the chain-link fence and NO TRESPASSING signs where the Ipswich
town dump begins.

"You ought to cut the lights," Soldier says and taps her Marlboro
against the rim of the ashtray. "You're gonna kill the battery, and I'm
in no mood to have to walk all the way back to town through this
shit."

Sheldon shrugs and switches off the headlights. The rainy night
swallows them at once, and Soldier gazes out at the marsh again,
waiting for her eyes to adjust to the darkness.

"I've never gotten the shakes," she says. "Not even once. The
Bailiff, he told me I would, but it never happened."

"Yeah? That's 'cause you're such a coldhearted little bit of jam."

"Fuck you, Shelly. It just never happened, that's all," and then
Soldier considers asking him to turn the radio back on, but she
doesn't. There's no more time for music. No more time for anything
but the job. Time to be quiet, to focus, time to get her act together
and find the frequency of this night. That's how she always thinks

of it, the frequency of the night, like turning the dial past static and white noise and all the crap you don't want to hear, turning the dial until you find just the right station.

"I still can't believe Bittern thought he could get away with this," Sheldon says. "I mean, I know he's not the brightest bulb in the pack, but Jesus . . ."

"What difference does it make? Ten minutes from now he's a corpse. Who gives a sick? The whys and wherefores aren't our concern."

"When he got tight with those assholes down in Jersey, I told the Bailiff then it'd come to this, sooner or later. A little creep like Bittern gets it in his head he's gonna play mobster with the big boys and—"

"*Stop it*," Soldier growls and snaps her fingers a few inches from his face; Sheldon shuts up and goes back to staring at the dump. "Hell, you go on like that long enough," she says, "and I *will* get the shakes." She decides she's had enough of the Marlboro and stubs it out in the ashtray.

"You got your goggles, right?" Sheldon asks her.

"I can see just fine without them. I'm going in first, but you better be right there to cover my ass; you understand me?"

"Yeah," he replies, crushing out his own cigarette. "I think I can handle it."

Soldier reaches beneath the seat and retrieves the bottle of Dickel. "Not a *word*," she says before Sheldon can remind her what the Bailiff told him about keeping her sober. Then she has one last drink before it starts, before the shitstorm barreling her way, one to keep her warm, and she tucks the bottle out of sight again.

"Let's get this over with," she says and pulls the black Beretta 9mm from the shoulder holster inside her jacket. Soldier pops the clip and runs her thumb quickly across the shells, counting off all eight Browning cartridges one by one.

"Man, I hope you're right about the lines," Sheldon says, reaching for the twelve-gauge Ithaca and the box of shells behind his seat.

"Tell me the last time I was wrong," Soldier replies and slides the clip back into the Beretta, then pulls the slide, chambering the first round. She flips off the safety, presses the gun to her lips, and shuts her eyes, whispering a short prayer to Mother Hydra.

"And no one walks out of there alive," Sheldon says, and one of the shotgun shells slips from his fingers and rolls away into the darkness between his legs.

"That's what the man said. No one walks. You've got the gasoline?"

"Five gallons. That ought to do the job."

"Yeah," Soldier says, returning her pistol to its holster. "That ought to do the job. Try to get a few of those shells *in* the gun, okay?"

"Yeah," Sheldon replies and almost drops another one.

"And hurry the hell up." She reaches for the other shotgun, the massive Mag-10 Roadblocker she picked up after some asshole Thelemite wearing Kevlar body armor and seven different deflection sigils had come at her with a goddamn Sears Craftsman chain saw a few months back.

"That's a scary fucking gun," Sheldon says. "You expecting something in there besides Mr. Bittern and his cardsharp buddies?"

"You just watch my ass, Shelly. Let me worry about the big scary monsters, okay?"

Sheldon finishes loading his shotgun and smiles a nervous smile at her. "It's a deal, lady. I'll look at your ass, and you'll kill all the bad guys."

"Yeah, you crack me up," Soldier says and opens her door. The rain is cold, colder than the November night, and she knows she'll be drenched long before they reach the door of Quaker Jameson's roadhouse.

"Do you see it?" Sheldon shouts at her across the roof of the hearse, shouting to be heard above the storm. "I don't see it any-where." She glances over her shoulder at him, and he's fiddling about with the resolution lever on his goggles.

"You just fucking follow me," she says. "Forget about those things."

The wind wraps itself about her, giving the rain teeth, whipping at her clothes and the exposed skin of her face as though this is something personal, like maybe the storm has decided it has a ven-detta against her. Soldier grits her teeth and squints into the stinging rain. She can see the path leading away through the marsh grass to a rickety, crooked catwalk and, beyond that, the low, sagging roof of Jameson's place. There's the faintest blue-white glow surrounding it all, a gentle, constant pulse of pale alabaster light, the last little bit of the glamour that she *can't* see through. Perhaps, she thinks, if the cheapskate son of a bitch would hire a halfway decent witch, then she might need goggles, too. But she doubts it.

"I still don't fucking see it," Sheldon mutters, but this time she ignores him. She's found her frequency, the clear channel she needs to see this whole mess through, and she knows that he'll follow her, that he'll be where she needs him to be when she needs him there. The big shotgun is heavy and solid and comforting in her hands, and that's something else she knows she can rely on.

Soldier can't hear the gravel crunching beneath her boots, not over the wind, but she can feel it. She steps across a deep puddle and into the tall grass, and the gravel is immediately replaced by mud. Even through the storm, she can smell the marsh and the backwaters of Paine Creek, that musky, fishy odor that's not so very different from the smell of sex. And all of it makes her stronger, the gun and the storm and the marshes, the knowledge of the flooded creek flow-ing to the river that flows, in turn, down to Plum Island Sound. Now that she has the frequency, now that she's so hard in fucking tune, there's no such thing as distraction, only these sensations and her concentration growing so sharp that it almost hurts. Ten more steps carry her from the mud and out onto the catwalk; she can feel the weathered old boards squeak and flex as she moves quickly towards the roadhouse.

"Hell, that place was stuck together back before the Revolution," the Bailiff said once, some other night when she'd had some other business out at Quaker Jameson's. "Started out as a whorehouse for the Masonic and Rosicrucian types, some place they could dip their wicks in whatever struck their fancies without drawing too much attention, if you get my drift. Mr. Benjamin Franklin himself had a few good pokes in that place."

Thirty-three more steps, and Soldier reaches the wide landing where the catwalk meets the front porch. The light from electric lamps leaks out through the milky antique windowpanes, and this is probably the only place in all of Essex County with electricity tonight, she thinks, wondering if it's an enchantment or just a backup generator. She steals a quick look over her shoulder, then, just to be sure, and there's Sheldon Vale in his ridiculous goggles. He motions towards the roadhouse with the barrel of his own shotgun, and Soldier gives him the thumbs-up. Sheldon nods his head, and she reaches for the door handle, something ornate cast in copper gone cancerous with verdigris, black and green shades of corrosion, and in the last instant before she touches it, the handle sparks. A single fleeting arc of sun-colored light that bridges the space between her palm and the handle, and she curses under her breath and jerks her hand back.

"*Fuck* this," she hisses and grips the handle, squeezing hard against the protective charm, collapsing it into something so small and ineffectual it couldn't even fry an ant. She feels the magick coursing through her and bleeding off into the night, losing itself in the turmoil of the storm. And then the door swings open wide, bathing her in yellow incandescence, and Soldier pumps the shotgun once as she steps across the threshold and points it at the first thing that moves.

A skinny, redheaded boy in a Sex Pistols T-shirt stares back at her from the other end of the Roadblocker. He drops the serving tray he's carrying, and five or six mugs and a couple of shot glasses shatter when it hits the floor, spraying beer and whiskey at her feet.

"On your fucking knees, faggot," she snaps at him, and a second later the boy's spread out on the roadhouse floor with all that beer and broken glass. Soldier swings the shotgun around and takes aim at the table where Joey Bittern and Quaker Jameson and two others have all put down their playing cards and drinks and are watching her. One of them's a morning gaunt, perched there on a bar stool like something that would happen if a stork knocked up an orangutan, and the other, seated across the table from the gaunt, is an orchid-skinned demon smoking a cigar and looking about twice as pissed off as anything she's ever had the misfortune to come across.

"You *told* us the door was locked," the demon says and turns away from her, glaring at Jameson from beneath its scaly beetled brows. "You *also* told us we'd hear her coming."

No one said anything *about demons*, Soldier thinks, channeling the thought the way that Madam Melpomene taught her years ago, sending it straight back at Sheldon, to the spot by the doorway where she hopes like hell he's still standing. *I'm pretty goddamn sure the Bailiff didn't say dick about any fucking demons.*

There's no reply, nothing rolling back from Sheldon's mind to hers, and Joey Bittern grins like a cartoon wolf and lights a cigarette. He's a big man, half Portuguese, half Narragansett Indian, one hundred percent asshole, and he blows a smoke ring at the rafters supporting the high ceiling.

"You're fifteen minutes late, Soldier," he says and pretends to check a nonexistent wristwatch. "What held you up, Mr. Vale? You miss that turn again?"

"Put your fucking hands down on the fucking table," Soldier says. "*All* of you. *Now!*"

"See, I'm thinking this game's a *little* steep for your tastes, sweetmeats," Bittern says and blows another smoke ring at the ceiling. "I'm thinking you talk like a big dog, but when the chips are down—if you'll excuse the pun—you got nothing to bring to the table *but* talk."

"That's a goddamn big motherfucking shotgun," Quaker Jameson says nervously.

"*You* said we'd hear the bitch coming," the demon says again, and then it picks its cards up off the table. "I like to pissed myself."

"I said put your hands on the *table*—"

"This is about the little Spooner girl, right?" Joey Bittern asks her. "Am I correct in assuming that those mangy curs down on Benefit Street have sent you out here to slap my paddies for pointing our friend Mr. Higginson in the right direction? That's all I did you know, point him—"

"Talk to me, Shelly," Soldier says, tightening her finger on the trigger. "Tell me that you're fucking back there somewhere."

"Oh, I'm back here, Soldier girl," Sheldon replies, "but I think you better be quiet and listen to the man."

And there it is, presto-change-o, abrafuckingcadabra, suddenly plain as daylight, and there's no time left to think about how fucking stupid she's been, how she should have seen it coming, how the Bailiff should have seen it coming a mile away. She's in the frequency, and she pulls the trigger, but the Mag-10 answers with a hollow, harmless click.

"Very thoughtful, Mr. Vale," Bittern says. "It's good to see you're the dependable sort. An eye for details and all that."

The morning gaunt makes a gurgling sound that's probably meant to be laughter. The air between her and the card table has begun to shimmer and twist back upon itself, like heat rising from blacktop on a summer's day, and so she knows that the four at the table have been removed from the reach of bullets, anyway.

"Shelly," Soldier says, speaking as calmly as she can still manage, "do you even begin to have any idea how much shit you're in?"

"You just let me worry about that," he tells her.

"Well said, Mr. Vale," Joey Bittern mumbles around the filter of his cigarette. "You're a man of few words, but you choose them well."

"Did you learn that from a fucking fortune cookie?" Soldier asks, her eyes moving quickly from Bittern to the orchid-colored demon, from the demon to Jameson to the gurgling night gaunt. "Give him a chance, he'll talk your goddamn ear off. Ain't that right, Shelly?"

"How about we *cut* the fuckin' la-di-da chitchat," the demon scowls, "kill the changeling bitch, and get back to the game? Or maybe, Joey, you think all this drama's gonna make me forget how far in the hole you are?"

"See, Soldier? Some people just aren't capable of savoring the moment," Bittern laughs and shakes his head. "They always have to be *rushing* things. Some people"—and he glares at the demon—"they just don't quite appreciate the sheer, astounding elegance of deceit done right."

"Whatever they decide to do with you, Shelly," Soldier says, reaching into her jacket for the 9mm, "I just hope it's going to hurt for a long, long time."

And then she hears Sheldon Vale take a step forward, the soles of his boots scuffing across the floorboards, her senses jacked up so goddamn high and tight that she even hears his index finger squeeze the Ithaca's trigger, hears the hammer fall, and then there's thunder—the night cracking open to show the storm precisely how it's done, to teach it something about tempest and destruction. There's no more than a foot between the muzzle of the shotgun and Soldier, and it tears through her easy as a hot knife through butter . . .

. . and she's stumbling, falling towards the demon's shimmering bulletproof barrier, driven forward by the force of the blast . . .

. . . and there's a wet spray of blood and bone and mangled entrails moving out before her, the lead shot opening her like a butcher's prize sow, like a bouquet of bloodflowers, like Noah's goddamn forty-day flood . . .

And seconds (tick)

have become (tock)

entire minutes.

Soldier shuts her eyes because she doesn't want to have to die looking at her own guts and stinking Joey Bittern's ugly, fucking grin. *He's killed me*, she thinks, and wonders if all that crazy shit Madam Terpsichore and Master Danaüs taught her about Mother Hydra and Father Kraken and the lives waiting for her out past death is anything more than pretty storybook tales designed to

make . . .

this . . .

easier.

I'll know in a moment, she thinks, and then all the world is pain.

And

then

"And no one walks out of there alive," Sheldon says, and one of the shotgun shells slips from his fingers and rolls away into the darkness between his legs.

"That's what the man said. No one walks. You've got the gasoline?"

"Five gallons. That ought to do the job."

"Yeah," Soldier says, beginning to remember things that haven't happened yet, an instant of déjà vu so strong that it's nauseating, so strong it almost seems to knock the breath from her lungs. She grips the Beretta, her hand trembling just the slightest bit, and she doesn't return it to its holster. "Yeah," she says again. "That ought to do the job. Try to get a few of those shells *in* the gun, will you?"

"Yeah," Sheldon says and almost drops another one.

"Christ, you're a clumsy asshole, Shelly," she whispers and swallows, her throat dry as August dust, and right now she'd give almost anything for whatever's left in the bottle beneath the seat. Sheldon slips an orange shell into the Ithaca 37 Classic and looks up at her.

"What's wrong?" he asks.

"What?"

"You look like you just saw a fucking ghost," he replies and takes another shell from the box. "I told you to stay sober. The Bailiff told you to stay sober."

"What the hell did they offer you?" she asks, and when he looks up again, Soldier raises the 9mm and puts two in his skull, right between the eyes. *Bang, bang.* Easy as falling off a log, exactly what the doctor ordered. Sheldon Vale slumps back against the driver-side door of the old hearse, and his whole body shudders once and is still.

"You sold me out, you bastard," she whispers. "You fucking *sold me out*."

She sets the pistol on the dash and reaches for the bottle of whiskey beneath the seat and sits drinking it, listening to the rain and watching the dim alabaster glow wreathing Quaker Jameson's roadhouse. The air trapped inside the hearse smells like cordite and blood, cigarettes and whiskey. When the pint's empty, Soldier lays the bottle down next to her and reaches for the Mag-10 tucked behind her seat.

"Five gallons," she says. "Yeah. That ought to be plenty."

V

Sparrow Spooner opens her eyes again when the man from Above begins to scream and pray to the Catholic god he abandoned more than half a lifetime ago. She isn't sure how long she's been huddled there, alone in this muddy, dark corner of the chamber, naked and shivering beyond the candlelight. Madam Mnemosyne laid her down here when they'd finished taking two fingers from her left hand, and she told Sparrow not to move a muscle and to keep her eyes tightly shut and her mouth shut tighter still, unless she wanted worse than she'd already gotten.

"When we are done, she *must* remain useful to us," Madam Terpsichore said to the other ghouls, before the cutting began. "She still has potential, this one, despite the gravity of her recent indiscretions." And Sparrow understood that Madam Terpsichore was the only thing left standing between her and the full wrath of the hounds. They would have seen her dead—Danaüs and Mnemosyne and that mongrel bastard Shardlace who'd sniffed out her forbidden liaisons with Mr. Higginson. They would have made a terrible example of her, something for the rest of the Children of the Cuckoo to see. Would have carved her up like a body taken for the dissection slab and then hung all the divided bits of her throughout the warren, her hands and feet and innards strung on baling wire and dried grapevines and left to rot, left for the other changelings to see again and again and again.

Master Shardlace wanted them to take her tongue, that she might never utter another of their secrets. Madam Mnemosyne suggested that a binding geas would be more appropriate and far more effective and would not so diminish her value as a courier and messenger. But, in the end, Master Danaüs left the decision to Terpsichore, and she asked only for two fingers from Sparrow Spooner's left hand, the pinkie and ring finger. They used one of the ceremonial knives, carved from greenish soapstone and graven with images of the writhing, many-eyed daughters of Mother Hydra. Madam Terpsichore cauterized the stumps with a pinch of belladonna and a few words of musical, alien language, some arcane tongue that Sparrow has yet to learn. The ghoul threaded the severed fingers onto plastic fishing line and hung them about Sparrow's throat.

"You will wear that until I say otherwise," Madam Terpsichore told her, and then Madam Mnemosyne carried her to the spot where she now sits with only the earthworms and tiny white mushrooms for company, listening to the man named Higginson scream.

Sparrow Spooner opens her eyes, even though no one's *told* her that she could, and she squints past the gloom and the ache in her hand that has begun to move slowly, steadily up her entire arm. Madam Terpsichore has spread wide her long, clawed fingers, jabbing them towards the night sky hidden by the ceiling of the chamber, above the fallen tree and the Old North Burial Ground, above Providence and the storm, and she's calling out the names of gods and darker things. As for Mr. Higginson, Sparrow sees that he's been given to the ghoul pups and changelings, all of whom have left the places where they were sitting and are clambering over his thrashing body. It isn't often that they get fresh meat, fresh and *living* meat, and it doesn't get any fresher than this; so this is one more part of her punishment, that she will not be permitted to take part in this rarest of feasts, even though it's her doing that the man's down here.

Madam Terpsichore asks almighty Father Kraken to let this

business end here, tonight, with no further repercussions. Sparrow knows that particular prayer, the snipping of a dangling thread, the tying off of a knot against any maleficent consequence. She begins to whisper it along with the *ghul*, then stops, too distracted by the man's screams and the vicious feeding noises of her peers. Two of the pups are wrestling over a slippery, fat length of intestine; Sparrow Spooner's empty stomach growls, and she licks her lips hungrily.

Madam Mnemosyne and Master Danaüs bark and yap their encouragement to the frenzied, blood-spattered pack, and Master Shardlace laughs and mocks the screams of the dying man. Madam Terpsichore squats next to Mr. Higginson, brushing aside two or three of her students, and she snatches the man's soul as it exits his right ear like a greasy puff of smoke. *So,* Sparrow thinks, *he'll be dead soon, and I won't ever get a father. I won't even get so much as a single mouthful of him.*

And then she feels something wash over her, something quick and dizzying and bittersweet that she's never felt before, something that she might almost have mistaken for simple déjà vu (which, she has been taught, is only the memory of the world flowing backwards through her from the end of time), if not for the way Madam Terpsichore turns and looks at her—a questioning, startled look from her red eyes to ask, *You felt that, too, didn't you, child?* The others seem oblivious, but last semester Sparrow Spooner ranked first in her Discord and Continuity class. She has often felt very faint things before, subtle or fleeting magicks and cosmic shudders that almost everyone else has missed. Things like the summoning that Mr. Higginson cast over the warren below the yellow house on Benefit Street, drawing her out into the day.

Be still, Madam Terpsichore's eyes say. *Be still and be silent. We will speak of this later.* And then she looks away again, squeezing the captured soul until there's nothing left in her palm but a dull green, pea-soup-colored stone, which she swallows at once.

One of the older changelings, a tall, blond-headed boy named Nehemiah Sweet, bites through the man's carotid artery, and Mr. Higginson is finally gone, gone forever, body and soul and everything in between. And then Sparrow Spooner closes her eyes again, shuts them tight as she can, just like Madam Mnemosyne said she should; she tries hard not to hear the delicious sounds of bone snapping and blood spilling and teeth ripping through sinew and gristle, tries to hear the storm still raging overhead instead. She doesn't let herself think about what she might or might not have felt, whatever it was or wasn't that Madam Terpsichore might, or might not, have felt as well. The pain from her missing fingers helps to distract her, the pain and the falling rain Above and the thunder, and before the others have finished with Mr. Higginson's carcass, she's asleep.

VI

When Soldier is finally done with the twenty-three incantations that have forever sealed the doors and windows of Quaker Jameson's roadhouse, the measured, angry stream of syllables to secure every loose board and ill-fitted sheet of corrugated aluminum—and maybe she's not much of a magus, but, by the Mother and Father, she *knows* how to plug a hole—she begins emptying the five gasoline cans. The demon and the morning gaunt have already gone, of course. This was never their fight, just something they came to see, a little mortal entertainment to interrupt the monotony of their long, long lives. The demon went down, vanishing into some deep, secret cavern or melding seamlessly with the weathered metamorphic strata below the marsh. The gaunt went straight up, a glittering, firework ghost climbing into the low clouds and disappearing with a distinct *crack*. Soldier knew better than to try to stop either of them.

By the time the last of the gallon cans is almost empty, Jameson and Joey Bittern have both given up trying to escape and have started making her promises, offers of power and money and sex and other things that she either doesn't need or has all she wants. They press their lips to the windowpanes and shout for her to see reason and stop. They make threats and curse the hounds and every changeling ever stolen from its crib or stroller or the arms of its mother. She listens for a little while, standing there in the rain, and then she turns and walks back to the muddy edge of the road, trailing the last of the gasoline behind her.

"I'm thinking this game's a little steep for your tastes, sweetmeats," she whispers and lights one of the highway flares from the Caddy's glove compartment. It paints the night with a sizzling ruby glow, and for a moment Soldier holds it at arm's length, staring into the heat and brightness, the dazzling inferno cocktail of potassium nitrate, magnesium, strontium, and sulfur.

"I'm thinking you talk like a big dog," she says, and imagines she hears the roar of Sheldon's shotgun again, imagines the pain as it tears her apart and the smirk on Joey Bittern's face. "But, when the chips are down, you got nothing to bring to the table *but* talk." And then she tosses the flare away, towards the tall grass and the catwalk, and Soldier watches as the flames rush hungrily back towards the roadhouse.

VII

Upstairs in the big gray house on Angell Street, Emmie Silvey lies in her bed, listening to the rain drumming against the roof and the bedroom window. Her father is sitting on the edge of the bed. He's been reading to her from one of her books, *Moon Mouse*, but he keeps pausing to listen to the storm. This last time there was a sudden cracking sound from the sky just as Arthur the mouse asked his mother how far away the moon is, a sound that might have been thunder, and he stopped reading and stared at the black, rain-slicked window.

"Deacon, it's only thunder," Emmie says. "What does Arthur's mother tell him?"

"Baby, how many times in the last three years have I read you this book?" he asks her, but his voice sounds sleepy and far away. He's been drinking tonight. She can smell it. She can always smell it.

"I don't know," she replies, because she doesn't. Sadie bought her the book before going away to New York, gave it to her for her fifth birthday. Inside the cover, Sadie wrote, *Happy fifth birthday, my beloved moonchild.* And she explained to Emmie that she'd been born on Halloween night, just as the full moon was rising in the sky.

"Deacon," Emmie says again. "What happens *next*?"

"Oh," her father says, turning away from the window and smiling sleepily down at her. "You know, I could read you another book tonight. How about some Dr. Seuss? Or *Where the Wild Things Are?*"

"No, I want to hear how far away the moon is."

Her father sighs and looks at the book lying open in his lap. "*Very* far," he tells her. "It was farther than the meadow. Farther even than the farmer's cornfield. Farther than the wheatfields."

"*Golden* wheat," Emmie says, correcting him. "Farther than the fields of *golden* wheat. I can tell you're only pretending to read."

"Yeah," he says and smiles at her. "Kiddo, you know this old book by heart. You don't need me to read it to you anymore."

"I need to hear the way *you* say it."

"Is that so? I think you're just being ornery."

"What's *ornery*?"

"What you're being," he replies.

"That's another of your Alabama words, isn't it?"

"Not really," Deacon says. "Lots of people who never lived in Alabama say *ornery*." And then he continues reading, and Emmie goes back to listening to his voice. There's a little bit of a slur from the beer, but it's still something comforting against the rain and wind and lightning. Arthur the mouse crosses the meadow and the cornfield and the *golden* wheatfield and finally climbs an old fire escape up to the moon, which is made of yellow cheese, just like his mother said that it might be. He shows her the picture, the big wheel of Swiss on someone's kitchen table, Arthur the mouse slipping in through an open window.

"It should be white," she says, as she almost always does, and her father nods and agrees with her, as he almost always does.

"Yes, but this is poetic license," he says.

"What's that?"

"Permission to lie," he tells her and goes back to reading. Arthur the mouse runs home to his mother, and he tells her how he nibbled at the moon.

"He would have broken his teeth on the rocks," Emmie says and rolls over on her left side to face the window.

"Yes, I imagine he would've," her father says.

"When is Sadie coming home?" she asks, and he sighs again. Whenever he sighs, the beer smell grows stronger, and she wrinkles her nose.

"Sadie lives in New York now, Emmie. You know that."

"We could go see her. We could ride the train."

"Maybe when the weather's warmer," her father says, and starts reading again. Arthur is alarmed at the half-moon, amazed that he managed to nibble so much of it away.

"We could go see the dinosaurs," she says, "when we go to see Sadie."

"We will. I promise. We'll go to see the dinosaurs. Do you want me to finish this?"

"I *know* how it ends," she says, wishing the rain would stop so she could see the moon again, to be sure it was still up there, so she could fall asleep without the sound of the storm in her ears. "He didn't eat it all. He only nibbled."

"I told you that you know this story by heart," her father says. "I told you that you were being ornery."

"You know everything," Emmie says and wiggles farther beneath the warm flannel sheets and blankets and the quilt that Sadie bought when she went to Tennessee. The quilt is white with autumn-colored maple leaves stitched one to the other.

"I don't know everything."

"You know magic," Emmie says.

"No, baby, I just know a few tricks. I've told you, it ain't nothing but tricks."

Emmie nods her head, though she isn't sure that she understands the difference. "I want to hear some music," she says. "I want to hear Doris Day."

"It's too late for music," her father says. "You have to get up for school—"

"It's not too late for music. Music isn't like stories. You don't have to look at the pictures."

"If I play Doris Day, will you go to sleep?" he asks, and she nods again.

"But you have to stay with me until I'm asleep," she tells him.

"It's only rain," her father assures her. "It can't hurt you, you know?"

She watches the rain streaking the glass a moment, pelting the windowpane like it wants inside, and she thinks maybe Deacon *doesn't* know everything, after all.

" 'You Are My Sunshine,' " she says.

"Yes, well," her father says, "it's very sweet of you to say so."

"No, silly," Emmie says and turns her head to frown at him. "That's the *song* I want to hear. I want you to *play* 'You Are My Sunshine.' "

"And you promise you'll go to sleep if I do?"

"If you promise to stay with me until I do."

"Then it's a deal," Deacon Silvey says and stands up, wobbling a little, and crosses the room to the shelf where Emmie keeps all her CDs. It takes him only a moment to find the disc with "You Are My Sunshine" on it, and that's something else that Sadie gave Emmie. She has three Doris Day CDs, and they were all gifts from Sadie. He hates Doris Day, and sometimes he thinks this whole thing, his daughter's fascination with Doris Day, is a plot to drive him the rest of the way insane. He presses a button on Emmie's pink and white Hello Kitty stereo, and the lid pops obediently open to accept the CD.

"When's it gonna stop?" Emmie asks.

"What? You mean the rain?"

And she doesn't answer right away; while he waits, Deacon forwards the CD to track five, sets it on repeat, and presses the button marked PLAY. In a moment the room is filled with the shrill din of accordions and the steady *thump thump thump* of a double bass.

The other night, dear, as I lay sleeping . . .

"Yeah," Emmie says. "When's the rain gonna stop?"

"Soon," he replies. "It'll stop tomorrow. By this time tomorrow, it'll have blown all the way out to sea."

"That's good," she says, and Deacon goes back to sit on the bed with her.

"It's only rain," she says.

"Nothing but," he assures her and leans over to kiss her forehead. In the lamplight, her yellow eyes seem almost golden. He brushes a few strands of ash blonde hair from her face.

"It doesn't scare me," she tells him, sounding as though she really means it.

"That's 'cause you're a big girl now, Emmie. Big girls don't have to be afraid of storms anymore."

And he sits with her, listening to the rain and thunder, listening *through* the rain for anything else that might be out there in the night, the things he's spent the past eight years listening and waiting for. The polka music fills the room, and he stays with Emmie until she's asleep. Then he switches off the lamp. The night-light will be enough until morning; Emmie's never been afraid of the dark.

You are my sunshine, my only sunshine.

You make me happy when skies are gray . . .

Deacon Silvey switches the stereo off on his way out of the room, pausing a moment to be sure that Emmie doesn't wake up. When she doesn't, he leaves her and pulls the door shut behind him.

I

Parallel Lives

One need not be a chamber to be haunted,
One need not be a house. . . .

—EMILY DICKINSON

ONE

Emmie

Emmie and Deacon sit together on one of the long antique benches lined up neatly inside the old Kingston Station, daughter and father waiting impatiently with all the other people headed south to New Haven or New York or wherever it is they're all bound at half past eleven on a cold Saturday morning in February. Old Kingston Station instead of Providence Station because Deacon says he likes the long drive, and, besides, he has a friend in West Kingston he hasn't seen for a while. He's sipping at a can of Diet Pepsi from a vending machine near one of the windows, and Emmie is silently wishing that the train would hurry up. She loves taking the train to see Sadie, even when she has to ride alone, even when her father is too busy with his shop to go with her. She pretends she's Eva Marie Saint in *North by Northwest,* or she pretends that all the sights rushing by outside the windows of the Amtrak are places that she's never seen before, exotic, far-off places from the books she's read, or she just sits listening to the reassuring drone of the wheels on the tracks and pretends nothing at all.

"Did you pack your toothbrush?" her father asks, and Emmie nods her head, even though she didn't pack her toothbrush because she has another one at Sadie's. "Did you think to pack clean underwear?" he asks.

"Yes," she says, wishing he wouldn't ask her questions about her underwear in public.

"More than one pair?"

"Yes, Deacon. More than one pair."

There's a round mirror mounted halfway up the wall directly in front of them, the sort of mirror she's seen in convenience stores so the clerks will know if anyone's shoplifting, stuck up there between a wide bay window and the door with a glowing red-orange exit sign mounted above it. Emmie watches herself and her father, the two of them caught in that distorted, fish-eyed reflection. She nods her head, and the girl in the mirror nods her head, too.

"Why are you nodding your head?" Deacon asks, and Emmie shrugs. The girl in the mirror shrugs right back.

"I just felt like it."

"Oh," Deacon says and sips his Pepsi. "I thought I might have missed something."

"No, you didn't miss anything," she tells him.

In the mirror, her father is wearing the gray wool sweater she gave him for his last birthday, the sweater and a pair of corduroys, and she can see the puffy reddish half circles beneath his green eyes, the half circles he gets when he's been drinking too much and sleeping too little. The half circles that mean he's spending too much time remembering things he shouldn't. Her own eyes are almost the same color as sunflowers, and they glint faintly in the morning light. She's the only kid in her school with yellow eyes, the only person she's ever seen *anywhere* with yellow eyes. Sadie says it means that her soul is golden, and she'll live to see more sunny days than rainy nights, but Deacon says that's bullshit and nonsense, that it doesn't mean anything at all that her eyes are yellow. He says *lots* of people have yellow eyes. The fat black tomcat that lives next door with a skinny old man named Mr. Bloom has eyes almost the same color as hers.

"Don't you talk to strange people," her father says, staring down at his soda can.

"How do I know if they're strange people?" she asks, even though she understands what he means. "What if they're just pretending to be normal and fool me?"

"Don't talk to people you don't know."

"Even the steward?"

"No, Emmie, not even the steward."

"But what if *she's* strange?" she asks, still watching their reflection in the round mirror on the wall.

"The damn train's late," Deacon says, though Emmie's pretty sure it isn't. She knows it means he doesn't want to talk about strange people anymore.

"You're gonna miss me," she says. Deacon shrugs his broad shoulders and takes another swallow of Diet Pepsi, then wipes his lips on the back of his left hand.

"Yes, you will, too," she tells his reflection. That *other* girl's lips move in unison with hers, the girl with the same yellow eyes and shoulder-length black hair and the same new pink-and-white, zebra-striped fur coat as Emmie. *Maybe it's not a mirror at all,* she thinks. *Maybe it's a window.* That's an old thought, one that she's never even told Deacon about, that mirrors might really be windows, that there might be some other world with some other her, and every now and then the two of them just happen to pass by the same windows and see each other and play this mocking game.

"You got the money I gave you?"

"Yeah," Emmie replies, suddenly bored with the mirror and looking down at her shoelaces instead. "I got it."

"And your cell phone's charged?"

"Mostly. It's charged enough."

"When you get back," her father says, setting the empty can down on the station floor between his feet, "we'll bake some of those snickerdoodle things you like. I'll take a day off and we'll see a movie or something like that. Maybe we'll drive out to the Beavertail Lighthouse and watch the waves. What do you think?"

"Sure. I guess so," Emmie sighs, not bothering with the least bit of enthusiasm because she's never thought watching the waves out at Beavertail Point is even half as much fun as her father seems to think it is, and she kicks at her backpack with the toes of her boots. "I think the train's late," she says.

"No, it's not," her father tells her, but he checks the clock on the wall anyway. "It's not quite time yet." Then he tugs at the zipper of Emmie's coat and smiles. "How's the new coat working out for you?" he asks. "Does Santa Claus have good taste or what?"

"I know all about Santa Claus," she says, and a small brown bird lands on the window ledge, flutters its wings, and then pecks at the sill.

"Do you now?" Deacon asks, and he cocks one eyebrow and rubs at his chin, rubbing at the rough and mostly gray stubble growing there because he hasn't shaved for a few days. She knows that *he* knows she doesn't believe in Santa Claus anymore, and that he isn't really surprised, but she doesn't say so. She smiles for him and kicks her backpack again. "Well, hell," he says. "I guess you *also* know all about getting too old for presents and toys and such, then, right?"

"No. I'm still a kid," she replies. "And kids get toys on Christmas, whether they believe in Santa Claus or not. It's a rule."

"A *rule*? Now, I don't know about that."

And then the train's pulling into the station, right on time, give or take a minute here or there, and the woman behind the ticket counter is talking loudly over the PA, reciting destinations and train numbers. Some of the people in the waiting room have started getting to their feet, shuffling their bags about, talking among themselves the way people talk whenever something's about to happen. And others, the ones who were already standing, are moving out onto the platform, out into the freezing Rhode Island morning. Emmie looks at the window again and realizes that all the noise has frightened the bird away.

"I don't have to go," Emmie says, turning away from the window and towards her father. "I could stay with you."

"What's wrong now?" Deacon asks her, the lines on his forehead wrinkling so she knows he's worried or confused or both. "You've got your ticket, Emmie. And Sadie's expecting you. All I've heard out of you for the last two weeks is how much you want to go to New York and see Sadie."

"But I *could* stay," she says, glancing back at the window, the place where the bird had been. "I could stay if you wanted me to."

"Are you sick?" he asks and presses a palm to her forehead.

"No. I'm not sick, Deacon. I'm fine."

"Then you're being silly," he says and picks her backpack up off the station floor, lifting it in a very decisive, end-of-discussion way. "I've got a lot of work to do this week. You'd have to spend half your winter break hanging around the shop with Jack."

"I *like* the shop," she says so softly she's almost whispering, wishing the bird had picked a different windowsill to land on.

"You'd be bored out of your skull, and you'd drive him crazy in the bargain."

"I said I like the shop, Deacon."

"You like New York, too. And that's where you're going. I know how much you've been looking forward to this. You and Sadie both."

"Yeah," Emmie sighs, admitting defeat, reluctantly admitting that Deacon's right, but also starting to relax a little. Seeing the bird there she felt confused, trying to clearly recollect something that she'd spent a lot of time trying hard to forget, and then, remembering, she felt angry and guilty and scared. She wanted to go back home with Deacon and lock herself in her room, wanted to forget about trains and New York City. But now the small brown bird is gone, and it seems to have taken all those bad feelings with it, and she can look forward to the trip again. Now she feels silly, just like her father said, and she smiles up at him and points at the door to the platform.

"I got a train to catch," she says, just like someone in a movie would say.

"You sure?" Deacon asks uncertainly. "If you really don't want to go—"

"I'm okay. I was worried about you, that's all."

"Yeah? Well, don't you do that. I'll be cool as a moose, kiddo. I always am."

"Okay," she says and smiles for him again. Emmie resists a last glance at the windowsill and lets Deacon lead her out into the cold, out onto the platform with all the other people.

She was almost seven when the thing with the bird happened, the thing that there was no way to take back and, she'd discovered, apparently no way for her to forget about, either, no matter how hard she tried. Deacon said that's how it always worked, that the harder you try to not remember something, the harder it is not to remember. "Just try not thinking of a white elephant sometime," he would say, like she was supposed to know what he was talking about. It hadn't been a white elephant. She'd never even *seen* a white elephant and thought he might have made them up. It had been a starling, a starling on a Saturday afternoon in October, the scraggly remains of the autumn leaves clinging stubbornly to the trees up and down Angell Street, all their bright colors turned dark and dull by the cold. Listening to the way they rustled against one another in the wind,

Emmie imagined that's what beetles would sound like, if beetles ever learned to talk.

The big rhododendron bushes growing around the front of their house were still green, though the ferns were turning shades of yellow and brown and dying back for the winter. She was playing on the porch while her father watched television, and at first she mistook the sounds the bird was making for the dry, rustling noises of the dead leaves. She had brought all her dinosaurs, the ones that Sadie had sent her, down from upstairs, and she'd lined them up on the porch rail—the *Styracosaurus* and *Triceratops*, the *Parasaurolophus* and spiny *Edmontonia*, the *Tyrannosaurus rex* and the *Apatosaurus* rearing up, enormous on its hind legs. She wasn't sure exactly what the dinosaurs were about to do, because she always liked it to be a surprise, whatever happened next, but she knew that there would be trouble. There was almost always trouble when she let the *Tyrannosaurus* too near the plant-eating dinosaurs.

And then Emmie noticed the starling, lying in the grass not far from the bottommost step. It was watching her nervously with its tiny black-bead eyes, and its breast feathers shimmered in the sunlight like oil on the road after a thunderstorm. Right off, she could tell that there was something wrong with it, the way the bird was holding its left wing crookedly, the way it was just lying there, watching her.

"Fly away, bird," she said, but it didn't. She tried to ignore it and go back to playing with her dinosaurs, moving the *Triceratops* in between the *Tyrannosaurus* and the other herbivores. The meat-eater was huge and his mouth was filled with teeth like knives, but his belly was soft, and he was afraid of the *Triceratops'* long horns. The frustrated *Tyrannosaurus* hissed, and the *Triceratops* let out a throaty bellow to say it wasn't going away, and if the *Tyrannosaurus* wanted something to eat, it would have to look elsewhere.

Down in the yard, the starling ruffled its feathers and hopped clumsily once or twice, then lay still again. Emmie looked over her shoulder at the front door and the living room window. She couldn't see Deacon and thought that he might have gone to the bathroom or to get something from the kitchen. *He'll be back in a second,* she told herself, and tried to concentrate on keeping the *Tyrannosaurus* from sneaking past the *Triceratops.*

The starling ruffled its dark and speckled feathers again, flapped at the air with its right wing, and made a hoarse sort of whistling *whooee* sound.

"Shut up, bird," Emmie said. "Shut up and fly away." The *Triceratops* lunged at the *Tyrannosaurus,* but her fingers slipped, because the starling was distracting her, and she knocked the horned dinosaur off the railing and into the ferns and rhododendron leaves below. "Shit," she hissed, hissing like the hungry *Tyrannosaurus,* cursing the way Deacon does when he can't find the remote control or whenever a lightbulb blows.

Whooee, the starling whistled.

"That's *your* fault," she scolded the bird, then looked again to see if her father had come back. He hadn't, and now she'd have to go down the stone porch steps and dig about in the bushes for the escaped dinosaur. Now she'd have to walk past the starling.

Whooee, it whistled, and then it made an anxious clicking sound and fluttered its right wing.

"If you were a *smart* bird," Emmie said, starting down the steps, "you wouldn't fly into windows. If you were a smart bird you wouldn't make so much noise." As she got closer, the bird tried to hop away, but kept tumbling over in the grass and weeds. It was easy to catch the starling, and Emmie knelt in the shadow of the house and stroked its back with an index finger. The bird stared up at her with its black eyes and trembled in her hand. She could tell that its left wing was broken, and probably one of its legs, too, and there was blood and bird shit matted in its feathers.

It was warm, and she could feel its heart beating, beating so fast it should burst.

I ought to tell Deacon about you, she thought. *Deacon would know what to do with a hurt bird.* But the words in her head felt more like something she'd thought a long, long time ago than something that she was thinking right then. She'd forgotten all about the lost *Triceratops;* it was getting hard to think about *anything* but the way the bird's heart was thumping against her palm, the fear in its glistening eyes, the way it trembled more when she touched it than when she didn't.

Gently she began to lift the wing that looked as if it might be broken, the left wing hanging limp and seemingly useless, but suddenly the starling stabbed at her hand with its sharp yellow beak. Emmie cried out, though she was more startled than hurt. Where the bird had pecked her, near the base of her thumb, there was blood, a single crimson drop welling out of her, growing larger and larger, and soon it would be running down her wrist and dripping onto the grass. She pictured the horns of the *Triceratops* piercing the leathery flesh of the *Tyrannosaurus'* belly, gouging wounds to drive it away and maybe even kill it, because, she thought, if you kill something, it can never try to hurt you again.

Deacon would know how to help you, bird.

The bird's heart was beating so fast now that Emmie couldn't tell where one heartbeat ended and another began. They had blurred together into one seamless sensation traveling out of the injured starling and into her. She felt a little dizzy, a little sick to her stomach, but she felt something else, too, something that felt good. Something that made *her* heart beat faster, and all at once the rustling of the dead leaves and the faded colors of the trees and the smell of the autumn day—everything—grew so perfectly clear, it was as though she'd never heard or seen or smelled anything in her life, nothing before that moment but the dim shadows of things and never the things themselves.

The front door creaked open, and she heard her father's footsteps on the porch, and Emmie almost turned to see, almost turned to hold the bird and her bleeding hand out for him to *fix,* but the starling pecked her again, harder than before, drawing still more blood.

And that's when she closed her fingers tight around its body and squeezed. Her heart was racing, beating almost as fast as the bird's had beaten, and the yard and Angell Street and the sky beyond the trees, all of it was so very loud, so vivid, so perfectly *defined,* that there was no room left inside her for the things that Deacon was saying. They were only another part of the whole, only splinters that would distract and ruin if she let them, splinters that would draw her back to that place where there was nothing but shadows waiting for her. Emmie squeezed even harder, breathless now at the ease with which the starling's bones snapped in her hand, at the contrast between cool, dry feathers and the warmth and wet leaking out of the bird.

Somewhere Deacon was telling her to drop it, drop it, drop it now over and over again. And then his hands were on her shoulders, pulling her up off her knees, shaking her so hard that her teeth clacked together and she bit her lip. The blood tasted almost as sweet and rich as chocolate syrup.

And then it was over—just like that—and Angell Street was only a street again, and there was nothing at all remarkable in the sound of passing cars or a leaf blower or the wind whispering through the maple tree outside her house.

"Drop it!" Deacon shouted again, and she did.

She wanted to tell him that she was sorry, because she was, because the starling was lying dead at her feet, as broken and empty as anything she'd ever seen, and *she'd* done that. She needed him to understand that she'd only wanted to help the bird, that its wing was broken, and it couldn't fly, and she'd wanted to find Deacon so that they could fix it. But her father was too busy cursing and dragging her up the stairs to listen, too busy to *hear* what she couldn't quite remember how to say. He dragged her past the dinosaurs, across the porch, and into the house. She almost tripped going over the threshold, but he caught her. He slammed the front door, and the lock clicked like breaking bones between his strong fingers.

He's going to kill me, she thought, certain that's just what she deserved for murdering a poor crippled starling, an eye for an eye, like she'd once heard someone say on TV, but then they were moving again, all the way down the hall to the bathroom. Deacon made her sit on the toilet seat while he ran hot water in the sink and found a bar of Ivory soap and a washcloth and a bottle of peroxide, and by the time he turned back to her she was crying.

He told her that he was sorry, held her and said that he hadn't meant to scare her, that *he* was frightened, too, and didn't understand. He was afraid, he said, and she needed to explain what had happened. But Emmie was sobbing too hard to talk, and after a little while Deacon stopped trying to make her. Instead, he used the soap and washcloth and hot water to clean all the blood and bird shit and feathers off her sticky hands, then cleaned out the places where the starling's beak had torn her skin, dabbed at the cuts with the peroxide, and that made her cry even harder. He put two Band-Aids on her hand, one across the other, hiding her wounds.

Later, after Emmie had stopped crying and he'd scrubbed her face and helped her change her clothes, after he'd brought her dinosaurs inside (except for the *Triceratops,* which had still been hiding in the bushes) and put the dead bird inside a green garbage bag, there was a trip to the emergency room and a tetanus shot.

"Birds and people can get a lot of the same diseases," he told her while they were waiting to see a doctor. "You should always leave them alone, especially the sick ones." And he did one of his magic tricks for her, the one where he pulls a nickel out of Emmie's ear and then puts it in his mouth and spits out a quarter.

That night she lay in bed, her arm aching from the tetanus shot, the Band-Aid cross gone and her hand wrapped up in gauze like an Egyptian mummy's, and she listened to Deacon talking on the phone downstairs. She knew that Sadie was on the other end, even though she couldn't make out many of the words. The words didn't matter. She could tell from the tone of his voice. Emmie lay there, listening, waiting for sleep and not wanting it to come, afraid the dead starling might return when her eyes were shut. It would get out of the green garbage bag and sit on her windowsill, pecking at the glass, watching her while she slept. It would call out, *Whooee, whooee,* so all the other starlings in Providence would come and do the same. If it could, it would change her dreams and make them into nightmares instead. It would haunt her, so she wouldn't ever be able to forget what she'd done. She listened to her father on the phone and waited for the birds. And the last thing Emmie heard before finally falling asleep was Deacon crying, and part of her wished that the starlings *would* come, that their hard yellow beaks would shatter the windowpane, and the birds would carry her aloft and away somewhere she'd never have to hear that sound again.

It's only been a short while since the train left Kingston when Emmie Silvey first notices the woman watching her, the woman seated on the other side of the aisle and one row forward. Emmie's been staring out the window, saving the book in her backpack for later on, when she gets bored with Connecticut. They've just passed the Mystic station, a handful of white sailboats bobbing listlessly in the little harbor, a few fishing boats moored at weathered piers, the wide gull-littered sky stretched out like a painting above the water and the shore. She's sitting on the landward side of the car and was glancing across the aisle for a better view when she caught the woman looking back at her. Not merely in her direction, and certainly not at anything behind her, but directly *at* her. When the woman sees that Emmie's caught on, she smiles and doesn't look away. The woman has curly brown hair tied back in a long ponytail, and she's wearing a black leather blazer with a gray turtleneck sweater underneath. Emmie's close enough to see that the woman's eyes are a pale hazel-brown; she doesn't return the smile, but goes back to looking out the window, wishing that there were someone sitting in the empty seat next to her. A big man with a red beard and wind-chapped cheeks, perhaps, or an old woman who might once have been a schoolteacher or a librarian, someone like that in the vulnerable space between Emmie and the brown-eyed woman.

She's not really looking at me, Emmie tells herself, though she knows it isn't the truth. *She was just looking around the train, that's all.* And then Emmie tries to make a counting game from the pattern printed on the back of the seat in front of her, the upholstery pattern that reminds her somewhat of a piece of hard candy or Sadie's rugs from Argentina. Broad bands of maroon on either side, then a riot of vertical stripes straight down the center, narrow and even narrower bands of purple and greenish blue, gray-blue, and rusty orange. She counts nineteen or twenty bands, though it's hard to be certain exactly how many there are, since some of the colors grade together, bleeding imperceptibly from one to the next. The blues and purples make up the outermost bands, with the orangey browns located at the center. But the whole time Emmie's really thinking about the brown-eyed woman, not the upholstery pattern, and, after only five minutes or so, she steals another quick glance in her direction. The woman is still watching and smiles a second time.

Emmie turns quickly away, not exactly frightened, not yet, because there are always the stewards and lots of other people crowded onto the train, but the woman's definitely making her nervous now. *Stop,* she thinks. *Don't look at me again,* pretending her mind can reach out all the way to the woman's seat, can reach inside her head and make her want to do anything but stare at people she doesn't know and has no business spying on. Then the train slows down and shudders once or twice, rolling up to the station platform at New London; some people get off and others get on, and Emmie sits with her fingers crossed, hoping that the brown-eyed woman is going only this far, or, at the very least, that someone boarding will take the empty seat next to her. She watches the busy platform and waits, but no one sits down beside her, and when the train is moving again, she risks another peek and sees that the woman is still sitting right there, so maybe she intends to ride all the way down to Manhattan. Emmie hauls her backpack up into the empty seat and tries to concentrate on the world rushing by outside the windows—beds of granite and slate carved to make way for the railroad; the twisted, arthritic fingers of bare limbs against the sky; brick buildings boarded up and scarred with graffiti; abandoned warehouses and gas stations; a tiny, neglected graveyard sheltered by enormous evergreens. At the crossings, automobiles wait impatiently for the train to pass so that they can go on about their business. Everything is just exactly as it *ought* to be, all the familiar sights and sounds of the trip, but she remembers her cell phone in the front pocket of the pack and thinks about taking it out and calling Deacon to tell him about the woman. And then she thinks about calling just to hear the sound of his voice.

"Would you mind if I sat here?" someone asks her, and "No, I don't mind," Emmie says eagerly before she even looks to see who it is, too relieved that the seat won't be empty anymore to care. But then she turns her head, turns to move her backpack from the seat, and she sees that it's the hazel-eyed woman. She's much taller than Emmie expected her to be, and there's a tattoo on the back of her left hand—two intersecting triangles, one red, one black, forming a six-pointed star, and there's something that looks like a T at the very center. For a moment Emmie doesn't move, trying desperately to figure out a way to tell the woman that she's changed her mind, that she wants to be alone, or the seat's taken, and her father will be back from the restroom in just a minute or two. But the woman's smiling, and her eyes are so bright that they almost make Emmie squint, and she moves the pack from the seat to her lap.

"Are you going to New York?" the woman asks, sliding easily into the seat. Her voice sounds a little hoarse, like maybe she's been crying or sick or she's only half-awake. "That's where I'm headed, and I've always hated not having anyone to talk to on the train." The woman holds out her right hand, the one without the tattoo, for Emmie to shake. "My name's Saben," she says. "Saben White. And you're . . . ?"

"You have a tattoo," Emmie says, not shaking the woman's hand.

"Oh, yeah. That," Saben White replies and looks down at the design worked into her skin. "I've had that for a long time. I forget about it."

"What's it supposed to be?" Emmie asks, hugging her backpack closer and wondering where Deacon is now, and if he's thinking about her, if he's *worrying* about her.

"Well," the woman says, frowning thoughtfully, examining her tattoo like maybe she's never looked at it closely before. "That's what's called the Seal of Solomon. It's called other things, too, but—"

"Who's Solomon?" Emmie asks, interrupting and not caring if it's rude, because it's also rude to stare at people you don't know and then sit down where you're not wanted.

"He was a king, the Israelite king who built a great temple in Jerusalem where the Ark of the Covenant would be safe. To the Hebrews, he's known as *chacham mi'kol ha'adam*—the wisest of all men."

"Are you Jewish?" Emmie asks.

"Not at all," Saben White replies.

"Then why do you have that tattoo on your hand?"

"Like I said, it's called other things, too. It means other things to other people besides the Jews. And it keeps me safe."

"From what?" Emmie asks, squinting skeptically at the woman.

"Oh, lots of stuff. All the things someone like me needs protecting from. You're a very curious little girl; you know that?"

"My father said I shouldn't talk to you."

"Did he? That's odd. I don't think your father even knows me. I mean, I don't know *him*."

"That's the point," Emmie replies, beginning to get annoyed at the way the woman seems to be talking in circles, the way she's only acting like she doesn't know what Emmie's trying to say. "I don't know you. He doesn't know you, either."

"Oh, *yeah*," the woman says and taps at her forehead with the ring finger of her right hand. "It's that old 'don't talk to strangers' routine. Okay—"

"So I think you should go back to your seat," Emmie says.

"Is that what I should do?"

Emmie sighs and looks out the window again. The train is crossing a bridge, but she isn't sure which one it is or which river it's ferrying them over. The woman distracted her, and now she's lost track of bridges and rivers and just about everything else. This one's wide enough to be the Connecticut River, but that would mean that they're almost to Old Saybrook, and she's not sure they could have gone that far already. It would also mean she's somehow missed crossing the Niantic, and she *never* misses the rivers, one of the ways she's learned to measure the train's progress so she knows how much farther until New York and Sadie, how much distance has accumulated between her and Deacon. She does the math in her head—it's fifteen minutes from Kingston to Westerly, ten minutes from Westerly to Mystic, then fourteen minutes from Mystic to—

"You're right," the woman says, and Emmie gets confused and

stops counting stations. "I don't know your dad, not personally, and he doesn't know me, but I do know who he is. He owns the old bookshop on Thayer Street, right? I've been in there a couple of times."

"Yeah, but lots of people know he owns the shop. That doesn't mean you're not a stranger. Kids who talk to strangers go missing. It happens all the time, every day."

"His name is Deacon Silvey," the woman continues, "and right now you're on your way to New York to visit your stepmom, Sadie Jasper. I've read all her books, by the way. So, see, you might not know me, but I'm really not such a stranger, either."

Emmie stares silently at the woman for a moment, wishing she could be sure which river is underneath her, feeling lost and sorry that she didn't lie and tell Deacon that she was feeling sick. He'd have taken her back home if she had, and she'd be safe in her own bed by now, and none of this would be happening.

"You *know* my name, don't you?" she asks the woman, who nods her head yes and picks a bit of fuzz off her gray sweater.

"I do," she admits. "And there's a good reason for that, but I probably shouldn't tell you what it is. Not just yet, anyway. I shouldn't tell you too much all at once. I don't want to frighten you."

"Too late," Emmie says, and now she's sure that it's the Connecticut River out there, and they'll be stopping at the Old Saybrook station in just a few more minutes. "You already have."

"I knew that I might, and I'm sorry about that. I promise, I didn't want to upset you or your father."

"What do you want?" Emmie asks, keeping her eyes on the window now, the bridge ending as the river gives way to land again.

"Just to talk to you, that's all. I swear. I'm not going to hurt you. I won't even *touch* you. You mean a lot to me, Emmie."

"Why is that, Saben? You don't even know me, so how could I mean a lot to you? That doesn't make any sense."

"Jesus," the woman says, "but you're a precocious one, aren't you?"

"I know what that means," Emmie says, because she does, and knows that sometimes adults pick words that they think kids won't understand.

"Of course you do. You're a smart little girl, Emmie. I know all about that, too, about the school and all." And now Saben White's voice is starting to sound hoarser than when she first sat down, and Emmie almost asks her what's wrong, if she's sick, then remembers that she has no business talking to the woman in the first place.

"I don't talk to strangers," she insists.

"Kids go missing every day," the woman says and nods her head again. "You shouldn't talk to strangers. Especially not to strangers on trains. They're probably the worst kind of all."

"Deacon never told me that," Emmie says, glancing back to the hazel-eyed woman.

"I expect there's all sorts of things he hasn't told you. And things he never will."

"What's that supposed to mean?" Emmie asks.

"It *means* that I need to remember why I have this thing," she says and points at the Seal of Solomon tattooed on her hand. "Do you know what the sacred number is, Emmie? Has anyone ever told you?" Emmie shakes her head; she's noticed that a man sitting across the aisle from them, an old Asian man wearing bifocals and a yellow scarf, is listening to what Saben White is saying.

I could ask him to help, she thinks. *I could tell him to make her leave me alone.*

"See these two triangles?" the woman asks her. "The one pointing up, the black one, stands for fire and masculine energy. Like your father. And the red one, that's for water and for feminine energy, like your mother. Or Sadie. Water and fire, so that's two of the elements, and if you look at the way the base of each triangle bisects the other just beneath its apex—that's what you call the top of a triangle—"

"I know that," Emmie says, still watching the old man, wishing that he'd say something, anything at all. It's rude to stare, and he should tell her to stop doing it.

"Okay," Saben White says hoarsely, "when you look at how the base of each triangle bisects the other just beneath its apex, you find the symbols for earth and air, which gives you all four of the elements—fire, water, earth, and air. And a triangle has three sides—"

"That's why it's called a 'triangle,'" Emmie replies, and the old man in the yellow scarf blinks at her.

"Right, Emmie. Now, what do you get when you add three to four?"

"You get seven."

"And seven is the sacred number," the woman says, and her eyes are shining like she's about to start crying. "So, this star here really has *seven* points."

Emmie looks from the useless old man back to the tattoo, counting off the points one by one. "No," she tells Saben White. "There are only six."

"Only six that you can *see*," the woman explains, and now the train has reached Old Saybrook, and people are beginning to move about. The man with the yellow scarf has started reading a newspaper, and Emmie gives up on him. "But there are still seven points there. Three *and* four, but the seventh, it's invisible."

"I don't think I believe in invisible things," Emmie says. "I don't think invisible things are real."

"You'll learn otherwise. Sooner or later you'll learn that invisible things can be a lot more real than the things you see. And sometimes that's *why* they're invisible."

"*That's* stupid," Emmie mutters, and turns to the window again, gazing out at Old Saybrook Station. "Now you're not even making any sense."

"I think I'd better get off here," the woman says. "I think it'd be best if I got off here."

"Yeah," Emmie agrees, relieved because the woman wasn't a kidnapper or a sex pervert after all, just some crazy person who can't count and doesn't know how to mind her own business. "It's probably best. I have a book in here I want to read." And she pats her backpack.

"You be careful, Emmie," the woman says. "And listen, I know this isn't going to make much sense, either, but you need to stay away from horses."

"What?"

"Just while you're in New York City this time, stay away from horses, okay? I think it's very important."

I think you're a nut job, Emmie almost says, never mind if it's mean to talk to crazy people that way, and she opens her mouth to say something else, but Saben White is already up and moving, pushing her way between the other passengers. In only a moment, Emmie's completely lost sight of her, so she turns back to the window and waits for the woman to appear on the platform, but she never does. A few minutes more and the train pulls out, rolling on towards New Haven and Bridgeport and Penn Station. Emmie forgets all about the book in her backpack, and the cell phone, too, and just watches the world through the train window as the morning turns quickly to afternoon, trying to remember everything the woman said about the Seal of Solomon, about four and three making the sacred number, in case she decides to tell Sadie or Deacon about it later. She might, and she might not. Sometimes she has no idea what the right thing to do is, and maybe it would only make them worry.

There are no clouds in the sky, but Emmie wishes it would snow, just the same.

*   *   *

Three years ago, not long before Sadie and Deacon finally stopped fighting, and Sadie left Providence and didn't come back, Emmie woke late one night to find her stepmother sitting alone at the foot of her bed. Emmie lay very still and quiet, unsure whether Sadie had realized she was awake, afraid that this was something important, something terrible, and as soon as Sadie knew she wasn't asleep any longer she'd begin talking, which would be the start of the terrible, important thing. Sadie was sitting with her back to the night-light, so Emmie couldn't see her face, even though she could see better in the dark than most people. Sadie's face was only a shadow, framed by her thick black hair, and Emmie tried hard to pretend that she'd come in to make sure everything was all right or because she'd forgotten to kiss Emmie good night (though she hadn't). Maybe she'd heard a noise outside, a cat rummaging about in the garbage cans or the wind brushing around the eaves of the old house, and thought that Emmie must have heard it too and might be frightened. Maybe that was all it was. She waited impatiently to find out, listening to one of her favorite Patty Duke songs set on repeat in her CD player—"The World Is Watching Us"—one of the songs she most liked to sleep to, turned down low enough so it wouldn't annoy Deacon, who hated Patty Duke just as much as Doris Day.

"Hey there, pumpkin," Sadie said very softly, and Emmie thought that she could almost *see* her stepmother's words, like wisps of red velvet in the darkness. "I'm sorry I woke you up."

"That's okay," Emmie replied. "It wasn't a very interesting dream."

"I hate those."

"This one wasn't even interesting enough to hate."

"Well, those are even worse," Sadie said, and then she didn't say anything else for a while, and Emmie lay there and waited, because she didn't know what else to do. Finally Sadie turned towards her, and Emmie could see her face illuminated in the glow of the night-light. Sadie's eyes sparkled like wet blue jewels. Emmie often wanted eyes the same color as Sadie's eyes; no one thought girls with yellow eyes were pretty.

"I need to ask you something, Emmie. I know that I can, because you're a very smart kid. Hell, I've never met a kid as smart as you."

And so it *was* something important and terrible. Emmie shut her eyes again, shut them tight, pretending this was just another part of the very uninteresting dream that Sadie had interrupted. Sometimes she'd rather she weren't so smart, or that Deacon and Sadie had never learned she was anything but a normal kid who couldn't be told the things that only grown-ups were supposed to know. Just another normal, unremarkable girl with Sadie's pale blue eyes.

"I might be leaving soon," Sadie said. "I might be better off living in New York. It might be better for my writing."

Emmie opened her eyes again. The Patty Duke song ended and immediately started over.

"What about Deacon?" she asked.

"I think Deacon might be better off with me living in New York, too. That's one of the reasons I'm considering it. I didn't want you to find out later and think I was keeping it a secret."

"Does Deacon think he'd be better off with you living in New York?" Emmie asked, though she was pretty sure that Sadie hadn't yet said anything to Deacon about leaving, which meant she *was* keeping it a secret.

"We still need to talk about it. I wanted to talk to you first."

"Don't you think that's kind of backwards?"

And then Sadie just stared at her for a moment, the same way her second-grade teacher had stared at her when Emmie had memorized the entire multiplication table in one afternoon, the same way that her father had stared at her when he discovered that she knew how to play the piano even though she'd never had lessons. Emmie didn't like that stare. It had always made her feel like something in a jar.

"I don't know," Sadie said at last and looked away again, the shadows hiding her face once more.

"He loves you," Emmie said. "He'd do anything for you. He told me that he would."

"He won't stop *drinking* for me. He won't do it for you, either."

And Emmie didn't argue, because she knew that was the truth, and there was hardly ever any point in arguing with the truth.

"You're going to divorce him?"

"That's not what I said," Sadie replied. "I just don't think it's good that we live together anymore."

Maybe this is the dream, Emmie thought. *Maybe this is the dream, and it's being awake that isn't very interesting.* She wished that could be how it was, that it could all be as simple as her getting turned around inside her head, and in the morning she'd wake up and tell Sadie, and Sadie would tell her what a very silly dream it had been.

"I won't leave him," Emmie said. "If that's what you came to ask me, I won't."

Sadie took a deep, hitching breath and wiped at her face with the front of her T-shirt. "Yeah," she said. "That's what I thought you'd say."

"Then why'd you have to wake me up, if you already knew?" Emmie asked, feeling suddenly more angry than sad or confused, and not caring if Sadie knew.

"I needed to be sure; that's why."

"You can't *make* me leave him either, Sadie. If you did, he would . . ." And she paused, not sure if she wanted to say what she was thinking, afraid that saying it out loud might be enough to make it so. But holding the words back was like being sick and trying not to vomit, and they came anyway. "He would die, if we both left him. He wouldn't have anything if we were both gone."

Sadie was crying now, and she shook her head. "I would never do that, Emmie. I'd never force you to come with me."

"But you *want* me to. You think that I *should*."

"I love you, sweetie, and I want what's best for you, that's all. But I'd never *make* you come, not if you want to stay."

"He's my father," Emmie said and sat up, pushing back the covers. "He's *my* father, and this is *my* house."

"It's my house, too," Sadie said, almost as though it was something she'd forgotten and was trying to remember, and she wiped her nose again. "Jesus, I'm sorry, Emmie. I promised myself that I wasn't going to cry."

"I think that was probably a dumb promise," Emmie said. "I don't see the point in making yourself dumb promises you know you can't keep."

"I can't stand the thought of being so far away from you," Sadie said, almost whispering now.

"Then don't *leave* us," Emmie replied, hearing the bite in her voice, the recrimination, and feeling only the smallest bit guilty about it. "Nobody's making you go. No one said you should."

Sadie took another deep breath and held it for what seemed like a very long time before Emmie finally heard her exhale. "This is hard, and you're not making it any easier."

"I'm not supposed to, Sadie. I'm just a kid, and you're my mother. I don't care what's best for your writing, not if it means that you're leaving me and Deacon alone."

Sadie turned back towards Emmie, and now her blue eyes were even brighter than before, bright with tears and anger and frustration and things that Emmie hadn't yet learned words for. Emmie flinched, as though her stepmother meant to strike her, as though something had been thrown. She almost called out for her father, but then the Patty Duke song ended again, and in the moment of silence before it started over, her panic dissipated, fading away like the red, used-up air that had spilled out of Sadie's nostrils.

"My *writing* pays the bills, little girl," she said. "My *writing* keeps your father in beer and whiskey and . . ." And then she held her good right hand up almost like a crossing guard, a gesture that Emmie understood at once—*stop, don't go any farther, don't say another word, shut up*—though she wasn't sure whether it was intended for her or for Sadie.

"Christ," her stepmother muttered, biting at her lower lip and shaking her head, and then she looked away from Emmie, staring down at the rumpled comforter instead. "I don't believe I just said that. I'm sorry, Emmie. That sounded like something *my* mother would have said."

"Maybe that's important," Emmie told her and scooted a few inches closer to her stepmother, close enough to be hugged if that's what Sadie needed to do next.

"Maybe so," Sadie agreed and then didn't say anything else for a couple of minutes, long enough that "The World Is Watching Us" ended again and started again. "But I'm still sorry. You should be asleep."

"I have school tomorrow."

"Yeah, you do. I shouldn't have awakened you. I shouldn't have brought this up in the middle of the night."

"I won't say anything to Deacon," Emmie said, hoping that Sadie wouldn't either. Hoping that by morning Sadie would have decided moving to New York was a ridiculous idea, that leaving them wouldn't help her writing at all.

"Thanks, pumpkin."

"Just don't give up on us yet," Emmie said, and Sadie did hug her then, held her tight and promised that she'd never give up on Emmie, no matter what, which wasn't particularly reassuring, since it still left the possibility that she might give up on Deacon and leave them anyway.

And later, after Sadie had left the room and there were only the outside noises and Patty Duke and all the strange creaks and thumps that an old house makes at night when it thinks no one is listening, Emmie told herself a story to make her sleepy again. It was a new story, mostly, not one she'd made up earlier or heard or read in a book. Sadie was in the story, but she was much younger, hardly more than a girl, and she hunted sea monsters with a pirate ship stolen from the Barbary Coast. Her bad hand had been replaced with a shiny mechanical contraption of cogs and gears with a timepiece set conveniently in the palm, and she searched the far horizon with a long brass telescope that had been given to her by the court astronomer of one sultan or another. The stolen pirate ship was called the *Harbinger,* because it was a word that Emmie loved and used whenever she felt using it was appropriate.

"Then turn not pale, beloved snail," the Sadie in the story howled boldly up at the fearsome Atlantic sky, "but come and join the dance!" (And Emmie had reluctantly stolen that part from *Alice's Adventures in Wonderland,* because she was too tired to think of anything better.)

She kept meaning to put Deacon in the story somewhere, because, as Sadie had taught her, telling stories was a sort of magick, a *powerful* sort of magick, and maybe doing so would help keep Sadie in Providence with them. But then the *Harbinger* suddenly ran aground on an island that was really the shell of an enormous man-eating turtle named Archelon, and by the time the giant turtle had been vanquished and the ship was on its way again, racing across the frigid Labrador Sea in search of seals and yetis and polar bears, she was falling asleep, sliding easily from the story into her dreams.

There were no pirate ships in her dream, or sea monsters, and Sadie didn't have a robotic hand, but her father was there, and her mother, too—the tall, plain woman who'd given birth to her, whom Emmie had only ever seen in photographs, because Chance Silvey had died the same day Emmie was born. She met her mother in dreams, sometimes, and sometimes they talked, and this time she told Emmie not to worry, that Deacon was a whole lot stronger than she thought. "He's slain dragons," her mother said, and smiled, and Emmie smiled, too, knowing it must be true, and the dream rose and fell like a French brigantine lost on the vast and briny deep, taking her places, and then on to *other* places, towing her soul slowly towards the dawn.

Sadie and Emmie take a cab from Pennsylvania Station, because Sadie said that she wasn't in the mood for the subway, and that was fine with Emmie. It was always much better to be aboveground, with the noise and movement of the city pressing in all around her, than stuffed into some dingy subway car hurtling headlong through the oily dark with no idea what might be going on overhead. The driver is a black woman with a thick Caribbean accent, and she asks Emmie how old she is before starting the meter. Then Sadie's cell phone rings, and she promises Emmie that it will take her only a second, just a minute, that it's someone from her agent's office, so she has to take the call. But Emmie knows that it always takes more than a second *or* a minute, and that's fine, too. There are far too many wonderful things to see, and if she talks to Sadie she might miss something. She'll have plenty of time to talk to Sadie later. So, the driver drives, and Sadie talks to the phone, and Emmie sits with her nose and lips against the cold taxi window and watches the city as the woman with the Caribbean accent navigates the crowded, steaming roads.

"Well, he *would* say that, wouldn't he," Sadie laughs, but not the sort of laugh that means she thinks something's funny, and then she digs about in her purse until she finds a yellow pack of Juicy Fruit gum. She gives a stick to Emmie and takes one for herself. "No, I've got my step-daughter down for a few days. He'll just have to wait until next week. They already said that I had until March, didn't they?"

The cab turns south onto Broadway, and Sadie laughs again and says good-bye to the person on the other end of the phone call. "I'm turning this damned thing off," she says, pressing a button on the cell phone and dropping it into her purse, then zipping the purse shut. "Now it's just me and you, pumpkin."

"We should get some pizza," Emmie says hopefully, reluctantly turning away from the smudgy cab window, from all those people and the other automobiles, the trash blowing along the sidewalks and the stunted little trees huddled in the lee of the tall buildings, the storefronts and restaurants. They've just passed a big yellow sign promising Ray's Famous Pizza, and Emmie wonders if the driver would go back if Sadie paid her extra.

"Pizza?" Sadie asks and wrinkles her nose. "You sure you want pizza? I thought we could get some sushi after we dropped your stuff at the apartment."

"I'd rather have pizza," Emmie replies. "Sausage pizza with lots of green olives. We can have sushi later, I promise. We'll have sushi tomorrow."

"I know you never get it, that's all."

Emmie smiles and starts folding the strip of silver foil from her piece of Juicy Fruit, working it nimbly between the tips of her fingers. "I don't eat *raw fish,*" she says, lowering her voice, imitating her father. "You can get goddamned *tapeworms* eating raw fish. You *want* a tapeworm, Emma Jean Silvey? You want a tapeworm *long as your arm*?"

And then they're both laughing so hard that Emmie drops her bit of foil and has to scrounge around on the floorboard behind the driver to find it again.

"You're going to get filthy down there," Sadie tells her. "You'll probably get a tapeworm long as your arm."

"Nope. I found it," Emmie says and holds up the foil so Sadie can see. Then the taxi hits a bump, and she almost drops it again. "Tapeworms hate pizza, by the way."

"Fine, you want pizza, then we'll get you some pizza." And Sadie sees that Emmie's almost finished folding the strip of foil into a tiny bird. A couple of months ago she sent Emmie a book on origami. Last time she spoke with Deacon, he complained that Emmie had folded a twenty-dollar bill into a kangaroo.

"Can I have that one?" Sadie asks, and Emmie nods her head.

"Sure," she says and gives the foil bird to Sadie.

"You're getting good at this."

"Yeah. I found more books in the library," Emmie tells her. "It's easy, once you get the hang of it. I'm teaching some kids at school."

"You are? How's school been working out these days?"

"Better," Emmie says, and then she catches the driver watching her in the rearview mirror.

"Just better?"

"Boring," Emmie adds, keeping her eyes on the driver's reflection. "Math is boring, history is even worse, and I hate playing goddamn volleyball."

"Everyone hates volleyball," Sadie says, still inspecting the precise angles of the origami bird. "That's why they make you do it. What about English? What are you reading?"

Emmie wishes that the driver would stop staring at her, wishes that Sadie would notice and make the woman stop. *It's just my eyes,* Emmie thinks. *She's noticed my eyes, and she's never seen a girl with yellow eyes before.* And that makes her think about the woman on the train again, Saben White and the star tattooed on the back of her hand. Seven points, even though Emmie could only *see* six. She starts to tell Sadie that the driver's staring at her, but then the woman with the Caribbean accent looks away, her eyes darting back to the road in front of them, back to the Manhattan traffic.

"Is something wrong?" Sadie asks, and Emmie almost tells her about the driver, and about Saben White as well. She knows that's exactly what her stepmother would *want* her to do, what Deacon would want her to do. Deacon almost got in a fight once with a guy on Thayer Street who was staring at Emmie's eyes, not just staring but pointing and making jokes about her. She remembers her father grabbing the man by the collar of his shirt and telling him that if he didn't apologize he'd be picking his teeth up off the ground. The man apologized, though Emmie had secretly wished that he wouldn't, had *wanted* to see Deacon hurt him for embarrassing her. Everyone on the street had stopped whatever they'd been doing and looked at them, looking at *her,* all those curious, peering green and brown and blue eyes brushing against her like dirty hands.

If I tell her, things will only be worse, she thinks, and so Emmie keeps it to herself for now and tells Sadie about her English class, instead, about Gulliver and *To Kill a Mockingbird* and a long poem by Robert Frost. Sadie gets her to recite part of the poem, the part that she remembers, and in a few more minutes the taxi is turning off Broadway, and the ride's almost over. When they reach St. Mark's Place, Sadie leans forward and tells the woman that this will do, this is fine. Emmie gets out and stands on the curb while Sadie pays the driver, stands staring up at the wintry slice of afternoon sky above the rooftops, and Emmie imagines that her eyes are that same color, like broken shards of china. There's an airplane up there, a black dot trailing white smoke, and as long as she's pretending, she makes it a spaceship on its way back to a planet where everyone has eyes like hers.

TWO

Soldier

"I'm asking you nicely—you need to stop staring at that damned watch of yours," Odd Willie Lothrop grumbles, plucking an unlit Winston from his thin lips. "You're making me jumpy."

"She's late," Soldier says for the seventh or eighth time since Saben failed to show for their two-o'clock. That was almost thirty-five minutes ago now, and the Bailiff's already called twice to see what the hell's going on, why the three of them aren't on their way from Cranston to Woonsocket. She's made Odd Willie take both the calls because she doesn't like talking to the Bailiff when he's pissed off—nobody does—but Soldier knows the next one will be for her, for her personally and no one else, and she'll have to come up with some sort of halfway credible excuse to cover Saben White's ass—again. This will make twice in one month, and Soldier doesn't know why the bitch hasn't already been handed her walking papers, why someone hasn't put a couple in her skull and left her floating face-down in a marsh somewhere.

"Jesus God, I fucking hate Woonsocket," Soldier says and takes another sip from her third cup of coffee, which has started getting cold and isn't doing anything at all for her hangover. "I don't know why this one couldn't have gone to Kennedy. He's sure as hell got a lot more experience up there than I do." She stares out the tinted, fly-specked plate-glass window of the Dunkin' Donuts at the squalor scattered up and down the gray asphalt strip of Warwick Avenue. Soldier only ever comes this far south when the Bailiff says that she has to, when he consults his tea leaves or his crystal ball, or whatever it is he uses to make up his mind, and picks a meeting place down here. Then she has no choice but to leave Providence and make the crossing into Kent County over the poisonous, filthy waters of the narrow Pawtuxet River.

"Kennedy's a *nebbish*," Willie says.

"And I'm up shit creek," Soldier replies and checks her watch again; Odd Willie shakes his head and puts the Winston back between his lips.

"Maybe she got stuck in traffic," he mumbles around the filter, and Soldier wants to hit him in the face. She takes another sip of coffee instead, something almost as bitter as her mood, and thinks about stepping outside for a smoke.

"You always been this high-strung?" Odd Willie asks. "I mean, were you this way before the winging with Sheldon and Joey Bittern?"

Soldier sets down her cup and stares at Odd Willie across the tabletop; he knows better than to start talking shit about Sheldon Vale, especially when she's sober and her butt's on the line. His shiny coal-black hair is slicked back into a crooked sort of duck's ass, his dewy sage-colored eyes peering out at her from beneath the place his eyebrows would be if he didn't shave them off once a week. He has a silver tooth right up front, and his cheekbones are so high and hollow, his face so pinched and drawn in on itself, Willie could easily score some extra cash renting himself out on Halloween. But pretty hasn't ever been very high on the Bailiff's list of desirable qualities in his underlings.

"Is it true," Soldier asks, "that people started calling you Odd Willie 'cause someone caught you fucking a dead cat?"

He laughs and makes a gun with his thumb and forefinger, then jabs it against his right temple. "Hell, I guess you done told me," he mutters around his cigarette. "Bang, bang."

"Hey, I'm just saying, you hear shit, that's all."

"And you heard that people started calling me Odd Willie 'cause I fucked a dead cat?"

"Something like that," she replies, looking out the window again. "At least, I think it was a cat. Might have been a dead raccoon."

"So, you're sitting there telling me you ain't never fucked nothing dead?" And he takes out the pink plastic comb he carries with him everywhere and runs it through his hair a few times.

Soldier nods her head. "I suppose," she says, "this is when you lose all respect for me, right? Alas, I have been forever diminished in your sight."

"Hey, baby, it ain't nothing can't be fixed."

"Don't do me any favors," she says, sick of Odd Willie and sick of the bright daylight making her headache worse, just fucking *sick*, and she reconsiders punching him in the face.

Odd Willie Lothrop shrugs, chews on the end of his cigarette, and puts the pink comb away. "Fine," he says. "Whatever. I already knew you were a tight ass. So, what you got against Woonsocket, anyway?"

"You're fucking kidding me, right?" But Odd Willie just shakes his head and grins a big, stupid grin for her, flashing his silver incisor. Soldier rolls her eyes. "Well, it's nothing that couldn't be fixed with napalm and bulldozers," she tells him, "maybe a few well-placed exorcisms here and there."

"I see," Odd Willie says and stops grinning. "Well, this'll be my first time up that way, so what do I know?"

And that's news to Soldier, the sort of news she wishes someone would let her in on before it's too late to make other, less suicidal arrangements. But this is how it's been since that night at Quaker Jameson's roadhouse. No one's ever come right out and said that any of it was her fault, almost walking into a trap that way, not being absolutely shit-sure what was what before she set out for Ipswich. And no one's ever blamed her for killing Sheldon, either, but there have been questions, questions she hasn't been very good at answering. So she keeps drawing these crap runs with the likes of Odd Willie Lothrop, and she gets stuck making excuses for Saben White because there's no way she's gonna blow it again, and whenever the Bailiff so much as *dreams* she's been at the bottle, it all gets a little bit worse.

"So, when do you tell me what this gig's about, anyway?" Willie asks. "I've never been much for drawing it out, savoring the razor's edge of suspense and all that happy crap."

"When we're on the road," Soldier says and checks her watch. "When we're moving, and when we're *not* sitting in fucking Dunkin' Donuts."

"You're kind of paranoid, too," he says and starts picking at the eviscerated remains of a Boston creme–filled doughnut lying on the napkin in front of him. The sight of it makes Soldier's stomach lurch, so she goes back to watching squalid Warwick Avenue for some sign of Saben, waiting for the phone to ring again.

"If you say so," she tells him.

"No, man, I'm serious," Odd Willie replies, giving up on the doughnut again. "People overhear some weird shit and ninety-nine times out of a hundred they're not gonna believe a single word of it. See, it just sails right on over their heads." He demonstrates by slicing the air above his greasy black hair with his left hand. "Someone hears us yakking about work, the kind of work *we* do, and you might as well be telling them the pope's a goddamn yeti. All this paranoid cloak-and-dagger, secret-handshake shit, you ask me, it's a total waste of resources."

"Like I said, if *you* say so. But I still don't talk shop in fucking Dunkin' Donuts."

"Maybe you'd be a little less *ap-pre-hen-sive* over at a Tim Hortons or a goddamn Krispy Kreme," Odd Willie snorts, wringing *apprehensive* until every syllable is bled bone-dry.

"Are you stoned?"

"Now, now," he says and grins, flashing that silver eyetooth for her, and he taps the windowpane hard with his knuckles. "Glass houses, Soldier. You always gotta remember about those glass houses."

"I'm sober," she tells him and reaches for the lukewarm coffee. "I haven't had a drink—"

"—since you passed out last night," Odd Willie says. "You're so hungover your hair hurts."

"I'm just fine," she lies, and Odd Willie nods his head and holds up what's left of the doughnut, just a few inches from her nose.

"Is that a fact? Wanna bite?"

And then her cell phone starts ringing again, and he drops the doughnut and licks his fingers, sits back in the booth, and points at the phone.

"Your turn," he says.

"One day we're gonna dance," she whispers, picking up the phone, speaking softly enough that there's no chance anyone but Odd Willie will hear her. "Just me and you and something sharp."

"So, you *can* talk dirty," he laughs, smug and dumb and entirely pleased with himself, laughs loudly and arches the prickly flesh where his eyebrows should be. "It's a date, girlo. Just you and me and a couple of pigstickers, but right now, you better answer that thing." And he points at the phone.

But when she looks, the number coming up on the display isn't one of the Bailiff's after all; it's Saben White's, and Soldier takes a deep breath, feeling something faintly like relief, and tosses the phone to Odd Willie. "You *tell* her she's got five minutes," and Soldier holds up all the fingers on her right hand for emphasis. "*Just five fucking minutes*. Then she's gonna have lots worse things to worry about than explaining this shit to the Bailiff."

Willie Lothrop nods, the humor in his face not quite draining completely away, and answers the phone.

"Yo, little miss slowpoke. You *know* you're screwed, right?" he chuckles, then waits while Saben White says whatever it is she has to say for herself.

"Five minutes," Soldier tells him again. "Not a goddamn second more." There's a fresh bottle of Dickel waiting for her out in the parking lot, wrapped in brown paper and tucked under the front seat of the old black Dodge Intrepid she's been driving the last three weeks. She can taste the whiskey, sweet and strong, burning her throat and her belly, easing the pain behind her eyes and the storm in her gut.

"No motherfucking way," Willie says and smacks himself in the forehead. An old woman sitting at another booth turns and stares at them. She has faintly lavender hair and a very large mole on her chin; Soldier stares back at her until she mumbles something under her breath and looks away. "That's fucked-up," Willie giggles, the way he does when he's nervous or scared.

"Just hand me the phone," Soldier says impatiently and holds out her hand.

"Rocky Point," Odd Willie says to Saben White, ignoring Soldier. "Right, yeah. Don't you worry; we'll find you. You just keep your ass put," and then he hangs up.

"What the hell was that?" Soldier demands, and Odd Willie smacks himself in the head again, even harder than before.

"We got trouble," he says, and before she can ask him what sort of trouble, the old woman with the lavender hair turns back around and glares at them. "What the fuck is your problem, lady?" Odd

Willie asks her, and the old woman narrows her eyes like an angry cat and doesn't say a word.

"Are you going to tell me—" Soldier begins, but Willie interrupts her.

"I swear to God, Soldier, if that old bat keeps staring at me like that, I'm gonna do her right here, in front of God and everyone."

"You're very unpleasant," the old woman croaks at him, and Soldier realizes that it's not a mole on her chin, but a dab of chocolate icing. "This used to be a *good* neighborhood."

"Yeah?" Odd Willie asks. "And just when the hell was that?"

"Let it go," Soldier says, her heart suddenly beating too fast, her palms gone cold and sweaty because she knows this is something bad, that it has to be something wicked bad to have Odd Willie losing his shit in public over a nosy old woman. "What did Saben say to you? Where the hell is she?"

"She's out at Rocky Point," he replies, glaring furiously back at the old woman. "She says she's got a fucking body in the trunk," and he raises his voice and yells, "Yo, Grandma, did you *hear* that over there? I said, she's got a *fucking* body in the trunk of her *fucking* car!"

The old woman shakes her head. "You Mafia trash," she sneers. "This used to be a *decent* neighborhood."

"I'm telling you," Odd Willie growls, "the bitch better stop looking at me."

And then Soldier sees one of the Hispanic girls behind the counter reaching for the telephone, and she grabs Odd Willie by one arm and hauls him up out of the booth. The old woman points a crooked finger at them, jabbing at the air like she means to poke it full of holes.

"That's right," she says. "You get out of here. Both of you, go on. I bet you got people to kill. I bet you got drugs to sell."

"Suck my dick, you shriveled old cunt."

"Wop trash," the old woman snaps back at him, then waves her finger about dramatically, like an incompetent magician finishing up a particularly difficult trick, before returning to her doughnuts.

"We're *leaving,*" Soldier says, speaking to Odd Willie and anyone else who's listening. "We're leaving right *now.*"

"She's calling the cops," he says and motions at the girl behind the counter with the antenna of the cell phone. "You better tell her to stop, or I'll have to shoot her. Hell, I'll shoot everyone in this dump."

And it *could* go that way, Soldier thinks, remembering all the crazy shit she's heard about Willie Lothrop. It could go that way, for sure, and maybe the Bailiff would be there to clean up the mess, and maybe he wouldn't. Maybe they'd both die waiting to find out, or maybe they'd die a little farther along, but it'd be their asses, either way.

She snatches her cell phone from Willie's hand and leans close, speaking directly into his right ear. His hair smells like a medicine cabinet. "Listen, you psycho shit," she hisses. "We're walking out that door, and you're not doing *anything* unless it's something I've fucking *told* you to do."

And Odd Willie nods once, *just* once, but it's enough that she lets herself start believing that maybe Saben White really is her biggest problem, and maybe she's not going to die in a Dunkin' Donuts on Warwick fucking Avenue.

"It's a priest," Willie says and giggles again, still watching the girl behind the counter.

"What? What's a priest?"

"The body locked in Saben's trunk. She killed herself a fucking priest."

And Soldier takes him roughly by the arm then, and leads him out into the February cold, out into the unwelcoming sunlight, her hangover and Woonsocket and the new bottle of bourbon all forgotten. Odd Willie gets into the Dodge as soon as she unlocks the doors; he takes a 9mm from the holster on his ankle and checks the clip. "I'm cool," he says. "I just can't stand people staring at me, that's all. It messes with my head." Soldier doesn't reply, doesn't say another word to him, doesn't even dare look over her shoulder until there are a couple of miles between the two of them and whatever is or isn't happening on Warwick Avenue.

"You're going the wrong way," he says, which is true, and Soldier turns around in the parking lot of a Shell station and heads for the old amusement park at Rocky Point.

Soldier first met the Bailiff when she was only five years old. So much of her childhood is only a vague, uncertain blur, but that first sight of the Bailiff, that's clear as moonlight through clean windows and uncloudy skies, as Sheldon Vale used to say. One night, she'd been told to put on her good calico dress, cornflower blue with tiny rosebuds, and then allowed to leave the tunnels and go into the basement of the yellow house on Benefit Street, up the creaky basement stairs into the house itself, and she found the Bailiff in a musty room filled with books and curio cabinets and an enormous globe cast in bronze, the whole world borne on the shoulders of a kneeling giant. When she'd opened the library door, the Bailiff stopped reading the book lying open on the writing desk in front of him and stared at her.

"Well now, child, exactly what would you be after?" he asked, and Soldier almost slammed the door, almost turned and ran back through the house, all the way back down to the safety of the tunnels. Instead, she squeezed the crystal doorknob and stared at the fat man, his smooth bald head and great gray beard, the biggest man she'd ever seen, and she imagined that he could hold the world on his shoulders, too, if it ever came to that. He was wearing a shabby navy blue seersucker suit and white tennis shoes, and he held a china teacup in his left hand, his pinkie finger extended like a small, plump sausage.

"Well, child? Are you dumb? Are you deaf? Do you have a name yet, or shall I just call you whatever strikes my fancy?"

"Soldier," she said and took one cautious step into the room.

"Soldier," the Bailiff replied, the way the word slipped from his lips making her think that perhaps he'd never heard it before and wasn't sure what it meant. He set his teacup down on a stack of books. "What kind of name is that for a pretty little girl such as yourself?"

"The name I chose," she told him.

"Then who am I to be asking questions? It's a fine name, Soldier. And which boneyard did you steal it from?"

She shrugged and eased the door shut behind her.

"Don't you even know?"

"Are you God?" she asked, setting his question aside for later, then glanced at the globe again. The painted continents were drifting across its surface, colliding with one another, pushing up new mountain ranges, tearing deep rifts for new seas to fill.

"Which one?" the Bailiff asked and sat up a little straighter in his chair.

She thought a minute, not having expected that particular question, and then she said, "The god of men. The church god. The one who let his son die, so that the people he'd made wouldn't go to hell." It was something that she'd overheard some of the older children and pups talking about one day when they should have been asleep, and though none of it had made any sense to her, she thought that it might be the right answer to the fat man's question. Or at least the sort of answer that would make her look like she knew about such things.

"Ah," the Bailiff said and rubbed thoughtfully at his beard. "And why would you ever think a thing like that, little Soldier, that I could be the god of man?"

"You look like him," she said, still watching the silent dance of continents and oceans over the circumference of the enormous globe.

"Do I?"

"Yes," Soldier replied. One of the pups had said that the god of man lived in a great house in the sky, where he was held prisoner by all the creatures that he'd created, and that he had a beard.

"Looks can be deceiving," he told her. "Our eyes are great liars and even worse judges of divinity."

"That's okay," Soldier sighed, finally turning away from the globe and back towards the Bailiff. "I don't think you're anyone's god. Not really."

"Well, I'm disposed to suspect you're correct about that," he told her and picked up his teacup again. "And don't you think I'm not grateful for that one small mercy, either."

"Are you the Cuckoo?" she asked.

"Why are you standing all the way over there?" he replied, watching Soldier over the rim of his cup. "Whatever I am, I don't usually eat little girls. Especially not one so full of questions."

Soldier looked back at the closed door, hesitating a moment more. It wasn't too late to leave, and she wasn't sure she was supposed to be in this room with this man. Maybe he was one of the house's secrets, and Madam Terpsichore had warned them all how dangerous secrets could be.

"Questions invariably give me indigestion," the Bailiff said and slurped his tea.

"Well, are you?" Soldier asked again, taking another two or three steps nearer the Bailiff. "Are you it? Are you the Cuckoo?"

"Not likely," he replied, sniffing at the contents of his teacup. "Have you ever seen a cuckoo? Nasty little things. Members of the family Cuculidae. Never met one yet was worth so much as a plug nickel and the time of day."

"I was . . . I was looking for something," she said, which Soldier thought was probably true. "They said I could come upstairs. They said—"

"They say an awful lot of things, don't they?"

"They do," she admitted reluctantly, hoping no one else was around to hear, trying to remember whatever it was she was supposed to be doing in the yellow house.

"The hounds are indeed damned garrulous beasts, and they do dearly love the sound of their own flapping tongues," the Bailiff muttered, half to himself, and held out the teacup to Soldier, who was now standing close enough to take it from him, if she wanted it. "Oh, it's a smidgen bitter, I warn you," he said, staring down into the cup and then back to Soldier. "Too much fenugreek in the mix, I suspect."

She took the cup from him and saw there was a little liquid left inside. It was very dark and smelled almost like turpentine.

"One thing's certain, though. We all got our burden of questions, little Soldier," the Bailiff told her and took a handkerchief from his breast pocket, white linen embroidered with tiny blue flowers, and he wiped at his wide forehead. "They follow us into this world, and damn it, they follow us out." Then he noticed that she wasn't drinking and frowned. "Don't you like tea?"

"Is that what this is?"

At that, the Bailiff laughed out loud and dabbed the handkerchief at the corners of his brilliant emerald eyes. "Well, that's what they tell me," he said. "But there's never as much truth in the telling as in the tasting, I've always heard. Have yourself a sip, and tell me what *you* would have it called if not tea."

Soldier, who had once taken a dare to eat a large spider that one of the pups had found beneath her bunk and then been sick for a week, sniffed the tea again and wrinkled her nose. "It smells like alley apples," she said.

"Oh, it's not quite as bad as that. I drink it almost every day."

"Is that why your hair fell out?" Soldier asked, sloshing the dark liquid about in the china cup. The cup had primroses painted on it, and there was a chip and a crack and the handle looked as though it had broken off and been glued back on again.

"Well," the Bailiff said, folding his handkerchief and returning it to the pocket of his seersucker suit. "They told me you had a mouth on you, child, and I daresay there's a wit to match."

And then she tasted the tea, because it seemed inevitable that she would, because this man might be the Cuckoo, despite what he'd said, or he might be the god of man and churches or a secret that shouldn't have been found out. Whichever, it was better not to make him angry, she thought, better if he didn't go complaining to the pale, silver-eyed people who kept the house that she'd interrupted his reading and then refused his hospitality.

It wasn't tea, and it didn't taste like turpentine. It tasted like something much, much worse.

"Such a face," the Bailiff said and shook his head. Soldier swallowed, gagged, coughed without covering her mouth, and then started to set the empty cup down on the edge of the writing desk, but, "No," the Bailiff told her. "That's not the last of it."

"Yes, it is," she said and wiped the back of one hand across her lips, as though she might wipe the taste away. "I drank it all. I wish I hadn't, but I did."

"Yes, you *drank* it," the Bailiff agreed, "but that doesn't mean the cup's quite empty."

"Oh," Soldier said and looked into the cup again. The Bailiff was right. The bottom was covered with a sort of sludge. It reminded her of the mud that got all over everything whenever it rained too much and the tunnels began to flood. It reminded her of the time she cut her thumb on a scalpel she hadn't had permission to touch. It reminded her of the empty skins snakes leave behind.

"They see something in you, dear girl," the Bailiff said, and she was dimly aware of the old, dry wood of his chair creaking as he shifted his bulk from one side to another. "It frightens them. It makes them wonder if it means their doom, what you are, what you may yet *become,* or if perhaps you can become a more perfect servant of the Cuckoo."

"I don't know," Soldier whispered, and her voice seemed to have shrunk down to a sound no larger than the scritching of insect legs against bare dirt walls.

"Nor do I," replied the Bailiff. "But we must endeavor to find out, don't you think?"

"I'm going to be sick," she told him and realized that the stuff in the bottom of the cup had become ashes or had been ashes all along.

"It would be better if you didn't. We'd only have to start this all over again some other time."

So she took a deep breath and struggled to think of anything at all but the wriggling sensation the dark liquid had left in her throat, the roiling, almost painful fullness much farther down inside. "I don't want to look at this anymore," she said and set the cup on the desk before he could protest, set it next to the book he'd been reading when she came in. The brittle paper was the color of ancient, rotting teeth, and she didn't recognize any of the words because they were all in Latin, and the ghouls held back Latin until the seventh year.

"Not to worry, child," the Bailiff said and ran the tip of one finger around the rim of the cup. "You've seen the start of it. The rest can wait." His skin against the porcelain made a high, clear ringing, and hearing it made Soldier's stomach feel better.

"They need their prophecies and portents," he said. "It keeps them on an even keel, if you know what I mean."

"That's pretty," Soldier said, meaning the ringing his finger was drawing from the cup. "I didn't see any bells in there," and she thought perhaps he was hiding them in his hand somewhere. A hand that big might hide almost anything at all.

"Do you recollect your mum?" the Bailiff asked. "Do you sometimes see her face?"

Soldier frowned. It was a stupid question, and whoever he was, he ought to at least have the sense to know that. Anyone who could read Latin ought to know that much. "No," she said. "The Cuckoo took me when I was a baby, just like all the others."

"Of course it did. But do you *recall* her face?"

"Our mothers are gone, gone, gone," she replied, repeating one of the first lessons the *ghul* had taught her. She didn't want to be talking, and she silently asked Mother Hydra to tell the fat man to shut up so she could listen to the music from the teacup. "Our mothers are gone from us forever."

"That's what they told you?" he asked.

"Yes. When the Cuckoo took me from her, he took all my memories of her, too. It made me . . ." And she paused, looking for exactly the words that Madam Mnemosyne had used. "It made us *hollow,* so we could be filled with other things."

"Did it now? Sure, that's what they say, all right, and you're a smart girl what knows all her lessons."

Soldier realized that the music had stopped, but she felt much better, just the same.

"You do what you're told," the Bailiff says, "and don't think I'm telling you to do nothing otherwise. You answer to the hounds, and you always will. That's the way of it, little Soldier, for better or ill. But you should know *this,* too," and now he lowered his voice, and his eyes seemed to flicker and grow dim. That frightened Soldier, those glistening emeralds bruising until they were almost brown, though she wasn't sure why it frightened her, and she took a step back from him, but then the Bailiff put a hand on her shoulder so she couldn't run away.

"They don't know even half what they pretend to know," he said, speaking in a hushed, conspiratorial tone. "And they've got no problem with making up the difference. They're something terrible, something more than this old world, just the way they tell it, but they ain't gods, no more than you or me. Don't you ever forget that, girl, no matter what they might say to the contrary."

"I'm sleepy," she said, because she was. Suddenly Soldier was very sleepy, and she wondered if she'd ever be able to find her way back downstairs before her dreams caught up with her.

"That's just the tea. The nap will do you good."

"Will I see you again?" she asked.

"You will," the Bailiff said, "and often. They want me to try to tell them if you're what they've been waiting for all this time, what they've been praying would never track them down."

"Am I?" she asked groggily.

"I guess we'll have to see about that, won't we?" he replied and laughed again. And then there was no use trying to stay awake even one minute longer, sleep grown so thick and warm and welcoming about her. He rose from his chair and took her in his strong arms, and the fat man who said he wasn't the god of men or the Cuckoo carried Soldier back through the yellow house and down the stairs to the tunnels far Below.

Near the dead end of Rocky Point Avenue, the ruins of the abandoned amusement park sprout like something cancerous, some gaudy, carnival-colored malignancy, grown wild and shattered from the banks of Narragansett Bay. There were rides and attractions and restaurants here as far back as the end of the nineteenth century, more than a hundred years of Rhode Islanders stuffing themselves with deep-fried clam cakes and doughboys, then getting sick on the carousels and Ferris wheels and roller coasters, until a bankruptcy finally shut the place down in 'ninety-six. Since then, the relentless vandalism of the seasons—snow and frost, rain and salt wind and summer heat—and the more random desecrations of teenagers have taken their toll. Now the park sits empty and forgotten by almost everyone but land developers and kids looking for someplace they shouldn't be. A few deer and the occasional coyote stroll the Midway, and rats nest in the boarded-up ice-cream stands. Something else for Soldier to hate about Warwick, another place she'd never go if not going there were up to her.

Saben White's rusty old Chevy Impala is sitting directly in front of the park's front gates—six vertical concrete columns painted hideous shades of blue and red and yellow, neons faded now almost to pastels, and there's a sagging cross span with giant red-and-white plywood letters and the gaps where other letters are missing to gaily spell out ROCK PO NT. When they pull up, Saben's standing near the rear of the car, smoking a cigarette.

For the last half mile, Odd Willie's been singing what he swears is an old radio and TV jingle for the park—*Come with your family, come with your friends. Rocky Point is open, 'cuz it's summertime again!* When he sees Saben, his voice rises to a strained, ear-rending falsetto, Frankie Valli on crack, and Soldier tells him to shut the hell up.

He giggles and lights another Winston. "Hey, I'm thinking maybe it's not a real priest," he says, talking through a cloud of smoke. "Maybe it was an impostor, and we're in the clear, safe as houses, cool as Eskimo poop."

"Oh, it'll be a real priest," Soldier replies, because she's been stuck with Saben just long enough to know that she never fucks anything up halfway, that with her it's all or nothing. "You just stay sharp and don't go freaking out on me again, you understand?"

"Roger-dodger, Captain Kangaroo," Odd Willie snorts and takes another long drag off his cigarette.

"You are such a fucking asshole," she says, pulling in close beside the Chevy, not certain if she means Willie Lothrop or Saben White but pretty damned sure it doesn't make any difference. Soldier shifts into park and kills the engine, and Willie rolls down his window and waves at Saben. Soldier unfastens her seat belt and opens the driver-side door, climbing out into the cold, sunny afternoon, all that clean blue sky overhead like some void her headache is working overtime to fill. She slams her fist down hard against the roof of the Dodge, and Saben sighs and drops the butt of her cigarette to the pavement, grinds it out with the toe of her boot.

"One good reason," Soldier says, "you give me one good god-damn reason why I shouldn't kill you right now and bury the both of you in the same hole."

"I didn't have a choice," Saben says, staring down at the ground instead of looking Soldier in the eye.

"Bull*shit*," Soldier growls and punches the roof again; this time Odd Willie yells at her to stop, and she yells back at him to get his lazy ass out of the damned car.

"It's fucking complicated," Saben says, glancing right, towards the amusement park's chain-link gates topped with glinting coils of razor wire. "I swear to you both, I did the only thing—"

"You gonna swear it to the Bailiff?" Soldier asks, coming quickly around the front of the Dodge as Odd Willie gets out of the car. "Or maybe you better just swear to the hounds and get it over with? What the hell were you doing in Connecticut in the first damned place?"

"Business," Saben replies. "I had business. I was going to call—"

"Saben, we are supposed to be in fucking Woonsocket right this very fucking *second*. Right now, all three of us, we're MIA. The Bailiff doesn't know where the hell we are. Those assholes up in Woonsocket don't know where we are."

"Maybe you should let her talk," Odd Willie says, and Soldier glares at him.

"Maybe *you* should stay the hell out of this," she barks back. "Maybe you should start worrying about your own problems, Mr. Goes-fucking-homicidal-psycho-in-a-goddamned-doughnut-shop-because-an-old-lady-looked-at-you-funny."

"I don't think I need you standing up for me, Willie," Saben says.

"Oh, I think you are gonna find out you're *very* wrong about that," Willie tells her and laughs. "In fact, I think you have no *idea* just how—"

"Shut *up,* Willie," Soldier says, and this time he does. For a moment the only sound is the wind through the high, bare limbs of the trees growing on either side of the Rocky Point gate. Soldier flares her nostrils and takes a deep breath, smelling the nearby bay, pushing back at the headache and the anger crowding her mind, the anger that's going to get her killed someday soon if she doesn't learn to keep it on a shorter leash. She watches Saben and tries to imagine what the Bailiff would say, what he'd tell her to do if he were here. Something simple and obvious, like, *You can fret about all the whys and hows and wherefores when you have the time for it,* or *The son of a bitch is dead, little Soldier. And that grave you've got to dig for him, it don't much care how he got that way.* Something like that. Something to get her moving and keep her from kicking Saben's ass until after they've dealt with the mess she's made.

"He's in the trunk?" Soldier asks, pointing at the Impala, and Saben White nods her head.

"Yeah, Soldier, he's in the trunk. I already told Willie he's in the fucking trunk. I can explain this. I really can, if you'll just stop and listen."

Soldier is standing very close to Saben now, close enough to hit her, close enough to knock out a few front teeth or maybe break her nose or both before Odd Willie would even have a chance to ask if that was really such a good idea. Her hands are clenched fists, and Soldier *knows* how good it would feel, Heaven in the force of the blow, release in the collision of her knuckles with that fragile construction of bone and cartilage and flesh. It would be almost as sweet as whiskey.

"And what good's that going to do us, exactly, me listening to more of your bullshit?" she asks Saben White and then takes a step closer, aware now that she's near enough to make Saben uncomfortable, that she's invaded the invisible, sacred bubble of personal space. To people like her and Saben, people who spend all their short lives waiting for the next confrontation, the next asshole who's come around looking for a piece of you, sometimes that's all it takes, and she silently prays to the nameless gods that Saben will swallow the bait and throw the first punch. "Explaining it to me, is that going to make this guy in your trunk any less dead? Will it get rid of the fucking body for us? Maybe it'll square things with the Bailiff, is that it?"

"Jesus," Odd Willie mutters around his cigarette. "How about let's just dispose of the motherfucker and get it over with. It's freezing out here."

"No, I want her to know how it is," Saben says, risking a glance at Soldier. "I want her to know this time it wasn't my fault."

Soldier spits on the ground at Saben's feet, and a white fleck of saliva spatters the shiny black leather toes of her boots. "Saben, I don't believe you could tell the truth if someone wrote it down for you."

Odd Willie laughs, then shivers and stares up at two big gulls wheeling by overhead. "You guys keep this crap up long enough, we're gonna end up having a chat with the fucking cops, okay?"

"Yeah, so how you want to do this, Willie?" Soldier asks him, not taking her eyes off Saben, thinking she might still get lucky. Saben

White's good at not knowing when to shut the hell up, even better at not knowing when she's in over her head.

"Christ. Why are you asking *me*? I didn't shoot the son of a bitch."

"You feel like digging a hole?" she asks Saben.

"Hell," Willie grumbles. "The ground's probably half fucking frozen," and he stops watching the gulls and kicks at the pavement. "It'd probably take the rest of the day to plant Holy Joe deep enough the dogs wouldn't just come along tonight and dig him up again. Lots of wild dogs out here."

"What about you?" Soldier asks, and steals another inch or two of the space separating her and Saben. "You killed him. Maybe you know what we should do with him."

"Put him in the bay," Saben replies, and Soldier can see how hard she's straining to sound like she has her shit together. "Gut him, fill the bastard with stones, then dump the body off Rocky Point. That's what I was thinking when I drove out here."

"I don't know," Willie says. "I never trust them not to float. Especially priests. Priests and faggots, they'll float on you every goddamn time."

"There've been a lot of fires out here," Saben says, and Odd Willie nods his head, then stares at the glowing tip end of his cigarette.

"She's got that part right," Willie says. "What with all the kids and the bums, it's a wonder there's anything left standing out here. It's a wonder it's not just a heap of charcoal."

"Right, so who's gonna care if there's one more fire?" Saben asks hopefully, looking straight at Soldier now. "We take his teeth and hands—"

"Yeah?" Soldier asks, speaking hardly above a whisper, and she leans close to Saben, sniffing at the air around her. "Is *that* what we do?" Soldier can smell stale tobacco smoke and expensive leather, cologne and the gun hidden beneath her blazer. The air about Saben stinks like fear and lies and desperation.

"Man, these days burning ain't much better than sinking," Odd Willie says glumly, looking up at the gulls again, "not unless you're dealing with some sort of serious expedient. What with the fucking DNA analysis and pathologists and all that shit, the goddamned cops might as well be magicians. Now, maybe if I had some time to lay my hands on a good accelerant, set up a delay—"

"Could you do it alone?" Soldier asks, and he answers her with a shrug and a scowl.

"Soldier, I heard you had pyromancy," Saben White says, and Soldier moves closer and sniffs at her hair.

"Did you? And where'd you hear a thing like that?"

"After Ipswich—"

"Ipswich was easy," Soldier replies, and now she's so close her lips brush against Saben's right ear. "There weren't any dead Roman fucking Catholic priests to worry about. All I used in Ipswich was a couple of cans of gasoline and a road flare. That's *all* the pyromancy I know, bitch."

"I'm not scared of you," Saben says, but it's obvious to Soldier that she is, that she's terrified—the way her voice trembles, the sweat standing out on her upper lip, her slightly dilated pupils, the faint electric reek of adrenaline.

"I think I want to see you on your knees," Soldier whispers. She can feel the other woman's body growing tense, fight or flight, resist or submit, and she nips at the top of Saben's right ear, not quite hard enough to draw blood, but hard enough to hurt, catching the soft curve of helix and antihelix between her strong incisors.

"Screw you," Saben says, her voice rattling like empty tin cans strung on baling wire.

Slowly, tentatively, Soldier releases her ear, and when it's free, Saben covers that side of her face with her right hand and turns her head towards Odd Willie.

"Is that what it's going to take?" Soldier asks her. "Do I have to actually fuck you to get your attention, to make you understand who's on top?"

"Willie, call the Bailiff," Saben says. "Tell him I had to do it. Tell him to get her off me."

Willie just shakes his head and flicks the butt of his cigarette at the curb, then takes his silver Zippo and a fresh pack of Winstons out of his coat. He peels away the cellophane wrapper and drops it on the ground. The wind whisks it away at once, and the crumpled plastic snags in a patch of dry brown weeds closer to the gate.

"C'mon, Saben. You know he's not going to do that. You ought to know he *can't* do that. He might be a lunatic, but he knows the rules. He knows your ass is mine if that's the way I want it. Ain't that right, Odd Willie?"

"Yeah, sure," he replies, and lights another Winston. "I know how it is. But, Soldier, I mean, fuck it, why don't we deal with the good Father Whoever-he-might-be in the trunk there before every cop in this end of Kent County shows up. You can still mess with Saben later, right?"

Soldier ignores him, only half hearing the words anyway, her own heartbeat too loud in her ears now, the taste of Saben's fear too sharp, entirely too immediate.

"Get down on your knees, Saben. Don't you fucking make me tell you again."

"No," Saben says, still watching Odd Willie like maybe there's some hope he's going to change his mind and come to her rescue after all. "I won't do it."

"Fine," Soldier says, "if that's how it's got to be, that's how it's got to be," and she slaps the left side of Saben's face so hard that she staggers and almost falls. Blood spurts from her nose and busted lower lip, falling in vivid crimson droplets across the blacktop. Odd Willie makes a disgusted, impatient sort of noise and retreats a couple of steps towards the Dodge. Saben slumps against her car, stunned, gasping through her bloody lips and nostrils, and Soldier seizes her by the back of her neck and forces her to her knees. She isn't surprised that it requires so little effort. She's learned that one good blow takes the fight out of almost everyone.

"How's that?" Soldier asks, bending over Saben. "Are you comfortable down there?"

"You know, just for the record," Odd Willie says, "it seems to me you got your priorities turned around."

"Duly noted," Soldier replies breathlessly and smiles at Odd Willie. Drawing blood felt even better than she expected it would, and the sight of Saben on her knees, Saben helpless and hurting and humiliated after all the weeks of bullshit, has her a little giddy. Part of her, the sliver of humanity that knows enough to keep its hands clean, reminds Soldier that there are limits to what she can get away with.

Don't worry, she thinks. *I'm not gonna kill her. Not today.*

"Maybe I should put it in writing," Odd Willie Lothrop says.

"Yeah," Soldier agrees, "maybe you should. There's a pen in the glove compartment. Probably some paper, too."

"But you're not gonna hold this against me?" he asks. "I mean, I know this sort of shit can come back to haunt a guy, taking issues with the powers that be and all."

"Oh, hell no," Soldier says, still smiling, and then she kicks Saben hard in the ribs. There's another gout of blood on the pavement, and Saben White's mouth is opening and closing, opening and closing like a fish caught out of water, fighting to draw breath back into her bruised, deflated chest. "I'm not vindictive," Soldier continues. "You ought to know that by now, Willie. I'd never *think* of keeping anyone from speaking his mind. I mean, that's the freaking First Amendment. That shit's sacred as George Washington and the goddamn golden rule."

"Never hurts to ask. I figure a guy's gotta watch his own ass," and then he slips quickly back inside the Dodge, shuts his door, and rolls up the window again. Soldier nods once in his direction and turns back to Saben White.

"Still thinking we should get the Bailiff's opinion on this situation?" she asks, taking her cell phone from her jacket and laying it on the blood-spattered ground in front of Saben. "It's easy. All you gotta do is press redial. Of course, I'll break your fucking hand, but nothing's free."

Saben, still gasping, starts to reach for the phone, then pulls her hand back.

"That's a smart girl," Soldier says, squatting down next to Saben White. "Who'd have ever thought it. Now, we're going stop fucking around and come to a mutual understanding, and *then* we're going to clean up this mess you've made, *capisce*?"

Saben only nods her head once, then gags and almost vomits. Soldier retrieves her cell phone and returns it to her jacket pocket.

"I . . ." Saben gasps. "It's . . . it's not . . ."

"You need to concentrate on breathing, babe, not talking. We're way past talking now."

Soldier leans forward and closes her jaws firmly around the back of Saben's neck, just below the hairline, just behind the point where her spinal cord enters the foramen magnum. She bites down hard, breaking skin and bruising muscle, sinking her insufficient teeth in as far as they'll go and tasting the warm, coppery sea trapped there inside that body. A low and threatful growl begins deep in Soldier's throat and rises very slowly; Saben White goes rigid, then, gradually, she begins to relax, accepting Soldier's rank, accepting her own position. They both know this drill, have both known it since they were children wrestling with other changelings and the ghoul pups in the tunnels beneath College Hill. It's almost instinct to them both. After only two or three minutes, Soldier releases her, and Saben crawls away, sobbing, still trying to get her breath, trailing blood and spit and snot.

"I'll give you a couple of minutes to pull yourself together,"

Soldier calls after her. "I wouldn't waste it crying." But the anger is deserting her now, and there's little left in its place but weariness and dread of all the trouble that's yet to come. Her phone call to the Bailiff. Keeping her mouth shut and taking it, whatever *it* may be, whatever he has to say. Whatever she has coming for letting all this happen on her watch.

She wipes her mouth, and her lips and chin leave a red smudge across the back of her wrist. Her throat's a little sore from the noises it was making only a moment before, the guttural canine sounds that it was never intended for. She thinks of the bottle of whiskey hidden beneath the seat and watches Saben White, who's sitting near the front fender of the Impala now, sobbing, her face hidden in her hands. Her tattoo, the Seal of Solomon, seems very bright beneath the afternoon sun, all those shades of ink shining from her skin like a beacon, like a warning. Soldier imagines cracking open the bottle of Dickel, imagines it filling her mouth, warming her belly, driving back the thought of the Bailiff's voice, and then she even manages to pretend she has that luxury.

The second time that Soldier met the Bailiff, he was wearing the same threadbare seersucker suit as before, the same white tennis shoes, but he offered her sugar cookies and grape soda instead of the foul-tasting, turpentine-scented tea. She'd been sent upstairs again by Madam Terpsichore, and one of the silver-eyed women who kept the house led her through the kitchen and a parlor and down the long hallway to the library where he was waiting at his writing desk. There was an oil lamp with a tall glass chimney sitting near the book he was reading, and it cast the only light in the room besides the waxing three-quarter moon slipping in through the parted draperies. He smiled when he saw her, smiled wide and thanked the silver-eyed woman, whose name was Adelaide.

"You're back so soon?" he asked Soldier, as though the whole thing had been her idea. "Why, it's hardly been a month, has it?"

In fact, it had hardly been a full week, but Soldier figured it would probably be best if she didn't correct him. A plate of cookies and a bottle of soda had been placed on the floor near his chair, and the Bailiff pointed at them and asked if she was hungry.

"Yes sir, I am," she said and sat down near the plate. She was missing her dinner, being sent up into the yellow house to talk with the fat man who claimed that he wasn't the god of men and churches or the Cuckoo, but whom she suspected could be either one and, perhaps, even both. She drank half the grape soda, taking care not to spill any on her blue calico dress, and ate one of the cookies before he said anything else to her.

"Have you been thinking about the things we talked about?" he asked. She told him that she hadn't and finished a second cookie.

"Oh," he said, sounding neither surprised nor angry. "Well, I don't suppose that much matters, does it? I suppose it matters much more what we talk about tonight. Before we begin, do you have any questions, little Soldier?"

And there *were* things that she wanted to ask him, such as why none of the other children had been sent up to the library, why only her, and whether or not he had a name besides "the Bailiff," which didn't seem like much of a name at all. But before she could think which question to ask him first, which might be most important, in case she got to ask only one, he was already talking again, so she started on her third cookie instead.

"That cup of tea you finished off," he said. "I trust it likely didn't agree with you. It's damned heady stuff, I'll grant you that. Sometimes, it knows the road into a person's dreams. Sometimes, it can leak straight into the soul," and then he tapped himself twice between the eyes with a pudgy index finger. "Unless, of course, you happen to be accustomed to it."

Soldier put down the unfinished cookie and stared up at him; his green eyes seemed even brighter than the last time. She wondered if they were real eyes, or if the Bailiff had somehow lost his own and these were only polished gems.

"I had a dream," she said. "Is that what you're asking, if I had a bad dream after I drank the tea? Were you the one who carried me to bed?"

The Bailiff hesitated a moment, as though confused at having been asked two questions at once. He rubbed at his beard and frowned.

"I had a dream," she said again, recalling the way her head had ached when she woke after her first visit with the Bailiff, waking confused, disoriented, and hurting, and sick to her stomach. She'd been excused from her lessons for the whole day, and Madam Melpomene had even made someone else take her chores. So she'd lain there in her bunk all night long, staring at the underside of the bunk above, afraid to sleep again, thinking about the Bailiff and trying to remember all the missing pieces of the strange, long dream. She knew it had come from the teacup, from whatever she'd swallowed. She didn't need him to tell her that.

"I might have warned you, I suppose," he said, those too-green eyes twinkling in the lamplight.

"Are these real cookies?" she asked him and poked at the one she'd left half-eaten. "Will they give me nightmares, too?"

"Do I look like the sort who would give a little girl tainted sweets?"

"Yes," she replied, and he laughed out loud, his laugh like a thunderclap, and leaned back in his chair. The old wood creaked alarmingly, and she thought for a second that it might burst apart in a hail of varnished splinters.

"The dream, then," he said, when he'd stopped laughing and had wiped his eyes with his handkerchief and put it back into his breast pocket. "Tell me as much of it as you can, little Soldier. Everything you recollect. Take care to omit nothing, no matter how nonsensical or insignificant it might seem to be."

"Nonsensical?" she asked, puzzled by the word because she'd never heard it before.

"Silly," he replied. "Ridiculous. Inane. Absurd."

"I see," she said, though she'd never heard *inane* before, either.

"Anyway, take care to leave none of it out. The devil is very often in the details, you know."

"Unless he's in this room," she said, deciding against finishing the sugar cookies and grape soda. The Bailiff laughed again, and his chair creaked and popped beneath him.

"Whatever in the hells have you gone and plucked from the wild, wild sea, my dear old Terpsichore," he chuckled, even though Madam Terpsichore wasn't in the room with them. And then to Soldier he said, "Child, you are a rare scrap, indeed. We shall have such delightful conversations, you and I."

"Do you want to hear about my dream or not?" she demanded, and the plate with the remaining cookies squeaked softly against the floor when she pushed it away from her.

"Oh, most assuredly," he said. "More even than I desire my next breath."

I could keep it for myself, she thought. *I could make it a secret and keep it forever, and no one would ever know. I'd forget he made me have that dream. I could try—*

"Whenever you're ready, dear," he prompted.

"It doesn't make much sense," she warned, but he said that didn't matter. "I don't remember *all* of it," she added, and he said that didn't matter, either. Of course, he'd told her both these things already, and she could tell he was losing patience. She didn't know what would happen if she made the Bailiff angry, the bald man, the one who might be the god of men and of churches, who might be the Cuckoo, who might only be a demon. She didn't know, and she didn't want to find out, so she took a deep breath, wished that she weren't afraid of drinking the rest of the grape soda, and cleared her throat.

"At first I was in a desert," she said, though that wasn't actually the beginning of it. The *true* beginning frightened her too much to put into words, so much so that it was better to risk making the bald man angry with her. "I was in a desert, and I wasn't a child. I was grown-up, and there was another woman walking with me. She was also a child of the Cuckoo."

"Did she tell you that?"

"Yes, I *think* so," Soldier replied. She told the Bailiff that the woman was the most beautiful person that she'd ever seen, dreaming or awake or anywhere in between, Above or Below. She was very, very tall, with long gray-white hair pulled back in dreadlocks to reveal her face and her golden-brown eyes. Her skin had, over the long ages that she'd wandered the sand, been burned black as pitch by the relentless desert sun and might as easily have been ebony or jet as flesh and blood. They'd walked together through the whispering sand, trudging over gigantic dunes that seemed to run on in every direction as far as Soldier could see.

As they walked, the woman told her a story about three witches and a changeling child named Esmeribetheda, an old story that Soldier had known already, though she'd never heard it told quite the way that the black woman told it.

"She was not a traitor," the woman said to Soldier. "That part's a lie. Esmeribetheda had good reasons for the things she did. The *djinniyeh* in their great domed city had set themselves against the *ghul,* who were interlopers, who'd come to the deserts from some world far away. Esmeribetheda was to be made a *djinniyeh* herself, when the *ghul* were all dead or driven back to that other place."

"How curious," the Bailiff said and lit a briarwood pipe with a kitchen match. He exhaled, and the air in the library smelled of brimstone and cherry tobacco. "And you've told none of this to the hounds?"

"No," Soldier replied, because she hadn't.

"Good. It's best we keep it that way for now. Continue, please."

"Are you sure?" she asked, hoping he'd decided that he'd heard enough and would send her away.

"Of course," he said around the stem of the pipe clutched between his yellow teeth. "You're doing very well. Don't stop now."

So she told him about the ruined walls and empty windows of a city half-buried by the sand. They passed it and then descended a particularly steep dune to stand together on the parched bed of an ancient, vanished lake or sea hidden deep within the endless desert, a vast plain of cracked mudflats and glittering salt and gypsum crystals. All around them lay the crumbling, petrified bones of the monstrous beasts that had lived there long ago, the beasts that had haunted deep places almost from the dawn of time until that last day when the sun had finally consumed the waters, and the things had perished in the mud and blistering heat.

The crooked, scorched trunk of a tree rose from the lake bed. There were symbols Soldier didn't recognize carved into the wood in long vertical columns.

"The *ghul* murdered her," the woman said, running her fingers across one of the symbols. "That part's true. Her bones turned to dust, and her ghost still murmurs in the night. In time, the *djinni-yeh* became distracted by other things—they're too easily discouraged—and didn't try again. But the hounds moved on, searching for someplace where they'd have no enemies to fear."

And then, Soldier told the Bailiff, the black-skinned woman had gone, and she'd been left alone and standing at the crest of a very high dune, the tallest one yet, the King of Dunes, she thought. She stood there, wrapped in silk and muslin robes that the dark woman had given her, looking down at a place where the desert finally ended, a place where the sea met the land, where the two were forever fighting a war and the sea was forever winning. The yellow-brown-white sand became a green sea capped with silvery waves, and she was starting down the far side of the King of Dunes when she heard something in the sky and looked up.

The Bailiff puffed his pipe and nodded his head.

"I'm not making any of this up," she said.

"I don't think that you are," he replied. "What did you see when you looked at the sky?"

"You don't think that I'm lying to you?"

"Of course not. But tell me now, what did you see?"

What she'd seen were two birds, or flying machines, or dragons, or prehistoric reptiles, or angels—it was difficult to be sure, and perhaps she'd seen all these things. Perhaps, she said, they'd been one thing and then another, changing constantly, and the Bailiff had thought this entirely plausible. The two things, whatever they might have been, were locked in an even fiercer battle than that being waged by the sea upon the sandy shore. One was wreathed all in flame and the other in a whirling veil of shadow. Bits of them were torn away and fell to the ground, sizzling, smoking, melting sand to glass on contact. She was very afraid, seeing them, not knowing what it meant, and Soldier told the Bailiff that she'd tried to reach the shore.

"Why? Did you think you'd be safe there?"

"There was a yellow boat waiting," she told him. "I thought that it might take me to the dark woman again. I thought she might have left it there for me."

"You wanted to be with her?" he asked, and Soldier nodded yes. "Do you wish you were with her now?"

"It was only a dream," Soldier said. "She wasn't a real person. You can't wish to be with a dream." But she knew that was a lie, and she'd missed the dark woman since the moment she'd awakened.

"Are you certain of that, it being only a dream?"

Instead of answering him, Soldier told the Bailiff how she'd lost her footing, had fallen and rolled a long way down the dune, getting sand in her mouth and eyes and nose; when she finally reached the bottom, she was sore and bleeding, dizzy, and her eyes were watering. Overhead, the two things, whatever they might have been, clawed and screamed and tore at each other. She understood that they might do this for all eternity, that they might have been at each other since the world began.

When she finally reached the beach, the boat was gone.

"Had it sailed without you?" the Bailiff asked, relighting his pipe, which had gone out.

"No, it just wasn't there anymore. I'm not sure it was ever really there."

And so, defeated, she'd sat down on the wet sand. There were stranded starfish and oysters and snails and ammonites all around, bits of coral and driftwood. She found a hermit crab huddled inside a snail's shell. The waves cooled her feet, which were bruised and raw from so many days or weeks or months walking in the desert, but the salt water also burned the blisters and the open, weeping sores. She'd become a child again, when she wasn't paying attention, a little girl sitting alone on a faraway beach while titans fought in the blue-white sky overhead. Digging her fingers into the sand, she found a single pearl and hid it in her robes.

"And then I woke up," she said.

"Yes," the Bailiff said. "I see," and then he said nothing else for a while. Soldier sat staring at the floor, at patterns she imagined she could see in the wood's grain, and the Bailiff sat smoking his pipe. She could hear a clock ticking loudly somewhere in the room, though she hadn't noticed a clock before.

Finally, the Bailiff emptied the bowl of his pipe into an ashtray and told her to stand up. "It's getting late," he said. "The sun will be up soon. Off to bed with you, little Soldier."

"Did I tell it right?" she asked.

"If you told the truth, and I think you did. But remember, say nothing of this to the hounds, even if they should ask."

"Lie to them?"

"Just do as I say. I need to think about this. Adelaide will show you back to the basement."

And Soldier almost asked him something else, almost asked what *other* secrets he was keeping from the ghouls, feeling a sort of thrill that the two of them were sharing a confidence, a conspiracy, that she'd been given instructions to *disobey* her masters and mistresses.

"Thank you for the cookies," she said, "and for the soda. Next time, orange might be nice."

"Ah, well then, next time, orange soda it will be."

"And arrowroot cookies," she added.

"If you wish," and the Bailiff had already turned away from her. The library door was opening, and Soldier could smell the faint acrid odor that all the silver-eyed people carried with them. Adelaide was coming for her.

"Thank you," Soldier said again, and this time the Bailiff only nodded his bald head and made a harrumphing noise that meant he was busy and she should leave. He was reading a large book lying open on his desk, squinting at the pages by the unsteady light of the oil lantern, peering at the print through the lens of a magnifying glass. There were other books on his desk, and an hourglass, and a bottle of red ink, and a calendar for July 2007, with all the days marked off through the nineteenth. Part of her wanted to ask him if she could stay, if she could sleep upstairs, but then Adelaide was leading her away, back down the long hallway to the parlor, and she was glad that she hadn't asked. He would call her back, if she did as he'd said and kept their secret. He would call her back, and there would be sweets and the smell of his pipe.

"You can find your way from here," Adelaide said.

"Yes," Soldier agreed. "I can. I know my way," and she went back down, through the basement doors, and descended the rickety stairs into darkness.

Soldier took Highway 117 west out of Warwick, shrugging it off like a long, dirty nightmare—the Rolling Stones blaring from the radio, just her and Saben White in the black Dodge sedan, because she left Odd Willie at Rocky Point to get rid of the dead priest and the Impala. She drove on past Apponaug, then took the interstate north, turning back towards Providence. Saben sat up front with her, with her and yet completely apart from her, pressed against the passenger-side door, keeping as much distance between them as possible. And that was fine with Soldier. It meant she'd made her point, so it was just as fine as fine could be, so long as Saben didn't start crying again. It was easily one of the most loathsome sounds that Soldier could imagine, women crying. It never failed to make her angry and always jabbed at the violence that was never very far beneath the uneasy surface of her; sometimes it was almost enough to make her physically ill. She'd once killed a woman for crying, a woman that she might otherwise have let live.

When they're finally clear of Warwick, when Cranston's sprawling bleak and ugly on their left and it won't be much longer before Providence comes in sight, Soldier takes out her cell phone and calls the Bailiff. He doesn't answer, of course. He never answers the phone himself. So first she has to talk to one of his lackeys, some shit-for-brains bootlick calling itself Cacophony who tells her how concerned they've all been, how they've been simply sick to death with worry. Soldier tells the boy to put the Bailiff on the line and then go fuck himself with the sharp end of a broken bottle.

"I was just this very minute talking about you," the Bailiff says. Nothing will ever seem as unnatural to Soldier as the Bailiff's voice coming through a cell phone.

"Guess that's why my ears were burning," Soldier replies and turns down the volume on the radio.

"I got a couple distraught calls from our friends up in Woonsocket," he tells her. "They aren't pleased at having been so neglected this afternoon. I trust it couldn't have been avoided, your dereliction. I trust it was at least a matter of life and limb."

"It was a matter of Saben," Soldier says. "Me and Willie, we were right there, ready to go. Then Saben showed up forty-five minutes late."

"Is that so? Then why am I only finally hearing from you more than two *hours* late?" he asks. "How, little Soldier, would you care to account for such a marked discrepancy in time?"

"It's a big fucking mess," she says, wishing there were any way at all around the words that have to come next, knowing that there's not, so she gets it over with fast. "She killed a priest somewhere down in Connecticut and brought him back to Warwick in the trunk of her car. We've been trying to deal with it."

"Well, now. That *is* a mess, isn't it. A *priest*, you say?" And the Bailiff laughs as though Soldier has just told him that this whole situation was the result of a blown tire or a stripped transmission or Odd Willie running over a fire hydrant. "Well, Miss White's certainly getting a bit more enterprising. Indeed. We'll have to see that she's rewarded for all this ambition."

"I'll reward her right now," Soldier says and glances at Saben. "All you got to do is say the word, and I'll reward her good and proper."

"And what about *you*?" he asks. "Those two are *your* responsibility. When they fuck up, you fuck up. I've been quite explicit about that, Soldier. So, then, how shall I reward *you*?"

"Good damn question," she says before she can think better of it.

"What about the earthly remains?" the Bailiff asks, and it takes her a second to realize he means the priest.

"Odd Willie's having some sort of barbecue. I don't think there'll be anything left to worry about when he's done. Listen, what am I supposed to do now? I can be in Woonsocket in half an hour, tops. Hell, I could be there in twenty-five—"

"No," the Bailiff says, and Soldier hears someone laughing in the background. "I'm afraid that won't be necessary. Our friends don't like to wait around. They're busy men. They've rescheduled for Monday at noon, that is, *if* you think you can make the time. If not—"

"No, no, Monday at noon," Soldier says, grateful that she'll have some time to recover from Rocky Point and the scene at the Dunkin' Donuts before she has to face Woonsocket. "Monday's totally fucking fine. I'm sorry as hell about this mess, Bailiff. But, please, I want her off my crew, okay? Right now, today."

"I've told you, she's your responsibility," the Bailiff replies. "Should I explain once more precisely what that means?"

Soldier looks over at Saben White again, Saben who's still staring out the window at the other cars or the bare trees along the side of the interstate, Saben with her swollen lip and blackening eye, the dried blood at the nape of her neck. And Soldier wonders if it would really turn out that much worse if she simply took out her gun and blew the bitch's brains out. After all, how much hotter can boiling water get?

How hot is summertime in hell? How hot do you think, little Soldier?

"Yeah, fine. My goddamn responsibility. So, what do you want me to do now?" Soldier asks the cell phone.

Saben White smiles, then, as though she's scored some secret victory. Soldier catches the smile out of the corner of her right eye, and it almost doesn't matter what would happen to her, because whatever it is, she has it coming, and it will surely find her sooner or later, anyway. On the radio, the Rolling Stones give way to Procol Harum, "A Whiter Shade of Pale," and Soldier turns the volume up again.

"I want you home as soon as possible," the Bailiff says. "I want you somewhere safe, somewhere visible, so I don't have to worry about you anymore."

"And what about Saben? What do I do with her?"

"*Your* responsibility," the Bailiff says for the third time. "Now, stop worrying so much about our wayward, trigger-happy Miss White. Perhaps she had good cause in this transgression. Perhaps there is a greater purpose here that we've yet to comprehend, little Soldier." And again, in the background, that high, girlish laughter.

> *And, likewise, if behind is in front*
> *Then dirt in truth is clean*

Soldier swallows, her mouth so dry there's hardly any spit left at all, and the bottle of whiskey is calling her so loudly now that it's a miracle she can hear either the Bailiff or the radio.

"Willie's a good man, so long as he has the right tools," the Bailiff reminds her. "You did well to leave the good father in his capable hands."

"Do I call you when he's—"

"You just go *home,*" the Bailiff says, that steel tone in his voice that says the matter's settled. "See that Miss White walks the straight and narrow. One priest here or there is hardly a sign of the Apocalypse, but I shouldn't want it to become a habit. Was he Catholic, Greek Orthodox, Russian Orthodox, or perhaps Episcopalian?"

"Catholic, I think." And Saben White nods her head yes. "Yeah, Saben says he was Catholic."

"Well, that makes it all a little easier," the Bailiff says. "Some wheels are much easier to grease than others, if you get my drift."

She doesn't, but isn't about to say so.

"And, Soldier, that bottle you bought this morning," the Bailiff continues, "you best leave that where it is for now. You may give it to me when next we meet. I'll consider it a gift, recompense for this inconvenience." And then there's silence, and she folds the phone shut and tosses it onto the dash. Saben flinches at the noise, and Soldier bites down hard on her lower lip because a little taste of her own blood is better than having to explain to the Bailiff how Saben's door just happened to come flying open, spilling her out onto I-95 at sixty-five miles an hour.

"Don't you worry, sweetie," Soldier says, putting a little more pressure on the accelerator. "It looks like someone's got your ass covered."

And then she notices the clouds building on the horizon, sweeping down towards Providence from the northwest; billowing hills of purple-gray, heavy with snow or freezing rain, and she wonders if Willie's found everything he needs to start his fire. And then the clouds make her think of an ocean, and an immense desert at her back, and monsters warring in the sky.

THREE

❧

New York

After the cab ride from the train station, after dinner and half an hour's worth of old Tom and Jerry cartoons on Sadie's little television, Emmie sits on the sofa and watches while her stepmother checks all the locks on the front door of her apartment again.

"Just in case," Sadie would say, or, "It never hurts to be careful," if Emmie were to ask her, but she doesn't ask because she knows better. She knows that Sadie paid extra to have all those locks installed on the door, because Deacon said so. He also told Emmie that it wasn't polite to ask questions about Sadie and her weird thing with the locks, but she'd already suspected as much.

"Something very bad happened," Deacon told her, "a long time ago. That's how her arm got hurt. I've told you that, Emmie. Now she needs to feel safe, that's all."

"Does she have OCD?" Emmie asked him.

"What?" her father asked back, furrowing his brow and scowling at her. "Where the hell did you learn about OCD?"

"From an abnormal-psychology textbook in the library at school. I know about schizophrenia, too, and paranoia—"

"Jesus." Deacon sighed and shook his head. "No, Emmie. She *doesn't* have OCD. She's just . . . she's just high-strung, that's all. She needs—"

"To feel safe," Emmie said, even though it annoys him when she finishes his sentences for him. Even when he's drunk and forgets what he was going to say.

"Are we gonna play some Scrabble now?" Emmie asks her stepmother.

"If that's what you want to do, then that's what we're going to do," Sadie replies, apparently satisfied with the assortment of dead bolts and chains on the door, because now she crosses the small living room to check the locks on both the windows again. From the sofa, Emmie can see the rusty iron zigzag of the fire escape, and there's golden light from the street lamps down on St. Mark's.

"I've been reading the dictionary a lot lately," Emmie says, "learning new words."

"New words?" Sadie asks, sounding distracted, staring at something down on the street, her good hand resting on the windowsill. "What kind of new words?"

"Well, Q-words, mostly. Especially Q-words without Us in them," Emmie tells her. She wants to ask Sadie what she sees down on the sidewalk, out in the street, but she doesn't, because Deacon would probably tell her that was rude, as well.

"What's wrong with Q-words with Us in them?" her stepmother asks, not turning away from the window.

"Nothing's *wrong* with them, except that there aren't enough Us in Scrabble, and I never have one when I have a Q and actually need one."

"Oh," Sadie says.

And then curiosity gets the best of Emmie, which happens a lot more than she'd like to admit. "Sadie, what are you looking at down there?" she asks.

"Nothing," Sadie replies, but she still sounds distracted, like she's thinking about everything in the world but playing Scrabble and what a pain in the ass Q-words can be when you don't have a U. "I was looking at a dog, that's all," she adds. Then she turns her back on the windows and smiles at Emmie Silvey. The smile comes out more than a little forced.

"Q-words like *qat*," Sadie says.

"Yeah, and *qintar* and *qoph*, too."

"Qoph? I don't think I know that one," Sadie admits, then glances over her right shoulder at the windows again.

"It's the nineteenth letter in the Hebrew alphabet," Emmie tells her, and her stepmother nods her head and turns back towards her.

"What about *qiviut*? Did you learn that one?"

"It's got something to do with a musk ox," Emmie says, and reaches for a magazine lying on the coffee table.

"You'll have to do better than that."

"Look it up." Emmie shrugs, opening the magazine, and maybe she doesn't want to play Scrabble, after all. This whole conversation about Q-words has reminded her how dull it can get sometimes, especially when Sadie's not really thinking about the game and it's too easy to win. "It's got something to do with musk oxes."

"Musk *oxen*," Sadie corrects her.

"Either way, *qiviut* has a U, and we were talking about Q-words without Us."

"Yes, you're right," Sadie says, cradling her bad arm, and she nods at the Scrabble box on a bookshelf in the corner. "But if it's Scrabble you want, it's Scrabble you'll get, even though we both know you'll only kick my ass again."

"Maybe not if you'd pay better attention and stop thinking about the locks and about dogs down on the street," Emmie says, immediately wishing that she hadn't, wishing she knew some trick for taking words back. She looks up from the magazine lying open on her lap, and Sadie is staring down at the hardwood floor now, still cradling her crippled left arm.

"I'll spot you," Emmie says, hoping maybe *that's* the right thing to say now that she's screwed everything up. She tosses the magazine onto the floor and gets up off the sofa, stepping quickly around the corners of the coffee table and a tall stack of books on the floor. "Fifty points. I *always* spot Deacon fifty points."

"Was that his idea or yours?"

"His," Emmie admits. "He wanted me to spot him a hundred, but I said, 'Uh-uh, no damn way am I spotting you a whole hundred points, Mr. Deacon Silvey.' "

"Good for you." Sadie laughs, and Emmie's relieved. She can tell the laughter is more honest than the forced smile was, that the laugh is *real,* something that Sadie feels instead of just something she wants Emmie to think she feels. Emmie's at the bookshelf now, standing on tiptoe, fishing the Scrabble box down from the shelf where her stepmother keeps all her tarot cards, copies of the books she's written and a couple more that she hasn't finished yet, a soap-stone scarab that she brought back from a trip to Egypt, three blue glass bottles, and her Book of Shadows. Emmie knows about the Book of Shadows—that it's filled with Sadie's spells and rituals—though she's never taken it down, never opened it, has never even touched it. She knows that her stepmother is a witch, has known that for as long as she can remember. Not the sort of witch you see on television shows or in the movies, of course, but the sort that's real, not make-believe. Deacon says it's all a load of horseshit and superstitious nonsense, but Sadie told her that she should wait and decide for herself when she's older. Seeing the Book of Shadows, Emmie's reminded of the strange woman on the train and the Seal of Solomon tattooed on her skin. Perhaps, she thinks, the woman on the train was also a witch.

"Have you ever heard of something called the Seal of Solomon?"

Emmie asks, managing to wiggle the Scrabble box out from under several heavy books without knocking anything over.

"Sure," Sadie replies and sits down on the sofa. "What do you want to know?"

"Well, mostly I was wondering if it really has an invisible point on it somewhere?"

Her stepmother glances towards the door, and suddenly she has that anxious expression she gets that Emmie knows means she wants to check all the locks again, that she's afraid she might have missed one, maybe that dead bolt up high that's a bit temperamental sometimes.

"That's what someone told me," Emmie says, "that the Seal of Solomon has seven points, even though you can only see six of them."

"Some things are like that," Sadie tells her, but doesn't look away from the door. "Sometimes you can only see part of a thing, even though it seems like it's all right there in front of you. Sometimes things will seem plain as day, and that's not what they are at all."

"So, it's something magick, like your tarot cards?"

"Everything's magick, Emmie, in one way or another. I've told you that before."

"But you *know* what I mean. Is it some sort of magickal symbol?" Emmie carries the Scrabble set back over to the coffee table, quickly clearing away all the magazines and papers and books cluttering the table, then sits down on the floor, opens the box, and begins to set up the game.

"Who told you about the Seal of Solomon?" Sadie asks her, finally looking away from the apartment door.

"Someone at school," Emmie says, pausing only a moment before deciding that the lie's probably better than telling Sadie about the woman on the train. "Do you want me to keep score?"

"Sure. You're better at it than me."

"Does it protect people?"

"That depends who and what you believe. Some people think it does."

"The Jews?" Emmie asks, choosing a pencil from the assortment of yellow and black stubs inside the box. She picks the sharpest of the bunch, one that even has a ragged pinkish stump of eraser left on one end.

"Some Jews, yes, and some other people, too. King Solomon is said to have had the star engraved on an iron ring. It gave him the power to command demons."

"I'm not sure I *believe* in demons," Emmie says and shrugs again. She writes her name at the top of a blank page in the notepad that Sadie keeps inside the Scrabble box with everything else. Then she draws a vertical line, dividing the page neatly in two, and she writes Sadie's name on the other side of the line opposite her own.

"It's just a word," Sadie tells her, and then her stepmother selects a wooden tile from the lid of the box where Emmie has laid them all facedown. "And like all words, it can mean a lot of different things—"

"To different people," Emmie says, and she points at the tile her stepmother has drawn from the box. "What did you get?"

"I got a P. Three points. Let's see you beat that."

Emmie draws a tile, but it's only an E, and she shakes her head and sighs. "Crap. I shouldn't have spotted you anything at all," she says, but she doesn't really care about not getting the first turn. At least Sadie seems to have forgotten about the doors and the locks and the windows for the time being.

"That'll teach you not to underestimate your elders," her stepmother says. Emmie draws six more tiles from the lid of the box and sets them up on the rack so that Sadie can't see what they are. They spell out POCSLEI, and she immediately begins rearranging them in her head, searching for something that will equal a halfway decent score.

"Maybe we should have played chess, instead," she says. "Or Chinese checkers."

"No, no. I'm feeling lucky," Sadie says, but her eyes have drifted back to the apartment door. This time Emmie looks, too, and sees that her stepmother forgot to reset the alarm when they came home from dinner. Emmie was talking, telling Sadie about a new video game. "Tonight I'm gonna take you down," Sadie adds, but the tone in her voice tells Emmie that she's no longer thinking about Scrabble.

"Then you can give me a word. A *new* word. One that I don't already know. That'll make it fair."

Sadie's pale blue eyes dart back to the game board, then nervously up at Emmie, as though she'd been caught doing something she shouldn't have been doing. "It's *already* fair, you little brat," she says. "I don't have to give you a word. You're too damned smart as it is."

"And it has to be a *magickal* word," Emmie adds, then begins rearranging her Scrabble tiles. She doesn't like it when Sadie's eyes look that way, like she's frightened and confused and trying too hard to seem like she's neither one. Now Emmie's tiles spell out IEPOCLS, so she starts over. She glances up at Sadie, and sees that her stepmother's staring at the door again, the red door painted almost the same shade as a ripe pomegranate, festooned with dead bolts and chain locks, the black steel rod she keeps wedged firmly between the door and a thick block of wood nailed directly to the apartment floor. The security pad is mounted just to the right of the door, beneath a framed black-and-white photograph of the three of them taken one summer day at Scarborough Beach, back when Emmie was hardly more than a baby. The alarm's ready light is green, but the armed light is glowing a bright, accusatory red.

"And, also, it has to be a real word," Emmie says, looking away from the door and the neglected alarm, back to her stepmother's face. "No made-up words. It has to be a word I could use to *beat* you."

"Tetragrammaton," Sadie says. "That's a real word."

"Are you sure? I've never heard it before."

"Well, if you'd heard it, Emmie, then it wouldn't *be* a new word, now, would it?"

"So, what's it mean?" Emmie asks her, sounding as skeptical as she can manage, hoping to distract her stepmother from the door again.

"It's the Hebrew name for god," Sadie says and chews at her lower lip. "It's supposed to have been part of the Seal of Solomon."

"Well, it has too many letters. You should have given me a shorter word. I'll never have all the letters I need to spell that."

"You didn't say it had to be a short word."

"I *should* have. I didn't think you'd take advantage of a kid. How do you spell it, anyway?"

And then her stepmother opens her mouth, like she's about to tell Emmie how to spell *tetragrammaton*, like Emmie's not smart enough to figure it out for herself. But then her eyes move rapidly from the door to the twice-locked windows and back to the keypad beneath the photograph again, and Emmie knows that they've both lost this round. For a second or two, it doesn't matter what Deacon's told her, and she almost asks Sadie why she's so afraid, what it was that ruined her hand and scared her so badly that she's still scared all these years later.

"Hold on," her stepmother says. "I'm sorry. This will only take me a second." And Emmie lets the questions dissolve, unasked, on her tongue while Sadie goes to set the burglar alarm.

"Do you still miss her?" Emmie asked Deacon one day in September, the last day of her vacation before third grade began. They were sitting at the kitchen table, eating the sloppy peanut-butter-and-grape-jelly sandwiches that Deacon had made for lunch, and she'd been thinking about school, because she'd been thinking about hardly anything else for a week, when Deacon had said something about the table being too big for only two people. She always sat at the chair beneath the window, and he always sat directly across from her. When Sadie had lived with them, she'd sat in the chair at Emmie's left. There was a stack of telephone books and old newspapers there now.

Deacon stopped chewing and stared at his plate a moment before answering her. "Sometimes worse than others," he said, and took another bite of his sandwich.

"And this is one of the worse times?" she asked, knowing the answer, and her father nodded his head.

"Don't you mind me," Deacon said, after he'd swallowed and washed down the peanut butter and jelly and white bread with a mouthful of milk. "Now and then I just think too much for my own good, that's all."

"Well, you know, it's not like she was my *real* mother," Emmie said, though, in fact, she thought it was exactly like that. It seemed like the sort of thing Deacon would want to hear, like something that might make him feel better and get him to thinking about something else.

"She did the best she could," Deacon told her, "under the circumstances. She did a hell of a lot better than—" But then he stopped, took another drink of milk, and wiped his mouth on the back of his hand.

"That's not what I meant," Emmie said, realizing that she'd only managed to make things worse. "I just meant, well, I meant—"

"Finish your lunch," her father said and stood up. "I need to get back to the shop," and then he took his saucer and empty glass over to the sink and rinsed them. Emmie sat looking at the uneaten half of her sandwich, wondering if third grade was when you finally learned when to keep your mouth shut.

Emmie lays her last five tiles down in a vertical line ending at the lower right-hand corner of the Scrabble board. R-E-D-C-A-P, and the P lands on "Triple Word Score." She grins triumphantly at her step-mother and taps her fingers loudly on the edge of the coffee table.

"Emmie, that's two words, not one," Sadie says, licking at her lips and already reaching for the paperback Merriam-Webster's dictionary because they've been playing Scrabble long enough that she knows Emmie won't ever just take her word on these things.

"No, it's not. It's only one word. Go ahead. Look it up. 'Redcap.' It's a sort of mushroom."

"Yeah, and it's also a sort of a fairie," Sadie adds. "I know that, but it's spelled as two words."

"It's also what they used to call Little Red Riding Hood," Emmie says, and Sadie stops turning pages and glances up from the dictionary at Emmie, who's still grinning.

"Go ahead. Look it up. But you're wasting your time. You'll just see that I'm right."

"You don't have to be a snot about it," Sadie tells her.

"Read me what it says. 'A poisonous species of toadstool.' I bet that's exactly what it says."

"Why don't you look it up," Sadie replies and hands her the dictionary. "I'd rather we wasted your time than mine."

"Fine," and Emmie takes the dictionary, which is already turned to the RE's, and she ticks off the words one after another—*redbreast, redbrick, redbud, redbug*—and there it is, just like she knew it would be, *redcap,* one word, two syllables. "Redcap," she says. "One word."

Sadie takes the dictionary back and frowns at the page as she reads it. "Okay, but you're wrong about the definition," she tells Emmie, then reads it aloud. " 'A baggage porter, as at a railroad station.' "

"I can still use it," Emmie says, adding up her score. "And I'm not *wrong,* because it is too a kind of mushroom. That dictionary just isn't very good. Maybe you should get a new one, one that knows about mushrooms and fairies."

"Yeah, maybe I should," and Sadie closes the dictionary and sets it aside. "Emmie, why even bother adding the score. We both know you won."

"It's still important. It's still important to know exactly how it turned out."

"Fine, but I have to go to the bathroom right this minute, or I'm gonna pop."

"Yeah, your eyes are starting to turn kind of yellow. Soon they'll be just like mine."

"Your eyes aren't yellow," Sadie says, standing up. "They're amber."

"Wrong," Emmie says. "They're yellow as butter. They're yellow as sunflowers." It's an old argument, one that Emmie's never really understood the reason for. Her eyes are not amber; she's seen amber at the museum, polished chunks of it with ants and ticks and flies trapped inside for millions and millions of years, and that's not the color of her eyes at all. And they aren't golden brown, either, or champagne, or any of the other things that Sadie has tried to call them so that she doesn't have to call them *yellow,* which is what they actually are. *"Yel-low,"* Emmie says, and then realizes that she's made a mistake in her arithmetic and begins rubbing hard at the notepad with the last stingy scrap of the pencil stub's eraser.

"Whatever. I'm going to pee now," Sadie sighs, sounding a little annoyed, and Emmie watches as she tries to make it past the front door without stopping to check the locks.

And later on, after Emmie has beaten Sadie again and the Scrabble set has finally been put away for the night, after a snack of Double Stuf Oreos and A&W cream soda, after Emmie's brushed her teeth and flossed and washed her hands and face and changed into one of Sadie's T-shirts that she likes to sleep in whenever she visits—after all these things, her stepmother sits on the edge of Emmie's bed in the narrow space between the kitchenette and bathroom. Emmie's bedroom, whenever she comes to Manhattan. It's hardly wider than a large closet, but Emmie likes the closeness. It makes the tiny room feel safe, makes it cozy, and sometimes she thinks she prefers it to her big room upstairs on Angell Street in Providence. A room this small has fewer shadows to wonder about when the lights are out, and there's still a place for her bed and a small chest of drawers, two red plastic milk crates stacked one atop the other to make a combination bookshelf and toy box. There are a couple of posters on the wall, Hello Kitty and a Japanese girl band, and Sadie has painted golden stars on the midnight-blue ceiling, one for each of her stepdaughter's birthdays.

"Do you want a story?" Sadie asks, and Emmie nods yes, because she doesn't want to be sleepy just yet, wants to lie there awake beneath the golden stars listening to Sadie read to her; Sadie reads aloud almost as good as Deacon.

"Read me the end of *The Voyage of the 'Dawn Treader,'*" Emmie says. "Read me 'The Very End of the World.' "

"Are you sure? I've read you that one at least a dozen times already."

"Not a dozen. Not that many times."

"At *least* that many times," Sadie says, but she's already taking the paperback copy of *The Voyage of the "Dawn Treader"* from its place in the topmost milk crate.

"Right near the end," Emmie tells her, "after Reepicheep has gone, when Aslan makes a hole in the sky. I think it's on page two forty-seven."

"You've memorized the *page numbers*?" Sadie asks, incredulous, and Emmie smiles a hesitant, flustered smile, wondering if maybe she should say it was just a lucky guess.

"Only a few of them," she says instead. "Only for the parts I like the most."

Sadie shakes her head and flips quickly through the dog-eared pages until she comes to page two forty-seven. When her stepmother begins to read, Emmie fixes on the largest of the painted stars, the one that stands for her birthday before last. It has seven points, but none of them are invisible.

" 'Oh, Aslan,' said Lucy. 'Will you tell us how to get to your country from our world?'

" 'I shall be telling you all the time,' said Aslan. 'But I will not tell you how long or short the way will be; only that it lies across a river. But do not fear that, for I am the great Bridge Builder. And now come; I will open the door in the sky and send you to your own land.' "

"Do you think it was like a black hole?" Emmie asks, but doesn't take her eyes off the star on the ceiling.

"No," Sadie replies. "I think you mean a wormhole. I think maybe Aslan's hole between worlds was more like a wormhole than a black hole. Hardly anything ever escapes a black hole."

"I *know* that, Sadie," Emmie says, annoyed at being corrected and embarrassed that she didn't get it right in the first place. "I forgot, but you know I know that. I read a book by Stephen Hawking."

"Yeah, I've read that book, too."

"So," Emmie continued, "Aslan made a wormhole for Lucy and Edmund and Eustace."

"I doubt that's what C. S. Lewis meant, but I suppose you could think of it that way."

"Right. A bridge between worlds, a shortcut, and there must have been another one—"

"Do you want me to read any more of this?" Sadie asks, and she glances at the alarm clock on the chest of drawers. "It's getting late. We have a lot to do tomorrow."

"Read just a little more," Emmie says and yawns without covering her mouth.

"Okay, but only a little bit more," Sadie says and turns the page. " 'Child,' said Aslan, 'do you really need to know that? Come, I am opening the door in the sky.' Then all in one moment there was a rend—"

"The wormhole," Emmie says, and then she yawns again.

"If that's the way you want to think of it. Yeah, the wormhole."

"They're *very* unstable things," Emmie says and squints at the birthday star. "That's what Stephen Hawking said. You couldn't just travel through one like that. Even in a spaceship, the gravitational forces would tear you to spaghetti if you tried."

"Emmie, you know this is a fairy tale. Maybe you're getting too old for fairy tales. Maybe science fiction would be better."

"I was just *thinking* about it, that's all. Go ahead. Read me some more, please."

Sadie blinks and rubs her eyes, and suddenly Emmie misses her father, misses her own room in her own house, and she almost asks Sadie if they can call Deacon, because he's always up late, but Sadie's already started reading the book again.

"Then all in one moment there was a rending of the blue wall (like a curtain being torn) and a terrible white light from beyond the sky, and the feel of Aslan's mane and a Lion's kiss on their foreheads and then—the back bedroom in Aunt Alberta's home in Cambridge."

"That's enough," Emmie says, deciding it's probably best not to call Deacon, even if he is still awake; the wave of homesickness has begun to pass, and she looks at the star again. Sadie closes the book and returns it to its place in the red milk crate.

"Stephen Hawking might be wrong," Emmie says.

"What do you mean?"

"I mean, some scientists think there might be ways to travel through wormholes without being torn apart. I think they might be right."

"Well, then, where do you think the wormholes would lead?" Sadie asks her. "Would they take us to Narnia?"

"Narnia's not a real place," Emmie sighs and rolls over, turning her back on her stepmother and the golden star, turning to face the wall because she knows that if she doesn't fall asleep soon she'll start missing Deacon again. "But they might take us to other places."

"Good places or bad places?"

"That remains to be seen," Emmie says, though she's thinking that her stepmother's old enough to know that places are neither good nor bad. That places are only places, and it's people that make them *seem* good or bad. "Leave the hall light on, okay?"

"Sure," says Sadie, tucking her in and kissing her on the top of her head. "Now, you'd better get some sleep, pumpkin. We'll go see the dinosaurs tomorrow."

"Night-night," Emmie whispers, and her stepmother switches off the reading lamp and leaves, shutting the bedroom door only half-way. Emmie stares at the wall, imagining a swirling, dinner plate–sized hole in it that might open out into their house on Angell Street. She imagines Deacon peering into the hole to be sure that she's all right and falls asleep to the sound of Sadie's footsteps.

"No," Emmie tells the rat in pirate boots. "I always know when I'm dreaming. It's easy to tell the difference." And when the rat glares skeptically back at her, she explains, "In my dreams, there are no limits."

"No limits to what?" the rat asks her, still glowering, and then it takes a sip of the peach-flavored soda it's been nursing since Emmie sat down at the kitchen table. Deacon's busy somewhere else in the house, and he doesn't know that she's having a conversation about dreams with a rat named Reepicheep. If he did know, he probably wouldn't care, but he might tell her to stop giving away sodas to talking rats, that those things cost money, and money doesn't grow on trees.

"See, that's what I mean," she tells Reepicheep. "Money *doesn't* grow on trees. So, whenever I see some money growing on a tree, I know that I'm dreaming, because in my dreams there are no limits to what's real and what's not."

The rat shakes its head and scratches at its chin, which is slightly damp and matted with the peach soda that keeps dribbling out of its mouth. "That seems awfully convenient, if you ask me," Reepicheep says.

"I didn't ask you."

"This stuff tastes like cleaning fluid," the rat shudders and stares into the bottle of soda. "Are you trying to poison me or something?"

Emmie's getting bored with the rat, who isn't nearly as interesting to talk to as she thought he might be when she offered him something to drink. She turns and looks out the kitchen window at the house next door and discovers that there's already someone at a window over there watching her. It might be the woman from the train, the woman who got off at the Old Saybrook Station. She waves, but whoever it is, they don't wave back.

"Have you ever been haunted by the ghost of a poisoned rat?" Reepicheep asks her. "Let me just tell you, it's not a pleasant affair."

"Go away now," Emmie says, and the kitchen gradually melts away like snow on a warm winter day, taking the talking rat with it.

"Six of one, half dozen of the other," she says, because it's something that Deacon says whenever he doesn't seem to care one way or another. He says it's something that people from Alabama say all the time. And the graveyard where she's standing now really isn't that much of an improvement over the kitchen and the talking rat and being watched from the house next door, so she says it again—*Six of one, half dozen of the other*. It's not Swan Point or the Old North Burial Ground or any of the other graveyards where she and Deacon sometimes go for long walks. All the headstones are jagged slabs of charcoal- or rust-colored slate, broken and covered with patches of lichen and moss. Hardly any of the names and dates carved into them are still legible, and that always makes Emmie sad, knowing that someone's dead and buried and so completely forgotten that even their tombstone doesn't know his or her name anymore.

Here's a whole cemetery of forgotten people, she thinks, and sits down in the grass beneath a maple tree, glad that at least it's summer in the dream instead of February.

"I was hoping you'd show up today," her mother says—not Sadie but her real mother, the woman who died the day that she was born—and Emmie looks up to see the tall woman standing over her. There's a rock hammer on her belt, just like the paleontologists Emmie's seen on television. "It's been a while," the woman says.

"I've been busy," Emmie tells her, wishing that the sun weren't so bright right there behind her mother's head, so that she could actually see her face this time. She knows it from photographs, but it's always hidden in the dreams, and sometimes that makes Emmie worry that maybe the woman in the dreams isn't her mother after all.

"You're a busy girl," her mother says.

"I don't believe in ghosts," Emmie says. "I know you're only a dream."

"It doesn't make much difference either way," the woman replies and turns away, the sunlight pouring fiery white about the eclipse of her head and shoulders. "A ghost or a dream, six of one, half dozen of the other."

"It *matters*," Emmie insists. "It's important to know the difference."

"There's something coming," the woman tells her. "You need to be ready when it gets here. You're a smart girl, aren't you, Emmie? You know the difference between dreams and what's real?"

"Yeah. I was just telling the rat—"

"Then I need you to try just a little bit harder. I need you to see who I am, not who you *think* I am."

"It's a *dream*," Emmie protests, and the woman turns back towards her. She doesn't seem so tall now, and the tool belt with the rock hammer's gone. There's a six-pointed star tattooed on the woman's left hand. "You're not my mother," Emmie says, a little disappointed, a little angry even though the dream woman never claimed to be her mother. She squints into the sun, trying harder to get a better look at the woman's face. "You're the woman from the train."

"You're a damned smart girl. But sometimes you talk when you should be listening."

"It's my dream," Emmie says.

"You also need to learn not to make quite so many assumptions."

"What's *that* supposed to mean?" And Emmie stands up, dusting bits of grass off her jeans, but the woman who's not her mother has already begun to fade away, just like the kitchen and the talking rat. Emmie tries to concentrate and make her stay, but the graveyard is *slippery* and has already become somewhere else entirely, the sun traded for shadows and mist in the blink of a dreaming eye. *An attic*, she thinks, because the ceiling's so very low, the vaulted house ribs of huge and rough-hewn crossbeams, cobwebs draped all about like a cartoon haunted house, and the only light is coming from a candlestick that the girl holding her hand is carrying. The girl, who's both older and taller than Emmie, is dragging her through the attic, leading her quickly from one somewhere to somewhere else, and Emmie stops and jerks her hand free.

"Who are you?" she demands. "And where are we going?"

"We can't very well stay *here*," the older girl says anxiously, impatiently. "They'll hear and come up to check. The clocks are ticking, Emma Jean. They'll find you *out*."

By the flickering candle, Emmie can see that the girl's skin is brown, skin like almonds or milk stirred into coffee, and her hair's black and cut into a bob. Emmie wonders if the girl's Hispanic or maybe part Narragansett, maybe a little of both. "Who? Who will find me out?" she asks the girl, who's beginning to look more than anxious and impatient—she's beginning to look scared. She tries to take Emmie's hand again, but Emmie snatches it away. "No, answer my question. Who's gonna find out I'm here?"

"It might be your dream, Emma Jean Silvey, but it might be someone else's, *too*. Did you never stop to consider that?"

"No," Emmie tells her. "That's stupid. This is my dream, and it isn't anybody else's."

The girl looks back the way they've come, and Emmie looks, too, but there's nothing back there except darkness and shadows, spiderwebs and dust. "Who are you so afraid of?" Emmie asks the girl.

"She told you that something's coming, and you need to listen to her. She told you about the horses, too, didn't she? You've already forgotten that, I'll wager?"

"She didn't say anything about any—" Emmie begins, but then she remembers the woman on the train—Saben White, *that* was her name, at least the name she *said* was her name—remembers her saying that Emmie should stay away from horses. "I'm in New York City at my stepmom's," Emmie says. "So I really don't think I have to worry too much about horses."

The candlelight glitters in the girl's eyes, eyes that are almost black, eyes that get Emmie to thinking about holes in the sky, holes punched in worlds by lion gods to send children home. The girl looks more frightened than Emmie has ever seen anyone look before.

"You need to calm down," she tells the girl. "You're gonna have a cardiac arrest or a stroke or a panic attack or something if you don't. It's just a dream. I promise. You don't even exist."

"You can hear them, can't you?" the girl asks. "You can hear the clocks ticking?"

"I don't hear anything," Emmie says, but then she stops and listens, and she does hear clocks, dozens of clocks, maybe more, but she can't tell where the sounds are coming from. "Yeah, so what? I can hear clocks ticking."

The girl groans, the same sort of noise that her father makes whenever he's tired of arguing with Emmie about taking a bath or doing her homework or cleaning her room. The end-of-his-rope noise, Sadie calls it. *Do it now, or you'll wish you had. That* sort of noise.

"You can get lost in dreams," the girl says and motions at the darkness with her candle. "If you're not careful, you can spend forever wandering about in dreams, and it hardly matters if they're yours or someone else's. Maybe this *is* your dream, Emma Jean, but it's mine, too, and maybe it's the hounds', and maybe it's even old Mother Hydra's, so you'd best hush up a minute and stop thinking things aren't connected just because you can't see the—"

"—shortcuts," Emmie says.

"That's not what I was going to say, but it's near enough. Those clocks shouldn't be ticking. You shouldn't be here. You're getting too far ahead—"

And then the brown-skinned girl's gone, and Emmie's alone in the sun-drenched cemetery again, and there's an empty soda bottle half-buried in the ground in front of every single one of the slate gravestones. There are black ants on the bottles—ants going in, ants coming out. Reepicheep's leather pirate boots are draped across one of the markers, and when she looks again at the lush green grass sprouting from the earth, Emmie can see that the ground has begun to leak something oily and red, *not* blood, no, but that's the first thing it makes her think of. The air crackles and smells like rain and a dead raccoon she once found out behind their house. There are rough voices drifting across the cemetery, guttural animal sounds that want to be words but haven't quite figured out the trick of it, and she tries not to hear what they're saying.

"She had a plan, your mother did," the leaves of the maple tree rustle in the voice of the girl from the attic. "And now I fear it isn't going so well for her. She made mistakes, and now it isn't going well at all."

"My mother's dead," Emmie tells the girl or the old tree or whomever she's talking to; she's angry now and getting scared, and when she gazes up into the limbs of the old maple, there are eyes there, gazing back down at her, eyes and grinning Cheshire cat jaws with sharp ivory teeth. "My mother's *dead*," Emmie says. "She's dead and buried, and she isn't planning *anything*."

"*Six of one,*" the tree whispers. "You said so yourself," and then something slips suddenly down from the branches, slithering snake-like along the trunk of the tree, something almost the same color of red as the stuff oozing from the ground.

"They must have heard the clocks," the girl from the attic says. "I *told* you they might. They have keen ears, and they're always listening. You know the way back. You'd best start running."

The red thing in the tree laughs and wriggles and vomits a slimy clump of fur and the half-digested bones of a very large rat onto the grass at her feet.

"Now would be better than later," the girl from the attic says.

And there's an ugly tearing sound—a *rending*, Emmie thinks—as she dreams a wormhole into the fabric of the stinking summer day, a shimmering hole filled with blinding white light. As the red thing from the tree coils about the roots and opens its mouth wide so she can see exactly what it's using for teeth, Emmie tumbles through.

                              *   *   *

By the time that Emmie's seen all the dinosaurs, saurischian *and* or-
nithischian, and all of the fossil mammals, it's almost noon. Sadie
buys her a hot dog, a bag of potato chips, and a Snapple from a silver
cart parked outside near the bronze statue of Theodore Roosevelt
on horseback, flanked by an Indian on one side and a black man on
the other. They sit on a granite bench beneath the tall Ionic columns
framing the archway leading back into the museum; the sun's warm
today, and the wind's not so bad that they can't have lunch outdoors.
Emmie tries to remember not to talk while she's chewing, but it's
hard, because her head's so full of all the things she's seen in the last
few hours.

"Hunter's meeting us in a bit," Sadie says. "You won't mind, will
you?"

"No," Emmie manages around a mustardy bite of hog dog. She
likes Hunter Fontana, likes her long salt-and-pepper dreadlocks, the
spicy-sweet clove smell of the Indonesian cigarettes she sometimes
smokes, and the fact that she knows lots of good stories that Emmie's never heard before. Hunter's a witch, too, and a writer, and
Deacon says that she's a lesbian. Emmie chews her hot dog, swallows, washes it all down with raspberry-flavored Snapple, then leans
back against the bas-relief sculpture of a pair of bighorn sheep.

"I didn't think you would," Sadie says and smiles. She points at
what's left of Emmie's hot dog. "Good?" she asks.

"Yep," Emmie says. "I could eat another one."

"We'll see," Sadie tells her and checks her wristwatch.

"I'm sure that I'll still be hungry when I'm finished with this
one."

"How about you finish it and find out."

"What do you think I'm doing?" and Emmie takes another big
bite. Deacon fixes hot dogs whenever she wants them, because he

likes them too, but they're never as good as the ones Sadie buys her outside the Museum of Natural History. Someone at school told her that the Mafia owns all the hot-dog stands in Manhattan, but she doesn't know if she believes that. It seems to her the Mafia would have better things to do than sell hot dogs.

"You can tell Hunter what you were telling me about the prehistoric horses," Sadie says, and Emmie shrugs and swallows.

"I'm not sure she'd be interested."

"Of course she would. You should tell her." Sadie didn't get a hot dog, just a Snapple and a bag of chips. She sips at her bottle of tea and watches the traffic moving up and down Central Park West, or she's watching the brown-and-gray edge of the park itself. Emmie can't be sure which without asking. She likes the park best in summer, when it's green and warm and there's Shakespeare and picnics; in winter, there's something hard and skeletal about it, just like the rest of the city. She finishes her hot dog and decides that she's probably full, after all.

"Tell her about the *Protohippius*."

"*Protohippus*," Emmie says, correcting her. "*Hippus* means 'horse' in Latin. Latin or Greek, I can't remember which."

"Well, so tell her about the *Protohippus*. Everything that you were telling me."

There's a sudden gust of icy wind then, sweeping down the street to remind them of February, blowing between the high buildings and the park. Emmie turns her face away from it, but it tugs persistently at her clothes and bites the tips of her fingers, snatches away her empty hot-dog wrapper and sends it scuttling like a pale, relish-stained insect across the sidewalk.

"Whoa," Sadie says and laughs. "Maybe we'd better hold on, pumpkin. Another one of those might blow us all the way to New Jersey."

Emmie doesn't laugh, because something about the wind has

reminded her of the bad dream—the girl in the attic, the clocks, the old cemetery, and the red thing in the maple tree. She hasn't told her stepmother about the dream, because she'd already forgotten it, mostly, by morning. And besides, Sadie always wants to make more out of dreams than she should. Emmie knows what dreams are, what she *believes* that they are, and they aren't portents or visions or anything like that. "Brain garbage," Deacon calls them, which seems about right to her.

"I don't want to litter," she says, "even if it's really the wind's fault," and Emmie chases down the hot-dog wrapper before it ends up in the street or across the street in the park. She catches it where it's snagged against the base of a flagpole, then glances back at Sadie, who points at a nearby garbage can.

She told you about the horses, too, didn't she? the dark-skinned girl in the dream asked her. *You've already forgotten that, I'll wager?* And she had, and she'd forgotten them again when she and Sadie were standing in front of all those fossil horse skeletons—*Hyracotherium, Mesohippus, Merychippus,* and the perfectly articulated skeleton of a *Protohippus,* not mounted on welded steel rods like the others but still encased in rock, half-exposed in right profile. Just behind the skeleton's rib cage, underneath its pelvis, were the skull and tiny bones of an unborn foal. Twelve million years ago, the mother horse had died giving birth.

She told you about the horses, too, didn't she?

I know this isn't going to make much sense, said the woman on the train, *but you need to stay away from horses.*

But Emmie *hadn't* stayed away from them, had she? And nothing bad had happened. She imagined telling it all to Deacon, imagined him rubbing his stubbly cheeks and nodding his head like it wasn't anything he hadn't heard a thousand times before. "Of course nothing bad happened," he would tell her, "because the woman on the train was crazy—and what have I told you about talking to strangers?—

and the dream was just a dream. Brain garbage." And then he'd tap on his forehead with one finger and tell her he was late for work but to try to stop worrying herself about horses and nightmares.

"Hello there," someone says, and when Emmie looks up, Hunter Fontana is standing over her, smiling. Hunter's a lot older than Sadie, and sometimes Emmie pretends that Hunter is her grandmother.

"What's that?" Hunter asks, and she points at the wad of paper in Emmie's hand.

"The stupid wind," Emmie replies. "I'm not a litterbug."

"Where's your stepmom?"

"She's right over there," Emmie tells her and jabs a thumb towards the spot where Sadie's sitting with the bighorn sheep. "We were waiting on you."

"Well, now I'm here. Let's put that in the trash and go see Sadie, shall we?"

Emmie smiles, her uneasiness from the wind already beginning to fade away. "We shall," she says. "She wants me to tell you about the museum, about the fossil horses."

"Eocene, Oligocene, Miocene, or Pliocene?" Hunter asks, following Emmie to the trash. It never surprises Emmie what Hunter seems to know, since she seems to know something about almost everything.

"Miocene," Emmie tells her. "I told her you probably wouldn't want to hear it. I'm sure you know about it already."

"Maybe," Hunter says. "You never can tell." And then Emmie drops the wrapper into the trash can.

"What about the Seal of Solomon?" Emmie asks, the words thought up, strung together, and spilling out of her mouth before she's even sure she wants to start talking about that again. Hunter seems only a little surprised.

"I thought we were talking about fossil horses?"

"Never mind," Emmie says, peering past the rim of the can into the trash, all the bits and pieces that people have thrown away, the bottles and drink cans and paper bags, discarded plastic and glass, aluminum and cardboard. And her hot-dog wrapper, crumpled into a ball and lying on top of everything else. She wrinkles her nose; something in there smells dead, and she wonders if maybe there's a dead pigeon wedged way down at the bottom, or a squirrel, or a rat.

"If you say so," Hunter tells her and takes Emmie's right hand, then leads her back to where Sadie's sitting, finishing her Snapple. "You know she's a weird kid, right?" Hunter asks her stepmother, and Sadie smiles.

"Takes after her dad," she says.

Emmie wishes that they wouldn't talk about her like she wasn't there, and that they wouldn't call her weird, even though she knows it's only a joke. *Lesbian witches have no damn business calling anyone else weird,* she thinks and turns loose of Hunter's hand.

"Is that a fact?" Hunter asks, sitting down on the bench next to Sadie. "When did Deacon Silvey take an interest in the Kabbalah?"

"Oh, I see. So I guess she's on about the Seal of Solomon again," Sadie says. "I don't know *what's* up with that. She—"

"You know, I'm standing *right here,*" Emmie says, interrupting her stepmother. "You could just *ask* me what's up with that."

"Did she tell you about the horses?" Sadie asks Hunter.

"She started to, I think. But then the other thing came up, and she didn't finish."

"You're *still* doing it," Emmie says, reaching for her backpack lying there on the bench. "It's rude, Sadie. How the heck am I ever going to learn how to act when all the adults I know are rude?"

"How about we go for a walk," Hunter suggests and points at the park. "It's such a nice day, we should take a walk in the park. How's that sound, Emmie?"

"We haven't seen the blue whale yet," Emmie protests, "or the meteorites, either."

"We could go for a walk, then come back to the museum later this afternoon," Sadie says. "Then we can still see the blue whale *and* the meteorites."

"And the Hall of Vertebrate Origins. And the planetarium," Emmie says.

"Right. And the planetarium."

"Sure," Emmie nods without a drop of enthusiasm. "Whatever." She's thinking about the dream again, the girl with the candle, the maple tree, and the rat sipping peach soda, and she doesn't want to walk in the park, just wants to go back inside the museum so maybe something interesting will distract her. They haven't even seen the Hall of Minerals or the Hall of Gems. But now Hunter and Sadie are talking about something else, laughing about some secret grown-up thing, and Emmie looks over her shoulder at the busy street, past the people and taxis and a long yellow school bus, to the place where asphalt and concrete give way to a low stone wall that seems to be holding back the grass and trees at the western edge of the park. *It's not the same as in the summer,* she thinks. *There's a whole hungry wilderness in there, hungry and waiting for me.* And then she remembers a book she read once about the history of Manhattan, how the island was saltmarshes and forest hundreds of years ago, how the land was drained by Dutch settlers and the Indians driven away so a city could be built here. How Central Park isn't really a wild place at all, but a garden designed by men who wanted to tame nature. *Maybe,* she thinks, *it isn't tame at all. Not really.* All those thousands of crooked, bare limbs clawing at the bright blue sky, the poplars and willows, oaks and *maples,* and suddenly Emmie Silvey is afraid of the park for the first time in her life.

"What about a carriage ride?" Hunter asks, and Emmie glances over at the statue of Roosevelt on his great bronze horse. "I bet that's something you've never done before. How about it, Sadie? My treat."

"What do you think, Emmie?" Sadie asks. "You want to ride in a carriage? Might be fun."

The statue is black and green with verdigris, and Theodore Roosevelt looks more like a Roman god of war riding off to battle than an American president. His head and shoulders are spattered with white smears of bird shit. *I know this isn't going to make much sense, but you need to stay away from horses.* His bronze mount is an enormous metal beast; no horse was *ever* that large, not even in prehistoric times. Emmie looks back at her stepmother and Hunter Fontana, trying to think of some way to explain, some way to get them to take her back inside immediately.

"Look, there's one now," Hunter says and points to a hansom cab making its way towards them, drawn by a muscular but weary-looking black mare, her iron hooves clip-clopping loudly on the pavement. The hack is wearing a gray top hat, and there are no riders in the carriage. "Just let me get his attention," Hunter says.

"We haven't seen the blue *whale*," Emmie says again, because she can think of nothing else to say.

"We will," Sadie assures her. "I promise. But Emmie, this is something you've never done before. You've seen that old whale lots of times."

"Three times," Emmie tells her. "I've only seen it three times." Her mouth has gone very dry, and the cold wind has started blowing again. An empty Coke can rattles past. The carriage has pulled over in front of the museum, parking in front of the statue of Theodore Roosevelt, and the driver pulls back on the mare's leather reins. Wooden wheels lacquered white as snow, white wheels with crimson hubs, and Hunter's already talking with the hack, taking money from her wallet.

"I don't want to go," Emmie whispers. "Please, Sadie, I don't want to do this."

Her stepmother looks confused, her smile fading slowly away

to some indistinct concern. "Why not, Emmie?" she asks. "You'll probably love it."

"I can't tell you. I just don't want to do it. Tell Hunter I don't want to do it, please. Make her stop."

"Oh, baby," Sadie says. "No, no, it's okay," and Emmie's crying now, and that's stupid and makes it all even worse. She's too old to be acting this way. She imagines the wind will freeze her tears, and tiny beads of ice will shatter on the sidewalk at her feet, imagines that they will make sounds like wind chimes when they break.

"He can't wait forever," Hunter shouts, and the mare snorts and shakes its head, pulling at the reins. "We'll just make a loop, once around the park, that's all."

"She doesn't want to go," Sadie calls out to Hunter.

"Why *not*?" Hunter shouts back. "I've already paid the man. Come on, Sadie."

"I *can't*," Emmie whispers, leaning closer to her stepmother. "I can't do it, Sadie. I can't *go*. If I do it, something bad's going to happen."

"That's silly," Sadie tells her. "Why would you think—"

"Hurry up!" Hunter yells.

"Just tell him we've changed our minds," Sadie shouts back at her, and she puts her good arm around Emmie and hugs her tightly. "I think she's tired. Thanks, but maybe some other time."

Emmie buries her face in her stepmother's lap, hiding from the wind and the hungry trees and Theodore Roosevelt. "I'm sorry," she sobs. "I'm sorry, Sadie. I'm sorry—"

"Pumpkin, there's nothing for you to be sorry about," Sadie says and begins stroking her hair. "Hunter thought it might be fun, that's all. No one's upset with you."

But then Emmie hears the squeal of tires, rubber burning itself to smoke against the blacktop, and she looks up in time to see the taxi swerve across the yellow dividing line. The mare sees it, too, and tries to bolt, but there's no time, too much weight hitched to her and nowhere to run, and a moment later the horse screams as the car collides with the hansom cab. The taxi's horn, the snap of wood, the wetter snap of splintering bone, the abrupt thud of metal against meat, and the mare goes down in a heap of flesh and tack on the sidewalk, just missing Hunter. Emmie knows from the emptiness in its lolling, dark eyes and the pool of blood spreading thickly across the concrete that it's dead. Sadie screams, her voice not so different from the dead horse's, and Emmie looks away.

Almost forty-five minutes later, and Emmie's sitting on her bed in Sadie's apartment, trying not to hear the things that her stepmother and Hunter Fontana are saying. They went into Sadie's bedroom and shut the door, but Emmie can still hear them. The apartment's too small for privacy.

"—would have been dead."

"Hunter, you don't *know* that."

"The *hell* I don't. If the two of you had come when I called—"
—we'd be dead.

They weren't, but the horse was, its ribs caved in and its neck broken, and the man who drove the hansom cab hauled off to the hospital in an ambulance.

"It was a fucking *coincidence*," Sadie hisses.

"You don't believe that," Hunter says. "You don't believe that for a moment, and we both know it."

"She's just a *child*."

"I want to go home now," Emmie says, speaking to no one in particular because there's no one there to hear. She's said it several times since they got back to the apartment, and that's why Sadie's packing. "I want to go home now."

"We would be *dead*," Hunter says again.

But Emmie's pretty sure she's missing the point. If Deacon were here, he'd say she couldn't smell the turds for the sewage or something like that. He always knows what to say when people are missing the point.

She told you that something's coming, and you need to listen to her. She told you about the horses, too. . . .

Just while you're in New York City this time, stay away from horses, okay? I think it's very important.

"She's missing the point," Emmie says, pretending that Sadie's standing there and can hear her. "Hunter's missing the point." Emmie's left shoe has come untied, and she starts to tie it, then stops and just stares at it instead.

"If I'd listened . . ." Emmie begins, but maybe it's not something she should say aloud, so she finishes the sentence in her head: *. . . the horse would still be alive. If we hadn't gone to the museum, where I knew there would be horses, Hunter never would have made the carriage stop.*

"Don't waste your life on regret," the dark-skinned girl from the attic says. Emmie looks up from her untied sneaker, and the girl is standing at the foot of the bed, watching her. "No good ever comes of that."

"If this is only a dream," Emmie tells her, "and I wake up, then the horse will still be alive."

"Six of one," the girl says.

"And I can tell Sadie I don't feel like going to the museum, that I'd rather go to Chinatown instead."

"Half dozen of the other."

"If I'm only dreaming, none of it has to happen."

"Unless it already has," the girl suggests unhelpfully.

"The hell with you," Emmie says, and it feels so good that she says it a second time. "The hell with you."

"You have a very foul mouth on you, Emma Jean Silvey. And,

just so you know, you won't ever profit from thinking that second chances are that easy."

"You're not real," Emmie growls at the girl, "so just shut up and leave me alone. And nobody calls me Emma Jean. If you were real, you'd know that."

She can hear Sadie crying now.

"Has anything like this ever happened before?" Hunter asks. "Sadie, the kid saved our goddamn *lives* today."

"You stop saying that," Sadie snaps back at her. "I don't want to fucking hear it again."

"What the hell are you so *afraid* of?" Hunter demands.

"You don't fucking know. You don't have any idea what you're talking about."

"If I'm dreaming, then I can change it all," Emmie tells the girl standing at the foot of the bed. The girl's wearing a black dress with a stiff white collar, like something a pilgrim girl might have worn to the first Thanksgiving dinner. She's also wearing black-and-white-striped stockings and old-fashioned black patent leather boots. She frowns and takes a purple Magic Marker from a pocket in her dress and hands it to Emmie.

"Show me," the dark-skinned girl says.

"What do you mean?" Emmie asks, staring at the marker. The label's mostly scraped off and the cap's missing.

"*Show* me, changeling. You know how it goes. '*I am the great Bridge Builder. And now come; I will open the door in the sky and send you to your own land.*'"

"You're a loony bird," Emmie says. She can smell the Magic Marker, and the purple ink smells like African violets and the ocean before a storm, which only goes to prove it's all a dream.

"Show me," the girl says a third time. "Build me a bridge, Emmie. I have long desired one."

And because this *is* only a dream, and almost anything's better than listening to Sadie and Hunter yelling at each other, yelling the way that Deacon and Sadie did before Sadie left Providence for good, Emmie turns and draws a circle on the wall with the purple marker. The felt tip squeaks loudly against the plaster. When she's done, it's not a bridge or a wormhole or anything else but a big purple circle drawn on Sadie's wall.

"See?" the girl from the attic says. "You're not dreaming," and when Emmie turns to tell her none of this proves a thing one way or the other, she discovers that the girl's gone, and she's alone again.

FOUR

Woonsocket

"It wasn't like that," Odd Willie mumbles indignantly, and lights another cigarette off the butt of the one before, crumpling the empty Winston pack and tossing it out the car window. "That sour old cunt, she needed a lesson in the finer fucking points of minding her own business, you know."

"Yeah, well, be that as it may," Soldier says, "don't think you're gonna make a habit out of shit like that." She squints through her sunglasses and the windshield of the Dodge at the cloudy afternoon, the sky still threatening snow. The Bailiff told her to keep driving the old Intrepid for now, even after what Odd Willie pulled at the Dunkin' Donuts and then the scene out at Rocky Point, and that was only one of the dozen or so unwelcome surprises in the last twenty-four hours that have Soldier wondering if maybe she's finally running out of luck, or if maybe the Bailiff's just running out of patience.

"You're wound way too tight, Odd Willie," she says. "You're like the center of a goddamn golf ball."

On the radio, Sam the Sham and the Pharaohs are singing "Lil' Red Riding Hood," and Soldier bumps up the volume a notch. The

Dodge rushes past the turnoff for the West Wrentham Road, and the final mile or so of I-22 before Woonsocket stretches out before her, gray and crooked and almost as narrow as her chances of coming out of this thing in one piece. Her eyes ache, and she could have used a few more hours sleep.

"I just can't stand people fucking staring at me," Odd Willie says, and then to Saben White, sitting alone in the backseat, "You make me sound like some kind of goddamn irrational lunatic."

"That's the way Soldier told it to me," Saben replies. "And you're not exactly known for your judicious conduct, Mr. Lothrop." Soldier glares at her in the rearview mirror, but Saben doesn't seem to notice. "You got that nickname somewhere."

"You're one to fucking talk," Odd Willie cackles and shakes his head. "Shit, Saben, I ain't never yet thrown down on a goddamned priest. And, you know, now that I think about it, that's probably why you don't hear people calling me fucking *Dead* Willie."

"You do what you have to do," Saben says and rubs at the gauze bandage on the back of her neck. "If you knew the whole story—"

"Yeah, well maybe that's the problem," Soldier says. "No one's bothered to let us in on the whole story."

"No one ever tells me jack shit anymore," Odd Willie mutters and sucks sullenly on his cigarette.

Soldier spares another glance at the rearview mirror, at Saben sitting there in the backseat, sitting up very straight and defiant in her neat black clothes, that one fucking outfit probably worth more than Soldier's entire wardrobe. The left side of Saben's face is swollen and splotched various bruised shades of red and purple, her lower lip split badly enough that it took two stitches to close. And the sight of her, all the damage done to that pretty, smug face, makes Soldier feel just a little bit better about almost everything.

"What *I* want to know," Willie says, "is why these goddamn beaver-beaters up in Woonsocket decided they couldn't wait until

Monday to do this thing, and, for that matter, why the fuck the Bailiff let them go and change their minds on him like that?"

"Likely as not, that's none of your goddamn business," Soldier tells him. "Anyway, what difference does it make to you? Did you have a fucking date or something?"

"*You* can suck my dick, the *both* of you," Odd Willie snorts and breathes out a cloud of smoke.

"You scared, Odd Willie?" Saben asks, trying to sound amused, but Soldier can hear the deceit.

"Damn straight, and if you aren't too, it's only because what precious little sense you ever had got knocked out of you yesterday. After I got back from Rocky Point last night, I started asking around about Woonsocket."

"What you mean is, you went looking for spook stories," Soldier says, and Odd Willie frowns at her.

"Jesus Christ, you're the one made the place out like it was the goddamned fifth level of Hades or something, so I just asked around, that's all. I talked to Patience Bacon, you know, that little creep used to run with Scarborough Pentecost back before he—"

"I *know* fucking Patience Bacon."

"Well, yeah, so he says it's never been much of anything, Woonsocket. Leastways, no one's ever given much of a shit what goes on up there. Boston leaves it alone. Providence leaves it alone. Bunch of inbred motherfuckers, he said, half-breeds and quadroons and messed-up shit like that. Total fucking *Deliverance* territory."

"Yeah, it's a shithole," Soldier says, wishing she'd made Odd Willie drive, because he doesn't talk so damned much when he's driving.

"Patience says it was a big mill town way back when, full of, you know, decent working-class folk," and Willie Lothrop snickers and taps ash onto the floorboard. "Give me your tired, your poor, your huddled motherfuckers yearning to get dicked up the ass by fat-cat mill owners, right?"

"We don't need a history lesson," Saben says. "Some of us know our own backyards."

"Shut the fuck up," Soldier says and smiles at Saben's reflection. "You keep right on talking, Odd Willie. Fancy-pants cunts that ride in the backseat never know half as much as they think they do."

"Hell, Soldier, I don't even remember what I was saying. What's the difference? We do what we're told, like good little henchmen, no matter *what's* on the other end. Into the Valley of Death rode the six fucking hundred, et cetera, et cetera."

"Whatever you say," Saben mumbles, meaning Soldier or Odd Willie or the both of them at once.

Willie Lothrop rubs at his nose. "Bad fucking mojo up there," he says. "That's what Patience Bacon says. Said that place was rotten to the core *before* the mills and the beaver-beaters and the fucking hounds showed up, said even the damned Indians knew that place was bad news, but *they* had the good sense to stay away. You know what Woonsocket means in Algonquin Indian talk? It means the fucking way down to hell; *that's* what it means."

"No, it doesn't, you moron," Soldier says and laughs. "It means 'place of deep descent,' because of the valley and all the damn waterfalls on the Blackstone River."

Odd Willie glares at her for a second or two and then gives Soldier the finger. "Fine," he says. "I didn't know we had Miss Hollywood fucking Squares in the car with us, Miss I'll-take-goddamn-geography-for-five-hundred-Alex. Jesus fucking crap. *You're* the one was telling me how messed up the place is."

"I never said it was the gates of hell. It's a rough neighborhood, that's all." Soldier knows better, knows it's more than that, *way* more than that, but doesn't see the point, at this late date, of telling Odd Willie the truth if he doesn't know it already. He'll see for himself soon enough.

"You want me just to shut the hell up?"

"No," Soldier lies. "I want to hear the rest of it. The history of Woonsocket as told by the illustrious and learned Patience Bacon. By the way, you know he's the same jackass who accidentally locked himself in a mausoleum over at Swan Point, right? He was there three days—"

"You're fucking making fun of me, and I hate that almost as much as crazy old ladies fucking staring at me."

"Oh, come on, Willie. Do it for Saben. She needs something to take her mind off being such a craven pain in my rectum."

Willie sighs and taps more ash onto the floorboard, ignoring the ashtray. "Patience Bacon says it's a bad place, that's all. He says it was always a rough neck of the woods, but after the mills left in the seventies, things kind of went to—"

"Hell?" Saben asks quietly.

"*If* you gotta put a goddamned name on it, yeah. Things kinda went to hell. It's fucking anarchy up there. Quadroons and octoroons wandering around in broad fucking daylight, buying their crack and crystal and shit right there on the street just like everybody else. The whole town might as well be a goddamn warren—"

"You curse an awful lot, you know that?" Soldier asks him. "You might just be the most foulmouthed bastard I've ever had to work with."

"Fuck you. You know about Ballou?" he asks her.

"Yeah, Willie. I know all about Ballou."

"Crazy son of a whore. Crazy as a shithouse rat. Way I hear it, he's spent the last couple of decades hidden away up here trying to open doors, doors no one's supposed to ever fucking open. *No one. Ever.* But there he is with his little inbred fuckfest, doing whatever he pleases, and the rest of us be damned. Lots of people go missing in Woonsocket."

"If I lived there, I'd go missing, too," Saben says.

"You might just go missing anyway," Soldier tells her, speaking to the rearview mirror.

"This guy Ballou, he's not even a changeling," Odd Willie says. "He's not a Child of the Cuckoo, and he's not a ghoul, either, just some half-breed mutt, and he's running the whole damn show, right? Descended from some kind of goddamn French Lancelots—"

"Huguenots," Saben White cuts in. "French Huguenots."

Odd Willie looks over his shoulder at her, peering past the rims of his expensive Wayfarers, and she gets the middle finger, too. "Soldier, if you want to pull over, I'd be glad to finish what you started yesterday."

"You'd be glad to fucking try," Saben tells him.

"Shut up, Saben. Interrupt Odd Willie again, and I'm not only going to take him up on his offer, I'm gonna lend a fucking hand."

"Whatever. Fucking *Huguenots*," Odd Willie says, turning back to face the windshield again. "They started all this textile shit way back in the 1840s, right? And they've been running the place ever since. Fucking half-breed loup-garou sons of bitches. Patience Bacon, he says there's this Precious Blood beaver-beater cemetery with some sort of big marble coliseum, you know, like a ruined Greek temple, and this Ballou fucker and his mongrels have been making human sacrifices there on the Full Worm Moons—"

"—trying to open doors," Saben says. "You're starting to sound like a bad monster movie."

"Oh, that's real fucking funny," Odd Willie sneers back at her.

"Ballou's a thug and a cunt," Soldier says, quoting the Bailiff. "Someone on the outside who's too stupid to know he's never getting in." Never mind how much it annoys Saben, she's tired of listening to Odd Willie. There's enough on her mind already without him making it worse.

"Okay. So, you tell me, why the hell does the Bailiff jump when Ballou says 'boo'?" Odd Willie asks. "Answer me that."

"There's some business we got to settle," Soldier replies. "That's all. So, please, as a personal fucking favor—drop the 'Valley of Death' shtick."

"Yeah, well, what about you, Soldier?" Saben asks. "Are you scared, too? Is he right? Are we really walking into something that bad?"

Soldier shrugs and pushes her sunglasses farther up the bridge of her nose. "Well," she says, "for someone who gets her kicks murdering men of the cloth, I suspect it might seem a little tame."

"I'd tell you," Saben says. "I'd tell you what really happened, if he'd let me."

Soldier glances at the rearview mirror again, and this time Saben's staring back at her. But there's more fear than bravado in her brown eyes, no matter how she's holding herself, no matter how straight her shoulders or high her chin. It's just bluster, and Soldier wonders how Saben White never managed to learn how to back down until *after* she's been bitten.

"Would you?" Soldier asks her. "Would you really do that? If you could, I mean. If he'd *let* you."

"I just said that I would."

"I think you're lying. I think it's possible you haven't even told the Bailiff everything. You look like someone with an awfully big secret."

"Did you tell the Bailiff that?" Saben asks, and then she looks down at her hands folded in her lap, the Seal of Solomon tattooed there like something that might actually have the power to protect her from whatever's waiting for them farther down the road. Soldier doesn't answer right away. Instead she listens to Sam the Sham, and the Dodge's tires spinning on the asphalt, the cold breeze rushing into Willie's window, which is still open a crack, and the roar of passing cars.

"I asked you if you told him that," Saben says, and now she's almost whispering. Odd Willie laughs and smokes his Winston.

"No," Soldier tells her. "I didn't say a fucking word." It's not the truth, but Soldier figures even a lie's more than Saben deserves to hear. "Whatever you did, why ever you did it, that's between you and him, because that's the way he wants it."

"Hey, ladies," Odd Willie Lothrop snickers. "How about a fucking joke to ease the tension?" and before Soldier can tell him to shut up, he's already started. "Okay, so, a Catholic boy and a Jewish boy were talking, you see, and the Catholic boy, being an arrogant Irish cocksucker, was like, 'Hey, man, my priest knows more than your rabbi.' And the Jewish boy, being such a wily cocksucker, he was like, 'Yeah? Well, of course he does. You fucking *tell* him everything.' " Odd Willie giggles and takes another drag off his Winston.

"Shut the hell up," Soldier says.

"Oh, come on. You know that was *wicked* funny," Odd Willie laughs. "I'm about to piss myself over here. Moreover, if you'll think about it a second, you'll see it was not entirely irrelevant to certain current events," and he turns and winks at Saben.

"Just shut up," Soldier says again, which only makes Willie giggle that much more.

"Thank you," Saben says from the backseat.

Soldier shakes her head and doesn't look at the rearview mirror. "Oh, no. It isn't like that, Saben. It isn't like that at all. Don't you dare start thanking *me* for anything."

"Yeah," Saben replies, and for a little while, no one says anything else.

"*Your* responsibility," the Bailiff had told her, no uncertain terms there, so Saturday night, after Rocky Point, Soldier drove Saben White to see the greasy old croaker over on Federal Hill who sews them up and sets broken bones and extracts bullets whenever something goes wrong. The basement where he works smelled like mildew and disinfectant, and Soldier sat in a moldering, duct-taped recliner in one corner while he cleaned up the mess she'd made of Saben's face and gave her an injection of antibiotics for the bite on the back of her neck. She'd heard the doctor had been a field medic in Vietnam, that he'd been sent home on a Section Eight after the My Lai Massacre back in sixty-eight. Now he works for the Bailiff, which means he also works for the ghouls and the Cuckoo, though, if his luck's improved any in the past forty-two years, the croaker knows nothing at all of the powers that held the Bailiff's leash.

"Human teeth are filthy things," the croaker mumbled gravely around his loose dentures while he filled the syringe with amoxicillin. "I'll tell you, I'd rather be bitten by a mangy, three-legged bitch than by a human mouth."

"Maybe it *was* a dog," Saben said and risked a glance at Soldier. "But I didn't count her legs."

"Just two," Soldier said, and then Saben winced when the old man jabbed her with the needle.

"That bite goes septic, missy, you won't be giving much of a shit if it had *six* legs and a pogo stick, now, will you?" the croaker asked Saben once he'd emptied the syringe.

Afterwards, Soldier drove across the Seekonk and left Saben on the sidewalk outside a renovated warehouse where she lived in a studio apartment on the third floor. All this time, except for the comments in the doctor's basement, neither of them had talked, because Saben was still too frightened, and there was nothing Soldier wanted to hear and even less she wanted to say. Soldier drove her home, left her on the sidewalk, and that, Soldier thought, was enough babysitting and fucking hand-holding for one night, enough *responsibility,* and she stopped at Fellini's for a couple of slices of pepperoni pizza on the way home. She drank Coke instead of beer, because a beer or three would only lead to the unopened bottle of whiskey beneath the front seat being opened, and she wasn't such a drunkard that the Bailiff couldn't scare her into staying sober for a few days every now and then. Not yet, anyway.

After the pizza, she went home to her own apartment, a dingy little hole on Lancaster Street. The Bailiff had rented it for her years before, the week she turned sixteen and was allowed to leave the warrens, just someplace to sleep until she could find something better. But Soldier had never really seen the point in looking for another place. It was quiet, and no one there ever fucked with her or got nosy. She had two rooms and a tiny kitchen, a bathroom and a view of the North Burial Ground past the rooftops. Soldier carried the bottle of Dickel in with her and set it on top of the television, then took a hot shower. The water and soap felt good, even if they weren't half clean enough to wash away the anxiety or the wall of angry black thoughts building itself high inside her head, but then, nothing was. Nothing ever was, not even the booze. She lay in bed naked, her wet hair and skin slowly drying in the not-quite-cold, not-quite-warm air of the apartment, and stared at the whiskey bottle on the TV. She imagined it stared back at her, taunting, tempting, reminding her how good it would feel, and all she had to do was crack the seal and take a few swallows. No one would ever know, it promised. Not a single soul, living or dead or anything in between. So then Soldier stared at the low water-stained ceiling instead.

A little while later she dozed, hardly more than half-asleep but dreaming about the night out on the Argilla Road, about Sheldon and the hearse, the cold November rain, and this time it all went more or less the way they'd planned it would, the way the Bailiff had laid it all out for them. At the end, Sheldon helped her burn down Quaker Jameson's roadhouse, and the gaunt and the orchid-skinned demon stood nearby, watching indifferently, and when they were done, the demon taught her a British drinking song that it sang to the tune of "The Star-Spangled Banner"—

The news through Olympus immediately flew;
Where Old Thunder pretended to give himself airs—
If these mortals are suffer'd their scheme to pursue,
There's devil a goddess will stay above stairs.
Hark! Already they cry,
In transports of joy.
A fig for Parnassus! To Rowley's we'll fly;
And there, my good fellows, we'll learn to entwine,
The myrtle of Venus with Bacchus' vine.

He offered to teach her another one, something bawdy the Free-masons sometimes sang to the tune of "God Save the Queen," but she was beginning to see where all this was headed, and she went back upstairs into the yellow house on Benefit Street. One of the silver-eyed women was waiting for her, and Soldier breathed into her palm, checking for the stink of whiskey. And of course she smelled like a fucking distillery, but the silver-eyed woman didn't seem to notice. A clock on the mantel rang the hour, and Soldier wondered if Sheldon had gotten lost in Ipswich again, if maybe he'd spend the whole night wandering about, lost in the rain. The silver-eyed woman, Miss Josephine, who'd lived in the house for more than a hundred years, offered Soldier a glass of brandy, and she said she'd rather have bourbon.

"Such a vulgar spirit," the vampire said disapprovingly, but poured Soldier a tall glass of Wild Turkey and left the bottle on the table so she could help herself if she wanted another. Soldier thanked her, drained the glass, belched, and then sat trying to recall the words to the demon's drinking song.

"I hear it did not go well tonight," the silver-eyed woman said, and when Soldier looked at her again, it was Sheldon Vale sitting on the other side of the wide mahogany dining table. There was a gaping red-black cavity between his eyes, the two overlapping bullet holes she could almost remember putting there. He wiped some of the gore from his face and then stared at the blood and brains and flecks of bone on his hands.

"Shoot first, ask questions later," he said and laughed. It made her think of drowning, that laugh, and she wondered where the silver-eyed woman had gone, and if she'd be coming back. "Of course," Sheldon said, "maybe *you* think it's better if you skip the questions entirely."

"You'd have done the same damned thing, and you know it," Soldier told him, and the clock on the mantel chimed again, fifteen minutes come and gone like a handful of nothing. The clock was strung together with baling wire and smoke, splintered wood from old tomato crates, three prickly white fish spines where the hands should be. Wheels and spindles carved from human bone, the fat pendulum a dead rat dangling headfirst, its stiff tail and some kite string for the rod. The clock's face had once belonged to a very pretty girl, and Soldier could see that the taxidermist had taken care to give her the finest glass eyes, irises the color of a broken china cup, before he'd tattooed a circle of blue-green Roman numerals onto her skin—XII perfectly centered on her forehead, VI on her chin. Or maybe she'd still been alive when that was done. Maybe they'd only killed her afterwards.

"But you *do* have questions, don't you?" Sheldon asked. "You've got questions gnawing you apart like maggots. You've got things in you *worse* than questions. I mean, at least a question is a place to start, right?"

"You're dead and full of shit," she told him and turned away from the clock because she was starting to think that the glass eyes could see her.

"That might be," Sheldon said. "But it doesn't change a word I've said. Do you even remember her?" and he pointed at the clock.

"Do I remember who?"

"The little girl in the attic, Soldier. The Daughter of the Four of Pentacles."

"Maybe I should be the one asking *you* the fucking questions—"

"So maybe you *are*. Maybe that's just exactly what you're doing. Do you *remember* her? The wizard's child?" And he rubbed at his eyes again, then wiped his sticky fingers on the table. The smear looked like chocolate and raspberry tapioca. He took something from the pocket of his jacket, a tarot card, and laid it faceup on the table between them.

"The Four of Pentacles," Sheldon said and tapped the card with an index finger like a magician getting ready for some sleight of hand. Soldier stared at the card a moment, a king seated upon a bench, a pentacle beneath each foot, one balanced atop his crown, and another wrapped up tight in his arms. Behind him there were low, tree-covered hills and the towers and parapets of a medieval city. The man's face was greed, she thought, greed and desperation, and then Sheldon tapped the card again.

"Yeah, so what?" Soldier asked him, losing patience, wondering how he'd made it back from Ipswich so goddamned fast. "It's a tarot card. I fucking hate riddles. You know that. You got something to say, spit it out or go haunt someone else, you backstabbing son of a bitch."

But the dead man only smiled and produced a battered paperback—*The Tarot Revealed,* by Eden Gray—from the same pocket that had held the card; he read silently from it for a moment, then laid the book on the table beside the card. "Maybe it's time you start asking a few of those questions," he said. "Maybe it's time for you to try and remember."

"Remember *what*?" she demanded, even though she'd been taught never to raise her voice in the yellow house on Benefit Street. "Just what the hell is it that you want me to try to remember?"

"I've got such a goddamned headache," he said, instead of

answering her question. "I should probably take some aspirin and find someplace to lie down."

"They've got these things called graves," Soldier said, glancing from the tarot card back to the clock on the mantel.

"Don't you even want to know why I did it?"

"Not particularly," Soldier told him and poured herself another glass of bourbon. The clock winked at her with one glass eye.

"Well, if that's the way you want it. You'll find out sooner or later, anyway. Right now, though, you'd better wake up," Sheldon said. "Looks like you've got company." And then he was gone, and Soldier was alone in the big dining room. She reached for the glass of whiskey, meaning to toast the clock, but opened her eyes instead, opened her eyes in another place and another time because now she could hear footsteps heavy on the floorboards of her apartment, footsteps and her squeaky front door being eased shut again. Adrenaline like a punch in the heart, brass knuckles to shatter her sternum, and she was awake in an instant, the dream already gone to gray tatters, nothing she'd be able to make sense of later. Soldier slipped her right hand beneath one of the pillows and pulled out the .357 Magnum she kept there, flipped off the safety, and cocked the pistol. The room was dark, even though she'd left the bathroom light burning.

"You would do me a great kindness," the Bailiff said, "if you'd please see fit to point that thing elsewhere."

"Shit," Soldier hissed, easing her finger off the trigger. She could smell her own sweat, the tinny stench of her fear, and she could also smell the Bailiff's cheap cologne like flowers and rubbing alcohol. "You scared the piss out of me, old man," she said, sitting up, returning the gun to its place beneath the pillow.

"I hope you don't mean that literally."

"I did what you said," Soldier told him. "I took her to the doc, and then I took her home."

"Would you like to turn on a light?" the Bailiff asked. "I can't see my hand four inches in front of my face."

Soldier reached for the floor lamp beside the bed, fumbling for the long cord with its frayed gold tassel, and a moment later she was squinting and cursing and shading her eyes against the dim glare of the twenty-five-watt bulb.

"It's right there on the television," she said. "I haven't had a sip. I haven't even opened it. It's all yours. Every goddamn drop, if you still want it."

The Bailiff turned to find the bottle of Dickel where Soldier had left it a few hours earlier. "Really? For *me*?" he asked, and smiled one of his great carnivorous smiles. "Why, little Soldier girl, how terribly, *terribly* thoughtful of you. I hope you won't mind if I share this with my boys. They do so appreciate a stiff shot of something now and then."

"I'm sure they do," Soldier yawned and picked up her lighter and a fresh pack of Marlboros from the cluttered nightstand. "Knock yourself out. Pour it down the fucking toilet, for all I care."

"You're naked," the Bailiff said.

"Thank you for noticing."

"Would you like me to give you a moment to dress yourself? The matter that's brought me here, it's nothing so urgent—"

"I'm fine," Soldier said, though the air in the bedroom was much colder than when she'd fallen asleep, and she wished that she'd bothered to bring her ratty green terry-cloth bathrobe to bed with her instead of leaving it hanging on its nail beside the shower stall. "Unless titties offend you, Bailiff."

He sniffed, cocked a bushy eyebrow, and set the bottle of whiskey down again. "It might not be my personal preference, as you should well know, but I have seen more than my share of womanflesh, and I'm not the squeamish sort, besides. So if it suits you—"

"I did what you said," Soldier told him again and lit a cigarette.

"Yes, I know. I just left Miss Saben White not half an hour ago. Somewhat worse for the wear, I might add. At the moment, I'm more concerned with the whereabouts of Mr. William Lothrop and the inconveniently deceased papist."

Soldier took a deep drag off her cigarette, exhaled, and stared through the smoke at the fat man standing near the foot of her bed. Beads of sweat stood out on his bald head, and his long beard was twisted into a short, stiff braid and tied with a rubber band. He was wearing a shiny blue suit of worsted wool.

"I haven't talked to Odd Willie yet," she replied. "He was supposed to call. But you know how he is. He gets caught up in his work. He forgets shit." And Soldier drew little circles in the air around her right ear.

"Yes, he does," the Bailiff said and nodded his head. "But he is a maestro when it comes to incineration, is he not? We can sometimes overlook eccentricities when matters of genius are involved, don't you think?"

"If it suits you," Soldier said, wishing the Bailiff would stop hemming and hawing and get to whatever was on his mind so that maybe she could go back to sleep.

"William is a troubled boy," the Bailiff continued, "but insanity and antisocial behavior have never excluded the likelihood of precocity, little Soldier. You should remember that."

"Fine," she said and took another drag off the Marlboro. "I'll remember that. Have I done something wrong?"

"No, no. Quite the contrary," the Bailiff said. "Why do you ask?" and then he looked about in vain for a place to sit down. Soldier pointed at the foot of the bed, and he eased his bulk onto the mattress. The box springs shrieked like a sockful of stomped mice.

"I asked because I'm not accustomed to waking up with you standing in my goddamn bedroom. *That's* why I asked."

"Yes, I suppose it *was* rude of me not to call," he said and tugged at his braided beard. "I'm sorry about that. But I believe, little Soldier, that I had cause not to trust certain information to the telephone."

"And it couldn't have waited until tomorrow?"

"No, as a matter of fact," he said, and then he told her that there had been another call from George Ballou up in Woonsocket, that she'd have to make the trip on Sunday instead of Monday. And then he said other things, and Soldier sat naked on the bed and listened. By the time he was done, the last thing on Soldier's mind was sleep. He took the bottle of Dickel, bade her a good morning and good luck, reminded her that if she fucked it up this time, she'd never have to worry about fucking it up again, kissed her on the left cheek, and then the Bailiff left. Soldier smoked another Marlboro, and when she was done, she picked up her cell and called Odd Willie Lothrop.

In the wan, cloud-filtered light of the winter afternoon, the winding, rugged course of the Blackstone River reminds Soldier of a gigantic coal-colored snake, some vast and immeasurably prehistoric serpent or biblical monster sprawled lazily across the land, and there's the city of Woonsocket held forever tight inside its iridescent coils. The water, which is really only its scales, glints darkly, and, here and there, she can see foam-white scars to mark the various waterfalls and cataracts. Soldier knows there's too much truth in the things Odd Willie said, and maybe when the Algonquin named this place, they meant hell after all. Seeing it now, postcard perfect between the steep, wooded hills and yet surely gone as sick and mean and insane as any town ever will, Soldier could believe just about anything at all about Woonsocket. There have been white men here, of one sort and then another, for almost four hundred years, and they have dug themselves in deep, almost as deep as the hounds and the things that were here before the hounds. The Dodge follows the highway down into the valley, out of the old forest, the trees that she imagines lean in towards the river as if their bare branches might hide it from the terrible gray and purple sky.

Odd Willie giggles anxiously and asks Soldier a question that she only half hears, something about swamp yankees and sundown, but she doesn't answer him, doesn't say a word. She follows the road past shoddy, weatherworn houses and boarded-up discount stores, fast-food joints and fading wooden billboards hawking "chowda" and clam cakes and lobster, out into the crooked streets of the city. The smokestacks and pitched rooftops of abandoned mills, towering church steeples and the brick-and-mortar corpses of long-dead factories rise up before her like some ingenious armor the serpent river has fashioned to keep itself safe, the symbiotic ruins of industry and avarice to guard a sleeping dragon.

"When are you going to get around to telling us what this is all about?" Saben White asks from the backseat.

"It's just a courier job; that's all," Soldier replies and stops at a red light. "As long as no one gets stupid and nothing gets fucked-up, it won't be anything but a simple drop and swap. We give them that leather bag in the trunk, and they give us a package for the Bailiff."

"What the Sam Hill could these yahoos have that the Bailiff wants?" Willie Lothrop asks her and shakes his head. She realizes that he hasn't combed his hair once since they left Providence, hasn't even taken out his pink plastic comb, and that's got to be some sort of record.

"That part's none of our goddamn business. You ought to know that much by now, Willie. That part's between Old Man Ballou and the Bailiff."

"Well, they should have sent *two* fucking cars," he says.

"Ballou said just one. One car, three occupants," Soldier tells him. "So that's the way we're doing it."

"We've got less than ten minutes," Saben White says, sounding more impatient than anything else, and Soldier nods, but doesn't look at her.

"Believe it or not, I can fucking tell time," Soldier says, then finds a gravelly place at the side of the road and pulls over, the wheels of the Dodge sending up a dense cloud of dust and grit. She lets the motor idle for a moment, as the dust settles again, before she turns the key and switches it off. The car's parked beside an old retaining wall, concrete covered with wild grapevines like a strangling network of dead, dry veins and capillaries.

"I want to talk to Willie for a moment," Soldier says. "*Just* Willie. You stay where you are, Saben. Unless I call for you, you stay right there where you are."

"Ten minutes," Saben reminds her, and Soldier shows her the middle finger of her right hand.

"Come on, Odd Willie. We need to talk."

"What the hell for?" he asks, reaching for the door handle, reaching so slowly that Soldier gets the impression that maybe he thinks she's going to change her mind and let him stay in the car.

"I need to stretch my legs. I need to clear my head before the drop, that's all."

She opens her door, and the cold air tastes like the highway grime stirred up by the Dodge, like the exhaust from passing cars and trucks, and, beneath that, there's the faintly rotten smell of the Blackstone River. Despite all her years in the tunnels, her schooling by the hounds, Soldier has never really grown accustomed to the smell of rot. Most of the changelings hardly seem to notice, but the smell of rot makes Soldier uneasy, and the smell of *wet* rot is the worst of them all. Odd Willie follows her along the road's shoulder for fifteen or twenty yards. He lights a cigarette and that helps mask the smell of the river a little, so she lights one of her own, then stops and stares back at the car and Saben sitting in the backseat.

"You think she's getting suspicious?" Odd Willie asks. "You think she knows something's up?"

"Well, you laid it on pretty thick," Soldier says, then looks away from the Dodge, up at the sky; she wonders how the car handles on ice and snow.

"Sometimes it's hard to stop," he says and puffs his cigarette. "Once I get started, it just keeps on coming."

"No, I think she's pissed off, but that's all. She thinks it's just something personal between me and her. And I guess that makes her half right." Soldier flicks ash at the gravel and takes a long drag off her Marlboro. She wants to walk back to the Dodge and put two or three in Saben's skull, but this is the Bailiff's show, and he's the one calling all the shots.

"I'm scared as shit," Odd Willie whispers and giggles softly to himself. "I'm sorry, Soldier, but that's the gods' fucking truth. I never signed on for crap like this."

"You never signed on," she reminds him, as if he might somehow have managed to forget.

"It was just a figure of speech. You know what I fucking meant."

"Sure," Soldier says, looking away from the sky, turning her attention once more to the walls and roofs and streets of Woonsocket laid out below them. "But I've never yet heard of one of us dying of old age. Makes it seem kind of silly to get too worked up over something like this." *That's Sheldon talking*, she thinks, his words from her mouth, something he said to her once or twice. *You ever heard of one of us dying from old age?*

"There's always a goddamned first time. I can't see the harm in being ambitious."

"Long as you're there when I need you."

"Shit, Soldier. All I said was I'm scared. I didn't say I was a coward. There's a great fucking difference between the two."

"That's all I wanted to hear," she says, studying the valley—the empty mills that are never really empty, the futility of a dozen ornate church steeples, the roaring white place where the Thundermist Falls were dammed in 1960, five years after a flood had almost destroyed the town. North of the dam, Soldier spots a low tree-shrouded hill rising from the rooftops and squalor, and she points it out to Odd Willie.

"Right there," she says, thinking that in the summer the trees would be lush and green, hiding the cemetery and all its secrets. But in winter, the old trees are little more than the weathered slats of a crooked fence, revealing the patchwork of headstones and less modest monuments to the dead and departed that crown the hill. Markers to signal mortal loss, and the way down to George Ballou.

"Fuck me," Odd Willie says and spits on the road.

"Don't you forget," Soldier tells him, still watching the tall trees surrounding Oak Hill Cemetery. "When the time comes, she's mine. Any of the rest of these assholes, you can take your fucking pick. But she's mine."

"I love it when you talk like Clint Eastwood," he says and snickers, then flicks the rest of his cigarette at a passing car. "It's absolutely fucking beautiful."

"Just don't you get all trigger-happy down there and forget what I'm telling you."

"Well," says Odd Willie, "as much as I'd love to do the honors myself—and I'm not gonna lie to you about that, no, ma'am—I learned a long time ago, you come between some cocksucker and the object of her passionate fucking need for vengeance, and pretty soon the hounds are gonna be shuffling your happy ass off to Mama Hydra—"

"You really believe that stuff?" she asks, interrupting him.

"Like I said last night, it's as good as anything else I've heard."

"Yeah," Soldier says and glances back at the car. Saben hasn't moved. "That other shit we talked about—"

"—stays between me and you," Odd Willie says. "I mean, until such time as they tie me down and some determined asshole comes at me with a pair of wire strippers and an acetylene torch."

"Guess that'll have to do," she says. "Let's get this over with."

Odd Willie Lothrop nods his head, and then he follows Soldier back to the car.

Odd Willie lives three flights up in a rat-infested Federal Hill tenement building that had been new when Calvin Coolidge was president and that should have been torn down long decades ago. It *had* been condemned, back in the 1990s, but that didn't keep out the squatters or the crackheads or Odd Willie. It didn't keep Soldier out, either. When the Bailiff had gone, she called Willie Lothrop and told him that she was on her way over. He sounded surprised, but not *too* surprised, and asked Soldier if she wanted to meet somewhere else, a bar or Swan Point or something more pleasant than his place. She told him no, his place was fine, that she just wanted to talk, that it was very important, and he told her to be careful on the stairs. "They're getting worse," he said. "I just about broke my goddamn ankle last week."

"You could move out of that shithole, you know," Soldier said, and she could almost hear him shrug.

"I got roots here," he replied and hung up first.

So, less than half an hour later, she was ducking under the boards nailed across the front doorway of the building, picking her way through the dark lobby cluttered with refuse and filth and broken furniture. She had a flashlight, but didn't turn it on. She could see well enough to find the sagging stairs leading up to Willie's apartment.

"Who the hell are you?" a gruff female voice demanded from the shadows. "You best stay the fuck away from me, bitch, or I'll cut you."

"Will you?" Soldier asked, speaking to the lightless place where the voice had come from, imagining the woman cringing there amid the peeling wallpaper and old cardboard and rat droppings. "Will you really?"

"I ain't messin' around with you, cunt. I'll slice you up so bad ain't no doctor ever been born be able to put you back together again." But the woman sounded more frightened than dangerous. Soldier imagined there were others, less bold, more frightened, cowering in the darkness of the lobby and the hallway leading deep into the ground floor of the building. She crossed the small room, stood at the foot of the stairs and squinted into the narrow stairwell that wound up and up and up, a right-angled whorl like the view from inside some geometrically improbable snail's spiraling shell.

"Don't you waste your time worrying about me," Soldier told the woman. "You got way worse things to worry about than me."

"Don't you tell *me* what I got to worry over, bitch."

Soldier laid her right hand on the banister and took the first step; she wanted a drink so bad it hurt, so bad she was beginning to feel sick, and she wondered what Odd Willie had upstairs. Odd Willie usually drank cheap tequila and cheaper malt liquor, but right now either one would be fine with her. She took a couple more steps.

"Who you is?" the voice asked. "You ain't no angel. You ain't no servant of the Lord Jesus."

"No," Soldier told the woman, "I'm not that. But you just wait. I expect someone else will be along shortly."

"You some kind of hoodoo," the woman sneered from her hiding place, and Soldier imagined her crossing herself or making some sign to ward off the evil eye. "You some kind of devil."

"Close enough," Soldier replied, and then she left the woman and climbed the stairs to Odd Willie's floor. By the time she reached his front door she was out of breath and thirstier than ever. She had to knock four times before he opened up.

"I was on the can," he explained, zipping his pants, snagging his underwear in the zipper, and having to start over again. Odd Willie was wearing black jeans and a black-and-white Buzzcocks T-shirt. There were several holes in the shirt, and he was barefoot.

"You know there's a fucking crazy lady downstairs?" Soldier asked him, leaning against the doorjamb, trying to catch her breath. "I thought she was gonna try to exorcise me or something."

"Yeah, that's Betty. Don't you worry about her," Odd Willie said and tried his zipper again. "When she's not high, which isn't very often, she's either seeing demons or waiting on the Second Coming or both."

"Charming fucking neighbors you got," Soldier said. "Now, you gonna let me in, or are we going to have to do this right out here in the hallway?"

He apologized and stepped to one side so that Soldier could get past, and then he shut the door and locked it. The apartment smelled like fried food and mildew and stale cigarette smoke, and the only light came from a few flickery fluorescent tubes he'd rigged up overhead.

"Like I said on the phone," Willie started, "it's taken care of. I set the timer for twenty minutes and left him inside the old House of Horrors—"

"That's not why I'm here," Soldier said.

"Oh yeah," Odd Willie said, and giggled, and then he sat down on the mattress lying in the center of the room, the mattress stained and torn and heaped with dirty sheets and a stolen blue U-Haul moving blanket. "You already said that on the phone," he smiled and nodded his head, made a gun with his thumb and forefinger and pressed it to his left temple. "You want something to drink?"

"You fucking know not to ever ask me that question."

"Yeah, but I got a brand-new bottle of Pepe Lopez Gold, hasn't even been opened," Odd Willie said and grinned at her. There was a blotch of something on the front of his shirt that looked like tooth-paste, though Soldier was pretty sure Odd Willie Lothrop had never made the acquaintance of a toothbrush.

"Might as well drink paint thinner as that shit," Soldier told him, and glanced about for someplace to sit down. Willie pointed her to-wards a three-legged chair propped against one wall.

"Hell, it *tastes* like fucking paint thinner," Odd Willie said. "But it generally does the job."

"I came over because I have to ask you a question," Soldier said, changing the subject because she had enough trouble right now with-out Odd Willie's cheap-ass tequila. She sat down on the three-legged chair, leaning slightly to one side so it wouldn't tip over.

"You could've just asked when you called."

"It's not that sort of question, Willie."

"Then maybe it's not the sort of question I want to get mixed up with."

"Saben's a spy," Soldier said, and there, it was out, a big enough bomb to shut Odd Willie up for a second or two. "She was screw-ing Sheldon. The two of them were working for these pricks out in Woonsocket, and they set me up."

"Fuck," Odd Willie Lothrop muttered and ran his fingers through his oily black hair. "Fuck all. Frankly, I never would've thought the cunt had it in her. And, hey, I was asking around about Woonsocket and—"

"The Bailiff said she's been in with that crowd for a long time, almost since the first night the hounds put her on the street," Soldier said and glanced up at the ceiling. In places, the plaster had fallen away, exposing the decaying lath beneath. "There's a kid. Saben got herself knocked up about nine years back. The daddy's part hound, and—get this—he's one of the Woonsocket mongrels."

"Oh, *man,*" Odd Willie groaned and shook his head. "I really don't think I want to hear any more of this shit." He reached for the tequila, which was sitting on the floor near the mattress, cracked the seal and opened the bottle. He tilted it towards Soldier, but she swallowed and shook her head.

"Fuck me," he said again and took a long pull off the pint bottle.

"There's more," Soldier said.

"There always is," Odd Willie told her and wiped his mouth, then screwed the cap back on the bottle of Pepe Lopez and set it down on the floor. "What I want to know is why the hell they didn't keep her out of Woonsocket after that?"

"The Bailiff claims he didn't know."

"And you believe him?"

"I suppose it's possible," Soldier replied.

"Yeah. Right. That bastard knows every time we take a dump, and he didn't know Saben was still getting her kicks in Woonsocket? Did they kill the little squealer?"

"No. They didn't. They gave it to the Cuckoo. That was part of Saben's punishment, and that's where the dead priest comes in. He was a mule."

"Yeah, well, at least I knew that much," Odd Willie said and rubbed at the stubble on his cheeks. "I saw the tattoos before I torched him. He had the wings and the eye, right here," and Odd Willie tapped his chest just below his sternum. "The wings and the eye, all in red."

"Red," Soldier said, wanting to get up and walk out, much too much said already, and she'd hardly even gotten started. She wanted to go back downstairs and maybe have some fun with crazy old Betty the junky, maybe show her a thing or two or three about devils and angels and keeping her goddamn mouth shut. She wanted to be home, or down in the tunnels below Benefit Street. She wanted to be driving, maybe down to Scarborough Beach or Napatree Point, maybe all the way the hell to Stonington. She could sit on the rocks, listen to the surf and watch the cold sunrise. She wanted to be any-where but Odd Willie's filthy little apartment.

"Yeah," she said, "I guess he would have been red, wouldn't he? The Bailiff said the old bastard had been whoring for the Cuckoo for almost fifty years. That would make him red."

"This is so many flavors of fucked-up," Odd Willie said, and this time when he giggled it made Soldier want to slap him. "So, when'd she start banging Sheldon?"

"Your guess is as good as mine."

There was an alarm clock on the floor, not far from the tequila bottle, and Soldier saw that it was almost four. "You want to get some breakfast?" she asked Odd Willie. "Maybe get some fucking pancakes?"

"Pancakes?" Odd Willie said, like he wasn't so sure what the word meant.

"Never mind," Soldier said.

"So why the hell did she kill the son of a bitch?"

"That was her paycheck for throwing in with Bittern."

"I thought you said she was spying for Woonsocket?"

"It's fucking complicated, Willie," Soldier sighed, and then she rubbed at her eyes, remembering the dream of the yellow house and the clock and Sheldon, wishing she could have gotten more sleep. "But in return for watching Bittern's back, for keeping him posted, she got information. She was trying to find the kid. I'm not sure the Bailiff *knows* why the hell the priest ended up dead. But if I had to guess, I'd say he's the one who muled out Saben's kid, and she just wanted revenge. Maybe he wouldn't tell her what she wanted to know."

"Okay. So, what's the Bailiff doing about all this?"

"We're going to Woonsocket tomorrow afternoon," Soldier said, and Odd Willie grimaced and then stared at the floor between his bare feet. "When we're done with business, when everything's squared away, then we take care of Saben White."

"Oh, Jesus," he said. "Jesus H. fucking Christ."

"You got a problem with that?" Soldier asked, but Odd Willie just shrugged and laughed again.

"Hey, man, I just do whatever the hell they tell me. They say, 'Yo, Odd Willie! Go fuck yourself,' I start studying up on contortionism. They tell me to blow my own goddamn brains out, and you're gonna find me sucking on the barrel of a gun."

"I'll do her, Willie. I'll pull the trigger. I just want you to know what's going down."

"That's awfully fucking thoughtful of you," he snorted and glanced up at Soldier. "But you *said* you were here because you wanted to ask me a question, and so far all you've done is delight and beguile me with all this goddamn good news. And, by the by, you do know it's supposed to fucking snow tomorrow, right?"

Soldier leaned forward on the three-legged chair, and the wood creaked and popped. Beneath the unsteady fluorescent lights, Odd Willie's skin made her think of some pallid, waxy cheese. She opened her mouth to ask him for the tequila, all the words she needed lying like ashes on her tongue, her right hand extended, but the Bailiff was there to stop her. The Bailiff standing at the foot of her bed, the Bailiff and his braided beard, and *there's* a fat, grinning devil that she'd like to introduce to Crazy Betty downstairs, something bad enough to make even the most demented, Jesus-loving crack whores sit up and take notice. Bad enough to keep Soldier's hands off the bottle, the bottle from her lips.

Maybe it's time you start asking a few of those questions, the dream Sheldon had told her, Sheldon Vale with two bullet holes in his head and a single tarot card on Miss Josephine's big table. *Maybe it's time for you to try and remember.*

"When's the first time you ever saw me, Odd Willie?"

And Willie Lothrop just stared back at her for a moment, and she could tell from the apprehensive shimmer in his eyes and the furrows in his forehead, from the way the corners of his mouth twitched slightly, that he wasn't sure what she was asking him.

"What do you mean?"

"I mean," Soldier said, measuring out her words like some powder or elixir that might heal or might poison, depending on the dose, "when's the very first time that you *clearly* remember seeing me in the warrens?"

"Fuck all if I know," Willie grunted. "What the hell kind of silly question is that?"

"How old do you think I am?" she asked him.

"None of us knows how old we are," he replied, looking even more confused, and he reached for the tequila again. "Not exactly. None of us knows that, Soldier. The Cuckoo—"

"Willie, I'm asking how old you *think* I am. Just fucking guess. We were warren mates, weren't we?"

"Sure," Willie replied, replying too quickly as he twisted the plastic cap off the pint of Pepe Lopez. "I mean, yeah, so we must be just about the same age, whatever the—"

"So, what's your earliest memory of me?" she asked again, her mouth as dry as all the deserts that have ever baked beneath the sun. Odd Willie took a drink of the tequila, and she watched his Adam's apple bobbing up and down as he swallowed. "It's a simple fucking question," she said.

Willie burped and set the bottle down without screwing the cap back on. "I don't know," he said. "Hell, Soldier. I'm tired, and I'm drunk, and I don't know what the fuck you're even getting at. We were kids. We fucking grew up together. How am I supposed to remember the first time I *saw* you?"

"So you remember me as a child?" she asked him, getting in one last question before she lost her nerve.

"To tell you the motherfucking truth," Odd Willie muttered and tapped once at the skin between his shaved eyebrows, "I'm starting to think maybe you exchanged a little more than just pleasant conversation with the freaks downstairs. Maybe Betty gave you a turn at her pipe."

Soldier nodded, then let the chair rock back on all three of its legs, and she took a deep breath and let it out again. She imagined that the last of her resolve went with it, out her nostrils and between her teeth, bleeding away into the ugly too-white light, the last bit of courage she could spare for the night, the night that was almost morning, and she had to hold something back for Woonsocket and George Ballou and Saben White.

"Forget it," she said. "This shit with Saben's got my head all over the place. Do me a favor and forget the whole damn thing, all right?" and Odd Willie shrugged and looked at his dirty feet again.

"Do you pray?" Odd Willie asked.

"You mean Mother Hydra and all that shit?"

"Yeah," Odd Willie said. "That's what I mean."

"No," Soldier told him, because she figured she owed him at least one honest answer. "I don't. What about you, Odd Willie? Are you a true believer? Do you await the cold fucking embrace of the vasty abyss?" and she smiled.

"Don't you fucking laugh at me," he said, almost whispering. He picked up the tequila bottle for the fourth time and began to peel the foil label off the glass.

"I'm not laughing at you. I'm just a faithless old cunt, that's all."

"What the hounds taught us, it makes about as much sense to me as anything else I've heard. And I need something, sometimes. Sometimes I need to at least pretend there's something more."

"Yeah," Soldier said, standing up, watching him peel the bottle and wondering if Odd Willie would still be drunk when they headed for Woonsocket, wondering if it mattered.

"Soldier, I just don't know what the fuck you were asking me," he said and flicked a shred of tequila label at the wall. "I mean, I've known you all my goddamn life."

"I said to forget about it," and he nodded, but she could tell from his expression that the very last thing Odd Willie was going to do was forget about it. "You better get some sleep. It's going to be a long day."

Odd Willie glanced up at her, rubbed his cheeks and smiled one of his crooked, sour smiles. "No shit. Hey, listen. You tell that whore downstairs, you tell her I said she better leave my guests the fuck alone, or she's gonna be looking for another building to occupy. Or worse. You tell her I said that," and Soldier said that she would, and then she showed herself out while Willie sat on the mattress, shaking his head and picking at the shiny label on the half-empty bottle of Pepe Lopez.

The entrance to the cemetery is a narrow paved road flanked on either side by run-down saltbox houses, one of them painted a drab peach and the other the color of a pigeon's egg, and Soldier thinks most people would probably mistake it for a private driveway. Probably no one in Woonsocket, of course, but the people who are only passing through, the outsiders, people who have no business poking about in cemeteries where no one's buried whom they've ever loved or known or to whom they are not even distantly related. There's a sturdy concrete pillar planted on each side of the road, just past the junk-strewn backyards of the houses, and a PRIVATE PROPERTY—NO TRESPASSING sign is hanging from one of them on a loop of wire. It looks to Soldier like someone has been taking shots at the sign with an air rifle, and the metal is crumpled at one corner and streaked with rust. There's no gate, no padlock, just the rusty sign; the warning would either be enough or it wouldn't, but she has a feeling that most people in Woonsocket don't need a warning to steer clear of the place. They'd know better. You could see it in the cast of the sky above the hill, in the way the trees grow a little too wild and a little too close together, and in the way that the patch of land beyond those two pillars seems always shaded by clouds that are nowhere to be found if you actually start looking for them.

"I want to go home," Odd Willie says and lights a cigarette.

"You think that sign's meant for us?" Saben asks. "Maybe we should stop and ask fucking permission." But no one answers her. Soldier cuts the wheel right, turning off George Street onto the road leading into Oak Hill Cemetery, and the Dodge's engine makes a sudden rattling noise deep in its guts.

"Oh, don't you fucking *dare*," Soldier growls at the car as they pass between the two houses. There's an old yellow sailboat parked behind one of them, behind the pigeon's-egg house, its mast broken and leaning to one side, and its name, the *Fly-Away Horse,* is painted along the prow in ornate crimson letters that have begun to crack and flake away.

"Patience Bacon said . . ." Odd Willie begins, but then they're through the pillars, past the pockmarked NO TRESPASSING sign, and his voice trails off as the bare winter limbs flicker like a few tattered frames from an old movie and are replaced by all the lush greens of midsummer. The pale, ice-thin light of the fading day has changed, too, has become the brilliant shafts and bright pools of a June or July afternoon, sunlight spilling through the rustling leaves and falling on the weeds growing along the sides of the road in warm shades of amber and honey. The engine sputters again and dies.

"What the *fuck*," Odd Willie says, reaching for the Bren Ten 10mm in his shoulder holster.

Soldier curses the Dodge and slaps the steering wheel, turns the key in the ignition switch, but the car doesn't make a sound. The Bailiff promised her that he'd told her everything she needed to know, everything to expect from Ballou and the cemetery, but he hadn't said anything at all about this. She turns the key again, pressing the gas pedal flat against the floor, and again the car remains silent and still.

"Stop freaking out, both of you. It's nothing," Saben says. "It's just a glamour, that's all."

"You can fuck that shit," Odd Willie laughs around the filter of his cigarette, flipping off the safety and cocking the pistol. "Talk to me, Soldier. Tell me what the hell's going on out there. Why didn't you let me in on this?"

"Because I didn't fucking *know*," Soldier spits back at him. She gives up on the car and turns her head, looking past Saben White to the place where the concrete columns and the rusty sign and the *Fly-Away Horse* had been a moment or two before. Now there's only the narrow road and the tall green trees bending low over it, and the road seems to go on forever. "Somehow, the Bailiff neglected to mention this part."

"Fuck," Odd Willie says. "Fuck, fuck, fuck."

"It's just a glamour," Saben says again. "We tripped it when we came in, that's all. It can't hurt us."

Odd Willie reaches for his door handle, then pulls his hand back. "Saben, if you don't shut the fuck up—"

"She's right," Soldier says, turning back to the windshield, and she closes her eyes and listens to her heartbeat—too *hard*, much too *fast*. She takes a deep breath and tries to remember everything the *ghul* have ever taught her about glamours and misdirection. But she never cared much for magick and was always a mediocre student, at best. The rituals and incantations too tedious and tricky, success or failure hinging on the most minute turn of a wrist or the slightest inflection. Better to settle things with her fists or a gun or a fucking sharp stick, she told the Bailiff once a long time ago. He frowned and muttered something about never realizing her full potential. Soldier exhales and takes another breath.

"We probably can't dispel this," Saben says, exasperated and impatient. "It's too big. There's too much of it. We shouldn't waste our energy trying."

"A bloody shame to see you squander yourself on account of laziness," the Bailiff said. "Stay ignorant, and someone will almost always benefit from your ignorance."

"You filthy old prick," Soldier whispers, casting the words like a net, her thoughts like impalpable graffiti, so that the Bailiff will have to stumble over them sooner or later. She opens her eyes to see that nothing's changed, nothing at all, the truth of things still hidden somewhere behind the glittering mask that Ballou has fashioned for this hill. But at least her heart's not beating quite so fast, and she's beginning to feel more annoyed than afraid. "Saben, don't you have some grounding with shit like this?" she asks without turning her head or glancing in the rearview mirror.

"No," Saben replies. "I don't handle glamours. I'm fine with *simple* photomancy, but this is something else. This is something much—"

"I didn't ask you for a lecture."

"He's *strong*, Soldier," Saben continues, and Odd Willie giggles. "You need to understand that; *both* of you need to understand that. Don't walk into this thing thinking Ballou's weak just because he's a half-breed."

"Is that your conscience talking?" Soldier asks her. It's getting hot inside the car, summer hot, and Soldier wipes sweat from her forehead and upper lip. Saben doesn't reply, and Soldier leans forward, resting her head against the steering wheel. She's tired of the masquerade, tired of pretending that she doesn't know what Saben's done, sick of waiting for her to die, and Soldier wonders if it would all really turn out that much differently if she just killed Saben right now.

"What next?" Odd Willie asks, and ash from the tip of his cigarette falls into his lap and he brushes it away. "What the fuck do we do now?"

"We get out of the car," Soldier says, because that *might* be the right answer; it's certainly the only answer she has for Odd Willie or for herself. "We do what we came to do and hope there are no more surprises. We get the bag out of the trunk, and we walk in."

"How about we walk the fuck *out*?" Odd Willie suggests.

"That might be difficult," Saben says.

"Soldier, will you please tell her to shut up before I shoot her? I'm totally fucking serious."

"We're going to get out of the car," Soldier tells him, and when she checks the rearview mirror again, she sees that Saben's drawn her own gun. "We're going to get out of the car now."

"Fine. Come on, girls," Willie says. "Let's all play follow the fucking leader," and he opens his door and climbs out into the shimmering day. Soldier does the same, and then she tosses Willie the keys across the roof of the car. He misses the catch, drops his cigarette and almost drops the Bren Ten, and has to search about on the ground for a moment to find them again.

"One minute," she says to Odd Willie. "That's all you've got, so stop screwing around," but he tells her to go fuck herself. Soldier takes another deep breath, filling her nostrils with all the scents and tastes of George Ballou's illusion. The summer air smells like dandelions and wild strawberries and is alive with the thrum of cicadas. Soldier looks towards the cemetery proper; the road curves sharply to the right before finishing the short climb to the top of the hill, and there's a low mausoleum not far from the car. Its granite roof is cracked, and the steel door is rusted the color of dried blood.

"Saben, you're going first," Soldier says, and Saben doesn't argue, so maybe she's figured out she's living on borrowed time. "I want you at least ten feet ahead of me and Willie."

"This is fucking insane," Willie grumbles as he tries to open the trunk and drops the keys again. "I'm telling you, Soldier. This is pay-back for Rocky Point yesterday. And hell, he probably heard about the shit at that Dunkin' Donuts, too. This mess is the Bailiff's way of showing us how fucking pissed—"

"Shut up and open the trunk," Soldier says, watching Saben. "I want the shotguns while you're in there."

"You really think that's such a good idea?" Saben asks. "Ballou might get the wrong impression, you come waltzing into the drop with a couple of scatterguns."

"I don't remember asking you, one way or the other."

Off towards the river, Soldier can hear the hoarse croak of a duck or some other waterbird, and the trees around them are filled with the raucous calls of catbirds and jays.

"You might want to hurry that shit up back there," she tells Odd Willie.

The trunk pops open, and Willie takes out a small black leather valise and drops it on the ground. Then he digs about for a moment, drops a lug wrench next to the valise, and starts cursing.

"What?" Soldier asks.

"There's only one fucking shotgun back here," he replies, even though she knows damn well there were two when they left Providence, the Mossberg twelve-gauge and her Ithaca Mag-10, the Road-blocker she had that night out at Quaker Jameson's.

"That's impossible," she shouts at Odd Willie. "Keep looking."

"I'm telling you, Soldier, it's *not* fucking back here, and I can keep looking from now till fucking doomsday, and it still won't be back here, so I still won't find it."

"They're watching us," Saben says, glancing up at the limbs of an elm. "They're listening."

"Don't you fucking move, not an inch," Soldier tells her, then walks quickly back to where Odd Willie's standing at the open trunk. In the trees, the birds are getting louder. And it only takes her a couple of seconds to see that he's telling the truth. He's holding the twelve-gauge cradled in the crook of his left arm, and there's nothing else in the trunk but the spare, a box of shells, a roll of duct tape, and the tire jack that goes with the lug wrench.

"It's a fucking setup," Odd Willie says. "Someone fucking set us up, Soldier."

"Don't start that," Soldier tells him, but it's nothing she hasn't already thought of herself. The Bailiff sending her off to Woonsocket with just Odd Willie Lothrop and Saben, not telling her about the glamour. And Saben still so cocky and self-confident when she ought to be broken, Saben smirking half the day like a fucking cat with blood and feathers on its paws. "It doesn't make sense," Soldier says. "It just doesn't make sense."

"Sure it does," Willie says, and then he points the 10mm at Saben. "She's in with Ballou, and she fucking double-crossed us. It all makes perfect sense to me."

"Tell him not to point that gun at me," Saben says, and she's calm, so calm it makes the hairs on the back of Soldier's neck twitch and stand on end.

"Saben, we fucking *know*," Odd Willie snarls. "The Bailiff told Soldier everything."

"Willie, don't do it," Soldier says, trying hard to think clearly through the shrill scream of the blue jays and catbirds overhead. There are words hidden in there, she thinks, important, powerful words disguised as squawking birds, if she could only tease the lie apart from the truth of things. "It's not that simple. It's just a trick, like the glamour, something else to distract us from what's really going on here."

"Soldier, you *told* me what she did," Willie says, not lowering his pistol. "You told me—"

"I *told* you to stop pointing that goddamn gun at Saben."

"You know I'm right. You know she did it."

"At the moment, Willie, I don't know my ass from a goddamn hole in the ground, and I'm not going to tell you again to stop pointing your gun—"

"Then it was the Bailiff," Odd Willie says, and Soldier can see the way his finger's begun to tremble against the trigger. "If it wasn't her, it was the fucking Bailiff did it, because *someone* fucking set us up."

"Soldier," Saben says, her voice still smooth as ice and milk, and Soldier realizes that the light around her has begun to bend and glimmer. "If he doesn't stop, I'm going to have to *make* him stop."

"We know about the kid," Odd Willie says, grinning the way he does when he's setting a fire or telling a joke he thinks is funny. "We know about you and Sheldon Vale. We know about the deal you made with these beaver-beater cocksuckers."

Saben's eyelids flutter, and her gun slips from her hand to the ground. "You know what the hounds *want* you to know," she says. "No more, and no fucking less."

"Did they tell you that you'd get the kid back?" Soldier asks her, trying not to sound scared, and she thinks they might have had a chance, if Willie had left the shotgun lying where she could reach it. If she had the shotgun in her hands right that second, and it was loaded, and there was already a round in the chamber, *all* that and a lucky shot and they *might* have a chance of making it back to the entrance of the cemetery. "Is that what they promised you? That you and Sheldon could hide up here in the boonies with your mongrel?"

"Put down the gun, Odd Willie," Saben says, and her eyes roll back to show the whites. "You don't have to die here today." An orb of blue flame has begun to writhe about her left hand, leaking from the Seal of Solomon, licking harmlessly at her skin.

"Fuck you," Odd Willie snarls and pulls the trigger.

The bullet explodes above the Dodge, spraying shrapnel and molten blue droplets. There are specks of blood on Odd Willie's face, and Saben White's wrapped in a writhing sapphire cowl of fire.

All lost, the birds scream from the trees. *Poor little soldier girl, all lost now,* and she can feel the tiny piece of steel embedded in her throat, a bit of Odd Willie's bullet, can feel the blood pumping from her body and spattering the grass at her feet. *All lost, lost, lost now, poor little Soldier girl. Should have stayed where you belonged . . .*

Her knees feel weak, and she reaches for her gun, blinking and squinting because the daylight and the fire from Saben's tattoo are blazing. Her hand closes around the butt of her pistol, but now Saben has turned towards her, and Odd Willie has slumped over dead into the open trunk. The light is blinding her.

Lost, lost, all lost, little girl.

"Let go," Saben says, and the blue flame coils and uncoils like snakes, weaving and unweaving, and . . .

. . . *All lost, lost, lost now,* George Ballou's fairie birds sing, their machete voices carving great slashes in the world. *All lost* . . .

. . . and she sets the glass of Wild Turkey down on the wide mahogany dining table, and looks up at the tall clock on the mantel,
the skin of a dead girl's face flayed and tanned and stretched taut,
and the fish-spine hands of the clock stop, and then begin to move
backwards. She reaches for the whiskey bottle . . .

. . . and Soldier opens her eyes, her forehead still leaning on the steering wheel.

"What next?" Odd Willie asks, and ash from the tip of his cigarette falls into his lap, and he brushes it away. "What the fuck do we do now?"

Soldier raises her head, an oily smear of sweat left behind on the steering wheel, and her right hand goes to the spot where the shard of the ruined bullet from Odd Willie's 10mm hasn't yet punched a hole in her jugular. She looks out the windshield, across the hood, and sees the black thing squatting in the road in front of the car, the thing that isn't a man and isn't a hound, either. It grins at her.

"No," Saben White says. "That's an awfully neat trick, Soldier, but it's not gonna save you this time," and the black thing stands up. Odd Willie screams and his gun goes off, blowing out the windshield and deafening Soldier in the instant before the butt of Saben's pistol connects with the base of her skull, and then there's only silence and winter cold and a bottomless, merciful oblivion.

FIVE

Angell Street

Emmie is sitting on the floor in her bedroom, her bedroom in Providence, home again after the three-hour train ride from Manhattan. They took the Acela Express, because it was so much faster, but the trip still seemed to take at least twice as long as usual. Sadie hardly spoke the whole way, and Emmie stared out the window at the countryside and the towns and the train stations rushing past. Somewhere in Connecticut, the sky turned stormy and dark; the clouds were like mountains piling up to crush the world. When they finally reached the Providence station, Deacon was there waiting for them. He looked worried and annoyed, but he hugged her tight, kissed her cheek and told her he'd missed her and was glad she was back so soon.

Home again, home again, jiggety-jog.

On Emmie's CD player, Doris Day is singing "Secret Love," and the volume's turned up loud, but she can still hear Sadie and Deacon arguing. They're downstairs in the kitchen, but their voices rise like warm air and get trapped in the heating ducts and travel all the way up to Emmie's room. She's shut the vent in the floor, but the voices are getting in anyway. She's sitting near the window, between her bed and the window, with her back against the wall. *I wish they'd stop,* she thinks. *I wish they'd just shut up and stop and Sadie would go back home, because that's what she's going to do, no matter how much they fight.* And then she wishes she were in school, that it wasn't a Sunday afternoon and it wasn't winter break. Then they could fight all they wanted, and she wouldn't have to sit here and listen to it.

"It wouldn't fucking kill you," Deacon says, and then dishes clatter in the sink. "You already have the week off. You could spend it here."

"No," Sadie tells him, the stubborn, angry tone she gets whenever Deacon suggests that she spend a night in the house with them. "You know I won't do that. It's not fair to ask me."

Emmie shuts her eyes and bites at her lower lip. *They could fight outside,* she thinks. *They could walk down the street and fight all day long.*

"It's fucking fair when you've already promised to take care of her this week."

"You know I won't stay here. There's no point talking about it, because you know I won't."

Emmie's already done the things she usually does whenever Sadie and Deacon are fighting. She's straightened her room, putting everything in its place because it always seems that creating order ought to help, even though it never has yet. She made sure all her toys and games and clothes were exactly where they should be. She checked to see that all her books were in alphabetical order, and all her CDs, too. She pulled the covers off the bed and then remade it.

"Hell, Deacon, I'll pay for you to hire a sitter."

"I don't want a sitter. You know I don't want strangers in the house. You know how I feel about that."

Emmie opens her eyes again and stares across her room at the closed door to the upstairs hall. If it were a door to somewhere *else,* anywhere else, she'd open it and step across the threshold and shut it behind her, and then run far enough away that she couldn't possibly hear Sadie and Deacon arguing. Emmie pulls a pillow off the bed—it doesn't matter that it messes up the blankets and sheets, because all the order she made isn't helping—and lays it over the heating vent. But she can still hear them.

"You know how rough things have been at the shop," Deacon says. "And you know damn well I've been counting on having this week to get caught up."

"She wanted to come home. What was I supposed to do? Tell her no?"

"I know it's news to you, but that *is* a fucking option," Deacon says.

On Emmie's CD player, Doris Day finishes singing "Secret Love" and "Teacher's Pet" begins. Emmie doesn't like that song, and she thinks about getting up and skipping ahead to the next track. She also thinks about making the bed again, just in case, but she stays where she is, listening even though she doesn't want to hear. Her stomach's beginning to hurt, and she has to pee, but their voices would only be louder out in the hall, louder in the bathroom because it's directly above the kitchen.

"It was horrible," Sadie says, bringing up the dead horse again, and Emmie chews her lip a little harder, chewing until she tastes a drop of blood. "That poor horse. Jesus, Deacon, I couldn't make her stay in New York after that. I just couldn't."

"That poor horse," Emmie says, and now she's thinking about the argument that morning between Hunter and Sadie. *It was a fucking coincidence,* Sadie said, and then there'd been the strange girl who wanted her to draw a bridge. It was getting hard to remember exactly what happened, and Emmie thinks she must have dozed off, listening to Hunter and Sadie, that she was tired and must have fallen asleep. She wishes she could fall asleep now.

"The two of you could rent a car and drive up to Boston or something," Deacon says. "You could spend the week in Boston."

"I can't fucking afford a week in Boston or anywhere else, Deacon, and neither can you. And Emmie doesn't *want* to be in Boston; she wants to be in her own home where she feels safe. It just about scared the hell out of her. Hunter said—"

"Don't fucking start with fucking Hunter Fontana," Deacon says, and then it sounds like he drops a skillet or a pot or something. "Right now, the last thing I want to have to hear is how that goddamn dyke thinks I should be raising Emmie. And how is it you could afford to pay for a sitter, but not a week in Boston?"

"Jesus, Deacon."

"You know, I've got enough to think about without the sage fucking advice of Hunter Fontana."

"It was a coincidence," Emmie says to no one and shuts her eyes again. "Co-in-ci-dence," she says, taking care to divide and separate each syllable from the other. "It was a coincidence." And even over the noise of her father and stepmother arguing, even over Doris Day, Emmie can hear the terrible, dull shattering sound of the taxi hitting the mare. She *remembers* the sound perfectly, and she doesn't think there's much difference between hearing it and remembering it. *I'm never going to forget that,* she thinks. *Not ever.* She opens her eyes and goes back to staring at the closed bedroom door. The girl from the attic, the brown-skinned girl, is standing near the foot of her bed, but Emmie tries not to notice her. Maybe if she doesn't say anything to the girl, she'll go away.

"That's an awful racket," the girl says. "Do they know you can hear them?"

"I'm not talking to you," Emmie tells her. "You're not real, and I'm not talking to you."

"I like this music," the brown girl says. "I've never heard such music. My father used to bring me music and play it on his Victrola. I liked 'April in Paris,' and 'Mood Indigo,' and—"

"I'm *not* talking to you," Emmie says again. *"Go away."*

"—'When the Moon Comes over the Mountain.' I like that one, too, but not as much as I like 'Mood Indigo.' "

Downstairs, Deacon curses and a glass breaks, and Sadie tells him to calm down and stop acting like a damned jackass.

"I could sing it for you," the brown girl offers, "if you'd like me to. I remember all the words."

"I know the words," Emmie says, which is true because she has a CD with Billie Holiday singing "Mood Indigo," one of the few CDs of hers that Deacon likes. "You don't have to sing it to me, because I know it already."

"Besides, it would be very hard to hear me over this awful racket," the girl says and frowns. "Do they know that you can hear them?"

"I don't know," Emmie replies, though she suspects Deacon and Sadie know perfectly well how sound carries in the old house, and they just don't care. "Maybe you should go downstairs and ask them."

"I would," the brown girl says. "But they probably wouldn't be able to see me or hear me. Your father might—"

"I wish you'd shut up and leave me alone."

"—he could do that, a long time ago, hear and see things no one else could see or hear. But he made it all stop. I guess he'd finally seen and heard enough."

Emmie stares at the girl. She seems solid, solid as anything else in the bedroom. She smiles at Emmie and sits down on the bed. The girl's wearing the same black dress with the same stiff white collar that she was wearing the first time Emmie dreamed about her. Maybe that's the only dress she owns, Emmie thinks and then silently scolds herself for thinking of the girl as if she were someone real.

"I didn't say you could do that," Emmie says.

"I was tired of standing," the girl replies. "And it was impolite of you not to offer me a seat."

"Stop it!" Sadie yells at Deacon, and Emmie flinches.

"Does he ever hit her?" the girl with brown skin asks.

Emmie shakes her head, getting angry, and she tries to stop imagining this, wishing now that she could just go back to having to hear the argument downstairs. "No," she says. "Deacon doesn't hit us. He's never hit either one of us. He doesn't do that sort of thing, not even when he's drunk."

"He's drunk a *lot*," the girl says.

"Yeah, he's drunk a *lot*. He's an alcoholic, but he doesn't hit us."

"The yelling's just as bad, sometimes," the brown girl says and stares past Emmie at the bedroom window. "You have a very fine house, Miss Emma Jean Silvey. I've never been inside this house before. My father once knew a man who lived across the street from here, a writer—"

"Don't you ever shut up?"

"I spend a lot of time alone," the brown girl says, still staring out the window at the house next door. "Well, that's not precisely true, because mostly it's not precisely time I spend alone. There's only time whenever someone visits me."

"I know about being crazy," Emmie says and glances past the girl at the closed bedroom door. If Sadie opened it, would she see the brown girl in her black dress, or would she see only Emmie sitting on the floor, talking to herself? "I've read books. You're a hallucination. It's probably because of stress, or maybe I have a brain tumor."

"You don't look sick," the girl says. "And I know that you aren't insane."

"How could you possibly know that? You're not even a real person."

Downstairs, the arguing has stopped. Someone slams a door, the front door, and Emmie figures that it's probably Deacon going out for a walk, going out to cool off and maybe have a drink. He'll probably walk for an hour or two, maybe follow Angell west to Hope Street, then turn north and walk all the way up to the Ladd Observatory, because he likes the benches there and being at the top of that hill. He'll stay away from Thayer, because it'll make him think of the shop, and she knows that's one of the things he'll be trying to forget. She's sorry that she couldn't have gone with him, not wanting to be in the old house right now, even with her hallucination for company and Sadie still right downstairs. But it's a relief that they've stopped fighting, relief like the battered silence after a bad storm late at night, and she feels herself start to relax a little.

"Something's coming, Emma Jean," the brown girl says. "Something terrible's coming."

"What are you on about now?"

The girl sighs and looks away from the window, looking down at Emmie. "I don't know *everything,* and I can't tell you everything that I know."

"Then what good are you?" Emmie asks her and goes back to watching the bedroom door.

"I've found a few flaws, cracks that I think perhaps my father intentionally left for me to find, cracks that the ghouls don't know anything about. I've come here to forewarn you, before it's too late for augury to be any good to you . . . or to me."

Now Doris Day is singing *"Qué Será, Será,"* and the brown girl looks over her shoulder towards the stereo.

"I read you somewhere," Emmie says. "I made you from different characters in different books, from people in different movies. There's no point trying to convince me otherwise. I'm not a moron, even if I'm going crazy."

"You're not insane," the girl says again. "And you have to trust yourself, because there's going to come a time, very soon, when you can't trust anyone else."

"My father can't afford a shrink," Emmie tells her and kicks at the side of the bed with her sock feet until the girl turns back around again.

"I like that song," the girl says.

"It's an old song. Haven't you ever heard it before?"

"I like it. It's very pretty, but it's not really the truth." And then the brown girl sings along with Doris Day for a couple of lines— *Whatever will be, will be. The future's not ours to see*—and her voice is high and sweet and reminds Emmie somehow of melting ice.

"What's not true about it?" Emmie asks her, wondering if Sadie will come upstairs, wondering if she'll apologize for the argument and try to explain, hoping that she doesn't.

"I mean that there are some people, and some other things that aren't people, who *can* see what will be, except there's not only one thing that will be; there's an infinity of things that *might* be. That's what I mean."

"No one can see the future," Emmie says, finally standing up, and she turns her back on the brown girl, who isn't really there anyway, and stares down at the driveway and the evergreen shrubs and the wooden slat fence dividing their yard from the house next door, the house painted an ugly color like blue Play-Doh. There's a robin down there, though it's too early in the year for robins in Providence, and it hops about a bit before stopping and gazing up at her.

"There's so much that you don't know, Emma Jean Silvey," the brown girl says. "There's so much you're going to have to learn, and you'll have to learn it quickly."

"I know too much already," Emmie says. "I'm just a kid, and I know too much already."

"What's coming, it doesn't care how old you are."

"Nothing's *coming,* and you're not *real.* I don't believe in ghosts."

"I'm not a ghost," the brown girl says. "I never claimed that I was a ghost."

"I still don't believe in you," and then the robin flies away, and Emmie looks up at the sky. There are clouds, the sort of clouds that usually mean snow, and she leans forward, flattening her face against the cold glass.

"Later on you'll believe," the girl says, and Emmie sighs because this is getting tiresome. She wonders whether or not she should tell Deacon or Sadie about the girl.

"My father's not a bad person," Emmie says, and her breath makes the window fog.

"No," the brown girl says. "No, he's not. He's only a man who's seen things men weren't meant to see. He's only very tired and very lonely and very worried about you, Emma Jean. He loves Sadie, but he misses his wife very much."

"Shut up," Emmie says, starting to cry even though she doesn't want to, because she knows it isn't going to make her feel any better about the poor dead horse or Sadie or Deacon or anything else. "You don't know about Deacon, and you shouldn't act like you do," she says, turning around to face the brown girl, but she's gone, and now there's no one sitting on the bed. There's a rumpled place in the blankets, a rumpled place where she imagined the brown girl sitting, but that might have happened when Emmie pulled the pillow off the bed.

"Go away," Emmie says, as if the girl were still there to hear her, as if she hadn't gone away already. "Go away, and never come back." And then Emmie lies down on the bed and cries until she finally falls asleep.

*   *   *

And in her dreams, Emmie feels herself rise slowly up from the bed, her soul grown suddenly lighter than air, and she drifts untethered and insubstantial, passing straight through the bedroom ceiling into the shadows of the dusty, disused attic, and then through the pitched roof of the house on Angell Street. She lingers there a moment, a few feet above the chimney, and the sky rushes by overhead like traffic, clouds filled with ice and snow and sudden patches of bright daylight. She isn't afraid of falling, because it's only a dream, though someone at school once told her that if you fall from a high place in a dream and hit bottom before you wake up, you'll die. When she asked Deacon about it, he said it wasn't true, that it was only a silly superstition, so she's not afraid. She looks down and sees that the brown girl is watching her, is standing in the middle of Angell Street gazing up at her.

I'm her balloon, Emmie thinks. *I'm her balloon on a string.* Though she can't see a string tied to her anywhere. *If she lets go, I'll float away forever and be lost.*

All lost, lost, lost now . . . And those were not her thoughts, so Emmie thinks they must be the thoughts of the brown girl, because in dreams she can sometimes hear other people's thoughts.

The girl waves at her, and then a gust of icy wind carries Emmie away, south and east and up and up, over rooftops and treetops. And in only a moment she's floated so high that she can see the Providence and Seekonk rivers going down to all the bays and islands and rocky coves before the ocean. And now she *is* getting scared, because this is much too high, even for a dream, and if she goes much farther, she might fall into the sea and drown, or end up floating away to some land so distant that she'll never be able to find her way home again. She starts to call out for Deacon, but knows he won't ever hear her, and the air's so cold her words would only freeze and fall to earth like hailstones.

The plink of words on sidewalks and lawns, a sentence heavy enough to shatter a windshield.

"Wake up now," she whispers, and Emmie's beginning to wonder if she'll float all the way out of the atmosphere and die in the near vacuum of space, looking down on the great blue ball of the world, when she realizes that she's standing on a sandy beach near the water, and the brown girl is standing a few feet farther out, the waves lapping about her ankles, soaking her black-and-white-striped stockings. And the air has grown very warm, and a brilliant white sun blazes overhead. It isn't winter here. *Maybe,* she thinks, *it's never been anything but summer here and never will be.*

"This is the place where Esmeribetheda saw the warriors in the sky," the brown girl says. "That's one of the parts of the story that the changelings are never taught. They're taught that she was hanged and burned alive because she betrayed the *ghul* to the *djinn,* but the ghouls know that's not the truth."

"Where am I?" Emmie asks. "What are you talking about?"

"You're only dreaming," the brown girl says and smiles and kicks at the salty, frothy water. "But you're in the wastes, near the battlegrounds. This place has other names, but I never learned them. Or I've forgotten them. Six of one, half dozen of the other. Either way, you're at the end of the wastes, the wastes at the very end of this world. At least you're not cold anymore."

"No, now I'm hot," Emmie says and sits down on the warm white sand. There's a conch shell nearby, half-buried, and she picks it up and runs her fingers carefully along the sharp spines spaced out along the conch's low spire.

"The Hindu people," the girl says, taking a step towards shore, "they believe that Vishnu, the god of preservation, has a conch shell named Panchajanya, and they believe that Panchajanya represents all the living things that have ever arisen from the life-giving waters of the seas."

"Are you from India?" Emmie asks. "Is that why your skin's so dark?"

The girl doesn't answer the question, but stares up at the cloudless blue-white sky instead. "There's something terrible coming," she says again.

"You told me that already."

"This is one of the places where it began, after the changeling child Esmeribetheda was murdered. After the ghouls fought a great war with the *djinn* and were driven out of the wastes forever. This is the place where the warriors *still* battle in the sky to keep balance against the destruction of all creation. This is where the sea meets the sand, where the two are always struggling to expand their earthly empires."

Emmie sets the conch shell back down. "There was a woman on a train," she says. "A woman with the Seal of Solomon tattooed on one of her hands."

The brown girl shakes her head and looks down at her wet feet. "We can't talk about her. Not just yet. Later. Soon."

"There's no point to this, is there? You should just let me wake up."

"I cannot stop you from waking, Emma Jean, but it's not pointless. There are things you need to see."

"Well, I don't need to see sand," Emmie tells her. "I've seen lots and lots of sand before."

"It's not the sand that's important," the brown girl says, and then Emmie's floating again, or maybe this time she's falling. There's no way to be sure exactly which, but now there's a lot more than sand. There are battles worse than anything she's ever imagined, men and horses and bristling hairy creatures that walk like men, blood and fire and the screams of the dying. Swords and spears, arrows and axes, and hungry crows and jackals waiting for their share. There are vast maelstroms in the sky, whirling clouds like hurricanes of flame, and monsters perched at the edges of the maelstroms, monsters tearing one another apart, and Emmie wants to shut her eyes, but it doesn't seem to make much difference. She is *seeing* these things, because the brown girl is *showing* them to her. The ruins of a city half-buried in the shifting dunes. The bed of a vanished lake, littered with the skeletons of water monsters. A girl tied to a tree and burned alive. The pages of a storybook, turned before Emmie's eyes, turned *behind* her eyes, and whenever it gets too scary, she reminds herself that it's only a dream, and she'll probably forget most of it when she wakes up.

"Open your eyes," the brown girl says, so Emmie does, and now she sees they're sitting on the roof of her house on Angell Street, sitting side by side, and there are fat, wet flakes of snow falling from the blue-gray sky.

"That was ridiculous," Emmie says and shivers. "None of that was real. You're not real, and none of those things were real, either."

"A long time ago," the brown girl says, as if Emmie hasn't said a word, "before you were born, Deacon Silvey was fighting a war, too. It wasn't that sort of war, but he was still a soldier, after a fashion, and he fought demons and worse things than demons."

"Bullshit," Emmie says, just like Deacon would say it, and scowls at the brown girl. "Deacon used to work in liquor stores and laundries, and now he owns a used bookstore on Thayer Street. He was never *in* the army or the navy or anything."

"That doesn't matter. He was still a soldier. He didn't want to be, but he was. He could see things, and so the policemen came to him, and he helped them catch murderers and rapists and thieves."

Emmie stares at the girl, at her dark hair now tangled by the wind and speckled with melting snowflakes. If any of that were true, Deacon would have told her. Deacon's told her lots of stories about before she was born, stories about when he lived in Atlanta and Birmingham, stories about her mother, whose name was Chance, and he's never said anything at all about helping the police.

"You're a liar," she says. "None of that's true."

"Once, he helped them find a woman named Mary English," the brown girl continues, undaunted, "a mule, a madwoman who worked for the Cuckoo, stealing babies to be hidden away in the dark places of the world and raised up by the ghouls. That day, he even saved a girl who should have become a changeling."

"You're full of it, and I'm cold, and I'm going to wake myself up now."

"There's not much time, and there are things you need to understand."

"I need to wake up," Emmie tells her and crosses her arms, trying to stay warm. "I'm gonna freeze to death up here."

The brown girl sticks out her tongue and catches a snowflake. She nods her head and points northeast, to the place where the clouds are coming from. "His daughter will come for you, Emma Jean. She may be dying, and she may not live, but if she does, she'll come for you, because you're a part in this. And there will be others, men who mean you harm, who will kill you if they can, and you have to be ready for them."

"Wake up," Emmie says. She's shut her eyes and is trying to think of nothing but her bed, her room, Doris Day on the CD player, the warmth inside the house. "Wake up, and forget all of this."

"You met your mother on a train," the girl says. "She gave the rest of her life to meet you just that one time. She gave her life to save you."

"Wake *up*," Emmie says, and she's started crying all over again. The tears are freezing on her cheeks, and they clatter down the steep sides of the roof and break on the driveway. "Wake up now. *Wake up now.*"

"There's a box," the brown girl says. "A cardboard box beneath his bed. When you see that I'm telling you the truth, Emma Jean, you'll know that you can't stay here in this house anymore. Something terrible is coming."

Emmie screams, opens her eyes and swings at the girl, both her hands clenched tightly into fists. The brown girl shrieks and breaks apart into a flock of robins and is swept away by the wind.

"Leave me alone!" Emmie screams after the fleeing birds.

All lost, lost, lost now . . .

"Just leave me *alone,*" she sobs, all the fight slipping quickly out of her, and the roof opens up like the maw of a hungry creature built of shingles and wood and nails, and it swallows her whole. She slides easily down its black gullet, and when Emmie remembers that the creature was only her house, she opens her eyes. And she's lying in her bed again, and Deacon's holding her. He smells like whiskey and cigarettes, and he's smiling.

"Hey, kiddo," he says. "You were having a bad dream. It's okay. You were just having a bad dream, that's all. How long have you been asleep up here? Do you know it's snowing?"

"Yes," she says, and Emmie starts to tell him about the brown girl and the endless desert beside the sea, the wars and flying high above the city, and then she remembers all the other things that the girl told her, all the crazy things she knows aren't true, but they're still too frightening to think about. Too scary ever to say out loud, and then she's crying again, crying awake and for real this time, and Deacon holds her and whispers soothing things until she stops.

By seven o'clock, there are two inches of snow blanketing Angell Street, and the house is quiet and still, the heavy, muffled silence it assumes whenever there's snow. Sadie's gone back to New York; she left while Emmie was asleep, and she told Deacon to tell Emmie that she was sorry she couldn't stick around and say good-bye, but she didn't want to miss her train. She promised to call later. And Deacon's gone to the shop, because Jack's sick or his car wouldn't start or something like that. Emmie told him it was okay, that she would be fine alone, and he said there was a frozen dinner, fried chicken with peas and apple cobbler, and that's what she should have for dinner. "You need something more than just a peanut-butter-and-jelly sandwich," he said, and she promised him she'd eat the frozen dinner, even though she hates fried chicken.

She's downstairs watching the snow fall through the tangerine light of the street lamps, watching as it hides the broad leaves of the rhododendrons growing beside the front porch. The leaves will freeze and begin to curl in on themselves by morning. It's hard to tell where the yard ends and the sidewalk begins, where the sidewalk ends and the road begins. She halfheartedly contemplates getting bundled up and going outside, even though it's after dark. Deacon didn't say that she couldn't, but, then again, she doesn't really feel like playing in the snow.

I could find the place where the sidewalk meets the grass, Emmie thinks. *I could find the place where the street begins.* And she considers carefully marking them off with sticks or rocks. But the snow would only bury her markers, because the Weather Channel says there'll be at least six more inches before morning. If the world out there is determined to erase all distinctions, she might as well let it. At least there are slushy, dark tire marks on the street, cars going one way or another; later, a truck will be along to salt the road. Emmie glances at the clock above the sofa. It's seven twenty-three, and Deacon won't be closing up the shop until nine, even though he was grumbling about how the snow would probably keep a lot of the customers away. She wanted to say, *You never have any customers, anyway,* but she didn't. Sometimes someone comes in and buys a book, but mostly people don't come in, and when they do, they usu-

ally walk about browsing and reading and leave without buying a
thing. "It's not a goddamn library," Deacon says sometimes. "I can't
pay the bills with their curiosity."

Emmie leans on the windowsill, resting her chin on her folded
hands, wiggling in the chair so the legs squeak against the dingy
hardwood floor. It seems pointless, but she wishes Deacon could have
stayed home, or that Sadie hadn't needed to rush back to Manhattan. The wind sweeps along Angell Street, making something like a
dust devil from the fresh snow; Emmie hears someone coming down
the stairs, and she turns to see who it is. But she already knows,
because that's what she's really been doing all evening, sitting here
waiting for the brown girl to come back.

"I never cared for the snow," the girl says. She's standing near the
bottom of the stairs, looking at the television as though she's never
seen one before. "It was snowing when my mother died."

"Your mother died, too?" Emmie asks, and of course the brown
girl's mother died, too. She had to have, because the brown girl is
only some part of Emmie that's decided it wants to be more than a
part, that it wants to be a whole person.

"My father tried to save her, but the doctors couldn't help, and
he couldn't help, either. It was the influenza, and she developed pneumonia. My mother was a powerful sorceress," the girl says proudly.

"Sure," Emmie says. "Every winter she rode about in the snow
offering children hot drinks and Turkish Delight, and that's how she
caught her death of cold."

"What's Turkish Delight?" the girl asks.

"Don't be stupid. If I know, then you know, too."

The brown girl stares at the television a moment more, then
glances back up the staircase. "You haven't found the box yet, have
you?" she asks.

"There isn't any box," Emmie tells her and turns back to the
window. "You made that up. I mean, I made that up."

The brown girl sighs and sits down on the stairs.

"I'm going to have to tell Deacon about you," Emmie says. "I'm going to have to tell him, and he's going to make me see a doctor or a psychiatrist or something."

"I wish you'd believe me," the girl says. "There's so little time left."

"I'm sorry that your mother died," Emmie replies, then watches a big yellow SUV moving slowly down Angell Street, its headlights shining through the falling snow.

"My father made a blood sacrifice to Father Kraken and Mother Hydra, and he used his strongest magick and some herbs that had come all the way from Persia and China, but nothing could save her."

"Who are Father Kraken and Mother Hydra supposed to be?" Emmie wonders aloud, trying to remember if she's ever read a book where she saw those names. For a long moment, the girl on the stairs is silent, and when she answers she sounds both amazed and like maybe she feels sorry for Emmie for being such an ignoramus.

"Of all the changelings," the girl says finally, "you may be the only one who would ever have cause to ask such a question. They are the Pillars of the Sea, Emma Jean, the Keepers of the Abyss, Mother and Father, destruction and conception and everything that lies anywhere in between. In the days of void and shadow, before the gods had grown weary of nothingness and pulled the land up from the sea—"

"I get the picture," Emmie says. "God didn't save your mother, but you still believe in him. It doesn't matter to me. I'm an atheist."

"An eight-year-old girl shouldn't be an atheist."

"Well, *this* one is," Emmie says and looks over her shoulder at the brown girl, who's staring at her between the banister rails. "Anyway, you could at least be consistent."

"What are you talking about?" the brown girl asks and scrunches up her face.

"I *mean, kraken* is a Norwegian word, which is sometimes used to refer to the giant squid, *Architeuthis,* or to mythical sea monsters in general. But the Hydra, on the other hand, is a nine-headed monster that Hercules had to kill. Killing the Hydra was the second of the twelve labors of Hercules. So, what I *mean* is that you're mixing Norse and Greek mythology, and that's inconsistent and stupid. Now, if you'd said Mother Hydra and Father Poseidon, well, that *might* be a little less silly."

The brown girl watches her for a moment, and Emmie can't read much of anything in her chocolate eyes, if she's insulted or angry or just confused. Then the brown girl shakes her head, the way one of Emmie's teachers might shake his or her head if a student is being particularly dense, and she stands up again.

"The Keepers have many names among the tribes of men," she says. "Names are only tools. Am I supposed to believe that you're a figment of my imagination, because Silvey is derived from a Spanish name, *Silva* or *Silvera,* but Emma comes from Old German and Jean is French? Or because Jean is a *man's* name—"

"That's not the same thing at all," Emmie says, her cheeks flushed, and she stands up so fast that she almost knocks the chair over. "You're not very smart if you don't see the difference."

"But a little while ago you said I *am* you," the brown girl reminds her, "so how can I be any less bright than you yourself?"

"Shut up," Emmie says, because it's a lot easier than trying to answer the girl's question. As a barb, she adds, "Deacon says that religion is a crutch."

"Why do you call him that?" the girl asks. "Why do you call him Deacon?"

"Because that's his name."

"Why don't you call him *Father* or *Daddy* or—"

"Why don't *you* mind your own business?" Emmie says, and the brown girl shrugs and stands up, straightening her stockings and black dress.

"Maybe it's because you know something, something you don't want to admit."

"That's a lie," Emmie tells her. "I call him Deacon because that's what he *wants* me to call him, because it's his name."

"We're wasting time we can't afford to squander," the brown girl says. "I was hoping you could find the box on your own, but you haven't even tried."

"I was busy. I was watching the snow."

"I've never much liked the snow," the brown girl says again. "My mother died when it was snowing."

"I might be schizophrenic," Emmie says, half to herself, and thinks about sitting back down in the chair. "If I'm hallucinating and having delusions and all, I might be schizophrenic."

"Or it might be something else entirely. Maybe you're like Deacon once was. Maybe you can see the things that other people can't. You know, it's a sad and unfortunate state of affairs that you have to live in a world where eight-year-olds refuse to believe in anything that they cannot touch or measure, and anyone who happens to see a thing that is invisible to most people is immediately branded a lunatic. Your stepmother still believes in magick."

"Sadie's a writer," Emmie says, repeating something else she's heard Deacon say. "Writers are different. They're supposed to be weird."

The wind is getting stronger, and it buffets the house on Angell Street and moans like a wounded animal as it slides around the corners.

"Come upstairs with me," the brown girl says. "I need to show you something. We don't have much time left."

"What if I want to stay right here and watch the snow?"

"The snow will still be out there when we're done."

Emmie glances about the small living room, surprised at how very dark it's gotten, the only light the shifting glow of the television set and the muted orange of the street lamps coming in through the windows. *I should turn on a lamp,* she thinks. *What if Deacon comes home, and all the lights are out? He might think that something's wrong.*

Something is wrong, the brown girl thinks, but Emmie can hear it just as clearly as if she'd said the words aloud. *Something's terribly wrong, and we need to hurry.*

"That's proof I'm hallucinating you," Emmie says, and then she switches on the old floor lamp near her father's chair, making a small pool of safe cream-colored light, before she follows the girl upstairs.

"Why do you have yellow eyes?" the boy asked, and Emmie told him she didn't know why, that they'd just always been that way, and she didn't have any idea why. She'd been asked the same question lots of times, and sometimes she'd been taunted and called names— *yellow eyes, yellow eyes*—lots more times than she could remember or cared to ever try. Sometimes, she made up elaborate stories to account for her yellow eyes, or told whoever was asking or bullying her that she had a contagious disease, like hepatitis or the plague, and they really shouldn't come too close. That was usually enough to make them leave her alone. But the day that *this* boy asked—which was the last day she went to the public elementary school on Camp Street, the last time someone asked before Deacon and Sadie finally moved her to the Wheeler School where hardly anyone ever asks about her eyes—*that* day, she didn't feel like lying, so she just told him the truth, that she didn't know why her eyes were yellow.

"I used to have an old tomcat with yellow eyes," the boy said. "Maybe you're part cat."

"I'm not part cat," Emmie replied. She was waiting out front, sitting on the stone front steps of the school waiting for Deacon to show up and walk her home. "I have yellow eyes, but I'm not part cat."

"Maybe your mama's a cat," the boy said.

"My mother's dead. She was a paleontologist, not a cat," Emmie told him, wishing that Deacon would hurry up or that the boy would get bored and find someone else to pick on.

"Maybe they just *told* you she was dead. Maybe they didn't want to tell you she was really a cat. Maybe they're ashamed to have half a cat for a daughter. Do they glow in the dark?"

"Do *what* glow in the dark?"

"Your eyes, dummy."

"Leave me alone," Emmie said, though she knew that he wasn't going to stop until someone *made* him stop.

"That would make you a monster," the boy said, "if your mama was a cat. Maybe they don't want you to know you're a monster. Maybe they think if you knew, you'd kill yourself or something."

"Lots of animals have yellow eyes," Emmie said. "Not just cats. *Lots* of animals have yellow eyes."

The boy smiled and sat down on the step next to her. "Yeah? So maybe she wasn't a cat. Maybe she was one of those other animals," he said. "But you'd *still* be a monster, because normal people don't have yellow eyes or animals for mothers." The boy was fat, a year older than she was, and he had a short, piggy sort of a pug nose.

"Maybe your mother was a sow," Emmie said, and the boy asked her what the hell a sow was. When Emmie told him it was a mama pig, he called her a freak and a retard and kicked her in the ankle.

By the time one of the teachers was able to pull her off the boy, Emmie had blackened both his eyes, knocked out a front tooth, and bitten him three times on the face. Two of the bites were deep enough that he would have to have stitches, but at least Emmie never had to go to school with him again. When Deacon finally arrived—almost fifteen minutes late because the toilet at the shop had backed up, and he'd had to wait on the plumber—he found her sitting in the grass, surrounded by three teachers, the vice principal, a crossing guard, and several other students. There was crusty, drying blood on her face and hands and the front of her white Curious George T-shirt. Her ankle was starting to swell and turn an angry cloudy color, but she wasn't crying. The boy was still screaming and rolling about on the ground, yelling that Emmie had almost bitten off his goddamn face, and now he was going to die of rabies because she was half cat.

Later, after they'd gone to the emergency room and knew that her ankle wasn't broken, Deacon took her home, and they sat at the kitchen table, eating grape Pop-Tarts and talking.

"He called me a monster," Emmie said. "He said you were ashamed of me because I'm a monster and a freak and a retard and because my mother was a cat."

Deacon chewed his Pop-Tart, washed it down with a mouthful of Coffee Milk, and then he scratched at his head. "And you think that was any way to show him different, acting like a zombie or something, trying to eat off half his face like that? You know you're not a monster. And you know better than to get in fights with assholes that call you names."

"I wouldn't eat his face," Emmie said, picking some of the purple filling out of her Pop-Tart. "You can get worms from eating raw pork."

And then Deacon was laughing so hard that Coffee Milk squirted out both his nostrils, which made Emmie start laughing, and by the time they'd both stopped, Deacon was out of breath and Emmie was beginning to feel a little bit better. He didn't punish her, told her that the swollen ankle was probably punishment enough, but he had to apologize to the boy's parents, and Emmie had to apologize to the boy in the principal's office. There were white bandages on the fat kid's swollen face, and he didn't look at Emmie once the whole time.

Emmie finds the cardboard box beneath Deacon's bed, right where the brown girl said it would be, and she pulls it out and opens it.

"There's very little time," the brown girl says. "You wasted so much of it, piddling about downstairs, staring at the snow."

Emmie nods her head, but she takes her time emptying the box and spreading its contents out on the floor of Deacon's bedroom, the room that used to be his and Sadie's, the room that never was his and her mother's bedroom. There are photographs, newspaper clippings, old letters written by hand, old letters written on a typewriter that punched out holes in all the Es and Os. There's a dried daisy pressed between two sheets of waxed paper. There's a much smaller box filled with ticket stubs from movies, and there's a beaten-up old copy of a Dr. Seuss book, *McElligot's Pool*. There's an envelope marked *WR* with a gold ring inside. There's a stack of "Calvin and Hobbes" strips clipped from the funny pages, all of which have something to do with dinosaurs. There's a Bullwinkle key chain with seven keys on it, and, wrapped in tissue paper, there's a reddish brown rock about as big as Emmie's fist with a dime-sized trilobite fossil embedded in it.

These are the pieces of a puzzle, she thinks. *Now, if I just knew how to put them all together—*

"But you don't," the brown girl says. She's sitting in the window seat, watching Emmie impatiently, "and there isn't time now to figure it out. You should look at the newspaper clippings."

"These are pictures of my mother," Emmie says, setting down the trilobite, returning it to its crumpled tissue, and picking up a stack of Polaroids. She knew her mother's face. Deacon kept a photograph of her on the table beside his bed, and there were others in a scrapbook downstairs. This was the same woman, the same bright green eyes, and in this picture she's smiling and holding a bottle of Coca-Cola. In the next one, her mother isn't smiling. She's sitting on a sofa reading a book, but Emmie can't tell what the book might be. In the third Polaroid, Chance Silvey is standing on a beach, and there's a dead pelican on the sand near her feet.

"You don't grasp how precious time is or how little of it we have left," the girl tells Emmie. "You're *wasting* it. Look at the clippings."

"But I've never seen these photos," Emmie says, still examining the Polaroid of her mother and the dead pelican. The ocean is flat and silver-blue in the background; the sky's almost the same color.

"That's because he hid all these things from you. Deacon's hidden many things from you."

"That's a damn lie," Emmie snaps at the girl, but she puts down the stack of photos and reaches instead for the nearest bunch of newspaper clippings. They've gone golden brown and brittle around the edges, almost like something that's been burned, but Emmie knows it's just because the paper's old and was so acidic to start with.

"Read the headline," the girl says.

And Emmie does, aloud—" '*Atlanta Police, FBI, Used Local Psychic, Source Claims.*' " Emmie stops and checks the date—August 23, 1989, twelve years before she was born. Deacon would still have been a young man, and Emmie does the math in her head; in 1989 Deacon would have been only twenty-seven years old. "This was almost twenty-one years ago," Emmie says, and the brown girl frowns.

"That's not the part that's important. Keep reading the article."

And Emmie looks back down at the clipping, but not, she promised herself, because the brown girl said she should. This cardboard box has been filled with secrets her whole life, filled with secrets and hidden all those years right here beneath her father's bed, where she could have found it on her own any day or night, if she'd only bothered to go looking.

"But you didn't find it on your own," the brown girl says haughtily. "If I hadn't come, you probably never would have."

"That's annoying, and I wish you'd cut it out. Stay out of my head. Anyway, they aren't *my* secrets. They're Deacon's secrets, and this isn't right. I think it's almost like stealing."

"You should keep reading," the brown girl says. "We're quite nearly out of time now. They'll be coming soon, and I need you to understand."

"Then shut up and stop talking to me," Emmie says, and she goes back to reading the article.

"I didn't come here to lie to you. If you'd have believed me, you wouldn't have needed to see the contents of this box."

But Emmie is no longer paying any attention to the girl, too busy with the words printed on that scrap of paper, a source close to the Atlanta PD claiming that the Mary English case had been cracked using a psychic named Deacon Silvey. The woman who was accused of having kidnapped and murdered fifteen children between 1982 and 1989, though no bodies had been found. The newspaper article said that Deacon had helped the police with other cases, and that he'd once been a student at Emory University. It also said that he was there with them when the cops found Mary English in the cellar of an old house in the woods, and that he helped save the life of a four-year-old girl named Jessica Hartwell. When she comes to the last line, Emmie puts the article on the bottom of the stack and begins reading the next clipping—"Inside Douglas County 'House of Horrors.' " There's a photograph of a very old house; the roof's sagging in the middle, and there are vines covering one side of the wide porch.

"Mary English was a woman in the employ of the hounds," the

brown girl says. "And the policemen never found the missing children because she didn't kill them. She merely delivered them to the Cuckoo."

"I don't know what the hell you're talking about," Emmie says, staring at a faded photograph of a doorway. An arch has been woven out of old dried vines, maybe some of the vines from the front porch; three human skulls have been nailed above the arch, each one wearing a crown of what appears to be rusted barbed wire, the words LAND OF DREAMS printed in neat black letters on the door underneath.

"Deacon Silvey never should have crossed that threshold," the brown girl says, "for in doing so he interfered in the dealings of the Hounds of Cain. His wife died because he went through that door."

Emmie lays the clippings down, because she doesn't want to read any more, doesn't want to *know* any more, even though she's still not sure what it all means. "He never told me about any of this stuff," she says quietly, and glances at the stack of Polaroids again.

"He was trying to do something kind, helping the police," the brown girl says. "He was trying to do something good. But he never *wanted* any part of it."

"But what he did, saving that girl, that got my mother killed?" Emmie asks, and she touches the dead-pelican photo with the tip of her right index finger.

"It's a very complicated story," the brown girl tells her. "There's not time for it now. But that woman is not your mother, Emmie. I know that you've always believed that, that you've been taught that she is, but that doesn't make it true. She's not your mother, and Deacon Silvey isn't your father."

"You're a goddamn liar," Emmie says and pulls her hand back from the Polaroid.

The brown girl stands up and goes to one of the stacks that Emmie has made, the stack of typed letters, and sits down on the floor. She takes an envelope from the stack and hands it to Emmie.

"Your stepmother wrote this to Deacon. You need to read it," she says. "Deacon's wife was pregnant when she died. It's a very long story, Emma Jean, but she died fighting a monster, a much more terrible monster than Mary English had been, a monster that tried to kill Deacon and Sadie and was trying to kill Deacon's wife and her child."

Emmie opens the envelope. The old paper crinkles loudly in the quiet room, all sound stifled and yet made somehow more distinct by the falling snow. There's no date on the letter, but it has Sadie's signature.

"The hounds took Chance Silvey's child for their own. They left you with Deacon, after Chance had died, and he has always believed that you are his daughter. But your mother is a changeling named Saben White."

"Yeah," Emmie says, remembering the woman on the train, the woman with the Seal of Solomon tattooed on her hand, the woman who knew about invisible things that were there even if you couldn't see them. "I met her on the train to New York," she says, and Emmie feels dizzy and sick to her stomach and has to shut her eyes a moment.

"I know it's a lot to have to hear, a lot to take in all at once like this," the brown girl says. "I'd have come to you sooner, had I been capable of doing so."

Emmie opens her eyes again and begins reading the letter. *You know that's not Chance's child,* her stepmother typed. *It isn't over. That isn't Chance's baby, and this all has something to do with Narcissa Snow and whatever she was trying to do. Jesus, I wish you would answer the phone. I wish you would just talk to me. I don't like writing this stuff down in letters and mailing it. I'm always afraid someone else will get the letters.*

"This is sometime after she left," Emmie says and chews at her lip.

"Yes," the girl says. "Have you seen enough? Do you believe me now?"

"I don't know what I believe," Emmie replies. "I don't even think I know what's for real anymore."

You can't doubt the blood and DNA tests, Sadie's letter reads. *She isn't your daughter, Deke, and she isn't Chance's daughter, either. I talked to the doctor. I know they weren't supposed to talk to me, but they did. Her blood work had them all a little freaked out.*

Emmie folds the letter and returns it to the envelope, returns the envelope to the stack on the floor. Then she picks up the trilobite fossil again. The weight of the rock feels good in her hand. There's a tiny handwritten label glued onto the bottom that she didn't notice the first time she picked it up: CRYPTOLITHUS GIGAS, CHICKAMAUGA LMS., RED MTN. CUT, BIRMINGHAM, SUMMER '73.

I won't cry, she thinks. *I'll cry later, when she's gone, but I won't cry sitting here in front of her.*

"There will be time to think about it later," the brown girl says, standing again. "But now you have to leave this house. The Bailiff is coming, and you must get far away from here before he finds you. I know a place where you'll be safe. You'll need warm clothes—"

"Then who *is* my father?" Emmie asks, interrupting and ignoring the brown girl. "If it's not Deacon, then who's my father?"

"We can talk about that later, when you're safe. It's nothing you need to know just yet."

"Was he a cat?" Emmie asks, and the brown girl stares at her, then looks over her shoulder at the bedroom window. Outside, the snow seems to be falling even harder than before. "Was he a monster?" Emmie asks.

The brown girl kneels down in front of her, unmindful of the clippings and letters and photographs she's crushing beneath her knees. Emmie wants to slap her, wants to tangle her fingers in the girl's ebony hair, wants to claw her and bite her and kick her until she admits that all of this is a lie. That *she* wrote the letter, that those aren't even real newspaper articles. Instead, Emmie only bites her lip and sets the trilobite down again.

"*Please* trust me," the girl says. "If you stay here, in this house, they'll surely find you before the morning, and they *will* kill you, Emma Jean."

"Who? *Who's* coming?"

"We need to get you dressed. It's very cold out there. It's still snowing. And it's only going to get colder, I'm afraid, before it gets any warmer."

"I'm going to call Deacon. I'm going to ask him if this is true. He won't lie to me—"

"*Listen* to me," the girl says, and now she leans close and grasps Emmie's chin in the fingers of her right hand. Suddenly, she looks very old, a shriveled old woman wearing a clever little-girl mask, and her eyes turn as red as ripe cranberries. "If they find you here they *will* kill you, and if they find Deacon, they'll have to kill him, too. If you leave now, and if they *know* you've left, they'll have no reason to come here looking for you, and Deacon will be safe. Now, get up and get dressed. We *have* to leave this house, Emma Jean."

And then another instant passes, and she's only the brown girl again, the girl from the attic, the girl from a dream, and she blinks once at Emmie and lets go of her face. "I'm sorry," she says. "But there's no more time."

"This isn't happening," Emmie says. "I'm asleep, asleep in my bed, and in a moment Deacon will come and wake me up. I'll tell him what I dreamed, and he'll laugh at me. I'll tell him I ran away in the snow with a crazy girl, and we hid so monsters wouldn't kill him, and he'll laugh at me."

"Yes," the brown girl says. "That's exactly what you'll tell him, but first you have to run away. First you have to hide."

"But it's *only* a dream," Emmie reminds the girl, and then she reaches for the envelope marked *WR* and takes out the gold wedding ring and slips it on her thumb. But it's too loose and falls off, so she puts it in one of the front pockets of her jeans instead. "I should clean all this up," she says. "Deacon will be mad if he comes home and finds this mess."

"There isn't time. He'll understand."

"But these are his *secrets*," Emmie says, and she knows that it's not right for them to be spread out all over the bedroom floor for anyone to see.

"*Now*," the girl says, and Emmie does as she's told, because it's only a dream, after all, and when she's awake again Deacon won't know about the box if she doesn't tell him. The brown girl disappears into the hallway, and Emmie goes to put on warmer clothes and find her coat.

And half an hour later, Emmie is walking east along Waterman Street, trudging forward with the freezing north wind pressing brusquely at her back, driving her, hurrying her along, and the snow swirls about her like fat white fairies. Her breath puffs out in foggy clouds, and the fairies slowly melt whenever they collide with the warm patch of exposed skin around her eyes and the bridge of her nose. This is the way the brown girl said that she had to go, east down Angell and then one street over to Waterman, east on Waterman to Ivy, south on Ivy to East Manning, and then on to Gano Street and the woods at the edge of the river, and there the girl would show her the place where they'd hide until it was safe to come out again. The snow's ankle deep, and she figures the monsters must have sent it to slow her down.

It's smothering everything just to get at me, Emmie thinks and stops walking, looking back to see if the brown girl's still following her. She's been harder to see since they left the house, but Emmie knows she's back there somewhere, because she can still hear her footsteps. From time to time the girl says something, not speaking out loud, just a few words whispered directly into Emmie's head.

Don't stop, Emma Jean. Keep moving.

Or: *You can't stop here. It's getting late.*

Emmie doesn't know *how* late it is—eight thirty, almost nine, maybe, and Deacon will be home soon. The streetlights spaced out along Waterman make pools of Creamsicle brilliance in the slippery, uncertain darkness. Overhead the sky is lost in the storm, and the bellies of the low clouds are the same soft orange-white as the light from the street lamps. Emmie walks a few more steps, wipes the melted snow from her eyes, then stops again beneath one of the mercury-vapor lights.

"Where *are* you?" she shouts back at the spot where she thinks the brown girl might be. "I can't *see* you."

You don't need to see me. I've told you the way to go.

"I'm freezing my rear end off," Emmie yells back, and she is, even though it's only a dream (she reminds herself), even though she has her good coat—not the pink zebra stripes, but her blue down-filled parka—and her mittens, gloves under the mittens, warm wool socks and her new winter boots, the blue ones from L.L. Bean that Sadie gave her, rubber and nylon and a drawstring to keep the snow from getting inside. She's wearing a sweater and a T-shirt under that, her toboggan cap and muffler, and she knows she *ought* to be warm. But the cold seems to come right through her clothes, right through *her,* as though she were no more substantial than the brown girl or the swirling snow.

You can't stop here, the brown girl says urgently. *It doesn't matter if you're cold and tired; you can't stop. You can rest when we've reached the tunnel.*

"What tunnel?" Emmie asks her. "You didn't say *anything* about a tunnel." It's getting hard to talk because her teeth have started chattering again and *tunnel* comes out more like *tuh-uh-uh-nel,* like a kid Emmie knew in second grade who had to have speech therapy because he stuttered.

You'll see. But you can't stop here.

"I got out of the house. You told me I had to get out so Deacon would be safe, and I'm out, so why do we have to hide?"

Because I also have to keep you safe, Emma Jean, because I also . . . And then the girl falls silent, and for the first time since they left the house, Emmie feels alone and scared and lost in the disorienting white blur of the storm.

"And because *what*?" she asks, but the brown girl doesn't answer her. Emmie looks up and down the length of Waterman Street, as far as she can see through the storm, but there's no sign of her anywhere. The houses, the trees, the fire hydrants, the cars parked along the side of the road, everything is rapidly vanishing beneath the snow. Everything is becoming something new, something indistinct and menacing, and Emmie wonders if she could find her way back home or if maybe she really is lost.

It doesn't matter if you get lost in a dream, she reminds herself. *You're found again as soon as you wake up.*

And then there's a flash of lightning and, only a few seconds later, a rolling, rumbling thunderclap that seems to begin at one end of the street and roll back and forth, back and forth, as if the simple sound of it means to crush everything flat and dead.

"What's happening?" she shouts back at the brown girl, at the murky place where she might have been. "I don't know what I'm supposed to do!" But the thunder steals her frightened voice and grinds it to silent pulp in the snow.

You can't be afraid of them, the brown girl says inside her head. *No matter what, you can't be afraid of them.* And then she's gone again, and there's only the storm and the snow-covered world and the thunder rolling up and down Waterman Street.

No, Emmie realizes, *not thunder. It's not thunder at all. Only something that wants me to* think *it's thunder, or something that can't help but sound like thunder when it moves.* And she remembers a book she has about mastodons and woolly mammoths, towering, shaggy things wandering about in the shadows of ancient glaciers, and Emmie also remembers a scary story that Deacon read her once, a story about the Wendigo, an enormous monster or Indian god that lived on the wind and snatched away people foolish enough to go too deep into the wild places it haunted.

"It's only thunder," she says. "It's only the storm playing tricks with sound, playing tricks on my mind." And then Emmie ducks quickly behind a sugary lump that was a holly bush before the storm began, and she crouches down and waits for the noise to stop. *Help me,* she thinks, hoping that the brown girl is listening and will hear her thoughts. *Help me. Make it stop. Make it stop looking for me.*

The brown girl doesn't answer her, and Emmie thinks that maybe it's because she's afraid to, that maybe the thunder monster can hear their thoughts, too, or maybe it's because it's found the girl already and has torn her apart or eaten her or whatever it does. Emmie peers out between the branches of the holly bush, at the abandoned white waste of Waterman Street, and she wonders why there aren't any cars. If there were a car or a truck or just someone walking by on foot, maybe there would be someone who could help her. This time of night there should still be traffic; even with the snow, there should be people coming home from work.

And then she sees it, the stilt-legged, tattletale gray thing that's making the noises she only thought were thunder. It isn't a mammoth or a mastodon—though it has long, shaggy hair—and she's pretty sure it isn't the Wendigo, either. It isn't anything she knows a name for, and maybe it *has* no name. Maybe you would die, if you even tried to name it. The creature seems to glide effortlessly out of the shadows, drifting along light as a wisp of radiator steam, moving like a whirl of fallen snow stirred up by the wind. But its footsteps are still thunder and lightning, betraying the weight of all the evil trapped deep in its roiling black-hole belly, betraying the gravity of the thing. Its footsteps are the shattering of stone by vast iron hammers, the grinding of pack ice at the bottom of the world, the collision of continental plates, the impossible gait of a thing so heavy that Emmie wouldn't have believed the universe could even *contain* it, that it doesn't simply tear a hole in space and time and vanish forever.

I'm dreaming, she reminds herself, *and when I'm awake, I'll forget it. I'll forget I ever saw it.*

It has no eyes that Emmie can see, and when the thing pauses near the holly bush and sniffs at the February night, its breath doesn't steam in the cold air. She doesn't dare move, doesn't breathe, does her best not to even *think*. Something pink and wet darts from a ragged cleft up high that might be its mouth, and then it bends low and licks at the snow and slush in the middle of the road. It lingers there a moment longer, as if considering whatever it might or might not have just tasted, and then a sudden strong gust of wind seems to catch the creature off guard and blows it away down Waterman Street, back in the direction Emmie's come, tossing it thundering along, weightless as a discarded candy wrapper and heavy as the heart of a collapsing star. Emmie doesn't move, crouching there beneath the holly bush as the snow slowly covers her. The creature's footsteps have become distant, faint fireworks heard from far, far away, and Emmie shuts her eyes tightly and shivers and wishes that this could be the end of the dream.

"It's not so cold anymore," the brown girl says, standing there with Emmie now, and she brushes snow from Emmie's lips and eyelids. "We're lucky," she says. "That was a very wicked place, indeed, but it didn't find us, and it won't come back. They never do."

"A *place*?" Emmie asks, and then she realizes that the brown girl's right. It *is* warmer now, only the cold of any snowy winter night, nothing more and nothing less. "What do you mean? I saw it. It wasn't a place. It was a monster."

"There's that silly word again," the brown girl says, and smiles at Emmie. "You use that word entirely too often, Emma Jean Silvey. You're going to have to try harder. Now hurry. We still have a ways to go."

"Will he be safe?" Emmie asks, glancing past the streetlights, peering deep into the night, towards the place where she thinks her house must be. "Will Deacon be safe now that I'm gone?"

"The Bailiff isn't looking for Deacon," the brown girl says. "He's looking for *you*, dear. Now come on. I don't like the snow. It was snowing when my mother died."

"What about *my* mother?" Emmie asks her. "Was it snowing when my mother died?"

The brown girl from the attic stares at her a moment, lost in thought or looking at something only she can see, and then she smiles and takes Emmie's hand. "I don't know," she says. "But I'm beginning to think it may turn out that way."

For twenty-eight years, the East Side railroad tunnel has sat half-forgotten beneath the streets of College Hill, a relic from a time when trains and trolleys were still used to carry people through the city. The two teams of workmen, one digging east from Benefit and the other west from Gano, met beneath Cooke Street on April 7, 1908, a full day ahead of schedule. Two hundred thousand cubic yards of hard Paleozoic bedrock were moved in the excavations, and when the workers were finally finished, the tunnel stretched more than five thousand feet from end to end. There were no casualties during the construction, which began in 1906, but there were persistent reports of peculiar noises, especially towards the western end of the dig, and a number of workers complained of foul odors, like rotting meat and ammonia, which seemed to leak in places from the freshly broken rocks. Others said that they often felt that they were being watched, and half a dozen men reported brief but unnerving encounters with doglike "goblins" or "devils" that never left tracks and always managed to lope away into the darkness and vanish before anyone was able to get a good look at them. There was a passing mention of the phantoms in an article published by the *Providence Journal,* mocking the Portuguese and Italian workers for not having left their superstitions in the old country.

The East Side tunnel was officially opened during a ceremony on November 15, 1908. Dignitaries were in attendance, ribbons were cut, speeches were made, and the stories told by superstitious immigrant workmen were quickly lost from the memory of Providence. For seventy-three years, as the restless world of men changed from one thing to another, passing from gaslights to electric bulbs to the fire of splitting atoms, the tunnel served the purpose for which it had been built. The men and women who passed through it, safe inside their rattling steel carriages, never reported anything strange, and certainly not the watchful eyes of subterranean demons. And then, when the world had at last changed enough that men no longer had any need for the tunnel, it was sealed off at both ends—for the public good—and the earth beneath College Hill became a secret place once again. There were padlocks, and gates were welded shut, but students from RISD and Brown would always break them open again, and parties in the tunnel became a routine occurrence. Sometimes the homeless sought shelter there, but it was wet and inhospitable, and there were usually better places to sleep.

Emmie Silvey crosses Gano Street, aiming for the scraggly patch of woods behind the baseball diamond and the soccer field, but the snow's falling so fast and heavy now that she's having trouble seeing more than a couple of feet in front of her. She follows the brown girl's footprints so that she doesn't end up somewhere she's not supposed to be, only catching a glimpse of the girl now and then, but Emmie can hear her, the girl's voice murmuring in her head, so she knows that she hasn't been left alone in the stormy night.

"It's not much farther," the girl tells her. "We're almost there. I promise."

Emmie's legs are beginning to ache and her lungs hurt, and she almost asks the girl why the woods aren't good enough for hiding. *I could sit down*, she thinks. *I could just walk over to the other side and sit down beneath a tree and wait to wake up.*

"It's not fair," Emmie mumbles, tasting the damp wool of her muffler. "Ghosts don't get tired."

I told you that I'm not a ghost, the girl replies. *And besides, you don't know that.*

"I know Deacon's not going to be happy when he finds out that I've run off in a damn snowstorm. I *know* that."

He'll understand, the brown girl assures Emmie.

"You think? You don't know Deacon. He's only gonna kill me, if I'm lucky."

It's just a dream, the brown girl reminds her. *Surely he won't punish you for what you've done in a dream.*

Yeah, Emmie thinks, reaching the far side of Gano Street and pausing beneath the snow-laden limbs of a big maple to catch her breath. *It's only a dream, and Deacon is my father, and that woman with the tattoo on the train wasn't my mother. It's only a dream, and there's no box of secrets beneath Deacon's bed.*

"I should've stayed in New York," Emmie says. "This is way worse than dead horses."

He would have come for you there, the girl from the attic tells her. *The Bailiff goes wherever he needs to go, wherever they need him to be.*

"Who's the Bailiff?"

"It's not much farther. We need to keep moving, Emma Jean. The tunnel isn't far." And Emmie realizes that the girl is actually *speaking* to her now. She looks up, and the brown girl is standing knee-deep in a drift.

"Aren't you even cold?" Emmie asks.

"We have to be going," the girl says. "We have to hurry."

So Emmie keeps quiet and follows her into the dark woods behind the park, too tired to argue anymore, and she's gone this far, so she might as well see what's waiting at the other end of it all. It certainly can't be anything worse than what she saw on Waterman Street. The girl guides her down a trail between the trees and underbrush, a narrow footpath leading them back towards the Seekonk River. The wind rustles through the dry branches, and just as Emmie starts to miss the streetlights, the brown girl begins to sing as she walks. Her voice is making Emmie a little sleepy, but it also helps to take her mind off the cold.

> *When the mistletoe was green,*
> *Midst the winter's snows,*
> *Sunshine in thy face was seen,*
> *Kissing lips of rose.*

> *Aura Lea, Aura Lea,*
> *Take my golden ring;*
> *Love and light return with thee,*
> *And swallows with the spring.*

"What was that?" Emmie asks her, when the girl stops singing. "I've never heard that song before."

"My father taught it to me. It was one of my mother's favorite songs. He sang it almost every single day."

"Is he dead?" Emmie asks. "Is your father dead, too?"

"No," the girl says. "But he's gone away. The hounds sent him away. He's coming back for me soon, though."

They're standing together at what first appears to be a fork in the trail, but then Emmie sees that it's actually a place where the trail ends at an old abandoned railroad track, one side leading off towards the river and the other back west towards Gano Street.

"We go *that* way," the brown girl says, sounding very certain of herself, and she points left, towards the glow of College Hill.

"But that's where we just were," Emmie protests and kicks at a stump buried in the snow.

"Yes, but nevertheless," the brown girl says, annoyed or insulted that Emmie's questioning her judgement, "that's the way to the tunnel. *That* way," and she points right, "only leads to the bridge. We don't need the bridge."

"I thought you *wanted* a bridge."

"Yes, but not that sort of bridge."

"I'm going home," Emmie grumbles.

"*No*. No, you're not. You *know* that you're not. Now stop dawdling," and, without another word, the brown girl heads off down the tracks. Emmie waits a moment or two, wondering if the girl bleeds, wondering if she can fight, and then Emmie Silvey takes a deep breath and follows. The brown girl is singing again.

> *Aura Lea, the bird may flee,*
> *The willow's golden hair*
> *Swing through winter fitfully,*
> *On the stormy air.*
>
> *Yet if thy blue eyes I see,*
> *Gloom will soon depart;*
> *For to me, sweet Aura Lea*
> *Is sunshine through the heart.*

Emmie concentrates on the girl's voice and the sound of her own boots in the snow, the wind and the brittle noise the snowflakes make as they fall. And before long they've come to a place where the tracks end at a rust-red wall of corrugated tin built within a high concrete archway set into the side of the hill.

"Here," the brown girl says. "They tried to seal it shut a long time ago, but nothing ever stays shut. Nothing that should be open."

"The tunnel?" Emmie asks, and she realizes that there's a light here, thin white light tinged faintly blue, light that doesn't cast any shadows that she can see. Emmie can't be sure where it's coming from, but it seems to be shining down from somewhere above their heads, near the top of the concrete arch, but when she looks up, there's only the black and snowy sky, the wall of metal and cement.

"Yes," the brown girl says. "You'll be safe in here till morning. The hounds won't look here. They won't think you'd ever come so near."

In front of the tunnel is a small clearing strewn with junk—the rusted remains of an automobile and a box spring, piles of beer cans, and the rotted carcass of a sofa. The land here is marshy, and there's dark and stagnant water on both sides of the tracks. The water looks almost like ink, ink with little blobs of snow floating about in it, and Emmie thinks of Frodo and Gandalf outside the mines of Moria, the black pool and the guardian of the West Gate.

"You're sure it's safe?" Emmie asks.

"I'm afraid nowhere's safe," the brown girl says. "But they won't look here tonight."

"And tomorrow?"

"We'll deal with that when it comes."

Someone has laid down wooden pallets, end to end, between the steel rails, and they lead to a door set into the wall of rusted tin. The door is standing ajar, and the strange blue-white light doesn't seem to reach inside. There's a red plastic milk crate, half-submerged, floating in the water on the right side of the tracks, and it reminds Emmie of her little room in Sadie's apartment in New York and makes her wish she were there. The brown girl steps gingerly across the pallets. She stops near the floating crate and looks back at Emmie.

"You should hurry," she says. "There are rules."

Emmie nods her head and takes one step forward. The lower part of the tin wall and the concrete of the tunnel are obscured by decades of graffiti, dull metal tagged and spray-painted with a drunken, looping neon tapestry of patterns and symbols and words that mean nothing to her, but it's an unexpected, distracting splash of color among the sleeping brown and gray of the trees and the snow and the stones.

"What kind of rules?" Emmie asks.

"There are *always* rules, especially in very magickal places," the brown girl tells her. "Don't you read?" And the brown girl takes something from a pocket in her dress, something that glints in the blue light, and Emmie guesses it must be a coin, and the girl from the attic drops it into the milk crate with a faint splash. "Don't worry," she says. "That's enough for both of us."

"Thank you," Emmie says, though she isn't at all sure she *should* be thankful, and the wooden pallets creak beneath the rubber soles of the boots that Sadie gave her as she walks towards the tunnel. She can see now that there's a black-and-white circle painted on the door, a white circle ringed by interwoven lines of black, and a cracked black heart at the very bottom. Inside, the circle has been painted black, and at its center there's a white horse that's fallen or been knocked down, a horse on its back with its legs in the air. Above the horse, in white lettering, is written, *The horse is dead,* and below the horse is written, *From here we walk.*

"What does that mean?" Emmie asks the brown girl, who makes a face like it's the silliest question she's ever heard.

"You were there," she says. "I don't think you need me to explain, Emma Jean." And then she steps through the doorway, and the darkness inside seems to swallow her.

"The horse is dead," Emmie whispers, glancing up at the snowy place where the blue-white light might be coming from, then down at the floating milk crate. "From here we walk." And she thinks once more about turning back, about turning and running all the way home again, before she says Deacon's name aloud, then crosses the threshold into the tunnel.

II

Lost Girls

My cocoon tightens, colors tease,
I'm feeling for the air;
A dim capacity for wings
Degrades the dress I wear.

—EMILY DICKINSON

SIX

Shadow and Flame

"Fucking dead," Odd Willie moans, somewhere nearby, somewhere in the river-scented darkness and the acrid stench of the mill-befouled Blackstone, and Soldier grits her teeth and shuts her eyes again. No sense staring into that black void until her eyes burn and she begins to imagine taunting, swirling colors that aren't there to see. No light left down here. No light at all. Only pain and the darkness and Odd Willie moaning about being dead. Both of them dangling headdown like fat hogs strung up for the slaughterhouse knife, her wrists tied behind her back, her ankles bound. Soldier's head and spine and shoulders are white fire, but at least she can't feel her hands or feet because she's been hanging here so long, and, besides, the nylon cord and electrical tape have cut off the circulation.

"Fuckers," mumbles Odd Willie.

They may have been hanging here only an hour, but it might have been much longer. She remembers the car and the cemetery, the glamour, the butt of Saben's pistol against her skull, then an indefinite, numb nothingness before being kicked awake and finding herself lying naked on the floor of the ossuary—a floor tiled with polished teeth, walls lined with long bones and skulls, a vaulted ceiling of ribs and vertebrae. And then she and Odd Willie were beaten and tortured and raped by Ballou's goons until the goons got bored and tied them up and left them alone together in the dark.

And *then*, later, she was dreaming, until Odd Willie's moaning woke her. She was dreaming about the musty library in the yellow house on Benefit Street, and the Bailiff was offering her a candy cane. She took it, translucent sugar the color of amethyst, and it was nothing she'd ever tasted before or since—not quite licorice and not quite peppermint, a bit like eating violets. She sat on a velvet cushion on the floor while he read to her from the big book lying open on his desk.

"She killed us," Odd Willie moans. "We're dead, dead as dog shit, and she fucking killed us."

Soldier opens one eye and tries to guess where his voice is coming from. "We're not dead," she says, though they could be, for all she knows. "Now shut up. My head hurts."

"She killed us both. That crazy, fucking, backstabbing cunt killed us both."

Soldier closes her right eye again, pretty sure Odd Willie must be somewhere to the left of her, anyhow, and tries to recall *exactly* how the candy tasted.

"Aren't you listening? Aren't you even paying attention?" the Bailiff asks and smiles at her. His green eyes are the kindest eyes that she's ever seen, and Soldier wishes that she could leave the warrens and live up here with him in the house forever. He could be her father, and she could spend every day listening to him read from his books. They could take long walks in the sunlight together, and he could tell her stories whenever she was having trouble getting to sleep.

"My fucking mouth tastes like puke and blood," Odd Willie says and makes a painful spitting sound.

"Someone keeps distracting me," Soldier tells the Bailiff, and he sighs and scratches at his beard.

"Well, you'd best try to ignore her, little soldier girl," he says. "She's trouble good and proper, that one. Lightning in a bottle. I don't mind saying it out loud. They should've slit her throat a long damn time ago, if you were to ask me."

"I didn't ask you anything."

"Too true."

In the darkness, the damp air is cold and smells like mud and mold and earthworms and the poisoned river, and Soldier wishes Odd Willie would shut the hell up. She couldn't hear him in the dream, in the library with the Bailiff, and she couldn't feel all the places where they've hit her or kicked her or sliced her with their knives, their nails and their claws. And then there's a *new* noise—dry twigs snapping, the living bones of a sparrow cracked open between a cat's teeth, thin ice breaking apart underfoot—and Soldier stares out into the darkness.

"Oh gods," Odd Willie whimpers. "They're coming back. Oh, fuck me, Soldier, fuck me—"

"Shut the *fuck* up, you fucking pussy," Soldier growls at him, and the effort makes her head pound and her stomach roll.

"Is this shit leading anywhere?" she asks the Bailiff, and he grunts and turns a page.

"Depends what you're asking me," he replies, then begins reading to her again, the poetry of demons transcribed by the hands of dead men, a meandering recollection from the last day of a battle in a city of ghosts that sleeps forever now beneath sand and blistering desert sky.

"What's the point?" she says, interrupting him. "*That's* what I'm asking you, old man. I'm sick of riddles and dreams and fucking symbolism. If you've got something to say to me, say it or shut up."

The Bailiff snorts and marks the page with a long white feather before closing the book and pushing it away across the wide desk. "The universe," he says, "and all those unfortunate beings locked up within it—cosmic inmates, if you will—have no purpose but the purpose which they imagine for themselves within the spiraling *dream* of time."

"That's very fucking nice," Soldier says, and she decides that the stick of candy isn't the color of amethyst, after all. "That's almost goddamn poetry. Did you find it scrawled in one of your books? Is it something else you learned from the hounds?"

"It's not a riddle," the child from the attic says, the Daughter of the Four of Pentacles, the girl whose name is never spoken, and now Soldier remembers her standing in front of the Bailiff's desk, running her fingers lovingly back and forth across the worn leather cover of the book. She's smiling, and Soldier thinks that maybe the girl is remembering the time before they locked her away and stopped all the clocks her father built for the hounds.

"You can't be here," Soldier says. The Bailiff doesn't seem to have noticed the girl.

"It wasn't easy," the Daughter of the Four of Pentacles replies, and suddenly she pulls her fingers back from the book, as if it's burned her. "I broke three of his bindings, and now those moments are lost forever. I simply dropped them on the floor and they shattered. It's the most wicked thing I've ever had to do."

"The universe," the Bailiff continues, "and, indeed, *all* universes, are at war with the consequences of their consciousness. Sometimes they fashion the most ingenious weapons for their regiments. But occasionally the weapons are reluctant to fulfill their purpose. Guns jam. Arrows miss their mark. Shots go wild, as they say."

He doesn't see her, Soldier thinks and opens her eyes again. *He doesn't see her, because she wasn't there.*

There's light now, warm light from a white candle held tight in the girl's hand, the flame flickering uneasily in the dank air far beneath Woonsocket. "It's simpler for me to move through dreams, usually," she says. "There aren't as many . . ." And the girl pauses a moment, furrowing her brow as though trying to recall a difficult or unfamiliar word. ". . . not as many *watchers*. At least, that's what my father used to call them."

"In the eyes of the hounds," the Bailiff says, "you have become just such a reluctant weapon. And I have failed to set you straight."

"You didn't fail, old man. You never even tried."

"Too true," he says again and smiles. "But that's most likely beside the point."

"Somehow, I doubt the *ghul* will think so," Soldier tells him, Soldier only five years old and seated on a velvet cushion on the floor, the tall bookshelves rising up all about her, so very tall that the tops are dappled with snow and lost in misty clouds. "You're a traitor," she says and licks the last of the candy off her fingers.

"Now, now," he frowns. "That's an awfully weighty word for such a small girl to be tossing about. Perhaps you should endeavor to avoid it in the future."

"Soldier, that was a long time ago, that day with the Bailiff," the Daughter of the Four of Pentacles says, and wax drips from her candle and puddles on the floor of molars and incisors and canines. "I need you here and now, with me. I need you awake. I have only a few moments left, and I can't come back to you once I've gone."

"She fucking killed us," Odd Willie says so softly that it's almost a whisper, and he laughs and then begins to cough.

"Do you want to *die* here?" the girl asks.

"No," Soldier says, and the Bailiff glares down at her from his seat at the desk, and she sees that what she mistook for kindness in his green eyes is something else altogether.

"Don't you start believing in fairy stories," he warns her. "It's a little late for that, child. They locked her away in that attic for a reason."

"Ask him why they put *you* there," the Daughter of the Four of Pentacles says, so much anger and bitterness for the voice of a child, and Soldier realizes that she can't see the girl anymore, only fluttering candlelight and her shadow stretched out across the floor of teeth.

"Where did you go?" Soldier calls out, and her voice echoes dully off the moldering walls of the ossuary.

"I'm here, behind you. Don't make so much noise. These knots are going to take me a moment."

"Don't you dare accept *her* help, Soldier," the Bailiff commands, "not *that* one." And he leans forward, towering above Soldier, who's only a child sitting cross-legged on a ratty velvet cushion. Only five and lost in an endless canyon of books and shelves, the taste of something sweet fading on her tongue, and all of heaven become the voice of a madman.

"Did you send me here to die?" Soldier asks him. The Bailiff licks at his lips, and her body sways a little as the wizard's daughter struggles to free her hands. *Like the pendulum of a clock,* she thinks, *like the clock on the mantel in the yellow house on Benefit Street, the clock with the face of a girl.*

"Oh, Soldier"—the Bailiff sighs—"don't you know you have meant all the world to me? Should any harm befall you, I could never forgive myself."

"How old am I?" Soldier asks, and the girl stops working at the knots and tells her, *No, no, Soldier, it's not time for that question yet. That question will come later.* The Bailiff narrows his glittering eyes and leans back in his squeaky chair.

"How old was I when you took *me* up to the attic?" Soldier asks, feeling sick, and her mind wriggles cold and slippery, a great, squirming fish caught between her fingers. She's blacking out again. "*Answer me,* you son of a bitch."

"You've had a very trying day," the Bailiff replies, and behind

Soldier the library door is opening, the silver-eyed woman come to claim her, to lead her back to the cellar steps and down to the Hounds of Cain. "We'll talk about this another time, when you're not so . . . excitable."

And then he's gone, and that day is gone, gone and almost forgotten, and Soldier is only hanging in the abscess carved out beneath a hill in Woonsocket, hanging by her ankles while the Daughter of the Four of Pentacles tries to loosen the knots that George Ballou's men have tied.

"Who is she?" Odd Willie mumbles. "Soldier, who the hell is that girl? Where'd she *come* from?" but Soldier ignores him and shuts her eyes and lets the world fall away.

"I hope you understand that this is an exceedingly special privilege," the Bailiff said as he closed the library doors behind them. "Very few changelings have ever been allowed into the house, and far fewer have seen the second floor, and the number who've visited the attic . . . well, I can say with confidence that I could count those souls on the fingers of my left foot." She smiled, imagining the mess that the Bailiff's left foot must be; he locked the library with a silver key, then slipped the key into his pants pocket.

"Is it true there's a ghost up there?" she asked.

"A ghost? Well, in a manner of speaking, I suppose. In a manner of speaking, there are many ghosts up there. More than you'd care to know. More than ever you could count."

"I wouldn't care to know any at all," Soldier said, and the Bailiff laughed and led her up a narrow staircase and down a long hallway hung with paintings and peeling Dresden-blue calico wallpaper. Soldier stopped to examine one of the strips of blue wallpaper, which she discovered was damp and sticky with something that smelled like soured milk; the Bailiff scolded her.

"Don't be greedy," he scowled. "And don't take liberties you haven't been offered."

"I just wanted to see," Soldier said, wiping her hand on the front of her dress. "I wanted to know why it was peeling off the wall, that's all."

"But that's a secret, Soldier girl, and this house and all those within its walls will reveal only the secrets they *choose* to reveal."

"It's only wallpaper. That's a pretty dumb secret."

"That's not for you to say, most especially not when you've already been accorded such grand and all but unprecedented honors." And the Bailiff took her hand firmly in his so that she'd have to walk beside him and couldn't stop to look at any of the portraits or urns or cut-glass doorknobs they'd have to pass to reach the end of the hall. "You wouldn't want to seem ungrateful," the Bailiff said.

"No," she agreed. "I wouldn't," and in only a few more steps they'd reached the far end of the hallway. There was a small wrought-iron table with a green marble top and a peacock green vase of dead roses, and all the wallpaper had been stripped away here to reveal the plaster underneath. The wall was marked with a confusion of red and gold runes that Soldier couldn't read. She was about to ask what they meant, when the Bailiff pointed at the ceiling; she looked up and saw the trapdoor. It had a length of rope for a handle, and there were more runes painted on it.

"I'm scared," she said, and the Bailiff made a concerned sort of face and knelt down beside her.

"I won't lie to you," he said. "There are plenty enough things in the house to be afraid of, and not a few of them are right over our heads. But your coming here today has been arranged. No harm will befall you, child, not so long as you mind your Ps and Qs."

"You'll be with me," she said and held his hand more tightly.

"As long as I can be, but I've told you already, there are places you must go without me. There are places you must see alone."

Soldier stared up at the entrance to the attic, and she wondered if he'd stop her if she tried to run away, if she turned and hurried back past the paintings and down the stairs, to the cellar and the tunnels and the shadows where she belonged.

"What is it, Soldier?" the Bailiff asked. "What is it you're not telling me?"

"The woman in the desert," Soldier replied, "I dreamed of her again yesterday."

"The black woman?" the Bailiff asked, and then he glanced up at the trapdoor.

"Yes, sir. The one who told me about Esmeribetheda and the *djinniyeh*. We were walking together in the ruined city, and she told me not to come here today."

The Bailiff watched her silently for a moment, then took a deep breath and rubbed at his beard.

"She said that a terrible thing was waiting for me here," Soldier added.

"Did she now?" the Bailiff asked and tugged at his whiskers. "Were those precisely the words she used?"

"Yes sir," Soldier said. "She said the hounds mean to take my life from me."

"But the hounds *already* have your life, child. You've belonged to them since the Cuckoo brought you from the home of your father and mother."

"Well, I know that," Soldier said, and the Bailiff shook his head. "I told her that."

"And what did she say?"

"That there are lies all about me, that my entire life has been spun from lies, and that the greatest lies, the ones which will take my life, are waiting for me with the ghost in the attic. She said that I can't trust you anymore," and then Soldier looked down, keeping her eyes on the dingy floral pattern of the rug because she didn't want to see his expression.

"And do you believe her?" the Bailiff asked, each word tumbling through the air like iron.

"It was only a dream," Soldier said. "All of it, it was only a dream."

"Are you quite sure?"

"Do you think that matters?" she asked and kicked at the rug with the toe of her shoe.

"And why didn't you tell me this sooner?"

"I wanted to see the attic. I thought if I told you, you might not show me."

"Look at me," he said, and she did. In the dim light of the hall-way, his face didn't seem quite so round, and Soldier could see the dark circles beneath his eyes, eyes that had gone the oily color of coal. "We play our assigned parts," he told her, "and that's all we get. My part was to bring you here, and your part is to enter. We all play our parts, little Soldier, nothing more."

"That's exactly what she told me you'd say."

"Is it now? Well, I guess that means she's a right smart nigger lady, doesn't it?"

"Sometimes," Soldier said, "she frightens me."

"I wouldn't worry your pretty head about her any longer," the Bailiff said, standing up, straightening his rumpled seersucker suit, and then he reached for the rope handle on the trapdoor and pulled. The rusted hinges and springs screamed and popped, stiff from long decades of disuse, and Soldier wanted to cover her ears, but she didn't. "Where you're headed, I doubt she'll be able to follow."

*   *   *

Soldier doesn't remember being lowered to the floor, doesn't remember the Daughter of the Four of Pentacles leaving her, doesn't remember the feeling coming back to her hands and feet, and whether or not it was the girl who untied Odd Willie or if maybe she did it herself—but none of that shit matters, none of that shit matters at all.

"I'm so goddamn cold," Odd Willie shivers, and she feels his forehead again. She's pretty sure he has a fever; maybe Ballou's men busted something inside him, and now Odd Willie is bleeding to death. "I'm freezing my fucking dick off."

"I don't know what you expect me to do about it," she says, and Soldier peers into the darkness beyond the muddy alcove where they're waiting, huddled together naked and hurting, waiting to see if anyone's coming back to finish the job, or if they've been left for dead. The alcove is just outside the ossuary. Soldier managed to pry loose the upper half of a femur from the wall, not much against guns and magick, but better than nothing, and she grips it tight in both hands and tries not to feel the cold.

"I'm gonna murder the bitch," Odd Willie says. "I swear, Soldier, if we ever fucking see daylight again, I'm gonna kill her with my goddamn bare hands."

"You're gonna have to get in line behind me," Soldier tells him. "Now, keep your voice down. I'm trying to hear something."

"What? What the hell are you trying to hear?"

"Anything," Soldier replies, "anything but you."

The dark is playing tricks with her eyes, painting sudden movements from the stillness, faking her out, and she ignores it and listens. The darkness is filled with sound—her heartbeat, hers and Willie's breathing, dripping water, a persistent, industrious gnawing that she knows is a rat wearing down its incisors against a piece of bone, and, occasionally, a distant splash. A low murmur that might be voices sifted through the cold and the black, and she leans close to Odd Willie and whispers in his ear.

"I don't think we're under the cemetery anymore," she says. "I think we might be beneath the river."

"Who gives a good goddamn?" Odd Willie says, and then he giggles, and then he moans very loudly.

Soldier lays the femur on the ground at her feet, and then she seizes Odd Willie by the jaw and forces his head around until she's pretty sure he's facing her. He makes a surprised, pissed-off noise, tries to jerk away, and she digs her nails into his face. With her left hand she grabs his testicles.

"What the fuck's your fucking problem?" he mumbles around her fingers.

"Right now, *you're* my problem, Odd Willie. We're in some pretty serious shit here, but we're *not* dead, not yet, and I don't intend to end up that way. Do you understand what I'm saying to you?"

"Jesus fucking *Christ*." Odd Willie grunts, and when he tries to pull free again, she digs her nails deep into the soft, hairy flesh around his scrotum.

"I *said*, do you *understand*?"

"Yeah bitch, I fucking understand," he growls back at her, growling like a wounded puppy. "I understand you're as big a psycho as that cunt Saben."

"Be that as it fucking may, Odd Willie, you're gonna keep your mouth shut, and if we're real goddamn lucky, we might still find a way out of this mess."

"Fine. Whatever you say. Now please just let go of my fucking balls, okay?"

"I *know* you're hurt," she tells him, slowly relaxing her hold on his face and his crotch. "And I know you're scared shitless, because I am, too. But we have to get out of here. We have to find a way out if we want to be sure that Saben gets what she's got coming to her."

"Fine," he says again, and when she lets go, Soldier feels him pull away, pressing himself against the damp stone wall of the tunnel.

"Something's gone wrong, Willie, something the Bailiff didn't see coming, something he couldn't anticipate."

"Fuck that," Odd Willie mutters and giggles very softly. "I think he sent us up here to fucking die. I think this is payback for lots of shit, Soldier. Cocksucker's probably in with Ballou, Saben, the whole stinking lot."

"It doesn't make sense," Soldier says, picking up the femur again. "I've been thinking the same thing, turning it over and over in my head, but it just doesn't add up."

"You fucking grab my balls again," Odd Willie mumbles, "I swear I'm gonna kill you."

"Yeah, whatever," Soldier tells him. "You better start thinking a little less about killing and a little more about keeping your own sorry ass alive and kicking. Remember your place—"

"Fuck that, too. Down here, ain't no *places* anymore, Soldier. Ain't no rank. No fucking *order*. Down here—"

"I'm gonna stand up," Soldier says, and she takes a deep breath, even though it hurts like hell. "Can you get up, Odd Willie? Can you walk?"

"I can fucking walk," he replies. "Christ, I'm freezing my ass off."

Soldier nods and listens to the suffocating darkness and the muffled, magnified tunnel noises, trying to fix a direction on what *might* have been voices, human voices or hound voices or something in between. They seemed to be coming from somewhere far away on her right, so she decides to try to keep to the left for as long as possible. Then Odd Willie vomits again, and she feels it spatter hot across her feet. Soldier waits until he's done, tells him to stay close to the wall, to keep his left hand on the wall and stay right there behind her, and she stands up. Both her knees pop, and she's suddenly so dizzy that she starts to sit back down.

"Just don't you leave me," Odd Willie says. "Whatever happens, don't you dare fucking leave me down here alone."

"I won't. I'm not going to leave you," she promises, though she knows that she will, if that's what it takes to make it out, if Odd Willie can't keep up. Soldier rests her weight against the tunnel wall until the dizziness isn't so bad.

"I'd rather you fucking killed me than leave me down here by myself, Soldier."

"Just stay close. Keep the wall on your left."

Beneath her feet the floor is an obstacle course of uneven, muddy cobblestones and puddles of icy water, and she almost slips twice. When she's gone forty, maybe forty-five yards, Soldier stops and lets Odd Willie catch up to her. She can hear the voices again, louder than before, though still not loud enough to make out whatever it is they're saying. But at least now she's certain that they're somewhere on her right, even if she can't begin to guess how close they might be. She's not even sure how wide or how high this tunnel is; she grips the broken thighbone and takes another step forward.

"You smell that?" Odd Willie asks, and Soldier stops and sniffs at the damp air.

"I smell mud," she says. "Mud and mold, and that's about it. What do you smell, Odd Willie?"

"Smoke. I smell fucking smoke. *Wood*smoke. Man, I wish I had a cigarette."

Soldier sniffs at the air again, and this time she catches the faintest whiff of burning, and she also realizes that it's not as stagnant as before. There's a draft here as the air's pulled weakly past them, back towards the ossuary or some side tunnel that they've missed.

"We get out of this shit with our skins, I'll buy you a whole goddamn carton," she tells Odd Willie, and she can hear the clumsy slap of his footsteps, so she knows that he's still following her. "I suppose you were never very good with all the hocus-pocus crap, either," she says.

"I can do a few things," he replies, wheezing a little now, and Soldier wonders if maybe the goons punctured one of his lungs.

"Yeah? Like *what*, precisely?"

"I'm no damn magician," Odd Willie says, "so don't go getting a hard-on or anything. But I learned a little here and there."

Up ahead there's a sudden loud, clattering commotion, like someone dropping a burlap sack filled with bones, and Soldier stops and lies almost flat on the tunnel floor, instinctively making as small a target of herself as possible; she holds the broken femur under her, gripped close to her chest. She can't hear Odd Willie's big flat feet anymore, so she assumes that he's done the same. There are smaller clatterings, then a whisking sound like a straw broom on wood, and she holds her breath and waits for silence or whatever's coming instead of silence.

Ballou's a maniac, the Bailiff said the night before they left Providence, early Sunday morning, and she was naked then, too. *He's a spoiled child fascinated with the smell of his own offal. But he's also a threat, Soldier, a threat that never should have been permitted to become anything* more *than a nuisance.*

You're telling me to kill him? Soldier asked, and the Bailiff smiled and rubbed at his nose.

Nothing too fancy, he said. *Try not to make a mess.*

Just the two of us? Just me and Odd fucking Willie?

The Bailiff stopped rubbing his nose, which seemed redder than usual, and nodded. *We have people up there. There won't be much resistance. We've been softening him from the inside. Trust me, little Soldier. You and young Master Lothrop will be quite sufficient to the task at hand. Nothing too showy, though.*

The sweeping sound has stopped, and Soldier exhales slowly, her breath escaping almost silently between her teeth. But she doesn't move, lies dead still on the uneven cobbles and mud and listens to the darkness.

Nothing more than is necessary.

And it's just gonna be me and Odd Willie against the whole damn warren? she asked him again. *Odd Willie Lothrop the firebug, the guy with no eyebrows?*

The Bailiff sneezed, then took out a white handkerchief and blew his red nose. *I shall expect you back by Sunday evening,* he said, *seven thirty at the latest,* and returned the handkerchief to the breast pocket of his jacket. *There will be a cleanup crew coming down from Boston sometime around midnight, and I want you out of there long before then.*

So, where the hell are they? she thinks, because it's surely long past midnight on Sunday. It might be past midnight on fucking Monday, for all she knows, and Soldier swears on the names of gods she doesn't believe in that she'd trade another half hour as George Ballou's punching bag for just one shot of Dickel. Just one shot of whiskey to make her hands stop shaking.

"It's *gone,*" Odd Willie whispers, and she can hear him getting slowly to his feet. "Whatever it was, it's gone."

Soldier waits another two or three seconds, then rolls over onto her back; a sharp corner of one of the cobblestones digs into a bruised spot beneath her left shoulder blade, bruised muscle and maybe something in there's fractured, as well, and she has to bite the end of her tongue to keep from crying out. The dizziness returns, and she lies still, waiting for it to pass.

"Soldier?" Odd Willie asks, his voice suddenly lost and close to panic. "Can you hear me? *Soldier—*"

"*Yes,*" she hisses around the pain in her back. "I'm right fucking here. Keep it down. Jesus . . ."

"I thought you'd left me. I thought maybe you'd gotten away and left me."

"I just fucking *said* that I wasn't going to leave you," and she shuts her eyes and swallows against the pain and a wave of nausea.

She imagines the Bailiff, holed up somewhere with his boys and their drugs, waiting for whatever it is he's started to blow over, the calm *after* the storm. She pretends he can hear her thoughts, pretends he'd care if he could. *I'm not going to die here in the dark and the mud, you bastard. I'm not going to die down here with Odd Willie while that bitch Saben is still alive somewhere.*

"I can do this one thing," Odd Willie wheezes. "Magick, I mean. There's this one thing I'm really pretty good with, but it makes me sick as a goddamned poisoned dog. So it's kind of a fucking last resort."

"Willie," Soldier says, "we're naked and beat half to fucking death, lost in the dark, surrounded by people that want us dead, and the only weapon I have is part of a damn rotten bone. Unless you've got a couple of nine-millimeters tucked up your skinny ass, I'm thinking, yeah, maybe this is pretty goddamned last resort."

"Sure," he says, "I know. You think I don't know how fucked we are?" And then he doesn't say anything else, and there's only the sounds of the two of them breathing and the steady *plip, plip, plip* of water striking water.

"Well, is it a fucking *secret*?" she asks finally, and she can hear Willie sitting back down again.

"No, it's not a secret," he says. "I just don't like to do it, that's all. So, you know, usually I don't let on."

Soldier opens her eyes, not that it makes any difference, and she sits up, raising herself with her arms and trying to ignore the pain from the bruised shoulder and just about everywhere else. The burning-wood smell's getting stronger, she thinks, either that or she's only noticing it more because now she knows it's there.

"Don't make me ask again," she says and glares at the place she thinks Odd Willie is sitting. "Spit it out."

"There's this . . . this fucking *thing*, right, this thing I can call up, summon, conjure, whatever the hell you want to call it. This *thing*."

"What kind of a thing?"

"Fuck all if I know. Maybe it's a demon, but I kind of doubt it. What kind of demon would take orders from me? Maybe it's a ghost, the ghost of something—"

"What does it *do*?" Soldier asks him, grasping at straws because they're all she has left to grasp, and Odd Willie giggles.

"Just the usual shit," he wheezes, coughs, then starts again. "Roll over. Fetch. Play fucking dead. Steal some beer. Kill a bunch of motherfuckers, if that's what I *tell* it to do."

"Fuck." Soldier laughs, wiping some of the mud off her belly and thighs. "Christ, and you were gonna get around to telling me about this little pet of yours *when*?"

"You don't know how it feels," Odd Willie says. "I've told the Bailiff. It's not a secret."

"Does it feel a whole lot worse than Ballou's dick up your ass? Or a bullet through your fucking skull? Does it feel worse than dying?"

"Yeah," Odd Willie says and coughs again. "Yeah, Soldier, I think maybe it does."

The janitors have been given the strictest instructions in this matter, the Bailiff said. *And they're very thorough agents. Nothing alive gets out. Nothing, Soldier. Not even a sewer rat. So, no stragglers, if you catch my drift. Get in, do what I've asked, and then get out. Do not expect help should anything happen to go awry.*

The hounds don't even know about this, do they? she asked him, playing a hunch, a queasy feeling in her stomach, and he raised his eyebrows and patted the pocket where he'd put the soiled handkerchief.

You're not a child any longer, he told her. *You're quite old enough, I suspect, to know something of the way of things. To be trusted, even, I suppose.*

They don't know, she said.

The Bailiff sat up straighter and tugged vigorously at his knotted beard. *I manage the affairs of those who manage the affairs of the hounds,* he said. *And the hounds don't want to know when there are problems. Most of the time it is sufficient that the problems are solved. The hounds don't want to know any more than they have to know. To their way of thinking, they have more pressing matters to attend.*

"I asked Madam Terpsichore to tell me what it is," Odd Willie says, "way the hell back when I was just a kid. I asked her twice to tell me. She said I was better off not knowing. She said I'd sleep better that way."

"But it *will* come?" Soldier asks. "If you *call* it, it'll come? And you can control it?"

"Yeah. I mean, you know, it always has before. But it's gonna make me sick as shit, Soldier. I might need your help after the—"

"Just fucking *do* it," she says, daring to raise her voice just enough to get Odd Willie moving. "Say the goddamn magick word or whatever. Do it now, before they come back for us. I already told you I'm not going to leave you down here."

"Yeah, you did," Odd Willie replies, and he sounds tired and ill and frightened. "You told me that. Good thing you're better at killing than you are at lying, Soldier, or the Bailiff would have run out of uses for you a long time ago."

"No shit," she says, slowly getting to her feet, leaning against the tunnel wall because she isn't sure how much longer her legs can support her. And then Odd Willie tries to clear his throat, coughs and suggests that she might want to cover her eyes and turn away until he says otherwise, and Soldier does as she's told.

"You're not a child any longer," the Bailiff said, when the trapdoor had been pulled down to reveal a rickety ladder leading up into the dark attic of the yellow house. The upper end of the ladder was attached somewhere overhead, and it had unfolded as the Bailiff had opened the trapdoor, seeming to Soldier almost like some small bit of magic. "We do not show children our secrets," he said, "as they cannot yet be trusted with the keeping of them."

"You can trust me," Soldier said, and she'd almost forgotten about the dream and the black woman with the long white dreadlocks, the warning that she shouldn't ever enter the attic. "I'm very good at keeping secrets."

"As well I know," the Bailiff said. "Elsewise, you would not be here today. You first, my dear," and he motioned towards the ladder.

"What *is* it?" she asked him, peering up into the gloom. The warm air drifting down from the attic smelled like cobwebs and dust, neglect and brittle, old paper, all familiar, welcoming smells, smells that Soldier had always known. But there was something else there beneath it all, something spicy and sour that made her wrinkle her nose. "What do they keep hidden up there?"

"You have merely to climb those nine rungs to find out for yourself."

"And you're coming up after me," she said.

"Of course I am," the Bailiff replied, and he smiled reassuringly and gave her an encouraging pat on the back. "As far as I can follow."

Soldier said a short, silent prayer to Mother Hydra, and then she climbed the ladder, though it seemed like many more rungs than nine. She started counting halfway up, and when she'd finally reached the top, she'd counted all the way to twenty-four.

"Go on," the Bailiff shouted up at her. "I can't start up until you're inside. This ladder's seen better days and won't hold us both at once."

So Soldier scrambled over the last rung and stood inside the attic at the edge of the trapdoor, gazing back down at the Bailiff and the floor of the upstairs hallway, a rectangle of light cut into the darkness.

"What do you see up there, Soldier girl?" the Bailiff asked, and she laughed and told him he'd have to come up and find out for himself, just the same as her. The Bailiff started up the ladder, the old wood complaining at the burden of him, and Soldier looked up, squinting into the colorless half-light of the attic. She could make out a few old packing crates and a steamer trunk, stacks of newspapers bundled with twine, and there was the sense that the attic was a very large place, perhaps even somehow larger than the house below, stretching away from her on all sides. But there were no ghosts, at least, not that she could see, and Soldier decided that whatever was in the attic probably wasn't all that interesting, after all. She looked down again, to tell the Bailiff to hurry, and saw that he was no longer coming up the ladder; the Bailiff was raising the trapdoor again, shutting her in. The rusty hinges squealed and screamed, and Soldier opened her mouth, because it seemed that she should scream, too. But there was no scream anywhere inside her, only the fruitless knowledge that there probably should have been, that some *other* child would have screamed at the thought of being closed up in the attic alone.

"Why?" she asked him, and the Bailiff paused and glanced up at her. He winked once, and, "All is mystery, wonderful mystery," he said, "and life is the revelation." And then he finished closing the trapdoor.

Soldier sat down on the dusty floorboards, waiting for her eyes to adjust so she could walk without tripping over some piece of junk and breaking her neck.

"Then I'm alone," she said, and a small voice—the voice of another girl, but someone who sounded quite a bit older than Soldier—answered her.

"No," the older girl said, "you're not alone, but you should have brought a lantern. They always bring lanterns when they come. It was silly of you to have forgotten."

"I suppose so," Soldier said, and then the brown girl stood up from the milking stool where she'd been sitting, unnoticed, waiting for whoever would come next, her father's gold pocket watch lying open on her lap, the hands frozen at precisely nine twenty-three and thirteen seconds.

"Are you a ghost?" Soldier asked her.

The brown girl, the Daughter of the Four of Pentacles, looked surprised or offended or both at once. "No," she said. "Certainly not. Are you?"

"Not yet," Soldier replied, and the girl took her hand and led her away into the murky depths of the attic.

The crackling, thrumming thing that Odd Willie has called up or down or simply *into* this world brings light with it, a soft, warm yellow-white light, like morning or butter, that pulses and ripples lazily along the tunnel. Soldier stands with her back to it and stares, transfixed by the miracle of her own shadow, her silhouette an eclipse thrown across rough-hewn rock walls and the paving stones and the sagging timbers barely holding up the low ceiling. She never truly expected to live long enough to see light again, and now she only wants to lie down and let it wash over her bruised, bleeding body, washing away the cold and the pain, the fear and dread knotted deep in her gut. She wants to turn around and let this light stream across her face and fill her eyes, fill her soul, if she has such a thing; she would gladly drown in this light, if it would ever have such a wretched creature as herself.

"Oh," Odd Willie moans. "Oh, Jesus . . ."

"What next?" she asks, because it's the only thing she can think to say to him, her mind clouded by the light and electric crackle. "What next, Odd Willie?"

"Oh," he says again, and then he begins coughing and the light flickers and dims, and for a moment Soldier's afraid he's going to let it slip away. But the coughing passes, and immediately the light grows brighter.

"Can you talk to it?" she asks him.

"You . . . you can turn around now if you want to," he tells her and makes an ugly hacking noise.

Do I? Soldier thinks. *Do I really want to see it? Do I really want to face all that light?*

You've seen a whole lot worse, Soldier girl, and, more than likely, you'll see a lot worse again.

"She won't bite," Odd Willie wheezes, "not unless I ask her to."

Soldier turns her head, and there's Odd Willie on his knees, pale as a corpse and a dark smear of blood and vomit down his chin, his throat, his chest. His eyes are shut, and he looks dead already.

"She doesn't like it here," he says. "That's going to make her hard to hold."

The thing reminds Soldier of a jellyfish, and then it reminds her of something else entirely, and she gives up trying to comprehend it. Her eyes water and burn when she looks directly at it, so she keeps them on Odd Willie instead.

"Tell her to get us the fuck out of here," Soldier says. "The faster she does that, the sooner—"

"She's *afraid.* Shit, Soldier. I've never seen her afraid before."

"Come on, Willie. What happens next? Show me what this bitch can do for us."

The crackling dynamo hum gets louder and rises an octave or two, and now the heat from the light is becoming uncomfortable. "She's scared," Odd Willie says. "She's asking me to release her."

"*No,*" Soldier yells at him, having to shout to be heard above all the noise the thing is making. "That's *not* going to fucking happen; you hear me? Not until we're out of here."

"She says it's Monday morning already. Six fifteen on Monday morning. Soldier, we've been down here—"

"It doesn't *matter* how long we've been down here," Soldier says, and never mind what the Bailiff said about the cleanup crew from Boston, whether they've come and gone, whether they ever even showed up, whether Ballou got them, too. "It only matters that we get out of here *now*."

"She also says Patience Bacon was right."

"Fuck Patience Bacon. We're not going to die in this stinking sump hole because your astral playmate here has the fucking heebie-jeebies."

Odd Willie takes a deep, hitching breath, and his eyelids flutter. "I'm sorry. Just do it," he tells the thing. "Just do it fast. I won't ever ask you for anything else, not ever again." His eyes roll back to show the whites, and the thing that isn't a jellyfish bobs and sways and begins making a sickly, mewling sort of racket.

There's a trickle of blood from Odd Willie's nostrils, and Soldier turns away again.

"Just kill them," Odd Willie mutters. "Kill them all. Every last goddamn one of them."

And then the thing is gone, a furious stream of fire rolling away down the tunnel, leaving behind steam and a sticky phosphorescent sheen on the floor and walls; at least they won't be in the dark again. The crackling sound is gone, too, but the air smells like ozone and hot metal.

"Can you walk?" Soldier asks Odd Willie, and his eyelids flutter again, and he sways a little, first to one side and then the other. "*Hey*, come on. Can you fucking hear me? I need to know if you can walk."

Odd Willie opens his eyes and stares up at her, but his expression is blank, distant, almost empty, and Soldier resists the urge to slap him hard. She wants to, but it might break whatever tenuous connection he has with the thing. And the way he looks, it might break him, as well.

"I'm gonna help you up, okay?" she says and stoops down, getting her right arm around him, and Soldier drops the broken femur and lifts Odd Willie Lothrop slowly to his feet. He's heavier than she expected, or she's weaker, and it doesn't help that they're both so slick with sweat and blood and the filth from the ossuary and the tunnel. She's afraid he's going to slide free of her grip. "I wouldn't mind if you helped out a little," she grunts and tries not to lose her balance.

"We should probably follow her," Odd Willie mumbles.

"That's sort of what I had in mind."

"She has a name," he says. "I can't fucking say it, not in words, right, but she has a beautiful name. She was born in the heart of a dying star. She's made of fire, hydrogen, helium, plasma, you know."

"Then George Ballou and his spaniels ought to be a stroll in the fucking park, yeah?"

"She even knows what killed the dinosaurs. I can't *tell* you, but she fucking knows, I swear."

Soldier shifts her weight, getting a better hold on Odd Willie, and she thinks maybe he's starting to support himself a little. But when she takes a step forward, he stumbles and almost pulls them both down.

"I can't carry you out of here. You're going to have to fucking walk."

"You said you wouldn't leave me," he moans and looks down at his feet. "You *promised*."

"But I'm a shitty liar, remember? That's what you said. Now, just fucking walk. That's *all* you got to do." And Odd Willie nods his head, the slow, measured nod of reluctant comprehension, and takes a step on his own, and then another, and another after that. Soldier's still holding him up, but at least she isn't having to try and drag him along an inch at a time.

"Hey, Willie, it ain't no goddamn foot race. Slow the fuck down," she says, and he coughs when he tries to laugh, and more blood leaks from the corners of his mouth.

"No way. You best keep up, bitch," he wheezes.

Good thing you're better at killing than you are at lying, or the Bailiff would have run out of uses for you a long time ago. And Soldier tries not to think about having to leave Odd Willie to die alone in the tunnel. *I wouldn't have done that,* she thinks. *I'm not that big an asshole. I'd take care of him myself before I'd leave him alive down here alone.*

"She knows what killed the dinosaurs," he says again. "Hell, she knows what happened to Atlantis. She saw it all. She's seen everything."

"Right now, you just keep moving," Soldier tells him. "You can tell me all about it later, when this shit's over and done with." She glances back at the discarded femur, lying behind them on the cobbles, and wonders if dropping it there was a mistake, if maybe she'll still need it later on. And then Odd Willie's body shudders, and he stops, and his eyelids begin to flutter again.

"Shit on me," he says, and his bladder lets go, spattering the tunnel floor and her feet and legs with hot urine. "She's found them, Soldier. I think she's found them all."

Soldier followed the Daughter of the Four of Pentacles through the attic of the yellow house, beneath great crossbeams carved from pines felled almost two hundred and fifty years before, past sagging shelves crammed with books and manuscripts and scrolls sealed in-

side baked clay tubes, past broken furniture and dozens more packing crates, an empty iron cage big enough to hold a lion, a bronze
bust of Triton balanced on a stone pedestal. *Perhaps,* she thought,
*this is the memory of the house. Perhaps this is where it keeps every-
thing that the rest of the house has forgotten or wants to forget.* She
knew some places were like that. Cemeteries were always like that.

"You knew I was coming?" she asked the girl, who shrugged and
paused to blow some of the dust off an elaborate wooden Noah's
ark laid out on the floor. The ark was at least ten feet long, and there
were hundreds of animals, two by two, carved with an exquisite attention to detail. Soldier stooped for a better look, and the older girl
sat down on the floor next to her.

"They told me. They always tell me when someone's coming up.
Of course, you're different. Usually they're only bringing me gifts,
candy or fruit or a length of red silk ribbon. But you're different."

"This has something to do with my dreams, doesn't it?" Soldier
asked her, but the girl didn't reply. She smiled and carefully wiped a
spiderweb off the shingled roof of the ark. Soldier sighed and glanced
back the way they'd come. She was thirsty and wondered how long
they'd been walking, how far they'd gone. *This must be the biggest
attic in the world,* she thought and then tried to remember a word
she'd learned from the Bailiff or one of the ghouls (she couldn't recall
which), a word for things that are larger on the inside than on the
outside.

"This was a gift," the girl said and pointed at the wooden Noah's
ark.

"Is it yours? Was it a gift to you?" Soldier asked.

"No, I don't think so. I'm just taking care of it. I take care of
almost everything up here."

Soldier leaned closer to the ark, trying to see all the animals more
clearly, the brightly painted menagerie filing across the floor and up a
long gangplank into the ship. She wished that there were more light.

But she could make out two elephants and two giraffes, a pair of hippopotamuses and a pair of moose, ostriches and alligators, horses and a couple of enormous brontosaurs, unicorns and leopards and bison.

"It was made in Italy," the Daughter of the Four of Pentacles said. "There's a signature on the bottom of the ark, and a date—Signior Anastagio Baldassario Moratti, 1888. All of the animals were made in Italy, too."

"They sent me up here just to see a damned toy?" Soldier asked.

"But it's not a toy," the girl said, righting a camel that had fallen over. "It's something else. It's sort of a metaphor, I think."

"What's your name?" Soldier asked the brown-skinned girl. She was growing bored with the Noah's ark and stood up, brushing the dust off her clothes.

"My name is Pearl," the girl said.

"You're the alchemist's daughter, aren't you? The Daughter of the Four of Pentacles?"

"Yes," replied the girl.

"They told me your name was Hester. Everyone down there thinks your name is Hester."

"People often believe silly, mistaken things," the girl said and shook her head. "Did you know that people used to believe that eating tomatoes would kill you, and that the whole Earth was created in only six days?"

"They said that your name was Hester. That's what they all seem to believe, down there."

"We should keep moving," the girl said. "It's never a good idea to tarry here very long. And we've still got a ways to go."

"A ways to go *where*?"

"Don't be impatient. You'll see," the girl said. "I want it to be a surprise. I never get to surprise anyone anymore. Not since my father went away and all the clocks stopped and—"

"There's no one up here but you?" Soldier asked, not particularly interested in surprises.

"Oh, there are very many people up here," Pearl replied—unless Soldier were to believe everyone downstairs and in the warrens, in which case Hester replied. "I'm not alone. I have company. All the people and things and places caught inside the constructions that my father fashioned. No, I'm not alone, Soldier, not at all. But it's all very complicated, I'm afraid. You're much too young to understand such complex metaphysical—"

"You're not that much older than me," Soldier said, interrupting her.

"I most certainly am," the girl said and then stared at her a moment, taken aback. "Soldier, I'm twelve years old, and you, well, you're still not much more than a baby, are you?"

"If I were only a baby, they never would have sent me up here to see you," Soldier said, angry that the girl would say such a thing, and besides, hadn't the Bailiff just told her that she *wasn't* a baby anymore, and that's why he could trust her with secrets?

"They've sent me babies before."

"Liar," Soldier said and then she kicked the Noah's ark as hard as she could, and animals fell over and flew through the air and tumbled about this way and that. The great boat swung to starboard and capsized, then rolled away into the shadows, leaving most of the animals behind.

"What did you do *that* for?" the Daughter of the Four of Pentacles gasped, and when Soldier didn't answer her, the girl just stood staring at her, and there were tears welling up at the corners of her eyes.

"What? Are you going to cry now?" Soldier asked her, and prodded a fallen zebra with the toe of her shoe. She thought about grinding it under her heel until it was only sawdust. "Are you going to cry like a great big twelve-year-old baby?"

"*No,*" the girl replied. "I'm most certainly not going to do anything of the sort," and she bent down and began setting all the animals upright again. "But that was a horrible, horrible thing to do. I've never shown this to anyone before. You were the very first."

Soldier watched while Hester (or Pearl) righted all the animals and then retrieved the ark from where it had rolled. There was a small bashed-in place on the left side near the prow.

"Guess Noah's going to have to fix that before the flood," she said, but the dark-skinned girl ignored her. "It's just an old toy," Soldier told her. "No one cares about all this junk up here. I bet no one even remembers most of it anymore. It's a wonder, really, they haven't forgotten *you.*"

"Follow me," the girl said coldly, when she was finished with the ark, when she'd undone as much of the damage as she could, and she led Soldier deeper and deeper into the attic of the yellow house. After a while they came to a gaping hole in the floor. There was a board laid over it for a bridge, and Pearl crossed it without comment. But Soldier lingered alone at the edge, looking down into the inexplicable cavity. There was nothing in that hole and no bottom to it; as far as she could see, it went on forever.

"Why can't I see anything down there?" she asked, shouting across the gap. "If that's a hole in the ceiling, I should be able to see the upstairs."

"Maybe it's not a hole in the floor," the girl replied. "Maybe it's a hole in something else. Now come on. I'm tired of standing here waiting for you. There are *other* things I could be doing."

Soldier reached into the pocket of her dress and pulled out one of the wooden animals from the Noah's ark, a wildebeest she'd picked up while the alchemist's daughter was busy with the mess she'd made.

"*Hey!*" the girl shouted from the far side of the gap. "What are you *doing* with that? That's not yours—"

"It's not yours, either," Soldier replied. "You told me so yourself."

"No, but it's my responsibility. We have to put it *back,* right now."

"Oops," Soldier said, letting go of the tempera-brown wildebeest. It fell into the hole and vanished.

"You beastly little *brat!*" the girl shouted at her, but Soldier wasn't listening; she'd sat down at the edge of the hole and was waiting for the sound the wooden wildebeest would make when it hit bottom. But there *was* no sound, unless she'd missed it somehow, unless all the noise the alchemist's daughter was making had covered it up. She waited awhile longer, what she figured must have been five minutes, at least, ignoring the brown-skinned girl, who was still shouting at her and stomping back and forth on the other side of the gap.

"I didn't hear it," Soldier said finally, when it had become clear that the hole went down much farther than she'd guessed. "But you were making such a commotion, it's no wonder."

"Cross the bridge, changeling," the girl said, standing there with her hands on her hips, glowering at Soldier from the other side. "Unless, that is, you're afraid that you'll fall. You might, you know. It's not a very wide board, and it isn't very sturdy, and you might end up like that poor animal, falling forever, wondering if you'll ever find the bottom."

"You don't scare me. It's just a hole."

"Yes, that's all it is. A hole. Now come across it."

Soldier set one foot on the board, because that's all it was, a hole, and all holes had bottoms somewhere.

"Don't look down," Pearl said and took a step back from the edge. "That will only make it harder. I'd hate to have to explain this to the Bailiff or Miss Josephine, if you should fall or the board should break and—"

"Stop talking," Soldier said, and she took another step, the board bowing almost imperceptibly beneath her. "How old are you?" she asked the brown-skinned girl again.

"I told you already. I'm twelve. In fact, I'm almost thirteen."

"Everyone down there says you've been up here a very long time. Twelve's not a very long time." And she took another step.

"It's a temporal contrariety," the girl replied. "That's what my father called it. Time's not the same up here. It's a part of his punishment."

Soldier took another step, keeping her eyes straight ahead, keeping her eyes on Pearl; she was almost a third of the way across now. "Because he betrayed the ghouls," she said. "Because he lied to them."

"It's all very complicated."

"Madam Terpsichore said that he was a villain, and that he has been chained in the deepest abyss for his crimes. She said that his daughter is a ghost, and that his wife was killed for his misdeeds."

"My mother died of a fever," Pearl said, and Soldier took another step.

"Did you *see* her die?"

"I was very young," the Daughter of the Four of Pentacles said, speaking now through clenched teeth. "My mother was a Montauk Indian princess that my father brought to Providence all the way from Long Island. She was a beautiful woman and—"

"Did you see what they *did* to her?" Soldier asked, and the board popped loudly beneath her, and she almost lost her balance. She glanced down, trying to see the board and her feet, but *not* the hole. She was halfway across now.

"It was consumption," Pearl said—Pearl, Hester, the brown girl, the alchemist's daughter, the ghostly Daughter of the Four of Pentacles whom Soldier had been taught lived off rats and spiders and devoured anyone who dared wander into her attic.

"Did they wait until she was dead before they ate her?" Soldier asked, and the girl shook her head and stared at the floor. "Did they let you have a taste?"

"You're horrid. You're a monster," she said, and Soldier figured she was probably right, but then maybe the brown girl was only a different kind of monster.

"What year did they take your father away?"

"Why won't you stop? Why won't you leave me alone?"

"Don't you even *remember*?"

The Daughter of the Four of Pentacles walked back to the edge of the bottomless hole and placed her foot firmly on the end of the board. She leaned forward suddenly, and the board bounced a little, and Soldier had to hold her arms out like a trapeze artist to keep from falling off.

"Don't *do* that," Soldier yelped. "Are you crazy?"

"August twelfth, 1929," the girl said, and then she made the board bounce again. "They took him away on August twelfth, 1929. It was a Monday night. It was raining."

Soldier pinwheeled her arms once, twice, then stood very still until she was sure she wasn't going to fall. She was good with numbers. Madam Mnemosyne said she was "quite precocious at arithmetic," and it took her only a moment to figure out that the brown girl had been shut away in the attic of the yellow house for more than seventy-eight years.

"You're an old woman," Soldier said. "You might look like you're only twelve, but you're really an old woman."

"I'm *not* an old woman," Pearl replied. "I'm not an old woman, because there's no time up here anymore, except when the attic door's open. The clocks only tick when the attic door's open. It's a temporal contrariety, and I'm not even thirteen years old yet." And then she bounced the board a third time, and Soldier had to squat down to keep from falling off.

"It would be very easy to make me fall, *Hester,* if that's really what you want. All you'd have to do is kick that end of the board over the edge."

"That's not why they sent you up here. The Bailiff said that—"

"Then stop jumping on the goddamn board," Soldier shouted as loud as she dared, even the effort of shouting enough to make her wobble and bob, and she *knew* the wildebeest would be falling forever. She was barely more than halfway across, and if she slipped, she'd still be tumbling after it, head over heels, ass over tits, when the universe had burned itself down to a frozen cinder. Her voice echoed through the ancient timbers, off the distant walls of the cavernous attic, and the Daughter of the Four of Pentacles cursed her, cursed all the changelings and the *ghul*. And then she turned and ran, vanishing in an instant into the gloom, as though the attic shadows were her *true* parents, and they would always be there to keep her safe.

In the tunnel beneath Woonsocket, Soldier marks time in footsteps, in Odd Willie's ragged, wheezing breaths, in her own heartbeats. She doesn't know how long they've been following the passageway, not in minutes and seconds, but it's been longer than she expected it would be. Odd Willie is muttering and snickering to himself, and the smell of smoke has grown very strong. It stings her sinuses and makes her eyes water, and it's no longer only the scent of woodsmoke; Soldier knows the smell of roasting human flesh, and the air inside the tunnel reeks of it.

"Yippee damn," Odd Willie croaks. "We're going to a goddamn barbecue."

"How about you shut up and concentrate on walking," Soldier tells him, and just then Odd Willie slips on a bit of the glowing slime and almost falls, almost pulls her down with him. "And watch your fucking step, please."

"Miss Soldier here, she don't *like* her no barbecue." Odd Willie snickers. "This lady takes it raw, or she takes it not at all."

And Soldier's about to ask him how much farther until they catch up with the familiar, if the thing can tell him that, when the main tunnel makes a sharp turn to the right and the incline grows suddenly much steeper. There are stairs cut deep into the stone here, slick and worn down the middle from centuries of use.

"I *think* she went thataway," Odd Willie says and points at the stairs, but that much is plain to see from the phosphorescent goo streaking the walls. And then he slides easily from Soldier's grip and sits down hard on the bottommost step, his long legs splayed out in front of him. "I can't climb those things, Soldier. Not for all the pussy in China could I climb those goddamn things."

"Well, I'm not carrying you."

"Then you'll just have to go on without me, Sarge," he says, and Odd Willie Lothrop hacks out a feeble laugh and wipes fresh blood from his lips. "Tell Laura I love her. Give my regards to fucking Broadway. Tell me dear old mum she was the last thought on me mind. But ain't no way I'm climbing those fuckers."

"It's right up there, isn't it? *He's* right up there, Ballou?"

"And don't you just fucking *hate* the irony," Odd Willie says, and coughs and wipes his mouth again.

"You should stop talking so much, Odd Willie. You're wasting your strength."

"And just what exactly, my lady sweet, am I supposed to be saving it up for? Are you perhaps hoping for one last go at the ol' arbor vitae here before the bitter end?" and Odd Willie waggles his limp penis at her. "One final ride on the ham bone of love before abandoning poor Willie Lothrop to his cruel, cruel fucking fate?"

"You're a sick fucking fuck," she says and shakes her head, and Soldier wants more than anything to sit down next to him and shut her eyes for maybe five or ten minutes, just long enough to catch her breath. But she's pretty sure if she does that, she'll never get back on her feet and moving again. So, she glances past Odd Willie instead, gazing up the long, uneven stairwell at the place where it ends two or three hundred feet farther on in a bright smudge of restless firelight.

"But we're so goddamn close. It's right up *there*," Soldier says and realizes that the draft she felt outside the ossuary earlier has changed direction, and now the hungry fire in front of them is drawing the air back towards it. "It's not fucking fair."

"Don't you go getting soft on me. Not this late in the game. I still can't climb those stairs."

"I promised not to leave you," she says, then pauses to swallow, her throat dry and sore and scratchy from the smoke and everything else. "I promised I wouldn't leave you alone down here . . . not alive."

Odd Willie stops playing with himself, spits, and lies back against the stone steps. "And that was truly very noble of you, my captain. So don't you think I'm not grateful. But I'm afraid you're gonna have to renege on that promise. You kill me, Sparky up there goes bye-bye, and she might not be done with Big Daddy Ballou."

"I'm sorry," Soldier says, ashamed that she feels relief at not having to kill Odd Willie, ashamed and confused. "I'll come back for you if I can. I swear, if there's any way."

"Yeah. And maybe I'll try crawling up those stairs, just as soon as I've found my second wind. Hope springs fucking eternal, right? Now, get the hell out of here, before I change my mind and make you do something unpleasant."

And so she leaves him there and climbs the stairs as quickly as she can. With every few steps, the light at the top of the stairs grows brighter, and it's getting hot, despite the cool, dank air being drawn up from the tunnels below. She doesn't look back, because there isn't any point, no matter how ashamed she might feel. No matter how fucked up things have gotten, and by the time Soldier reaches the brick and mortar landing at the top of the stairs, she has to shield her eyes from the light and can feel the heat of the flames beginning to sear her bare skin. There's a stone archway and then a great chamber spread out past the landing, what she takes to be a natural cavern uncovered during the ghouls' tunneling. There's thick black smoke, oily and choking, and steam, and a blistering curtain of heat that makes it hard to be sure what she's really seeing and what's only a mirage. The crumpled, blazing bodies of several of Ballou's changelings and mongrels lie near the landing. Soldier steps past them into the cavern, which seems to have been long used as a burial chamber, moldering bodies wrapped in winding sheets and skeletons tucked into hundreds of nooks in the walls, and now she's walking on stone that's hot enough to scald her feet if she stands still too long.

In the center of the cavern are the remains of a bonfire, a guttering mound of charred wood heaped seven or eight feet high, and a very tall, broad-shouldered man is standing directly in front of it. Glittering embers swirl around him, filling the air, and he raises his right hand so that Soldier can see what he's holding. It's a stoppered bottle, and even through the smoke and heat haze, she can see that there's something fiery trapped inside. His yellow eyes glimmer triumphantly, and he smiles.

"It was a damn good try," he says, shouting to be heard above the roar of the flames. "I've *always* said, an honest man gives credit wherever and whenever it's fucking due. Mr. Lothrop is to be commended. I lost some good men before I finally managed to get this beast under control. A goddamned *elemental*. I ask you, now, who'd have thought such a thing from a twerp like Willie Lothrop?"

Soldier looks around the chamber, and sees that there are others, crouched in the shadows or slinking in through the entrances to other tunnels, emerging through cracks in the walls. Some of them are human, some of them aren't, but most she couldn't say for sure.

"The Bailiff sent me here to kill you," she shouts back at George Ballou.

"Yes, I know. Miss White was very clear on that point. She insisted we should have killed you straight out. Why take chances, she said. Why fuck around? She's usually a cautious woman, but me, I do admit I like a little sport now and again."

"They sent me here to *kill* you," Soldier says again, and Ballou nods and sets the bottle holding Odd Willie's familiar down on the ground at his feet. The assembling crowd of changelings and half-breeds and ghouls begins to chatter and bark excitedly among themselves.

"Well then," says George Ballou, and he slips a very large hunting knife from a long scabbard on his belt; the blade flashes in the firelight. "Let's start the fucking dance, shall we?"

SEVEN

Star

It's a little warmer inside the old tunnel, if only because Emmie's finally out of the storm, out of the wind and snow. But the subterranean air is stale and stinks of neglect and the tiny, long-stemmed mushrooms growing from the old railroad ties. Their caps are neither red nor white, but not exactly pink, either, and Emmie figures she'd probably die if she were to eat one of them. The tunnel is flooded on either side of the tracks, but the brown girl has assured her the water isn't deep. The smooth cement walls rise up around them, converging overhead in a wide arch encrusted with icicles and stained with the soot of forgotten trains. Emmie can see because the brown girl is carrying some sort of fist-sized flashlight or lantern, something she pulled from a pocket of her dress shortly after they entered the darkness. Emmie thinks it looks more like a snow globe with a lightbulb sealed up inside than any sort of flashlight, but when she asked the girl what it was, she wouldn't say, only that it was one of her father's experiments, and she really shouldn't have brought it down from the attic. No one was ever supposed to touch her father's things, she said, not even her. The brown girl holds the light above their heads and walks toe to heel, balanced on one of the steel ties, and the yellow-white light rains down around them. Emmie stays off the rails, because they look slick with moisture and a fuzzy sheen of charcoal-colored mold; the thought of losing her footing and falling into the scummy black water makes her feel queasy. So, instead, she follows the girl by keeping to the half-submerged string of wooden pallets laid down over the railroad ties.

The only sounds are their footsteps and a steady dripping from somewhere nearby, but the tunnel makes the most of it, seizing every footfall and the irregular xylophone beat of water striking water, magnifying, reverberating, and, "I bet this is where the King of Echoes hid from the Queen of Silences," the brown girl says.

Emmie glances back over her left shoulder, but they're far enough inside now that she can no longer see the pale glow of the entrance.

"Where are we going?" she asks the girl. "How much farther is it?"

"Well, truth be told, I've never been down here," the brown girl confesses. "But I can't imagine it could be *very* much farther. Barnaby said to just keep walking the tracks westward, and we'd come to it, eventually."

"Who's Barnaby? And what are we looking for, anyway?"

"You really do ask an awful lot of questions, Emma Jean Silvey," the brown girl says, and the light in her hand bobs and sways when she almost loses her balance. The shadows on the walls bob and sway, too, and Emmie holds her breath for a moment until she's sure the girl isn't going to fall.

"Be *careful*! If you drop that thing, if it broke, we'd never find our way out of here in the dark."

"Oh, don't be so melodramatic. All we'd have to do is walk back out the same way we came in. We might misstep and get our feet wet, but I *know* the way back. So do you, Emma. And besides, if *this* broke," and she nods at the globe, "we wouldn't have to worry about finding our way back. We wouldn't live that long."

Emmie almost asks her what she meant by that, that they wouldn't live that long, but then decides she doesn't want to know.

"Barnaby's just a ghoul, that's all," the brown girl continues. "They aren't all completely terrible. Some of them are decent enough people. I helped him find something that he'd lost, and, in return, he helped me get out of the house to assist you and Soldier."

"Who's Soldier?" Emmie asks.

"You'll see," the brown girl replies. "We shouldn't get too far ahead of ourselves."

"I'm tired," Emmie says and stops walking. "I'm tired, and I'm sick of riddles, and I'm hungry, too."

"Barnaby said that there'd be a little food. He put it there himself. If the rats haven't found it."

"Deacon's probably looking for me by now," Emmie says, and peers over her shoulder again; there's nothing back there but the dark. "He's probably already called the police."

"You shouldn't worry about the police," the brown girl says. "They won't find us here. They likely couldn't if they tried. But they won't. Try, I mean."

"He'll think I'm lost. He'll think I'm freezing to death out in the snow." And Emmie imagines Deacon searching the big house for her, searching it twice over, top to bottom, then searching the front yard, the backyard, and finally looking up and down the length of Angell Street, banging his fists on doors, talking to people he doesn't know because maybe one of them saw her. She imagines him getting scared, shouting her name over and over until he's hoarse. Then he'd go back home and call the police. He'd call the hospitals. He might call Sadie; he'd think it was her fault.

"There it is," the brown girl says and points at something rising from the gloom and the water at the right side of the tracks.

Emmie stares at it a moment, trying to make sense of the strange, twisting angles and unexpected bulk of the thing. Her first impression is that she must be seeing the rusty red-brown carapace and jointed legs of some gigantic lobster or crab that's dragged itself up from the icy water, which must be much deeper than the brown girl said to ever hide such a thing as that. And now the monster is perched right there at the side of the railroad tracks, waiting to devour them both.

"I told you. I knew that Barnaby wouldn't lie to me," the brown girl says and smiles.

It's only a car, Emmie realizes. *Only a shitty old car that someone's dragged in here,* her mind slowly making sense of the snarl of rusted metal, slowly recognizing the familiar made unfamiliar by the dim light and years of corrosion. A stripped and burned-out wreck missing its roof, not a giant crustacean after all, not something with pinching claws and blazing eyes set on twitching stalks. Emmie's legs feel weak, and she imagines Deacon trying to tell the police what she looks like, what she might be wearing, Deacon trying to remember what her coat looks like, wondering which coat she's wearing. And maybe the police would ask if he'd been drinking. Maybe they'd figure out he was drunk, or think he was crazy and was only hallucinating that he had a daughter who was lost somewhere in the snow, being chased by monsters and hiding in old railway tunnels.

"I know it doesn't *look* very inviting," the girl says, "but, sometimes, looks truly can be deceiving, Emma Jean." And then she steps off the rail and over something crushed and folded in upon itself that Emmie thinks might once have been the driver-side door.

"You're gonna cut yourself and get tetanus," Emmie tells her, because that's what Deacon would say—*You'll get lockjaw climbing around on something like that*—but then the girl's staring back at her from the middle of the wreck, and Emmie reminds herself it's all only a dream. You don't catch diseases in dreams, and even if you do, you don't wake up sick.

"It's got to be here somewhere; I'm sure of it," the brown girl says, holding the ball of light out in front of her as she examines all the crannies and corners and the gaping holes torn in the metal. Emmie isn't exactly sure what the brown girl's looking for, so she waits and watches at the edge of the train track instead of following her inside the wreck.

"What's your name?" she asks.

The brown girl stops looking for whatever it is she's looking for and stares at Emmie a moment without replying.

"Forget it. You don't have to tell me," Emmie says, "not if you don't want to, not if it's a secret or something."

"No, it's not a secret," the girl replies. "It's just not something I have much use for anymore. Sometimes I almost forget about it. Isn't that odd?"

"Well, you know *my* name," Emmie says and leans closer, and now she can see that someone's gone to the trouble of wrapping what remains of the car's front seat beneath a couple of heavy blue blankets. "I could sit down there," she says, "if you don't mind?"

"Of course," the brown girl says and shakes her head. "Why didn't I think of that?" And it takes Emmie a couple of seconds to realize that *of course* wasn't an answer to her question. The brown girl gets down on her knees and holds the globe so she can see whatever's under the front seat. When she stands up again, she's grinning and holding a brown paper bag.

"See?" she says. "Barnaby's the most reliable ghoul I ever met." The top of the bag is rolled closed, and the brown girl unrolls it and looks inside. "My name's Pearl," she adds.

"You're not really going to eat something you *found* in here, are you?" Emmie asks and points again at the seat wrapped in blue wool blankets. "Is it okay if I sit down?"

"If that's what you want to do. I'd wager Barnaby put those blankets there for us, too. He can be very thoughtful."

Emmie steps off the pallet onto the rail, which is at least as slippery as it looked, and then she works her way carefully past the sharp edges of the twisted door frame to stand beside the girl whose name is Pearl.

"There are sandwiches," Pearl says, still staring into the paper bag, "and two pears, and I think that might be . . . oh . . . well, ghouls have their own idea of food, you know. But the sandwiches are probably fine, and the pears."

Emmie sits down; the springs beneath the blankets make a soft, crunching sort of sound, and she sinks a few inches into the seat. It feels good, being off her feet after the long walk, better than sitting down has ever felt before, she thinks, and it would be easy to shut her eyes and go right to sleep. She pulls off her mittens and gloves and stuffs them into her coat pocket.

I'm already asleep, she tells herself, *so maybe if I shut my eyes, I'd wake up instead.*

"I hope you like liverwurst," Pearl says, and Emmie sees that she's taken one of the sandwiches from the bag and is peeling back the waxed paper it's wrapped in. "Because I think that's what we have here. Liverwurst and cheese and horseradish sauce."

"I've never eaten it," Emmie says, leaning back in the seat, "but it sounds disgusting."

"It's just sausage made from pigs' livers, mostly."

"No, thank you," Emmie says and makes a face. "Besides, I don't eat food someone left lying around in a boarded-up train tunnel full of rats and mushrooms and who knows what else."

"Suit yourself," Pearl tells her. "But you said you were hungry," and then she sits down beside Emmie, and the car seat creaks again. The brown girl sets the glowing orb on what's left of the dashboard, puts the bag on the seat between them, and takes a big bite of the sandwich. Emmie ignores her and watches the snow globe thing instead. Up close, it doesn't look like it has a lightbulb inside. It *looks* like there's a *sun* trapped within the orb, a star no bigger than a very large jawbreaker. She starts to touch the snow globe, and Pearl mumbles something around a mouthful of liverwurst and bread, and Emmie pulls her hand back and apologizes.

"What's *in* there?" she asks. Pearl swallows and wipes her mouth. "It almost looks like a star," Emmie says.

"It is a star. That's one of my father's later experiments, and he's extremely proud of it. He was careful to take a star none of the astronomers had ever seen, so no one would miss it. It came from somewhere near the constellation Cassiopeia, I believe."

"That's impossible," Emmie says and squints at the bright thing suspended at the heart of the orb.

"Be that as it may, it's still a star," Pearl tells her and tears away a piece of waxed paper to expose more sandwich.

"Your father put stars inside snow globes?"

"It's not a snow globe," Pearl says, glancing up from her sandwich. "It's all very complicated, but my father moved places and moments. He was studying spatial and temporal translocation for the ghouls," and the way she says *translocation* makes it sound like the most important word in the world. "But you shouldn't stare at it too long. It could hurt your eyes. You might even go blind."

"Yeah," Emmie says very softly, not quite whispering, "if you say so."

"You might at least have one of the pears," Pearl tells her, looking into the brown bag again. "They're perfectly fine, I promise, and you ought to eat something. You'll need your strength."

"No, Pearl. I need to go *home*. I need to wake up."

Pearl sighs and takes another bite of the sandwich. Emmie stares at the snow globe again, at the star. "Well, you should at least make up your mind," Pearl says with her mouth full.

"What?"

"Make up your mind. Whether you want to go home or wake

up. Whether you're really here in the tunnel with me, or whether you're only having a bad dream."

"This doesn't *feel* like a dream anymore," Emmie says, and immediately wishes that she hadn't, that she'd kept that thought to herself.

"There's a reason for that, I suspect. But what do I know? I eat garbage and drag frightened little girls away into blizzards when they have perfectly safe, warm houses."

"If I believe you, Pearl, what happens next?" Emmie asks the brown girl, turning away from the snow globe, and her eyes trail yellow-orange afterimages that refuse to go away when she blinks.

"That's not an easy question to answer," Pearl tells her, "not even if you believe, and I don't think that you do, which makes it harder."

"But if I *did* believe you?"

Pearl drops what's left of her sandwich back into the brown paper bag, then rolls the top closed again. "I hate liverwurst," she says. "My father never makes me eat liverwurst."

"I *want* to go home," Emmie says. "I want to know if Deacon's safe. I want you to tell me what happens next. I want to know when it'll be safe to go home again."

"You want a terrible lot of things," the brown girl replies. "You may have to settle for less."

"Fine. I want to know what happens next."

There's a loud booming sound then from the darkness waiting at the limits of the snow globe's radiance, and Emmie covers her ears and grits her teeth. She can feel it in her bones, that sound, and it makes her think of the thing she saw on Waterman Street, the thing that wasn't a mammoth or a mastodon or the Wendigo, the thing riding the wind. The booming fades slowly away, but Emmie's ears are still ringing painfully, and something about the sound has left her slightly sick to her stomach.

"Be very, *very* quiet," Pearl whispers and reaches for the snow globe with the star inside. It seems to glow the smallest bit brighter when she's touching it. "They don't know we're down here, and it can't see or smell through solid rock, and it loathes the tunnel. So, we'll probably be safe if we just stay quiet."

"I want to go home," Emmie says again.

"I know," Pearl tells her and holds the globe up, pushing back the darkness a scant few feet. "I *know* you do. I want to go home, too, Emma Jean."

"Hold my hand," Emmie says, and the brown girl does, her hand colder than ice, colder than the silty bottom of the deepest sea or the empty heart of a solar system whose star has been snatched away, leaving behind only ice and the endless twinkling night and dead planets frozen straight down to their cores. But Emmie doesn't let go, and they sit together in the wrecked car, hand in hand, shivering and waiting for the booming to come again, waiting for whatever's supposed to happen next . . .

. . . and when Emmie opens her eyes again, the cold and damp are gone, and she's staring up into the widest night sky that she's ever seen. There's a cool breeze—cool, but not cold—a wind that smells like cinnamon and jasmine and dust, and when she sits up, she sees that she's lying near the crest of an enormous sand dune. The old railroad tunnel has vanished, the tunnel and the wrecked car and the girl named Pearl. Instead, a vast desert stretches out around her, countless grains of sand to mock the stars overhead, and there's something dark sparkling wetly on the horizon, something she thinks might be water, a river or the sea. The moon is high and white and only a few days from full.

"Damn it," she says, lying back down in the sand, which is still warm from the day before. "I'm not awake. Maybe I'm dead now, and I won't ever wake up again."

"You're awfully young to be so concerned with what is and isn't a dream," someone says, an old woman's voice or only a woman's voice weathered and worn until it *seems* old. Emmie rolls over onto her left side, and the woman, who doesn't look old at all, is squatting in the sand only a few feet away. Her skin is black—not any shade of brown, but skin as perfectly, truly black as an obsidian arrowhead or a licorice whip—and her amber eyes shimmer dimly. Her eyes remind Emmie of her own, though they're more golden than yellow. The woman is dressed in white muslin, and her hair is white, too, not gray, but white, arranged in long dreadlocks reaching down past her shoulders, framing her high forehead and cheekbones.

"I *know* the difference," Emmie says, surprised that she's not afraid of the woman, who she's certain wasn't there only a moment before. "I know when I'm dreaming."

The woman smiles and takes a deep breath. "That's a lot to claim," she says. "That's a mighty conceit, child."

"I was here once before, wasn't I?" Emmie asks. "These are the wastes at the end of the world."

"It's true some people have called them that," the woman replies. "And some other people have called them other things. Myself, I've never thought them a waste, and this is hardly the end of the world. The world goes on *far* beyond this place."

"But I *was* here before?" Emmie asks her again, growing impatient and noticing that the woman's earrings are the sharp teeth of some tiny animal strung on loops of silver wire. They glint in the bright moonlight.

"Were you?" the black woman asks. "Or was *that* only a dream? If you know the difference—"

"Yes, it was a *dream*," Emmie sighs, exasperated and in no mood for games, and she sinks back down onto the warm, welcoming sand. "That's what I meant to say. I was here before in a *dream*, just this afternoon, when I fell asleep in my bedroom."

"Well, if you say so, since you claim to know the difference."

"Where'd the tunnel go?" Emmie asks. "Where's Pearl?"

"It hasn't gone anywhere. It's right there beneath the hill, where it's always been. And Pearl's where you left her, asleep beside you. Don't worry about Pearl. She's safe, for the time being."

"That's the prettiest sky I've ever seen," Emmie says, though it's more than that, more than pretty, but she can't think of the words that would do it justice. Staring up at all those stars, at the brilliant swath of the Milky Way, makes her a little dizzy, and for a moment Emmie thinks it would be easy to fall, the sand and sky reversed, and all she'd have to do is stop trying *not* to fall.

"It comforts me," the woman says, glancing up into the night. "When I'm lost, it helps me find my way."

"I'm afraid Pearl's not right," Emmie tells the black-skinned woman. "She's even weirder than me, and that's saying a lot. I think there's something wrong with her."

"She misses her father," the woman suggests.

"I'd be worried about her, if she were real."

Then neither of them says anything for a minute or two, and Emmie lies still, listening to the wind blowing through the dunes. *I could lie here forever,* she thinks. *I could lie here forever, counting stars, and never go back to that smelly tunnel. Never go back to the cold, or my room, or—*

"But what about Deacon?" the woman asks. "Wouldn't you miss him?"

"Of course I'd miss him. I'd miss him more than anything. But maybe he'd be better off. Maybe things would be easier for him if I wasn't there, if he didn't have to worry about me all the time."

The woman picks up a handful of sand and then lets it sift out between her fingers; some of it is carried away on the breeze, and some of it falls back onto the dune. "I'm going to ask something of you," she says.

"I don't even know who you are," Emmie replies.

"It's not important *who* I am. I can't tell you that, not tonight. But I'm still going to ask something of you, something important."

"You mean a favor?"

"You could think of it that way, I suppose."

"Deacon says I shouldn't talk to strangers, so I doubt seriously I'm supposed to go around doing them favors."

"When you first met Pearl," the black woman says, "the day the horse was killed, do you remember what she said to you? She said, 'Build me a bridge, Emmie. I have long desired one.' "

Emmie starts to ask the woman how she knows that, then decides there's no point, that it doesn't matter anyway, and she nods her head instead. "I told her she was a loony bird," Emmie says.

"But she was telling you the truth. You *are* a bridge builder. Indeed, you are a bridge yourself. You span the distance between humanity and the creatures Pearl calls the Hounds of Cain."

"The ghouls," Emmie mumbles and works the fingers of her left hand into and under the sand.

"Yes," the black-skinned woman says. "And they've been seeking a bridge as well. They have been seeking a bridge desperately for thousands of years. Some among them believe they have found her, but they're mistaken."

"I don't know what you're talking about."

"Child, *listen* to me," the woman says; her words have become urgent, half whispered, and she's dropped down onto her hands and knees, her lips near Emmie's left ear. For an instant she seems like something more animal than human, some night-colored, reptilian thing that sleeps away the days in caverns beneath the shifting sand and slips out at sunset to stalk the desert. Her breath smells of ashes and sage. "Listen to what I'm *saying*, child. Your mother is a changeling, and your father was the son of the union of a changeling and a hound. There is a secret locked up in your soul, a terrible secret that would free the *ghul,* if they could only reach it. The hounds believe the bridge builder is the daughter of Deacon Silvey, but they're mistaken."

"*I'm* the daughter of Deacon Silvey," Emmie says.

"One among them suspects the truth, I think, and he is the one you must fear above all the rest. He is not a hound, but he keeps their counsel."

"This is a big fat load of baloney," Emmie says. "I'm going to wake up now. And not in that damned tunnel, either. I'm going to wake up in my *house,* in my *bed.*"

"He'll have you *dead,* Emmie, if he gets his way."

And Emmie's about to tell the woman to shut the hell up, to stop talking and go away and leave her alone so that she can wake up, when something rises from the sand a few yards from her feet. The keels of its dusky scales scrape roughly across the sand, and its eyes shine bright and red, two holes burned deep into the fabric of the night. Emmie has never imagined a snake even half this big, and she's seen pythons at the zoo, pythons and even an anaconda from Brazil, but this snake makes them look like the worms she finds dying on the sidewalk whenever it rains. The snake, if it *is* a snake, grins and flicks its long forked tongue, and she can see there are at least a thousand needle teeth set into its jaws.

"Whatever have you found *this* time, old whore?" the huge snake hisses, dragging more of itself up from the sand, and the sides of its neck open wide like the hood of a cobra. Emmie begins to scramble backwards away from it, but the woman lays a strong hand on her shoulder and tells her not to move.

"You can't ever outrun it, child, though it would be pleased if you were to try. Be still. Be still and wait."

"It's only a dream," Emmie says and shuts her eyes. "It's only a dream, and I'm going to wake up now."

"Share it with me," the snake hisses. "It's a plump little thing.

There's plenty enough for us both, and maybe even a few scraps for the jackals and vultures left over."

"Stay away from her," the woman says to the snake. "She's not for eating," and the serpent makes a sound that isn't a laugh, but Emmie knows it was meant to be.

"No?" the snake asks. "That's too, too bad. But tell me, if it isn't for eating, then what's it for? Is it for diversion, perhaps? For play? It's so *soft*, so *pale*, so, so *young*."

"Go, Emmie," the black-skinned woman says. "Go *now*. This instant. You know the way back across. I don't expect you need me to show you."

And she's surprised to find that she does know the way, sure as she knows all the scars that Deacon says he got the day she was born or the winter-sky color of Sadie's eyes, sure as she knows the way from one side of Angell Street to the other. She could do it blindfolded. She could do it in her sleep.

"Who were you talking to just then?" Pearl asks, and Emmie rubs her eyes and blinks, trying to remember where she is and why she's so cold and hungry. "Where did you go, Emma Jean? What did you see?"

"I didn't go anywhere," she mutters, remembering the railroad tunnel, the long walk through the storm, the desert and the snake and the woman with amber eyes. "I fell asleep, that's all."

"You were talking to *someone*. I heard you."

"I was *dreaming*," Emmie says, and then she tells herself that she's *still* dreaming, that this is only the outer dream wrapped around that darker inner dream. There could be a lot more than two layers, she thinks. It might go on forever, dreams within dreams within dreams, like letting go of the sand and falling up into the sky. "Anyway, it's none of your business what I was dreaming."

Pearl looks annoyed and offended, frowns, then turns away from Emmie and reaches for her father's snow globe, which is still sitting on the dashboard. "I do have my *own* dreams," she says. "I certainly don't have any need of yours. But we'd better get moving soon, changeling. Something's coming. We shouldn't have slept so long."

"*What's* coming?" Emmie asks her, sitting up, hugging herself against the dampness and the chill.

"At first I thought it might only be Barnaby," Pearl says, lowering her voice, and then she rubs her bare hands over the surface of the glowing ball, as if to warm them. "But there's more than one of them. The tunnel connects with the warrens, back towards Benefit Street."

"You said we'd be safe—"

"Actually, no. I said that we'd be safe until morning, which it may well be by now, for all I know. By now, Emma, they've probably figured out where we are. If you sit there talking long enough, you're sure to find out."

"*Christ*, Pearl. Just slow down, okay? I'm not even awake yet. I'm freezing and—"

"Swearing is a sign of a poor upbringing. And, in any case, you probably shouldn't talk so loud. They have very good ears, the hounds. They can hear—"

"My upbringing is something else that's none of your business. My upbringing has been just fine."

"Well, Deacon's a drunkard, and your stepmother's a witch who runs away whenever things get too scary," Pearl says and glances at Emmie.

"And just what the hell was *your* father, Pearl, putting stars inside that . . . whatever that is . . . and leaving you locked up in an attic. People who live in glass houses—"

"Point taken," Pearl says and shrugs. She stares down at the globe, looking deeply into it despite her earlier warnings about damaged eyes and blindness; her face is underlit, washed in the softly pulsating yellow-orange-white light shining from the ball. Emmie squints and rubs her eyes again.

"We're still in the tunnel?" she asks.

"Where else would we be, dear? Can't you hear them?"

Emmie listens, holds her breath and listens for at least a full minute, but she doesn't hear anything at all except the water dripping from the concrete ceiling to the flooded floor of the tunnel. "No," she says. "I can't. Maybe you're wrong." Her hands are cold, and she takes her gloves and mittens from her pocket and puts them on again.

"Maybe your ears are full of wax and fluff," Pearl says and stands up. "There's still a pear left in the bag that Barnaby brought for us, but I'm afraid we don't have time for breakfast, even if you'd deign to eat garbage I found in—"

"*What* will they do if they catch us?" Emmie asks, standing up and peering into the darkness farther along the railroad tunnel.

"They'll put me back in my attic. They aren't allowed to hurt me. But I can't say precisely what they'll do with you, except that it likely won't be pleasant. It won't be pretty."

"I was dreaming about a woman in a desert," Emmie says, and looks back at the brown girl. "And a giant snake that wanted to eat me. The woman was about to ask me a favor, but the snake came along before she got around to it. Now will you please stop acting like such a bitch?"

Pearl pushes back her bangs, which have fallen across her eyes, and then she glances at Emmie. "A woman with skin as black as a lump of coal?" she asks. "A kind woman with white hair?"

"She didn't seem very kind to me," Emmie says. "But her skin was black and her hair was white. Why? You know who she is?"

"We should go now," Pearl tells her, instead of answering the question. "Maybe if we head back the way we came, they might not try to follow. If the sun's up, they won't follow us outside."

"No. First, you tell me who she is," Emmie says. She still hasn't heard anything but the dripping water and is unconvinced that someone's coming for them. "Tell me what she wants."

"These days, they don't get fresh meat very often," Pearl says, and begins climbing out of the car and back onto the tracks. She moves slowly, the snow globe cradled in the crook of her left arm so both hands are free as she picks her way through the wreckage.

"I could have held that for you," Emmie says and points at the globe.

"No, you couldn't have. There are rules. Hurry along, Emma. They're coming fast now."

"Is she one of them?" Emmie asks, stealing another look into the darkness beyond the car before she follows Pearl. "The black woman in the desert? Is she one of the ghouls?"

"Hardly," Pearl replies. She's standing on the wooden pallets between the rails now, holding the snow globe in her right hand. "Now stop your dillydallying, unless you want to wind up on Miss Josephine's vivisection table."

"Why won't you tell me who she is?"

"There's not time. I can tell you later, unless they catch us, in which case it won't matter."

"I don't know about you, but I'm smart enough to walk *and* talk at the same time."

"Sticks and stones, dear heart," Pearl says, and then she flips her head to one side and smiles a conceited, insincere smile.

I hate you, too, Emmie thinks, thinking it hard and sharp so maybe Pearl will overhear, wondering if she's ever hated anyone or anything half as much as she's starting to hate this strange girl. Emmie wishes that she'd brought her cell phone, because then she'd know what time it is. If she had her phone, she could call Deacon and tell him where to find her, and he could stop worrying whether she'd been kidnapped or murdered or worse.

"Nothing's coming," she says. "I have pretty good hearing, too. The doctor said so, and if there were *anything* coming, I'd have heard it by now." But then she *does* hear something—a wet and breathy sound like panting dogs, the splash of feet moving quickly through the flooded tunnel. Her heart seems to pause between beats, her mouth gone dry and cottony, her left foot dangling halfway between the wrecked car and the slick steel rail.

"You'll have to do better than that," Pearl says and pulls her the rest of the way down to the tracks. Emmie almost falls, her feet slipping, balance lost, and she would have gone down face first in the mud and gravel ballast and splintery, rotting pallets if the brown girl hadn't been there to catch her. "We'll try to go back to the entrance," Pearl says. "Maybe we can get outside and make it across the river. Barnaby said there are places to hide over there."

"Let me go home," Emmie says. Her legs are shaky, and she wants to sit down, wants to cry. "Please, Pearl. Just let me wake up and go home. I can't do this anymore."

"Stop whining and follow me," the brown girl says and begins towing her along the tracks, back the way they entered the railroad tunnel. Emmie stumbles once or twice, the toes of her boots catching on the edges of the pallets, but then she's running on her own. The panting sounds are getting louder, and the splashing feet, too, and Emmie doesn't know why it took her so long to hear them. *Maybe,* she thinks, *I didn't hear them because they weren't there to hear. Maybe it's only Pearl making those noises, making me hear them.* But she doesn't stop moving. There's no way to be sure of anything anymore, and she'd rather run from make-believe monsters than find out that she's wrong. The soles of their boots are loud against the boards, her bulky winter boots and the brown girl's old-fashioned lace-up boots.

"We waited too long," Pearl says, out of breath, and she stops and looks hastily back over her shoulder. The noise the ghouls are making is much louder now, and Emmie can hear them calling back and forth to each other in guttural animal voices. "You shouldn't have wasted so much time."

"No, Pearl, we can make it. It's not that far. We should be almost there."

"Then tell me, why can't I see the doorway out? We should be able to see it by now, but it's not there."

"Maybe someone shut it," Emmie says and reaches for Pearl's hand, because they can't stop running now, not with those splashing, yelping things bearing down on them.

"No, they've changed something, Emma Jean. They've changed the tunnel. Maybe there isn't a door out anymore. Maybe the tunnel just loops 'round and 'round. Maybe—"

"That's crazy. They couldn't have changed the whole tunnel. We just haven't gone far enough; that's all."

Pearl sighs, and her breath steams white in the cold air, a sudden rush of mist visible in the light from the snow globe, there and gone in only an instant, and she looks down at the alien sun inside the glass ball.

"They can see it, can't they?" Emmie asks, pointing at the snow globe. "We should hide it, get rid of it or something. If they can see it."

"Of course they can see it. But hiding it wouldn't make any difference. They see better in the dark than in daylight. We're in *their* element, Emma. And even if they were blind and deaf, they'd still find us by our smell alone."

"Why are we just *standing* here?" And Emmie takes two or three steps farther along the tracks, but Pearl doesn't move. "Come on," she says. "You don't *know* the door's shut. You don't know for sure."

"Sometimes," Pearl says, her words wrapped in a veil of white breath, "sometimes, Emma Jean, I think that they've killed him. Sometimes I think my father's never coming back because they've killed him, or they've sent him so far from me he can never find his way home again."

"No place is that far away," Emmie tells her, and one of the pallet boards cracks loudly beneath her feet, and she takes another step. "You can fly all the way around the world in just a couple of days, so nowhere's that far away."

Pearl watches her a moment, her expression enough to say that she's not sure if she knows what Emmie's talking about. "My father never learned to fly," she says. "Once, a demon offered to teach him, but he was never interested."

"*Airplanes,*" Emmie says. "I meant flying in airplanes."

"Oh, aeroplanes. Yes, of course that's what you meant. But there are many, many places where aeroplanes cannot go, Emma Jean Silvey. Most places, in fact."

"Hester? Hester, can you hear me?" a voice calls out from the murk, someone or something half barking, half speaking, and Pearl bites at her lower lip and sighs again.

"That's Barnaby," she says and smiles, but not a relieved or happy smile, a sad, disappointed sort of a smile. "They probably threatened him. He must have lost his nerve. He didn't have that much to start with. Do you know the way back to the desert, back to the black woman?"

"Pearl, that was only a *dream.*"

"*You* think *this* is only a dream."

"Hester, you must stop running now. No one wants to see harm come to you, I promise. They'll take you home again; that's all."

"Home again. Back to the attic," Pearl says softly and looks from the glowing ball to Emmie. "If you know how to return to her, perhaps you should go. Sometimes there's no point running away, because you can't run fast enough or far enough to make any difference."

And then Emmie grabs her arm and tries to drag her forward. But Pearl shakes her head and digs her heels in. The ghouls are very close now, close enough that Emmie thinks she can smell them, a stink like spoiled meat and wet dog, like old cheese and boiled cabbage.

"No," Pearl says, wrenching her arm free of Emmie's grip. "I told you, they won't hurt me. They wouldn't dare, and maybe I can stall them here. And if you can find your way back to her . . . Here. Take this. . . ." And she shoves the snow globe that isn't a snow globe into Emmie's hands. Emmie's so surprised she almost drops it. It's much heavier than she expected and so cold that she can feel it straight through her mittens and gloves, so cold it almost burns her skin.

"But you just said I couldn't touch it," Emmie protests, wanting to give it right back. The cold's bad enough, the cold and the weight, but there's something more coming from the orb, something she could almost mistake for music, the most dreadful music she's ever heard. "You said there were rules."

"For pity's sake, there's not time left to argue," Pearl snaps and pushes her so hard that Emmie almost loses her footing. "*Run*, you silly little idiot. If you can find the way back, run as fast and far away from this place as you can go."

And then something lopes out of the shadows and into view, something moving on all fours that stops a few feet from Pearl and stands up straight and tall on its long and spindly hind legs. Its matted belly fur is dirty blond in the starlight from the globe, and its thick black lips fold back to reveal teeth the color of antique ivory. Its eyes are the color of fire.

"Where's Barnaby?" Pearl asks the thing, turning away from Emmie. "I heard him. Where is he?"

"Barnaby will be along directly," the thing barks back at her and wrinkles its nose. "Don't you fret about Master Barnaby. But that one *there*"—and the ghoul points a claw at Emmie—"that one has become a matter of significant concern. Step aside, Hester."

And so Emmie runs, the freezing ball of light clutched tight to her chest, her head quickly filling up with its song. But she's gone only a few feet when one of the pallet boards snaps beneath her, and she pitches forward. Behind her the ghoul has begun to howl, and before her the railroad track has dissolved into a sky full of stars, opening wide to take her back. Emmie shuts her eyes and lets it have her.

"I always knew you'd be back, someday or another," the black-skinned woman says and smiles. "It was really only a matter of *when* and *where*."

Emmie's standing with the woman at the very top of an extraordinarily high sand dune, watching as Pearl's snow globe rolls away down the steep slope, throwing up a fine spray of sand as it goes. It slipped from her mittened hands when she opened her eyes and saw the wide blanched sky and the yellow-brown expanse of the desert, the undulating dune fields broken only by a few scattered outcrops of weathered rock. This time the woman is wearing a long-sleeved, ankle-length thobe dyed a very pale blue with tiny red and silver beads embroidered about the neckline. She's barefoot, and there's a short sword or a long dagger tucked into a length of cloth cinched about her waist.

"Crap," Emmie says and begins unwinding the alpaca muffler from around her throat, because the sun here is bright and hot, and she's already sweating underneath her heavy winter clothes. "I wasn't supposed to drop that."

"Don't worry. It won't go very far," the woman says. "No farther than it can roll. We'll fetch it back."

"But if it breaks—"

"It's not going to break. Trust me."

Emmie drops the muffler to the ground at her feet and unzips her coat. "Pearl pushed me," she says, sliding her arms free of the sleeves. "I told her we could make it if she'd run, but she *pushed* me."

"She must have been very afraid for you," the woman says. "I expect the alchemist's daughter knows well enough what the hounds would have done had they caught you."

Before, in the dark with only the waxing moon for light, Emmie hadn't realized how beautiful the woman was. By daylight, the sun glints off her ebony skin and catches in the dazzling topaz facets of her irises. *She might be the most beautiful woman in the world*, Emmie thinks and sits down in the sand. She might be an Ethiopian or Egyptian princess disguised as a Bedouin bandit.

"It's a long way down," Emmie says and points at the orb, still rolling towards the bottom of the dune, the place where this dune finally ends and the next begins. "Is that big snake still around here?" she asks and glances up at the woman.

"Oh, don't you bother yourself about him. That was far ago and long away. A lot has changed since then."

Emmie pulls off her gloves, the right and then the left, and she lays them neatly on top of her mittens. "You mean *long* ago and *far* away," she says, and then she takes off her sweater, folds it, and puts it on the ground next to her coat and gloves and mittens.

"I think that I know what I mean, child," the woman replies, and squats in the sand next to Emmie. "Anyway, the stone drakes are all but extinct. He was one of the last."

"This is like Narnia, isn't it?" Emmie asks and wipes her sweaty hands on her pants. "Like when Lucy and Susan and Peter and Edmund go back to Cair Paravel, and it's only been a year for them, but in Narnia it's been ages since they left, and everything's changed."

"I certainly wouldn't say that everything's changed," the black-skinned woman tells her. "In fact, it's pretty much the same around here as it has been since the sea dried up and the dunes and salt flats came to take its place. But, yes, the drakes are gone, which is really only a good thing. They were foul, intemperate beasts."

"It wanted to eat me."

"Well, you can't really blame him for that. A creature, even a wicked one, cannot be faulted simply for wanting to eat, and out here, very few creatures can afford to be picky."

Emmie stands and brushes sand and dust off the seat of her pants. She doesn't feel like arguing with the woman about whether or not the snake had a right to try to eat her, and she points at the orb again, which has finally stopped rolling and lies partly buried at the base of the dune. "I should go get it now. I probably shouldn't just leave it lying there like that."

"No," the woman says. "You probably shouldn't."

"You never did tell me what the favor was, what you wanted to ask me to do." And then Emmie starts down the dune before the woman can reply. Each step she takes triggers a small avalanche of sand that spills out before her in gleaming fan-shaped flows. Narrow rivulets break free and meander rapidly towards the bottom, and Emmie thinks it's almost a miracle, all these millions or billions of grains of sand balanced here by the wind, laid one atop the other and nothing to hold them in place but gravity.

"I thought you didn't do favors for strangers," the woman says, starting down the dune after her.

"I've decided Deacon might approve of you," Emmie replies and stops so the black-skinned woman can catch up. "You told the snake it couldn't eat me."

"I see. Then I suppose that was very shrewd of me, wasn't it? Do you still think you're dreaming?"

Emmie stands staring at the streams of sand winding their way downhill, and she notices a small gray lizard that her footsteps have disturbed. It scurries away and burrows into the dune.

"I think maybe it doesn't matter," she says. "If it's all a dream, then I'll wake up sooner or later, unless maybe I'm in a coma or something. And if it's not a dream, I won't wake up. But either way, I think that I should at least try to do the right thing. Just in case."

"Emma Jean, do you believe that you *know* what the right thing is?"

"I'm only a kid. I know what Deacon and Sadie tell me is right, but sometimes they contradict each other. I know what I've read in books. I know what my teachers say."

"And, more important, you know what you *feel* in your heart is right," the woman says and continues past her down the dune.

"I'm only a kid," Emmie says again. "So I might be wrong. I might have it all turned around backwards."

"I'm wrong all the goddamned time," the woman laughs and looks over her left shoulder at Emmie. "Don't you start thinking that getting older makes much difference about knowing the right from the wrong."

Emmie watches the woman for a moment, then follows her, and when they reach the foot of the dune, Emmie picks up the orb, but immediately drops it again. Even after baking under the desert sun, the thing's still freezing cold to the touch. "I don't know if I can carry it," she says and blows on her fingers. "I'll get frostbite if I try to hold that thing for very long. I don't know how Pearl was doing it."

"I'm afraid you'll need your gloves after all," the black-skinned woman says, and Emmie looks back up the towering dune to the spot where she left the discarded pile of clothing and groans.

"Crap," she says and sits down beside the orb. There's sweat dripping from her face, speckling the sand, and her T-shirt's already soaked straight through. "I'll have a heart attack."

"I can carry it back to the top for you," the woman says. She kneels beside Emmie and lifts the glowing orb, blows some of the dust and sand away, and then rubs it clean against the front of her blue thobe.

"Doesn't it burn you?" Emmie asks, and the woman shakes her head.

"Getting old might not teach you right from wrong, but it can give you thicker skin."

"You don't look old."

"Which should be a lesson to you, child." Then the woman gazes into the glass ball and licks her lips. "Amazing," she whispers. "Such an amazing and blasphemous thing this is. Perhaps it's best, what the hounds have done with the magician."

"I don't believe in god," Emmie says.

"A thing can be blasphemous," the black-skinned woman tells her, "whether there's a god involved or not. *This*," she says and taps a fingernail against the orb, "this *thing* is a perversion, a blasphemy. The mere fact of its existence is a crime against the world. It's *wrong*, Emmie."

"I thought so, too. But I don't think Pearl agrees."

"Pearl loves her father, and sometimes love can blind us to the truth of things."

Emmie looks back towards the top of the dune again, squinting at the sun reflected off the sand. "I suppose we should get started," she says, "if we have to walk all the way back to the top for my gloves. And if you're still going to ask me for a favor, maybe you should ask me for it now, just in case I *do* have a heart attack or a heatstroke and die."

The woman nods her head and blinks, looking away from the orb. "There's a changeling woman whom the hounds call Soldier. You have to go to her, Emma Jean Silvey. And you have to carry this thing to her. She's close to death and in great danger, and there's not much time left."

"Pearl said something about her. I asked who Soldier was, but she wouldn't tell me. She said we shouldn't get too far ahead of ourselves."

The woman turns towards the orb again. "Soldier's the true daughter of Deacon Silvey," she says. "She's the one the hounds thought might at last build their bridge away from this world. She's paid an unspeakable price for their beliefs, and your fates, yours and Soldier's, are bound almost inextricably one unto the other."

"Deacon is my father," Emmie says, standing up.

"He loves you," the woman says. "You mean everything to him."

"And you have no right saying he's *not* my father."

The woman sighs, and for a moment the sun sealed inside the orb dims. "That's the favor I ask of you, child. It's more than anyone should ever ask of another, but these are desperate times. If you do as I've asked, you'll learn the truth of things, and in the end you'll curse me for that knowledge. Would there were any other way."

"She's really dying?" Emmie asks.

"Yes. She's dying and lost in a dark place, and very soon she'll stand before a foe almost as blasphemous as this vile thing," and the woman nods at the glass orb. "I can show you the way down to her, the correct where and when, but it has to be your choice."

"This isn't really like Narnia at all, is it?"

"No," the woman says. "It's not."

"Could you also show me the way home, if I were to say no? Could you show me the way back to Providence?"

"There's no need. You already *know* the way home."

"Crap," Emmie says again, and then she begins climbing the dune, but the sand shifts and slides out from under the soles of her boots, and three steps only carries her right back to the bottom.

"I know a shortcut," the black-skinned woman says.

"Do you have a name?" Emmie asks her.

"Oh, I've had many names, but I've found it's usually best I keep them to myself," and then the woman takes Emmie's hand in hers, and the desert dissolves, collapsing into stars and empty space the same way that the railroad tunnel dropped away after Pearl pushed her. The scorching desert day is replaced by night, a twinkling indigo sea of constellations, and Emmie thinks about all the questions she wishes she'd asked the black-skinned woman with topaz eyes and waits for the long fall to end.

EIGHT

Intersections

And from the starry place, all things are possible, and, perhaps, all things are also probable. Possibility is infinite here, and possibility collides, in spiraling space-time fusillades, with probability at every turn. The unlikely and the never-was become, for fleeting instants, the actual and the inevitable and the black facts of a trillion competing histories, each entirely ignorant of all the others, each confident that it's the only *true* history. Emmie is wearing her gloves and down coat again, her alpaca muffler and her mittens, and she clutches the glass orb as she slips between everything that was and is and never quite shall be. Sometimes she shuts her eyes, because there are things she cannot comprehend and would rather not see, and sometimes she opens them wide and wishes that she could see more clearly and more fully understand *what* she's seeing.

The stars, and the almost empty spaces between the stars.

Light and darkness and things that are not exactly either one or the other.

Countless detours on the road the black woman has told her to follow . . .

~ A girl in an attic, a girl who isn't Pearl, holds a wooden animal out over a wide hole that has no bottom—and she almost drops it in, then decides the wooden animal isn't hers to drop. Instead she sets it down on the dusty floor and steps back from the edge of the abyss.

~ Sadie is reading Emmie *The House with a Clock in Its Walls* by John Bellairs, but this Sadie has only one hand, and she turns the pages with two shiny steel hooks strapped somehow to the stump of her left wrist. This Sadie has red hair, like her red door, like the red of pomegranates.

~ "What about a carriage ride?" Hunter Fontana asks, and Sadie says no, she's heard terrible things about the way the horses are treated, and the three of them go back inside the museum to see the blue whale instead.

~ A careless elbow, and a paperweight that isn't a paperweight at all rolls off the edge of an alchemist's workbench. There's a breathless moment when the air smells like gardenias and millipedes, and then a blinding flash of light, and the world vanishes, and Emmie is never born and Deacon is never born and the solar system is only an ember.

~ The woman from the train, the woman with the Seal of Solomon tattooed on her hand, presses the barrel of a gun to a priest's head. Her finger tightens on the trigger, and she curses him. The priest is begging for his life, begging her to understand that he had no choice, that he *never* had a choice. Then he wets himself and sinks to his knees, his tears and urine dripping to the floor of a darkened room. She spits on him, and a few moments later, she places the gun to the soft spot beneath her jaw. The priest screams when she pulls the trigger.

~ Saturday afternoon in the Kingston Station, and Emmie tells Deacon that she's sick to her stomach, that she thinks she's going to vomit, and wants to go home. On the way back to Angell Street, he talks about blackbirds.

~ Another gun, this one in the hands of a tall, pale man in a Dunkin' Donuts, and he shoots an old lady first, then the woman behind the cash register, then . . .

Concentrate, the woman in the desert tells her. *You get lost out there, and you'll never get found again.*

But there are so many diverging paths.

There are so many choices.

        . . . and yo
                u'll
                    ne
                        ver
                        get
                    fou
            nd
    again.

Emmie tries to look away, fights to keep her eyes on the invisible, intangible current pulling her along towards wherever it is she's meant to be. But faces flicker and moments flash all around her.

~ An albino girl in sunglasses, hitchhiking beneath a scalding Southern sun. At first, Emmie thinks the girl is alone, but then she sees the thing following her. The albino girl thinks it's an angel.

~ Deacon, but he's a young man, and he stands at a rusted iron gate leading into a tunnel, into the limestone heart of a mountain. It's raining, and he lifts a pair of bolt cutters and clamps them shut on the hasp of a lock. The padlock falls away and splashes in the mud at his feet. Someone giggles, and the gate creaks open.

~ A snowy night at the edge of the sea, and a house burns, a very old and haunted house, evil beyond reckoning, and inside a girl named Narcissa Snow dies with her grandfather.

~ On the train to New York, a woman watches Emmie from

across the aisle. Emmie wishes that she'd stop, because there's something about the woman that makes her nervous, something that frightens her. The woman smiles at her and starts to stand up, but then someone takes the empty seat next to Emmie, and the woman sits down again. She gets off at Old Saybrook.

~ Deacon's bedroom in their house on Angell Street, and he's taken the box from beneath his bed, his cardboard box of secrets. He carries it downstairs and out the front door to the place where they leave the garbage cans by the curb. Emmie's watching him from a living room window. She's only six years old, and she decides that whatever's in the box, it's probably nothing but old clothes or worn-out shoes or something else she has no interest in. He comes back inside and fixes them hot dogs for dinner, and he tells her a very funny story about how her mother once thought she'd found a dinosaur bone, but it turned out she'd only found part of a fossil tree stump instead.

~ A woman who looks a lot like Chance Silvey is sitting in a hearse at the end of a country road, talking to a man named Sheldon. "Something's wrong," she says and rolls her window down just enough to toss out the butt of a cigarette. "I don't know what, but something's gotten fucked-up." It's raining hard, rain slamming loud against the roof of the hearse, and a flash of lightning reveals the marshes at the edge of the road and a ramshackle building farther out. "Fuck it, Shelly. Let's get the hell out of here," the woman says, and the man named Sheldon shoots her in the face.

~ "She died when you were still just a little baby," Deacon tells Emmie and sips his beer. "Her name was Sadie, and she wanted to write books. I'll be damned if she wouldn't have gotten a kick outta you, kiddo."

Emmie looks back, hoping to see the black-skinned woman and the warm desert sun, hoping it's not too late to turn around and head back that way, hoping she knows *how* to turn around. But behind her there is only the void, the slipstream of her passage erasing a trillion possible outcomes to a hundred thousand worldlines.

~ Deacon is standing on the front porch of their house talking to two policemen, and he's barefoot despite the snow piled high in the yard and at the edges of the porch. He's been drinking, and he calls one of the policemen a son of a bitch and a cocksucker, and the two officers exchange glances and frown at each other. "We need you to come with us, Mr. Silvey," onc of them says. "I'm sorry. I know how hard this must be, but we need you to come down and look at the body, to be sure that it's your daughter."

No, Emmie says and squeezes her eyes shut, her voice lost in the clamor of all these possible existences playing out around her. *That's not what happens. That's a lie.*

Then you'd better start looking where it is you're putting your feet, the black-skinned woman says, or maybe it's really the girl from the attic who's talking, or her stepmother. There's no way to be sure. But Emmie keeps her eyes closed and drifts in the current, letting it drag her

forward

(or backward   or sideways,

there's no way to know which).

This

is

what

it's

like to

be

sucked

up

through

a straw,

she thinks, and then there's heat and light and the smell of meat cooking reminds her how hungry she is. In an instant, all potential collapses around her into

one moment

and

one place,

and she opens her eyes in the hollow carved out beneath Woonsocket.

"I have to admit," George Ballou says, his face a grinning mask of blood and grime and soot, "I *was* expecting just a wee bit more from ol' Terpsichore's prize bulldog. You've got me kind of fucking disappointed here." He's squatting next to Soldier, who went down fast and hard shortly after Ballou decided that he'd be better off fighting her with incantations than with knives. She's lying naked at his feet, her back and buttocks beginning to blister on the hot stone.

"You're breaking my fucking heart," she mumbles around a busted upper lip, and he slaps her again.

Firelight fills the burial chamber and casts wild, shifting patterns across the high walls as Ballou's mongrels feed a mix of cordwood and corpses to the hungry flames. Some of the men and women and half-breeds have begun a frenzied summoning dance, cavorting around and around and around the fire, shouting and howling, taunting an unseen sky, cackling and recklessly calling out the names of gods that Soldier's been taught never to speak aloud. The very few full-blooded ghouls present stand apart from all the others, lingering in twos and threes near the periphery of the chamber, watching and waiting, patient and curious as all immortal things.

"Now look what you've gone and done," Ballou sighs. "You

made me lose my goddamned train of thought. No damn wonder the Bailiff decided he'd be better off without a mouthy little cockshy like you."

"So why don't you kill me, and then maybe I'll shut the fuck up," Soldier says; she keeps her eyes on the dancers and the bonfire because she's already seen more than enough of George Ballou. He's a mountain, a living mountain dressed up in muscle and bone, as if that might be enough to hide the truth, and his eyes blaze bright and vicious as any ghoul's. His long gray hair is pulled back in a ponytail that hangs down past his waist; his huge knuckles are a patchwork of scars and fresh gashes, knuckles like the gnarled roots of an ancient willow tree, if any willow ever bled.

"Down here, Providence, we do things in *my* time," he replies and leans closer. His breath smells like bad teeth and wintergreen. "Down *here,* you die when I *say* you die. And I'm thinking maybe that's gonna be a while longer yet, seeing how you're hardly the hellcat I was led to expect. You might even make a halfway decent meretrice, once the dogs have softened you up a little. We can always use fresh breeding stock down here. And who'll be the wiser, eh?"

"Kill her," one of ghouls barks out above the roar of the fire. "That was the bargain."

George Ballou glares at the ghoul, then glances back down at Soldier. "Is that so?" he asks. "See, I don't remember the exact wording. In fact, I don't seem to remember anything quite that goddamned specific at all."

"Kill her," the ghoul barks again, louder than before.

"*You* shut the fuck up!" Ballou shouts back. "She'll die. When I'm done with her, she'll die just fine."

"Maybe the leash is a little shorter than you thought," Soldier says, wincing at the heat and all the raw and wounded places where his magick brushed against and through her. He grabs hold of her chin, forcing her head up, forcing her to look into his glittering holocaust eyes.

"Don't you think for a goddamned minute I don't know *that* game," he snarls, baring his crooked yellow teeth. "That mouth might get you hurt a little more, but it won't get you dead, Providence, not until I'm good and ready for you to *be* dead."

"Just seems like that collar of yours might be getting tight," she says through clenched teeth, and Ballou slaps her again, this time opening her left cheek with his long nails.

"See what I mean? That hurts, but you're still breathing. Want to try again? Who knows, you might get lucky."

Soldier doesn't answer him. She rolls over on her left side and watches the dancers and the flames and the darting, swooping shadows they're painting on the walls. There are tears streaming from her eyes now, and she begins laughing out loud so she won't start sobbing.

"Yeah, that's what I thought," Ballou snorts. He shakes his head, and beads of sweat and spittle, snot and blood spatter Soldier's naked body. "Damn, but those Benefit Street cunts are gonna wish they'd been choosier about their messiahs. They're gonna wish they'd put their money on a horse that could actually fucking run, aren't they, Providence? Maybe if they'd ever gotten around to teaching you what to do with that special rewind switch you got, if they hadn't been too afraid to *try,* you might not be in this predicament. Fuck it, you could just send us all back to next fucking Friday and be done with it."

"I don't know what the hell you're talking about," Soldier says and blinks back salt water and pain. "Maybe you've got the wrong mouthy cockshy. Maybe—"

"Oh, no. No, don't you worry your pretty head about that. I've got just exactly who and what I want," he says and gets to his feet. "George Ballou does his homework, yes, ma'am, and your friend Saben, she might be a sloppy killer and a lousy fuck, but she's pretty good at keeping her promises. *You're* the one, all right, the holy god-damned changeling whore that's supposed to lead them all back to the land of milk and fucking honey. Now, how about you hush up for half a second or so, and I'll see if I can't loosen you up myself." And he unzips his pants.

There's a sudden keening sound from the direction of the bonfire, something loud enough to rise above the din echoing off the walls of the cavern, and a cloud of sparks swirls up from the flames and hangs a few seconds in the smoky air. The dancers cry out trium-phantly and begin moving faster, their bare feet slapping ash and paving stones, arms and legs a drunken blur, their matted hair and contorted faces rendering them all but indistinguishable from one another. Soldier doesn't shut her eyes, and she tries not to flinch as a few of the embers settle on her exposed skin.

Ballou leans close again, and his penis slips out of his pants and dangles limply between his legs. It's tattooed to look like the head of a serpent.

"Seems to me like they've done sent you straight on down to hell, Providence," he says, screaming at her to be heard over the keening sound and all the noise the dancers are making. "But maybe you better shut your eyes now. You're a tough piece of snatch, all right, but everybody's got a breaking point, and I'd like you sane and fully fucking cognizant of your situation when I finally do get around to slitting that sweet little throat of yours."

Soldier blinks, and there's the Bailiff watching her from the far side of the bonfire, and it's almost like seeing him from underwater or seeing a ghost of the man, the way the heat makes the light bend and writhe.

Stay ignorant, he says, *and someone will almost always benefit from your ignorance,* and then she realizes that it's not the Bailiff at all, just one of the Woonsocket *ghul,* a thin and mangy bitch waiting to see what happens next.

"What do you want from me?" Soldier asks, asking the Bailiff who isn't there, but Ballou thinks she's asking him.

"No more than your masters and mistresses have ever wanted," he says. "Your soul. Your heart, my dear. Every iota of your being. A little sport, while we're at it. Your flesh and bones when there's no more sport to be had."

"I wasn't talking to you."

someone will almost always benefit

"Whatever were they thinking, Providence, leaving you all alone, unprepared and unprotected? They've dithered your life away, unable to make a simple decision. It all might have gone another way, but for the turn of a friendly fucking card."

Occasionally, the weapons are reluctant to fulfill their purpose. Guns jam. Arrows miss their mark. Shots go wild. . . .

Ballou touches her, his calloused palm moving slowly across her flat, hard belly, moving down towards the bloodied tangle of her pubic hair, and he nips at her right shoulder with his sharp teeth.

"What *do* you want, George Ballou?" Soldier asks him. She's noticed that the bonfire is expanding, its circumference steadily increasing like the pupil of some giant's eye dilating as it forces the world into focus—whatever the Woonsocket half-breeds have summoned, waking up, shaking off aeons of sleep. Bright tendrils of fire and glowing ash slither across the floor, licking tentatively at the feet of the dancers. Then Soldier sees that one of the mongrels has the stoppered bottle with Odd Willie's captured elemental inside, a silver-haired woman with a bristling gray mane. She holds the bottle high and casts it into the bonfire.

"Only the respect due to me and mine," Ballou mutters in her ear. "That, and maybe just a little fucking more. Right now, I'm in the mood to watch the whole goddamn world burn, so we'll just have to see how it goes."

Do you want to die here? the Daughter of the Four of Pentacles asks, the words that Soldier dreamed or only imagined, delirious and half-awake, because the girl is locked away in the attic of the yellow house, locked away forever or near enough. But that doesn't change Soldier's answer to the question.

George Ballou bites down on the back of her neck, and his hand slides roughly between her legs.

It's a simple spell, something she doesn't even remember having learned, only a few lines of Tadjik to set an elementary alchemy in motion. She doesn't even have to say the words aloud, just follow through with the pantomime, the silent interplay of her lips and teeth, her palate and her tongue. A simple spell, a very small magick, but there's nothing simple or small about the pain, the searing white ache in her hands as molecular bonds are broken and reforged, and she opens her mouth wide and screams.

The thing the bonfire is becoming screams back at her, but no one else seems to notice.

"Whoa," George Ballou laughs, and then he laps at the damage he's done to her neck. "Slow down, girl. You're getting ahead of me."

When she turns on him, her fingers have become lightning and molten steel, and Soldier screams again and drives both her hands deep into his rib cage until she finds his spine. It snaps like a rotten branch in the hands of a child. For an instant, Ballou only stares at her, surprised and disbelieving, and then his whole body shudders violently and his yellow-orange eyes roll back in his head; Soldier feels his soul slipping free of its tethers, and she lets it go.

Emmie Silvey stands alone in the entrance of the cavern, the stone stairwell at her back, the brown girl's glowing orb cradled in her mittens, and she watches as the naked woman pulls her hands free of the dead man's shattered chest. The woman and the dead man and all the rest of what she sees, the great fire and the monsters skip-ping and hopping and dancing crazy circles around it, the burning whirlwind rising from the center of the fire towards the high ceiling. And Emmie knows that wherever this is, wherever and whenever she's emerged from the starry place, it's the very worst part of the dream so far. The naked woman glances up at her, looking Emmie directly in the eyes, and for a second Emmie thinks that the woman has knives for fingers.

"Soldier?" Emmie whispers, her voice immediately lost in the pan-demonium, swallowed by the mad wails of the dancers and the train-whistle bellow of the fire. The woman looks confused, but she nods her head and then glances down at the dark blood and clots of gore dripping to the floor from the ends of her fingers (which aren't knives after all). Then Emmie sees the two hairy, dog-jawed creatures stand-ing together near the wall, and she knows immediately that they're the same sort of beasts that came for her and Pearl in the old railway tunnel. She takes a step backwards, and the naked woman looks up at her again.

"Help me," Emmie says. "I don't know what to do. I don't un-derstand any of this," and she holds out the glass orb because the black-skinned woman said she was supposed to find someone named Soldier and give it to her.

One of the ghouls shakes its head and makes an ugly mewling sound. It glares at Emmie and bares its long teeth.

"Don't move!" Soldier shouts at her, and then she turns towards the ghouls, and they snarl and whine and huddle against the wall. *They're afraid of her,* Emmie thinks. *They're monsters, but they're still afraid of her.*

Soldier has turned to watch the immense and crackling thing dragging itself free of the bonfire, the thing that has begun to coalesce *from* the fire itself, and she stands silhouetted against the conflagra-tion. Emmie wants to run back down the stairs, vanishing into the darkness behind her. Maybe there would be a place to hide, a cold and lightless place where it won't ever be able to find her. Maybe she could even discover a way out of the dream.

Some of the dancers have started to burn, their thrashing bodies wreathed in tendrils of blue-white flame.

"We have to get *out* of here!" Emmie screams, and Soldier looks back over her shoulder.

You have to go to her, Emma Jean Silvey. And you have to carry this thing to her.

Don't move, the naked woman says again, but Emmie can't hear the words, can only see the shapes her lips are making. *Don't move,* but the heat has begun to sting Emmie's eyes and make them water, and she can feel it getting in through all her heavy winter clothes, pushing past her coat and sweater and T-shirt, touching her. She knows that in a minute or only a few more seconds, the fire thing will be done with the dancers, and then it'll eat the woman named Soldier, and the ghouls, and then it will eat her, too.

"*We can't stay here!*" Emmie screams, squinting against the light and the heat, but Soldier only shakes her head and points at her ears—*I can't hear you.*

And then the ground begins to lurch and roll, ripples passing quickly through the stone as though it were only mud, the shock waves beginning at the bonfire and racing out towards the walls of the chamber. Emmie almost falls, and the snow globe with a star inside it slips from her clumsy, mittened hands and hits the floor hard enough that a labyrinth of hairline cracks opens up on its glassy surface.

If this broke, Pearl said, *we wouldn't have to worry about finding our way back. We wouldn't live that long.*

Emmie reaches for the orb, but then the ground begins to shake and roll again, and this time she does fall, goes down hard, and her chin strikes her left knee; she bites her tongue, and her mouth begins to fill with blood. The floor groans and tilts towards the scrabbling fire thing clawing itself free of its bonfire womb as the last of the dancers are incinerated alive, and the orb pulses once, twice, and rolls away towards Soldier.

Emmie begins crawling on her hands and knees, heading for the stairs, and even though there are only a few feet between her and the wide landing, it might as well be a hundred times that far, the way the floor is pitching and rolling about underneath her. All she had to do was give the snow globe to the woman named Soldier, but now she's screwed it up. She's broken the orb, ruined the fragile shell of glass and magick spun by Pearl's father, and soon the star imprisoned inside will escape, and Emmie knows there's no point in running from a star. But she runs anyway, crawls because she *can't* run; she's been brave too long, and now there's no courage left inside her.

"I want to go home," she says, because maybe that's all it will take, just like Dorothy and Glinda and the ruby slippers. In the desert, hadn't the black-skinned woman told her that she already *knew* the way, that she didn't need anyone to show it to her? "I want to go home and wake up," she says. "I want to be home with Deacon now. I want to be *home*."

Another convulsion racks the cavern, and dust and sand and bits of rock and roots pepper the floor all around her. Emmie stops crawling towards the stairs and lies down flat, despite the heat of the stone against her cheek, trying to hold on because she's afraid if she doesn't she's going to start slipping back towards the bonfire and the thing coming *out* of the bonfire.

"*Now,*" she says. "I want to go home *now*. I *know* the way, and *I want to go home*."

"Kid, I don't know who the hell you are, but I think I know exactly what you mean."

Emmie looks up, and there's a very thin, tall man kneeling next to her. He's naked and filthy, too, just like the woman named Soldier, and he's holding half a long human thighbone clutched tightly in his right hand. He smiles at her, but Emmie doesn't smile back. For all she knows, he's just another crazy person or some other sort of monster. For all she knows, he's someone else who wants to hurt her.

"Stay away from me," she says. "You leave me alone."

"*Duck,*" he says, then puts his free hand on top of Emmie's head and forces her back down onto the hot floor. He swings the thighbone, and there's a dull thud, barely audible above the noise from the fire. Emmie rolls over, and one of the ghouls is lying crumpled at her feet, the left side of its face caved in. There's a rusty carving knife, the wooden handle wrapped in duct tape, lying on the floor beside it.

"Holy mother of crap, I've always wanted to do that," the tall man says and grins. "Just haul off and let one of the ugly motherfuckers have it."

"You saved me. It was going to stab me. It was gonna kill me, but you saved me."

"Don't take it personally," he says. "Now, maybe you can tell me what the hell she thinks she's doing," and he points and Emmie follows his finger, looking past the dead ghoul, and sees that the woman named Soldier is holding the cracked orb and standing much nearer the fire than before. All the dancers are dead now, smoldering, twisted heaps scattered in a charcoal ring, and the whirlwind of sparks and smoke and flame is spinning faster, gathering momentum.

"I don't know," Emmie says, and then the thing that the dancers have summoned turns towards Soldier, and it opens three simmering eyes the color of nothing that Emmie's ever seen, and she turns away.

"Aren't they wonderful?" the girl in the attic of the yellow house on Benefit Street said to Soldier when they'd finally reached the place where the alchemist had worked. They stood in front of the wooden shelves and the tall cases holding hundreds upon hundreds of glass or crystal spheres, most of which seemed to Soldier to be filled with fog or some milky whitish liquid.

"Aren't they simply the most wonderful things you've ever seen?"

"What are they?" Soldier asked, and the Daughter of the Four of Pentacles smiled a secretive smile and shrugged her shoulders.

"I'm not supposed to tell you that. But maybe you could try to guess."

"I don't like guessing games," Soldier said. "If you don't want to tell me, then I don't want to know."

"I'd tell you if I could. They told me not to."

"You could tell me anyway."

"Why? Why should I do that? You've been nothing but dreadful since you climbed up that ladder. And besides, they're not the reason that you're here. I just wanted you to see. My father is so proud of them."

"I think you don't *know* what they are," Soldier said. "You don't know, and you're lying about being told not to tell because you don't want to look stupid."

"You're impossible," the girl replied. "Of course I know what they are."

"Then prove it."

"I shouldn't even have shown them to you. A brat like you doesn't *deserve* to see anything this wonderful. Anyway, we should get started soon. There's an awful lot to be done before the Bailiff comes back for you."

"He's never coming back," Soldier sighed and took a step nearer the shelves. One of the spheres had caught her eye. It seemed less foggy than the others, and she thought maybe there was something moving around inside it besides the milky stuff. "He's left me here forever. We have to be sisters now."

"Frankly, I'd rather have a spider for a sister," the alchemist's daughter said and made a face like she'd bitten into something bitter. "No, wait. I like spiders. I'd rather have an old *toad* for a sister."

"What's in there?" Soldier said, ignoring the insult and peering into the glass ball, at all the specks moving about inside. She thought they must be bugs—ants or fleas, maybe. But then she saw that they weren't bugs at all.

"Hey," she said, "those are *people*. Those are tiny little people."

"We're wasting time, changeling. I'm a very busy person, you know."

"But that's what they are. They're a bunch of tiny little people in a glass ball."

"Don't you dare touch it," the Daughter of the Four of Pentacles said sharply, because Soldier was reaching for the sphere. "You mustn't ever touch any of them. Not *ever*, you hear me? It can be very dangerous."

"How'd they get in there?" Soldier asked.

"Never you mind about that. That's not any of your business."

Soldier leaned as close to the sphere as she could without her nose bumping against it, and stared at the scene inside. There were rooms within it, and there were tiny people in most of the rooms—people who seemed no larger than ants or fleas. Some of them appeared to be talking to each other. Some were running about, as if they were being chased by something invisible, something that Soldier couldn't see. Some were sitting alone on miniature chairs or sofas or lying on tiny beds. One was on its knees, praying at an altar festooned with minuscule candles.

"You've seen enough," the Daughter of the Four of Pentacles said and took Soldier by the arm. "You're here for a reason. We need to get started."

"Do they *know* they're inside a glass ball?" Soldier asked and tried to pull free, but the girl was holding her too tightly.

"Who cares? What difference does it make? Now come on. I have other things to do."

Soldier frowned and glanced at the glass ball one last time, then let the alchemist's daughter lead her away from the shelves and the tall cabinets, towards whatever it was the Bailiff had sent her up into the attic to see or do.

"And what the hell did he put inside you?" Soldier asks, staring down at the orb in her hand. The glass is freezing, so cold that it hurts to hold, but she holds it anyway. A fine mist has begun leaking out through the cracked surface, and the reek of ammonia rises from it to mix with all the hot, burning smells. She can see that there's some sort of fire sealed in behind the glass, a bright mote drifting in a sea of night, and she wonders if it might be something like Odd Willie's elemental. Soldier looks up at whatever it is that Ballou's mongrels and the Woonsocket *ghul* have midwifed and finds it gazing furiously back down at her. Three gaping holes leading nowhere, holes that must be its eyes, and they open and close, close and open, one after the other in a fierce counterclockwise gyre.

Right now, I'm in the mood to watch the whole goddamn world burn, so we'll just have to see how it goes.

A thin blue wisp flickers from the thing in the bonfire, like the stinging, phosphorescent tentacle of some deep-sea creature, and it briefly grazes the left side of her throat, then disappears again. Soldier winces, but after the beating in the ossuary, after the tunnels and George Ballou, it's only a very small pain.

"I know that you were invited," she says and swallows, her throat so sore and dry it's getting hard to talk. "But I'm afraid we've changed our minds. Here. Take this for your troubles," and Soldier heaves the freezing glass ball at the gyre of blinking eyes. It sinks into the thing, passing straight through flesh that's still mostly flame, and disappears.

"You can go now. We don't want you here."

The three eyes shut in unison and then open again, much wider than before. Chasms of hate, the most perfect expression of hatred that Soldier has ever seen or imagined, malevolence in the absence of any other sentiment that might taint or dilute its purity. Above the thing, the whirlwind breaks apart, scattering cinders across the burial chamber, and she instinctively covers her face with her hands. The floor trembles and tilts again, then seems to drop several inches all at once, and Soldier is hurled to her hands and knees.

This is it, she thinks. *This is where I'm going to die,* and the thought's not so very terrible, not even so unwelcome, after everything that's happened since she drove through the gates of Oak Hill Cemetery and straight into Ballou's glamour. There *is* regret, though—that she's not going to live long enough to murder Saben White, that she'll never understand why the Bailiff let her walk into this mess or what the hell George Ballou was up to down here, what he thought he could accomplish by summoning beings he could never hope to control. And other questions, too; the nagging, unanswerable questions she might never have remembered, except for the dream of Sheldon Vale's ghost and a clock with a dead girl's face.

A sound fills the cavern, then, a sound like the world dying and being born again, a sound like tumbling cataracts and falling leaves and the grinding teeth of sleeping gods. Soldier clenches her hands into fists and whispers half-forgotten prayers she's never believed, supplication and benediction, a mumbled litany for Mother Hydra and Father Kraken waiting in their silent, flooded halls at the bottom of the bottom of the sea.

And then the fracturing, rending sound ceases as suddenly as it began, and the thing writhing inside its birth caul of fire howls one last time and breaks apart, dissolving, collapsing into itself, becoming no more than tattered, glimmering shreds of ash and slag. The bonfire is only a bonfire again, and in the instant before Soldier loses consciousness, she can hear Odd Willie calling her name. It sounds like he's at least a thousand miles away.

When it's over, when the brown girl's snow globe has been swallowed by the fire, and the monster has been destroyed or driven away or whatever it is that Soldier has managed to do, Emmie carefully picks her way up the split and buckled sections of flooring to the landing and sits alone at the top of the stairs with her back to the dead bodies and the sputtering remains of the bonfire. She takes off her coat and mittens and gloves, and lets the cool, moist air flowing up the dark stairs wash over her.

The handful of surviving ghouls have fled the chamber through narrow fissures in the walls, and the thin man who told her that his name was Willie is wearing the clothes of the man that Soldier killed, though they're much too big for him and the pants keep sliding down. He's wrapped Soldier in a long linen robe that he stripped from the body of the ghoul he killed with the thighbone, and then it takes him at least half an hour to carry her over the rubble and up to the landing. He lays her next to Emmie and sits down, slicked with sweat, looking sick and gasping for breath.

Emmie brushes hair from Soldier's face. "Is she going to be okay?" she asks him.

"Maybe," Willie Lothrop says and wipes at his sweaty face. "Maybe not. I'm not a doctor, kid. I'm not even sure *I'm* going to make it."

"My name's Emmie," she says. "The black woman in the desert sent me here."

Odd Willie laughs and wipes at his face again. "Is that a fact? Well, I have no idea what the hell you're talking about, Emmie, but perhaps we'll figure it all out later. Unless we die down here."

"She can't be Deacon's daughter," Emmie says, speaking to herself now instead of the skinny man with no eyebrows. "She's too old. She can't *possibly* be Deacon's daughter."

"She ain't nobody's daughter, nobody except the hounds. Jesus fucking Christ, did you *see* that shit?"

"I saw," Emmie says. "I don't know what any of it was, but I saw it."

"Yeah, me either. Me and you both. But it was sure some crazy, fucked-up shit; I know that much."

"She's hurt," Emmie says, then pulls off her right glove and lays her palm against Soldier's forehead. Her skin is pink, like someone with a sunburn, and she has a fever. "I think she needs a doctor."

"Hell, at this point she probably needs a goddamned exorcist. Whatever the shit that thing was, it most certainly wasn't a goddamn hobgoblin. Nobody goes up against something like that and comes out. . . ." And then he stops wiping his face and stares at her a moment or two. "Who the hell *are* you?"

"I told you. I'm Emmie Silvey. The black woman in the desert sent me to help Soldier."

The man named Willie takes a deep breath and spits. "You ain't one of Ballou's bunch?"

"I've never heard of anyone named Ballou, except for that bear in *The Jungle Book.*"

"Oh, that's fucking cute. That's just precious."

"Well, it's the truth."

"Are you a witch?"

"No, I'm Emmie Silvey. I live in Providence with my father, Deacon. He runs a used bookstore."

Odd Willie laughs again and cracks his knuckles. "Well, Emmie Silvey from Providence. I'm Odd Willie, also from fucking Providence. Now, just let me get my breath, and then we'll see if we can't figure out how to get Soldier out of here. How's that sound to you?"

"Okay," Emmie says, and the skinny man nods and shuts his eyes. She sits with Soldier while he rests, and tries not to think about the monsters or the lost snow globe, Pearl or the woman in the desert, tries not to wonder where she is or how hard it's going to be to get home again. There'll be time for that later. There are strange noises from the darkness beyond the stairs, sounds like animals or people or both, and she tries not to think about those, either.

Emmie opens her eyes, and at first she's unable to remember where she is, and then, remembering, panics that she must have dozed off, and she has no idea how long she might have been asleep. But then she sees that the skinny man is standing over Soldier, who's still unconscious. He's holding a torch, and the landing and archway are bathed in its warm yellow light.

"I fell asleep," she says.

"Yep, you sure as hell did."

Emmie rubs at her eyes, then asks him where he found the torch.

"There were a few pieces of furniture," and he nods towards the devastated chamber. The bonfire has almost burned itself out, and it's mostly dark in there now, only a single shaft of white sunlight getting in from somewhere far overhead. Emmie thinks it might be coming in through a sort of chimney.

"This used to be a table leg," Odd Willie continues. "Toss in a couple of rags and some candle wax, and presto-changeo, abraca-fucking-dabra, voilà, and what's the difference between me and a goddamned Boy Scout, I ask you?"

"Your goddamned dirty mouth," Emmie replies. "I don't think Boy Scouts curse. I think it's against the rules."

"Hey, fuck that," Odd Willie says. "I have it on good authority that Boy Scouts curse like drunken sailors. Hell, there's probably a goddamn merit badge for profanity."

"I'm hungry," she says, wishing she had one of the sandwiches or pears from Pearl's brown bag, and he shrugs.

"Sorry. I can't help you there. First things first. I want you to carry this," and he waves the torch at Emmie; the flames make a loud whooshing noise in the air. "I'll carry Soldier best I can. We need to get out of this place before one of those beaver-beater fucks stops licking its wounds and decides to come back looking for us."

Emmie stands, stretches, puts her coat on again, and then takes the torch from Willie. It's heavier than she expected.

"You gotta be careful with that thing. Hold it out away from you," he says, and she does.

"Can you carry her?" Emmie asks.

"I think so. I'm starting to get some of my strength back. Right now, I only feel like *one* truck ran over me. She's just real fucking lucky I didn't make her shoot me before she came up here."

"I don't even want to know what you're talking about," Emmie says and holds the torch up as high as she can, trying to get an idea how far down the stone stairs go. She can see that the steps are slick, and there are patches of moss or algae growing on the rock.

"Smart kid," Odd Willie says. "Ignorance is fucking bliss." And when Emmie gets tired of watching the stairs, staring at the murky place at the limit of the torchlight where the stairs blend imperceptibly into the darkness, she turns back to find that he's managed to lift Soldier off the ground and is holding her slung over his left shoulder. Her head's dangling towards the floor, her chin resting against his back and her mouth half-open, and he has both hands clasped together firmly beneath her butt.

"You go first," he says. "And keep that light on the stairs. I gotta be able to see where I'm putting my feet."

"Those steps are slippery," Emmie warns.

"No shit, the steps are slippery. You just make sure I can see where I'm going," and then he curses and shifts Soldier's weight so he has a better grip on her.

So Emmie starts down the stairs, forgetting her mittens and the glove she took off, and Odd Willie follows her. He slips only once, but he doesn't fall. It seems to Emmie that the steps go on almost forever, down and down, curving along the side of the rocky wall. When they finally reach the bottom, Emmie sits on the damp ground, and Willie leans against the side of the tunnel, his eyes shut, gulping air like a goldfish that's jumped out of its bowl.

"How much farther?" Emmie asks.

"How the hell should I know?" he wheezes.

"Left or right?" she asks.

"Do I look like fucking Ranger Rick? Your guess is as good as mine. Flip a coin."

"I don't *have* a coin," Emmie says and stares at her reflection in a puddle. Her face is streaked with mud and soot, and she's lost her toboggan cap somewhere. Maybe she left it back in the desert; her hair is tangled and sticking out in all directions.

"Well, we can't stop here," Odd Willie says and coughs. "We gotta keep moving, or I'm never going to make it. Left or right, kid. You pick."

Emmie picks left, for no particular reason, and leads Odd Willie Lothrop down the long tunnel, which seems to slope gradually upwards. The air is dank and smells like mud and mold, and there's a chemical odor that burns Emmie's nose and eyes, like the place beneath the sink where Deacon keeps the bottles of Clorox and detergent, Mr. Clean and Drano and Formula 409. When she asks Odd Willie about it, he says it's from the river, that the old textile mills along the Blackstone dump all their toxic sludge right into the river, and that's what she's smelling.

Once, they cross a narrow wooden bridge, pine boards gone slick and punky, and Emmie pauses to look over the edge. But there's only blackness down there, as far as she can see, and the rushing of flowing water far below.

"Shake a leg, kid. Ain't nothing down there you want to see," he says, then grunts as he shifts Soldier from one shoulder to the other. "And, more important, there's nothing down there you want to be seen *by*."

The tunnel rises, turns left, then right, then left again, and when they come to an archway leading to another chamber or a side tunnel, Willie tells her to keep going straight. There's a skull resting on a small ledge above the arch, and Emmie tells herself it's only the skull of a coyote or a big dog, but she knows better. The next time the tunnel turns right, they're greeted by a gust of cold, fresh air.

"This must be the way," she says. "I think I can even smell the outside. It smells like snow."

"What the hell does snow smell like?" Odd Willie asks, and stops again to get his breath.

"Clean," Emmie tells him. "Snow smells clean."

Odd Willie shuts his eyes and licks at his lips. "Christ, I wish I had a goddamn beer."

"I'd settle for a Cherry Coke," Emmie says, "or some birch beer."

"I thought we were fucking dead back there," and he tightens his hold on Soldier. "If you hadn't come along, you and that goddamn crystal ball of yours—"

"It wasn't mine," Emmie says, interrupting Odd Willie. "It was Pearl's, and it wasn't a crystal ball, either."

"You saved our sorry skins," he says and opens his eyes again. "We owe you one, Emmie Silvey."

"I just want to go home, that's all."

"Then that's where you're gonna go," Odd Willie tells her. "Just as soon as we can get out of this shithole, I'll drive you myself. Hell, I'll even get you that bottle of birch beer. You like Polar?"

"Yeah, Polar's good. Are you ready now?" she asks.

"As I'll ever be, which isn't saying very goddamn much." And she starts walking again, heading in the direction the clean, wintry air is coming from, and he follows.

Odd Willie left Soldier and Emmie in the woods not far from the north side of the cemetery. When she asked where he was going, he told her that he had to steal a car, unless she'd gotten it in her head to walk all the way back to Providence. The day was bright, but it was still snowing—a white sky and whiter ground—and Emmie wondered if it was only the next day, only Monday, or if maybe she'd been gone a long time and it'd been a whole week or more since she left Pearl in the railroad tunnel. Maybe it had been snowing for days. She sat with Soldier, the two of them beneath an old poplar tree that Odd Willie had picked because he said ghouls hated poplar trees. When she asked why, he wouldn't tell her, so she had a feeling he was lying and had only said that so she wouldn't be afraid. Soldier was still unconscious, and her fever was worse. Sweat trickled across her face, and she shivered so hard that her teeth chattered. Emmie wrapped her tighter in the robes that Odd Willie had taken off the ghoul he'd killed, and told her about Aslan defeating the armies of the White Witch. She felt silly doing it, but she was scared, and it was all she could think of to talk about, and it made the time go faster.

And then Willie was back much sooner than she'd expected, back in the cemetery and blowing the horn so she'd know it was only him coming—two short honks, one long. She followed him through the snow as he carried Soldier up the hill again. He laid her in the backseat of the purple Chevrolet Malibu, spread a blanket over her (Emmie didn't ask where the blanket or the car had come from), and then they drove away from Oak Hill and Woonsocket, and no one and nothing tried to stop them.

It's Wednesday, and they've been at the seedy little motel just outside Uxbridge, Massachusetts, for almost two days now. Willie drove north on icy back roads until he found the place, and he told Emmie they'd probably be okay there until Soldier felt better and he could figure out what to do next. The walls are the same shade of green as lime sherbet, and the carpet is orange. Emmie's sitting on one of the queen-sized beds with Soldier, swabbing her bruised and blistered face with a damp washcloth, and Odd Willie's on the other bed, talking on his cell phone, having another argument with the man he calls the Bailiff. The television is on a channel that's been showing nothing but Tom and Jerry cartoons for two hours, but the volume's turned all the way down.

"What I *want* is some sort of fucking security," he says again. "I've told you that, what, like a hundred goddamn times already? I keep fucking telling you that. I want a fucking guarantee that it's safe to come in. *That's* what I want."

There's a long pause while Willie chews at a thumbnail and stares at the TV screen. Emmie lays the washcloth back across Soldier's forehead; she's sick of Tom and Jerry and wishes he would change the channel.

"Damn straight, I'm paranoid. Right now, I'm the most paranoid motherfucker in New England. *You* weren't there, and you have no goddamn idea what we walked into."

Another pause, shorter than the last, and then Odd Willie says he'll call back later and hangs up. "Fucking mouse," he says and points at the television with the antenna of his cell phone. "It's just a game to him."

"He doesn't want to be eaten," Emmie says. "That's all, he just doesn't want to be eaten."

"Then maybe he ought to live somewhere there isn't a damned cat. Lots of people don't have cats. Christ, man, I hate that little brown fucker. He's fucking sadistic; you know that, right? You know what 'sadistic' means? That is a sadistic fucking mouse."

"It's almost suppertime," Emmie says. "You should let me call my father now."

Odd Willie frowns and sits up, swinging his long legs over the edge of the bed. "I told you I can't let you do that. We'll get you home, I swear. There's just some shit has to be cleared up first, so no one else gets hurt."

"Deacon's gonna think I'm dead. He's gonna think someone kidnapped me."

Odd Willie looks at the clock radio on the table between the beds. It's almost seven o'clock. "Well, then, just think how much happier he'll be when you show up safe and sound. Want a hamburger?"

"No. I'm *tired* of hamburgers," Emmie says and watches Soldier's eyelids flutter. They've been fluttering all day, but she still hasn't opened them.

"Then how about some fucking McNuggets? Those are pretty good."

"They taste like shit," Emmie tells him.

"There's some sort of pizza joint—"

"I don't *want* pizza. I want to call Deacon. I want you to take me home."

"Kid, you're just gonna have to be cool, all right? When I get this crap straightened out—"

"If you don't get Soldier a doctor soon, she's gonna die," Emmie says. "She's in a coma. Her fever's up to a hundred and two again. The aspirin aren't working."

"I need a fucking cigarette," Willie says and reaches for his shoes, because Emmie won't let him smoke in the room. He got some clothes and shoes that fit from a Salvation Army in Uxbridge;

there's also a pair of Levi's, a black sweater, and some scuffed-up old cowboy boots for Soldier, if she ever wakes up. He tosses Emmie the remote and tells her to find something else to watch.

"Hey, you're the one who wouldn't change the channel," she tells him. "I hate Tom and Jerry. I told you I hate Tom and Jerry."

"Well, I hate them worse than you do. You're a kid. I thought kids liked fucking cartoons and shit. Just change the channel. I'll be back in five."

"You know it's almost suppertime," she says again, and Odd Willie rolls his eyes.

"Decide what you want, and I'll go get it. I'll be back in five minutes." And he stands up, puts on the Red Sox jacket that he also found at the Salvation Army store, and leaves Emmie alone in the room with Soldier. Before he pulls the door shut, she sees that it's snowing again. She turns the sound on the television up loud and flips channels until she finds a documentary about the planet Mars, then lies down beside Soldier and stares at the television a few minutes before glancing at the phone sitting useless on the bedside table. Odd Willie disconnected it and hid the cord somewhere. She's tried to find it, whenever he leaves her alone, but she's starting to think he must have hidden it out in the car.

"What's going to happen to me?" she asks Soldier, pretending that Soldier can answer her, pretending that Soldier might *know* the answer. Soldier's eyelids flutter, her lower lip twitches, and then her face is still again.

"You know I'd help you, if I knew how. Right now, there are lots of things I'd do, if I knew how." Then Emmie stares at her a moment, her face like someone who's only asleep and having a very bad dream.

"You look like my mother," Emmie says. "You look like her a lot." She's been thinking it since she first saw Soldier beneath Woonsocket, but she's been too afraid to actually *say* it out loud, too afraid of what it may mean to allow herself to even think about it for more than a few seconds at a time. But it's true. Soldier's face isn't *exactly* her mother's face—the face of the woman in the old photographs that Deacon's shown her and the ones that she found in the box under his bed—but it's close enough. *Too* close. And Soldier doesn't have yellow eyes. She has green eyes like Deacon. Green eyes like Chance Silvey.

Emmie remembers the gold wedding ring she took from the box, and reaches into her jeans pocket, afraid suddenly that she might have lost it somewhere, in the black woman's desert or one of the tunnels. But the ring's still there, and she takes it out and stares at it for a moment.

On the television, the narrator is talking about a time, billions of years ago, when Mars might have had an ocean.

"Willie's not so bad," she says to Soldier. "He's not nearly as big a creep as he wants everyone to think he is. If he was, he'd have left me down there to die, right? He wouldn't have saved me. He's mostly just scared all the time, and that's why he acts the way he does."

Emmie doesn't have to touch Soldier's skin to feel the heat coming off her; it's almost like lying next to an oven. Emmie thinks about taking her temperature again, slipping the digital thermometer beneath her tongue and watching the numbers go up, waiting to see just how bad it is. Willie bought the thermometer at a CVS the day before, when he bought aspirin and Tylenol, Neosporin and gauze bandages and a tube of something smelly he keeps combing through his hair. She hasn't asked him where he's getting the money. She hasn't really cared.

"You can't die," Emmie whispers. "You can't. If *you* die—" and then she makes herself stop, because Sadie has told her that words are magick and she should be careful how she uses them. She slips the ring into her pocket again and goes back to watching television.

And she holds Soldier's hand, no matter how hot it is, and waits for Willie to come back.

Dreaming, dreaming so long now that Soldier has forgotten that there was ever anything before the dream. There was fire somewhere back towards the beginning, an unimaginable, devouring fire that would have burned away the universe and still been hungry, and now some fraction of the fire is trapped inside her. Perhaps no single fire—Quaker Jameson's roadhouse in flames, the fire Odd Willie set at Rocky Point and then the sizzling being he summoned, George Ballou's bonfire and the beast rising from it, and, finally, a star inside a crystal ball. Fire to destroy and purify, fire to deliver and condemn, and she breathed it all in, and it might never find a way out again.

Dreaming, she has drifted through years and months, days and hours, and sometimes it seems that she only drifts and there's no *time* at all. She's never entirely alone, because she has the fire that she swallowed for company, and she has the Daughter of the Four of Pentacles, too, who comes and goes, rattling on about things that Soldier only occasionally understands. She has memories and things that can't be memories because they haven't happened yet or will never happen.

"I sent her to you," the alchemist's daughter says, but Soldier isn't at all sure she believes her. "The poor child," the girl continues, "she was lost and alone on the sea in a tiny yellow boat named the *Fly-Away Horse,* bobbing and lost in a hurricane tempest upon the wild, wild sea. There was a whale that wanted to swallow her alive, and there were monsters, and a phantom mariner who catches mermaids on fishhooks and cooks them in his skillet."

Soldier watches herself sitting on the floor in the Bailiff's study, a child in a blue calico dress eating sugar cookies and drinking grape soda while an old man talks. But here he has silver eyes, like the vampires do, and his words are black and living, and there's a nasty plopping sound as they drip from his lips to lie in a squirming heap on his desk.

She walks the long, narrow path down to the dragon, old Root-nibbler waiting for her on the night of the Full Hunger Moon, the last confirmation before she passes from childhood into the service of the ghouls. At the bottom of the pit, she kneels and thrusts her arms into the twin holes in the earth, one ringed in gold, the other in platinum, and holds her breath, expecting the dragon to take her hands. Expecting to die there with all the ghouls and the other changelings looking on.

"Strictly speaking, this has never happened either," the Daughter of the Four of Pentacles says and shakes her head. "You're the only adult changeling alive who hasn't had to make the passage through the three trials, fire and blades and teeth. The *ghul* imagine you're much too precious to risk on such dangerous formalities."

"They sent me to Woonsocket to fucking die," she replies, and "No," the girl says. "The Bailiff sent you to Woonsocket. *Not* the ghouls."

"The Bailiff serves the ghouls. Whatever he does, it's nothing that isn't their will."

"Oh, don't be such a silly sap," the girl says, and then she wanders off again, leaving Soldier alone on the *Fly-Away Horse,* and the fisherman who only catches mermaids scowls at her and goes back to wrestling with the tiller. The rain's falling so hard now that she can barely see him, even though he's only a few feet away from her, squatting in the stern of the dory. The boat rises and falls on waves so high that their white crests scrape at the low clouds; then it races back down the steep sides of watery canyons, plunging into troughs that carry them almost all the way to the seafloor. The tattered sail, shredded by the wind, flutters uselessly in the gale. She doesn't know the fisherman's name; she isn't even sure that he has one. She paid him a dollar and a handful of dead spiders to get her from one side of Block Island Sound to the other, but now she thinks that they'll both drown before they ever see land again.

"I ought to have known better," the fisherman growls and chews the stem of his soggy corncob pipe. "I ought to have my sorry skull stove in, takin' on the likes of you."

"I was only looking for the way across," she says, surprised that she doesn't have to raise her voice to be heard above the storm.

"Well, I hope you're pleased with yourself," he grunts, but Soldier doesn't know what he means. The voice of the storm is the same as the voice of the fire, the fire from the beginning, and soon it will fall on them like a hammer. The water seethes with the restless coils of great eels and serpents and the eternally searching arms of Mother Hydra and Father Kraken.

"My father caught this boat in 1922," the girl from the attic says, and smiles. "It was one of his earliest experiments with translocation. He was only trying to catch a bit of the sea. He said the boat was pure luck."

Sand blows down from the dunes, which have never been waves, no matter how much they might emulate or envy them. The *Fly-Away Horse* lies on its starboard side, half-buried in the beach, its mast snapped in two and its rigging and canvas scattered all about, and Soldier is sitting cross-legged in the shade of the boat, hiding from the desert sun. There are dead mackerel and jellyfish and trilobites baking in the noon heat, stranded by the tide. The Daughter of the Four of Pentacles told her to wait here if she wanted to speak with the black woman, the woman who is ancient and unaging and who wanders the desert looking for lost dreamers.

"I never said I was lost," she tells the girl.

"You certainly don't look particularly found," the girl replies and kneels in the sand in front of Soldier. The noonday sun gathers in her hair like honey and washes gently across her almond skin. She doesn't make eye contact with Soldier, pokes at the corpse of a blue-gray starfish instead, flipping it over to expose all the hundreds and hundreds of wriggling tube feet to the sun.

"I don't need *your* help," Soldier says.

"What I did to you—"

"Is ancient fucking history. Go away. Leave me alone."

"They said they would kill my father if I didn't help them, if I didn't work the contraption. No one else knew how. They said they would send assassins all the way to Weir to find him. They said—"

"Leave me alone," Soldier tells her, and the black-skinned woman kneeling in the sand picks up the dying starfish and sighs.

"It used to make me very sad, finding all the helpless little things that the sea spits out, all the things cast up to die. I used to think, perhaps I could save them all. I'd walk this beach for days and days," and she motions at the shoreline stretching away on either side. "I would find them and carry them back down to the water where they belonged. I would try to give them back to the sea."

"Do you have a point, old woman?" Soldier asks her, and the woman from the desert smiles and shrugs her shoulders. She sets the starfish back down on the sand, then wipes her hand on the hem of her thobe.

"A lot of them died anyway," she says. "That's all I wanted you to know. The world makes orphans of us all, sooner or later. It puts us where and when we don't belong, and even if we manage to find our way home again, we might discover home doesn't want us anymore. That's the truth, and there's not much we can do about it."

Low waves break against the edge of the desert, speaking in a secret language Soldier thinks she might have understood once, a long time ago, before the Bailiff took her up to the attic. A warm wind whispers through the dunes at her back and tugs at the black-skinned woman's pale dreadlocks.

"She was a fine little boat," the woman says and pats the hull of the capsized dory. "A *fine* little boat, was the *Fly-Away Horse*. She sailed all the seven seas. She saw typhoons and maelstroms. And she even got *you* this far."

"And just how the hell far is that?" Soldier asks, and she starts to reach for the starfish, but the sun is much hotter than she expected, and Soldier pulls her hand back into the shade of the wrecked dory.

"Far enough and then some," the woman says, standing up. She shades her amber eyes with her left hand and gazes up at the sky. "Far enough you have to make a choice how this thing's gonna end. That child's mother's coming for her, Soldier, and she means to have the girl."

"What's that to me?"

"Well, now that would seem to be the most important question," the black-skinned woman replies, still watching the wide and simmering sky. "But don't you sit here too long thinking it all over. She's a natural-born sorceress, that one, and she knows well enough how to ride the coattails of a snowstorm. The child is hers, and she believes that you are the last and only thing standing between them. She has a fearful hatred for you."

And then the woman's gone, as are the *Fly-Away Horse* and the sand and the sea and the blue starfish. The falling snow confuses Soldier for only a moment—a passing dislocation, the half blink of a sleeping eye, a breath—and she's glad for the cold and the winter night after so much sun, lost in fever and grateful for cool air, and the weight of the Winchester shotgun feels good in her hands. She's standing in a parking lot, cars and trucks half-buried in snow, everything veiled in white and countless shades of blue and gray trailing off to black, everything except the soft orange pools from streetlights and the flashing red and green neon of the tall motel sign at the edge of the road. The Daughter of the Four of Pentacles is there, too, walking in circles, catching snowflakes on her tongue. She stops and looks at Soldier.

"We make a fine pair, don't you think?" the girl asks. "Me with too much childhood and you with hardly any at all. That almost makes us sisters, of a sort."

"I'm still dreaming," Soldier says.

"Of course. Otherwise, we wouldn't be having this conversation. They apprehended me in the old railway tunnel. Miss Emma Jean Silvey slipped away, but they caught me—because Barnaby's a coward and a louse—and then they shut me away again. But all that *time* was wonderful. I aged almost an entire day and night."

Soldier pumps the shotgun, chambering a round, and stares into the swirling, shifting gloom. The storm is filled with shadows and the less distinct shadows of shadows, with almost endless possibility and potential. It is a crucible, like all storms, dreaming or awake.

The Daughter of the Four of Pentacles stops and stares down at the pattern her boots have pressed into the snow and slush—two intersecting triangles to form a six-pointed star. And Soldier realizes that she hasn't been walking in circles at all.

"Saben," she says, and the alchemist's daughter holds one finger up to her lips and frowns.

"Not so *loud*. She's coming. She's probably already here somewhere," and the girl glances nervously over her shoulder. "There's no need to *call* her."

"Ballou's dead. Why didn't she just run?"

"She wants her daughter back, and besides, she knows you'd come after her. She knows that if she runs now, she'll never be able to stop running."

At least she got that part right, Soldier thinks and shuts her eyes, or she dreams she shuts her eyes, and she's back in the yellow house on Benefit Street, sitting across the mahogany dining table from the ghost of Sheldon Vale. He lays a tarot card on the table—the Tower—and tells her what it means.

"Saben *chose* to face me in a dream, didn't she?" Soldier asks him.

"Yeah," he says and taps the card once, twice, three times. "It was her idea, if everything went to shit and she wound up with you on her ass. She understands that you're much weaker here, sleeping. You have to be awake to do that . . . that *thing* you do." And he makes a staccato *tick-tock-tick-tock* noise with his tongue, his index finger up to mimic a clock's second hand moving steadily backwards, and then he winks at her. "No hard feelings, though. We made a fine pair while it lasted, don't you think?"

"Come back," the Daughter of the Four of Pentacles says and shakes Soldier so hard she almost drops the shotgun, almost squeezes the trigger. "You can't keep wandering off like that. She'll kill you if you do. She began the dream, so the labyrinth always works to her advantage."

Two triangles to make a star, you see? Two intersecting dreams, and one angle remains always invisible—the overlap—a shared point in space and time and sentience, the Bailiff said and pulled at his beard.

"You should go now," Soldier tells the girl.

"Are you sure? You may yet have need of me."

"Then I'll find you when I do," Soldier says, and the girl comes apart in a sudden gust of icy wind, becoming briefly something bright and sparkling and even less substantial than the snow.

And Saben White is standing ten or fifteen feet away, on the other side of the star traced in the snow. Her clothes are torn and dirty, and there's dried blood on her face and hands. She isn't alone. One of the Woonsocket mongrels is crouched on either side of her.

"You should've run," Soldier says, and the half-breeds bristle and bare their teeth.

"Haven't you ever loved anything?" Saben asks bitterly. "Haven't you ever once loved something so much that you'd die for it?"

"You can't have the girl, Saben. She belongs to the Cuckoo, just like you do. Just like me. And even if she didn't, after all this bullshit, I still wouldn't let you have her."

"She's my fucking daughter," Saben says, and the mongrel on her left cries out, an ugly, feral shriek that Soldier knows is the nightmare of Saben's loss and denial, and it lunges, bounding through the snow on all fours. Soldier pulls the trigger, and for a heartbeat the roar of the shotgun drowns out every other sound. The half-breed thing goes down in a spray of blood and shredded flesh, becoming only a faceless, broken heap in the snow.

"See what you made me do?" Soldier says, the echo of the Winchester fading away across the shell-shocked winter night.

"After everything they've done to you," Saben says, "you're still willing to fight for them?"

"This isn't about them. You tried to kill me, Saben. *Twice* now you've tried to kill me. And, unless I'm mistaken, you came here tonight to kill me. That makes *three* times," and Soldier holds up three fingers.

"I came here for my child."

"Like I said, she's *not* your child. She belongs to the Cuckoo."

"Soldier, how can you stand there and say that? They've stolen so much from you. You don't even fucking *know* the things they've taken away from you. Your whole life is lived in a fog they've spun to keep you ignorant. And now the Bailiff—"

"Am I going to have to shoot that one, too?" Soldier asks and points the barrel of the gun at the second Woonsocket mongrel. It snarls and retreats, cowering behind Saben.

"Listen to me, Soldier. You think he didn't *know* exactly what Ballou was doing? You think he believed you'd ever be coming back to Providence alive?"

"Right now, I don't exactly know. But I figure all that shit's between me and the Bailiff."

"You have to understand," Saben says, "they want to leave the world," and she draws a circle in the air with her left hand as she speaks, a ring of silver fire that hangs suspended above the snow. Soldier takes a step back and pumps the shotgun again.

If you fully comprehend the sum of these angles, and if you can see all the points of convergence simultaneously, then the game may always be turned to your advantage, the Bailiff said, and Soldier stopped nibbling at the cookie and watched what he was doing with his hands. *It's a bit like origami, only without the paper. See? A fold here, a bend there—*

"Don't make me kill you," Saben White says, and her ring of silver flame grows brighter. She draws another with her right hand.

"Jesus, Saben. You've *tried* to kill me three goddamn times now, and you want me to think you're feeling merciful?"

—it's simple. Valley fold the left side of the first triangle so the edge falls on the closest crease. Now, Soldier, simply mountain fold the right side of the second intersecting triangle without severing—

"You were in my way before. All you have to do is let me have her. She's my *daughter.*"

There's a tug at the shotgun, the tidal drag of Saben's spell, and Soldier doesn't resist it. A moment later the Winchester slips from her hands and falls to the ground.

—to make a new crease and complete that side of the star. It's up to you where you want the star point to be realized, where you wish it to appear.

"Let me have her, and you won't be in my way anymore."

"Suck my dick," Soldier says and folds the star that the Daughter of the Four of Pentacles trampled into the snow. It's much easier than she remembers—*valley fold, mountain fold*—and she shuts her eyes again as the geometry of the dream begins to ravel and fray. She feels the sudden eddy when Saben's wheels of silver fire shift into another range of the spectrum. And she hears Saben scream when the fire folds back upon her.

Soldier stands between the desert and the sea, and the black-skinned woman smiles and kisses her softly on the lips. "You see, that wasn't so difficult. That wasn't hard at all."

"But it's not over," Soldier tells her.

"Child, it's never over. You'd better get used to that."

And the *Fly-Away Horse* moves across a calm green sea, a school of dolphins racing one another at its prow. The old man at the tiller puffs his pipe and tells her about the time he sailed all the way to the Pillars of Hercules.

Deep beneath Providence, on the night of the Full Hunger Moon, Soldier begins the long walk down to the dragon, the walk she never had to make.

These and a thousand other cusps spaced out along a tissue-paper star with seven points, and in the end, she finds her way back past George Ballou's fire in the cavern and the greater fire trapped inside a cracked glass sphere, the twin fires burning at the beginning of the dream, which she sees now are *all* fires and all dreams. She breathes out an inferno, and in the great emptiness beyond the heat, she can rest and heal and remember herself. And she can hear the girl's voice calling her, the voice of the child who saved her, Saben White's daughter, and she wakes up.

NINE

The Bailiff

The clouds have gone, and the sky above the highway is a bright shade of blue, a cold and perfect cloudless blue spread out above the sagging power lines and bare tree branches glistening with ice. The snow is piled high along the sides of the road, and Emmie thinks it'll start melting soon, if it hasn't started already. Odd Willie's driving, and Soldier's riding up front with him, so Emmie has the backseat all to herself. The stolen Chevy sedan glides over brown slush—ice and salt and sand—and the black streaks of asphalt showing through. There's a Beatles song playing on the radio, "Hey Jude," and Odd Willie is humming along to it. Every now and then he smiles at Emmie from the rearview mirror.

"I'm sorry," Soldier says again.

"She was my mother," Emmie replies, but no matter how many times she says the words, it doesn't feel any less unreal. "She was my mother, and she'd come to find me, and you killed her."

Soldier lights another cigarette and rolls her window down an inch or so. She doesn't look much better than she did the night before. Her face seems somehow pale, despite the sunburn that isn't a sunburn, and there are too many bruises and scrapes to even bother counting. The edges of the long gash Ballou made in her left cheek are swollen and scabby. Odd Willie stitched the wound closed with dental floss, but it looks fevery and infected.

"She didn't leave me any fucking choice," Soldier says again, but Emmie's not sure she believes that. Sadie's told her that people always have choices, even when they believe that they don't, that sometimes they just say they don't because it helps them feel better.

"You could have let her come to me like she wanted; you could have let me . . ." But then Emmie trails off, all these things already said once or twice or three times since they left the motel in Uxbridge, and she knows that repeating them over and over isn't going to do anything to chase away the empty, confused feeling. It isn't going to change what Soldier's done. It isn't going to bring Saben White back from the dead.

"I did what I had to do," Soldier says firmly and exhales. Most of the smoke is sucked out through the open window, but some hangs about her head like a veil.

Odd Willie stops humming and glances up at Emmie again. "You better listen to her, kid," he says. "She knows what she's talking about. Believe me, you're way the hell better off without that bitch."

"She was my *mother*," Emmie says quietly and shuts her eyes. The bright day is swallowed in darkness, and there are only sounds— the tires against the frozen road, the spray of sand and salt pinging against the wheel wells and the undercarriage of the car, the music from the radio. "Willie, please, just take me home now."

"He can't do that yet," Soldier replies. "We'll do it when we can, but not yet. Maybe after we see the Bailiff, maybe then."

"But none of this has anything to do with me," Emmie tells her, even though she knows that it does, that maybe, somehow, it has an awful *lot* to do with her. She opens her eyes, and Soldier's watching her across the seat, watching her with Chance Silvey's green eyes.

"Emmie, you have to be patient," Soldier says. "There's too much at stake here. We have to try to do this the right way. I still don't know exactly how you fit into this mess, or where you got hold of that sphere, and I have to find out before you can go home."

"I didn't want to run away," Emmie says and opens her eyes. The day seems even brighter than before. "I didn't *want* to go into that tunnel. I only did it because Pearl said they'd hurt Deacon if I didn't."

Soldier nods her head. "She was right about that. The way things stand, you're a loose end, and the ghouls don't like loose ends. They'd have come for you and killed anyone else they found *with* you, because, like I said, they don't like loose ends."

"But now you're *taking* me to them?"

"I'm gonna find out what the hell's going on, that's all. I'm not going to let anyone hurt you."

And Odd Willie glances at Emmie again from the rearview mirror, a flash of something guarded and uncertain on his face, something she catches despite the sunglasses hiding his eyes. *He doesn't believe her,* Emmie thinks. *He doesn't believe a word she's saying.*

"Like I told you," Soldier says, "I think someone tried to kill me and Willie, and until I find out precisely what—"

"I'm not *deaf,*" Emmie snaps at her. "You don't have to keep telling me the same damn lie over and over and over like I'm a retard. I heard you the first time."

"Fine," Soldier says and turns away. She takes another drag off her cigarette and fiddles with the volume knob on the radio. "Hey Jude" ends, and now the dj's talking about a wreck and a traffic jam at the Thurbers Avenue curve.

Last night, Emmie thinks, *last night my mother died. Last night Deacon's real daughter killed my real mother.*

In the motel room, she waited almost a whole half hour for Willie to come back from having his smoke, and then Soldier started talking, still unconscious but talking in her sleep, muttering about starfish and storms and drowning while her eyelids fluttered and her hands trembled. Emmie thought that maybe she was having a seizure or a stroke or something, and went outside to find Odd Willie. He wasn't standing by the purple Malibu, so she walked from one side of the motel parking lot to the other and back again, calling his name, but he didn't answer, and she couldn't find him anywhere. She gave up and started to go back in the room to see if Soldier was still alive when there was a scream, a woman's scream, and a brilliant flash of blue-white light from the woods directly behind the motel.

Just go back inside, she told herself. *Go back inside the room and watch TV and wait for Willie to come back and tell me not to worry. Do that, and everything will be okay.*

Instead, she went around to the rear of the motel, pushing her way through the snow and a dense tangle of wild grape- and greenbrier vines, past the sleeping trees. Emmie found Odd Willie sitting alone in a little clearing smoking a cigarette. The night was dark, but the dark has never kept her from seeing, not Emmie Silvey, the girl with yellow eyes, and she clearly saw him sitting there on a rock, and she also saw the thing scattered across the snow, the thing that had once been Saben White. There were tracks everywhere, footprints that Emmie had learned enough to know only *looked* like the tracks of dogs. Odd Willie sighed and tossed the butt of his cigarette into the woods, then turned to look at her. But she didn't take her eyes off the broken, bloody thing on the snow. It had been folded somehow, white bone and red flesh folded into something like a six-pointed star.

"What . . . what happened?" Emmie asked him, trying to keep her teeth from chattering.

"Soldier did what Soldier does," Willie replied. "Don't ask me how. I don't know, and I don't want to know how."

Emmie continued to stare at the mess in the snow, and the wind through the trees made her think of whatever it was she'd seen back on Waterman Street. "But Soldier's still in bed," Emmie whispered. "She hasn't left the room."

"You really shouldn't be out here," he said. "You're gonna get sick. You're gonna catch your death of cold. Haven't you ever heard of pneumonia?"

"But she never left the room."

"Yeah, well, she's a talented lady," Odd Willie nodded and stood up, dusting snow off the seat of his pants. "Stop looking at it. That ain't nothing a kid like you ought to see," and he took her hand and led her back towards the motel. When they got to the room, they found Soldier in the bathroom, awake and vomiting into the toilet bowl.

Stop thinking about it, Emmie tells herself. *Forget you ever saw it. Forget you ever saw anything at all.*

"He's still not fucking answering," Soldier says and throws her cell phone at the dashboard. It beeps loudly, bounces off the vinyl, and lands on the floorboard at her feet.

"It's your decision," Odd Willie tells her.

"Hey, if it were my motherfucking decision, asshole, we'd be all the way in goddamn Mexico by now."

"Then we're going in?"

"What the fuck do you think?"

It's a dream, Emmie tells herself. *The worst dream anyone's ever had.* And she watches the bright February day, the clean morning sun sparkling off so much ice and snow, the wide blue sky above the rooftops of Providence finally coming into view. She thinks about the black-skinned woman in the desert, and wishes that she knew the way back to her.

They stopped at the Cumberland Farms on Reservoir Avenue because Emmie said that she had to pee, and, she said, if they made her wait any longer, she'd end up wetting both herself and the car seat. "I have a weak bladder," she lied, so Odd Willie cursed and pulled into the parking lot.

"If they've got it, grab me pack of Black Jack gum," Odd Willie says, and Soldier tells him if he wants fucking chewing gum he can damn well get it himself. Then she leads Emmie inside, out of the cold and into the stuffy, crowded warmth of the convenience store. The air stinks of disinfectant and bad coffee, and something about the shadowless white wash of the fluorescent lights hurts Soldier's eyes even more than the sun, even though she's wearing a cheap pair of sunglasses Odd Willie picked up for her in Uxbridge. Her confrontation with Ballou and the fire thing beneath Woonsocket has left her half blind and headachy, and she squints behind the black plastic lenses, squinting through stinging, watery eyes. People at the counter turn to stare—curious, prying, unwelcome eyes for the battered, sunburned woman and the disheveled eight-year-old.

"I'm hungry," Emmie says.

"Yeah, well, you can eat later. We didn't stop so you could get something to eat."

"But as long as we're here—"

Soldier gives her a little push, and the woman at the register frowns and shakes her head.

"In and out," Soldier says, hurrying Emmie down one of the narrow aisles towards the restrooms all the way at the back of the store. "You said you had to piss. Do it, and let's get the hell out of here."

Emmie snatches a bag of ranch-flavored corn chips off one of the racks.

"Put that right back where you got it," Soldier tells her, but Emmie's already opened the bag.

"Is that your plan?" Emmie asks and pops a triangular chip into her mouth. "To starve me to death so you don't have to take me home?"

Soldier looks over her shoulder, and the staring people up front are still watching them. So is a man one aisle over. When she turns back to Emmie, she's gone. The restroom door clicks shut, and Soldier sighs and decides to give her three minutes alone. She turns to face the plate-glass windows and there's Odd Willie, waiting outside in the car, singing along to whatever's playing on the radio and slicking back his hair with his pink comb; he probably couldn't be any less inconspicuous if he set his head on fire.

"What now, Soldier girl?" the Bailiff asks, and Soldier spins around so fast that she almost trips over her own feet. The Bailiff is standing only a few feet away, standing there between her and all the people at the register. He's wearing a gray corduroy suit with a silk vest the color of ripe raspberries, bright yellow galoshes and a wool hunting cap with the left earflap pulled down. He grins and picks at his teeth with a pinkie nail.

"You look ridiculous, old man," Soldier says and takes a step back. "You look like a goddamn circus clown."

"Have you perhaps been anywhere near a mirror lately? From the looks of it, Old Ballou must have put up quite a struggle."

"Yeah, well, he's dead," Soldier says, and the Bailiff flickers and almost fades away entirely. Then, in an instant, he's back again. He stops picking at his teeth and nods his head once or twice.

"And Saben? How's she doing on this fine winter's morn?"

"Why didn't you tell me what we were walking into?" Soldier asks him, and the Bailiff smiles again and shrugs his broad corduroy shoulders.

"Soldier, dear. You know the refrain. Ours is not to question why—"

"*Bullshit,*" Soldier hisses, and the Bailiff holds an index finger up to his lips.

"*They* can't *see* me, you know," he says. "Perhaps you should keep your voice down."

Soldier glances around the convenience store, staring back at the half dozen or so people who apparently have nothing better to do than stand around in Cumberland Farms gawking at strangers. The woman behind the register points straight at Soldier, then leans forward and whispers something to the moonfaced man who's just set a box of Slim Jims and a six-pack of bottled springwater on the counter, and he laughs out loud.

"Since when did minding your own damned business cease to be an option?" Soldier shouts at them, and the cashier immediately stops whispering and goes back to pushing keys on the register. The moonfaced man snickers, covers his mouth, and stares down at his shoes.

"You're still a paragon of subtlety," the Bailiff snorts and pulls a white handkerchief from his breast pocket. The edges are embroidered with tiny bluebirds, and he blows his nose loudly.

"Saben's dead. I killed her, too," Soldier tells him. "We've been trying to call you all morning."

"I've been occupied," the Bailiff replies, then stuffs the soiled handkerchief back into his pocket. "As you may know, there's been some trouble with the alchemist's daughter. Do you have Saben's little brat?"

"She's taking a piss."

"How precious. When she's done, bring her to me. You *and* Master Lothrop, please bring her to me at once."

"You still haven't answered my question."

"No," the Bailiff says. "I suppose I haven't, have I? And perhaps I never shall. We'll just have to see which way the wind blows, as they say."

And then the air before her shimmers and the apparition of the Bailiff dissolves, leaving behind a smell like cinnamon and castor oil.

"Fucking *bastard*," Soldier whispers, suddenly dizzy and nauseous, a tinfoil aftertaste in the back of her mouth, and she figures that's probably the Bailiff's doing as well. She leans against a sturdy cardboard ziggurat built of red-white-and-blue cartons of Pepsi-Cola, and the things that Saben said to her the night before come rushing back. . . .

They've stolen so much from you. You don't even fucking know the things they've taken away from you. Your whole life is lived in a fog they've spun to keep you ignorant.

Soldier takes a deep breath, swallows, exhales, and then looks at the restroom door. It seems farther away than it did before, and one of the fluorescent bulbs overhead has begun to buzz and flicker.

Listen to me, Soldier. You think he didn't know exactly what Ballou was doing? You think he believed you'd ever be coming back to Providence alive?

"Time's up," Soldier says, and she quickly traces a protective symbol in the air with her left hand before she goes to retrieve Saben White's mongrel daughter.

Emmie's sitting on the closed toilet lid in the Cumberland Farms' women's restroom. She chews the last of the salty corn chips, wishes she had something to drink, and crumples the empty Mylar bag. The woman named Soldier has started knocking at the door, trying to get her to unlock it, trying to draw her out. Emmie drops the crumpled bag to the gray tile floor and then kicks it hard with the toe of her boot; it bounces off the restroom door and rolls under the sink.

"Open the door," Soldier whispers. "We don't have time for this."

Emmie shakes her head no, even though Soldier can't see that she's doing it. She went into the restroom planning to escape through a narrow window, just like she's seen people do in movies. But there aren't any windows in this restroom, narrow or otherwise. There's only the toilet and sink, the mirror above the sink and the gray tile floor. She flushes the toilet again so she can't hear Soldier, and for a few moments there's only the gurgling sound of water racing itself around and around the porcelain bowl.

Six days ago, she sat in Kingston Station with Deacon, waiting for the train that would take her to see Sadie, waiting for New York City and a week without homework, a week of museums and galleries and food that Deacon won't eat and all the other sights and sounds and tastes and smells of the city. Only six short winter days ago, but it seems like it must have been weeks and weeks. And the things that have happened since she boarded the train, since she noticed she was being watched by the woman with the Seal of Solomon tattooed on her hand, have changed everything forever, and nothing is what it was. She's beginning to understand that this is permanent, this shift, that there's no going back, no matter how hard she pretends it's only a dream. Saben White, the girl from the attic, the black-skinned woman in the desert, Soldier and Odd Willie—all of them have torn her loose somehow from everything that was real and true before, and now *this* is what she has instead. All the hours since Saturday morning and Kingston Station have made her someone and something else, and she's not even sure she knows what she means when she says that she wants to go home.

"Emmie, open this door," Soldier says, louder than before.

"No," Emmie replies flatly. "Go away. Leave me alone."

"You *know* I can't do that. *Now open the damn door.*"

Or I'll huff and I'll puff and I'll . . .

"I can find my way home from here," Emmie says. "I can walk or call Deacon to come get me."

"I'm not going to keep asking you. . . ."

Emmie flushes the toilet again, drowning out Soldier's voice. She stares at the silver knob and the restroom door that's the same shade of gray as the floor and tries hard not to think about the bleeding, folded thing lying in the snow behind the motel. Odd Willie took it deeper into the woods before they left and burned it.

"I don't want to be in this story anymore," she says, but then the door opens easy as you please, just like she hadn't bothered to lock it. Soldier steps into the restroom and shuts the door behind her.

"How did you do that?" Emmie asks her, much more angry than surprised. "I locked it. I made *sure* that I locked it."

"Listen, you smart-mouthed little runt," Soldier says, and, behind her, the door locks itself again. "I don't have time for this crap. I don't know what you know and what you don't know and what you *think* you know, but, right now, it doesn't fucking matter one way or the other."

"Stop yelling at me," Emmie says very softly, and then she looks down at the gray tiles and pointy toes of Soldier's thrift-store cowboy boots. "You don't have any right to yell at me. I did exactly what she told me to do. I brought you the snow globe thing, because she said you'd die if I didn't, and now I just want to go home."

"Emmie, I can't expect you to comprehend what's happening. Hell, I don't understand half this shit myself. But I haven't got time to hold your hand and coddle you. I need you to do what I tell you to do and stop being such a pain in my ass."

"I know that you and Willie are lying about taking me home. You killed my mother, and now you're going to kill me, too."

Soldier squats down so she's at eye level with Emmie. "Listen," she says. "It's not up to me, whatever happens to you. I'm not going to lie and tell you that I *wouldn't* kill you if that's what I was supposed to do. But the hounds put you where they did for a reason, and if I hurt you I'd be interfering with their plans, and that, Emmie Silvey, would be the end of me."

"Maybe I understand more than you think I do," Emmie says. "Maybe Pearl and that woman in the desert told me things about you that even *you* don't know."

"Then maybe you should be so kind as to unburden yourself and fucking enlighten me." And Soldier sounds more than pissed off now. She sounds like Deacon did the night that Sadie left them. She sounds dangerous.

"I'm *not* getting back into that car with you," Emmie tells her and then looks away again.

"Yes, you will, little girl, even if I have to drag you kicking and screaming all the way."

"But I *did* what she told me to do. I *brought* you the star. I brought you the star so you could stop that monster."

"And now you're going to do what *I* tell you to do."

Emmie squeezes her eyes tightly shut, silently counts to four, then opens them again, something Sadie taught her, a trick to settle her mind whenever she's too scared to think clearly.

"I saw the way all those people out there looked at us," she says, turning to face Soldier again. "If you try to make me go with you, I'll tell them all that you kidnapped me and won't let me go home. I'll tell them you're a murderer."

Soldier shakes her head and smiles, a resigned and weary smile that seems to bleed away some of the fury in her battered face, and for a second Emmie thinks that maybe she's won the game, that maybe Soldier's finally had enough, and now she'll get up and leave Emmie sitting on the toilet. That Soldier and Odd Willie will drive off in their stolen car, and Emmie will never have to see either of them again.

But then Soldier pulls a big black pistol from the waistband of her jeans and holds it only a few inches from Emmie's face.

"You're a smart girl, and you know what this thing is, right? You know what I do with it?"

Emmie nods, her victory dissolving in the dull glint of the restroom light off the barrel of the gun.

"You do that—you start telling people things about me and Odd Willie—"

"And you'll kill me," Emmie says.

"No, I *won't* kill you. But I will have to kill everyone else in here, every last person who hears what you say. And everyone who *sees* me killing them, I'll have to kill those people, too. Men, women, children—at this point, I really don't give a rat's ass. And *all* those deaths, every one of them, will be because *you* couldn't keep your mouth shut, Emmie. Now, you tell me, do you want that on your conscience? Do you really, truly want to have to think about that fucking day in and day out for the rest of your life?"

"You'd do that?" Emmie asks, though she already knows the answer.

"In a heartbeat. I'll do whatever it takes. I've done worse things."

"Are you proud of that?"

"You should wash your hands," Soldier says instead of answering her question. "You've got that Frito crap all over them. I'll give you a minute to wash up."

"They weren't Fritos," Emmie tells her and looks down at her fingers, dusted with salt and the ranch dressing–flavored powder. "The horse is dead," she says. "From here we walk."

"What the hell's that supposed to mean?" Soldier asks, returning the pistol to its hiding place.

"I thought maybe you might know," Emmie replies, then gets up to wash her hands.

"Why are we going to the museum?" Emmie asks from the back-seat of the Malibu. She's sitting directly behind Odd Willie, putting as much space between herself and Soldier as possible. It's the first thing she's said since Soldier led her from the restroom back out to the car. "This isn't even a very *good* museum. Mostly, they just have a lot of old junk."

"I thought that's why people *built* museums," Odd Willie snorts. "To have someplace to keep all the old junk."

"You'll see, Emmie," Soldier says and flicks a cigarette butt out the car window as Odd Willie comes to a stop directly in front of the museum building. It seems worn and out of place in the city park, like some peculiar temple to the Victorian scientific enterprise, maybe plucked from the streets of nineteenth-century Paris and meticulously reassembled, stone by stone, in Providence. The steeply pitched roof is covered in black shingles, and the yellow-pink granite facade is decorated with bas-relief Corinthian columns and elaborately carved acroterions. There are stained-glass windows set deeply into the semicircular arch above the entrance, dormers higher up, and a great clock tower front and center.

There are no other cars in the parking lot, and no sign that the museum's even open.

"It's not the museum we've come for," Odd Willie says and kills the engine. "It's where the museum leads."

"The museum leads to the Bailiff?"

"Like I said, you'll see," Soldier tells her.

"I heard your stepmother's some kind of witch," Odd Willie says. "If that's true, she must have told you that things aren't always what they seem. Never judge a book by its fucking cover and all that. So, you might see a run-down, rinky-dink little museum, but me, I see a passageway, a secret avenue—"

"You stay right by me," Soldier cuts in, and she turns around in the seat and glares at Emmie. "None of that shit you pulled back at the gas station, you understand?"

Emmie nods her head but doesn't say anything.

"I'm not fucking kidding with you," Soldier says, and then she turns around again. She pops the clip out of the Smith & Wesson 9mm that Odd Willie picked up in a pawn shop back in Uxbridge and counts the rounds—six, seven, eight—then slides the clip in again. The Model 439 has seen better days, and Soldier wishes she had half the firepower Ballou took off them in Woonsocket. Right now she'd give her eyeteeth for a good shotgun. When she looks up, she sees that Odd Willie's frowning at her.

"What the hell's your problem?" she asks him.

"This is just dumb," he replies, and his eyes drift from Soldier's gun back to the museum building. "I mean, if it *was* a setup—"

"We don't know that."

"I know we don't *know* it, but it's what we're both sitting here thinking. Don't you try to lie to me and say that it's not."

"You know I wouldn't dream of lying to you, Odd Willie," Soldier says and sticks the pistol back into the waistband of her jeans.

"Yeah, well, I just don't see what good fucking guns are gonna be. If he's got it in for us, we won't be shooting our way out of there."

"Chance favors the prepared," Soldier says and looks at Emmie again. "Ain't that right, little girl?"

"Don't call me that. You know my name."

"Okay, Emmie. You behave yourself, and that's a deal. Now, listen, when we go through the front doors, there's a staircase on the other side of the lobby—"

"I *have* been here before," Emmie says and sighs.

"Then you know where the black bear is, right?"

"No. I don't remember a black bear."

"But you just said you'd been here before."

"Yeah, but I still don't remember a bear."

Soldier takes a deep breath and clicks her tongue once against the roof of her mouth.

"I'm *sorry*. I don't remember a *bear*," Emmie says again.

"Well, trust me. Halfway up those stairs there's a stuffed black bear, okay? You know, taxidermied."

"Looks like it's got the fucking mange," Odd Willie adds and opens his door, letting in a gust of cold air.

"That's where we're going, Emmie," Soldier continues. "Half-way up those stairs. We're going in the front door and then straight to the bear."

"Why are we going to see a dead bear?" Emmie asks and opens her door, too.

"We're not going to see the goddamned bear. We're going to see the Bailiff and—"

"But you just said—"

"Things aren't always what they seem," Odd Willie tells Emmie again, and he grins at her from the rearview mirror. "Just like the lady said," and he nods at Soldier, "you'll see. It's magick."

"Fine," Emmie replies, "but I don't remember a dead bear," and she starts to get out of the Chevy.

"Hold up," Soldier says. "Give me another second or two." She stares out the smeary windshield at the museum. *You're just like everyone else,* she tells herself. *You're afraid of him. Everyone's afraid of him, everyone except the hounds, and he knows it. He banks on it.*

"Jesus, I just want to get this over with," Odd Willie groans and pulls his door shut again.

You're scared half to death of the bastard, Soldier thinks, *and he knows it.*

"Emmie," she says, keeping her eyes on the hands of the clock mounted high above the museum doors. "You got that glass ball you gave me from a woman in a desert, a black-skinned woman. Not a black woman, but a woman with black skin."

"No, that's not what I said. I got it from Pearl. The woman in the desert told me to bring it to you, but I *got* it from Pearl. She said it was one of her father's experiments."

Odd Willie giggles to himself and shakes his head.

"Did she tell you her name, the woman in the desert?" Soldier asks.

"She said she had a lot of different names, but she likes to keep them to herself."

Willie Lothrop leans forward, resting his forehead on the steering wheel. "Anytime one of you ladies wants to tell me what the hell you're talking about, I'll be sitting right here."

"And she told you something about me?" Soldier asks Emmie, ignoring Odd Willie. The clock's hour hand is at one, and the minute hand is at four, but the clock's been broken for as long as she can recall.

"Yeah," Emmie says. "She did."

"Well, we'll talk about it later," Soldier tells her. "If that's cool with you. When all this is over, we'll talk about exactly what she told you."

"If I'm not dead yet," Emmie grumbles.

"Just stick close to me." And then Soldier opens her door, and the sky above the old museum in Roger Williams Park seems to shudder and stretch for a moment, like something that's grown too ripe and is almost ready to burst. And then it's only sky again, and she gets out of the car.

"It's a tough row to hoe," the Bailiff said and then leaned back in his squeaky chair. *One day,* Soldier thought, *it's gonna break, that old chair, and he'll end up on the floor.* He gazed down at her over the rim of his enormous belly and smiled.

"Being a Child of the Cuckoo?" she asked. "Is that what you mean?"

"I do," he said. "I mean that very thing, little Soldier. The universe is a cruel old cunt, she is. But for the random vagaries of happenstance, you might have been any girl, safe and snug at home with a loving papa and a loving mama to watch over her."

Soldier wondered about it for a moment and chewed thoughtfully at the arrowroot cookie he'd given her after the vampire named

Adelaide had led her into the study. "Maybe," she said. "Or I might have ended up like Cinderella, with a wicked stepmother and three wicked stepsisters. Or like Hansel and Gretel. Or the pretty daughter in 'Mother Hulda' who has to spin until her fingers bleed."

"Ah, yes," the Bailiff replied and nodded his head, seeming to consider what Soldier had said. "But all those stories have happy endings."

"That depends who's telling them."

The Bailiff chuckled and tapped the side of his nose. "Too true, too true," he said. "You are wise far beyond your years, child."

"I had another dream last night," Soldier said, because she knew that was probably the reason he'd called for her. He rarely wanted much of anything but to listen to her dreams. "You were in this one."

"Was I now?" he asked and leaned forward again, one bushy eyebrow cocked, and she thought perhaps he looked more worried than curious. "Do tell. Whatever was I doing in one of your dreams?"

"I didn't understand all of it."

"Then let's start with the parts you *did* understand, and we'll get to the confusing bits later on." He tugged at his beard and licked his thin lips like a hungry dog.

So she told him about a winter day, still many years off, and a lost mongrel girl, and a demon of fire and cinders that she'd slain with nothing more than a crystal ball. There was something about the mongrel's mother, something that had upset her so much she'd forgotten most of it, and, she said, she'd realized, in the dream, that she wasn't a child anymore, that she was a grown woman who could barely even recall ever having been a child.

"But you said that I was a part of this dream," the Bailiff said impatiently. "So far I've not heard one word about me."

"I was coming to that part," she said, annoyed that he was hurrying her, and swallowed another bite of arrowroot cookie. The Bailiff frowned and tugged on his gray beard.

"You wanted to kill me," Soldier told him. "We were standing in a room, and there was incense burning and silk pillows and all these pretty boys who at first I thought were girls. And we weren't *here*."

"You mean we weren't in this house?"

"No, I mean we weren't *here*. We were somewhere else. Somewhere you had called me to. Somewhere you went to be away from the hounds."

The Bailiff laughed and took out a handkerchief. He wiped fat droplets of sweat off his face, then laughed again. He'd begun staring at a particularly old book lying open on his desk instead of looking at Soldier.

"Are you feeling well?" Soldier asked, and he wiped his face again.

"Tell me the rest," he said. "Tell me all of it."

But Soldier waited a moment, wishing that she had another cookie or maybe a piece of fudge or something else she'd never tasted.

"Is there a problem?" he asked.

"No," she told him, "not really," because she was pretty sure there was no point, this far along, in asking for fudge. So she told him that in the dream the hounds were leaving, going back to someplace they'd been before they'd found a way into this world. They were all going away forever and leaving him behind, and then he would only be a strange fat man with no work left to do.

"I saw Madam Terpsichore," Soldier said, "who was the last of the ghouls to leave, and she told me to watch after you, that you had become dissipated and decadent and careless, that you'd sunk too deeply into your appetites, forgetting—"

"She said that?" the Bailiff asked, his lower lip trembling, and she saw that his hands were shaking.

"If she hadn't, I wouldn't have told you she had."

"Pray tell, was there anything more?" he asked, laying his palms flat on the desk, on the pages of the old book.

"Yes," she replied, and Soldier watched him and considered whether or not she should say anything more. She'd never seen the Bailiff like this. Even if he wasn't the Cuckoo or the god of men and churches, she'd thought he was *something*, something powerful enough that he certainly didn't have to be afraid of the dreams of children.

"Well?" he said. "I'm waiting."

Soldier picked a stray speck of cookie off the front of her dress and then continued. "You said to me, 'We have fallen on hard times. Our lords and ladies have all deserted us, and our purpose lies in ruin. A masque which has endured down untold ages is ended here this night, and now we are castaways in our own land.' "

"I said all that?" he asked and wiped his forehead with the damp handkerchief. "Quite the mouthful, don't you think?"

"Yes sir," Soldier told him. "But you said it. Then you cut your throat from ear to ear, and the pretty boys whom I'd thought were girls went down on their hands and knees and lapped your blood from the floor. When they were done, they saved some in a little blue bottle. They locked the bottle in a lead box and dropped it into the sea. When I asked why, one of them told me it was so your soul would go down to the Mother and the Father, and so you'd not come back to haunt them."

"You are an ill wind, indeed," he said, but she wasn't sure what he meant, and since she wasn't finished with the dream, she didn't bother to ask.

"And then," she continued, "I remembered a magic trick I knew, and I . . ." And she paused, the words eluding her, the language she needed to describe something that seemed all but indescribable.

"Oh, don't stop *now*," the Bailiff laughed and slammed the big book shut, startling Soldier. "Surely," he said, "there's some snippet of cataclysm yet to be revealed."

He's scared, she thought. *He's really scared.* And she knew then that the Bailiff was only a man and nothing more.

"I *unhappened* it," she said, making up a word because she could think of none that fit. "And you were back, and I took the knife away before you could hurt yourself with it. I promised to watch over you, because when I was a little girl you'd been good to me and given me cookies and candy and soda."

The Bailiff dabbed at his sweaty cheeks. "And that's all?" he asked.

"No, but I've mostly forgotten the rest. It wouldn't make any sense if I tried to tell it. Can I have another cookie, please?"

"No," he said, standing up, and the handkerchief slipped from his fingers and fell to the floor at his feet. "You may not have another cookie. We're quite finished for tonight." And then he called out for the silver-eyed woman, who came and led Soldier back down the basement steps to the tunnels.

And the next time the Bailiff called for Soldier, he took her to the long hall on the second floor of the yellow house and opened the foldaway stairs leading up into the attic. . . .

Through the heavy front doors of the museum, into shadows and the musty smell of very old things, past whale bones and mastodon tusks leaning against the foyer walls like the crooked walking canes of leviathans—through the doors and across the lobby, just like Soldier told her, and Emmie goes up the stairs with Odd Willie in front of her and Soldier behind. The girl in the gift shop, just past the entrance, doesn't ask them to pay admission. She doesn't even seem to notice them, and Emmie suspects that's because she can't see or hear them. *We're invisible,* she thinks, *like the seventh point on the Seal of Solomon,* but it doesn't seem nearly as remarkable as it ought to. Then she spots the black bear, a neglected, moth-eaten thing rearing up on its hind legs, swiping at the air with its shaggy forepaws, its muzzle frozen permanently in an expression of mock ferocity. The bear is exactly where they said it would be, halfway up the stairs on a wide landing, but she still doesn't remember it ever being there before. There are six stained-glass windows behind it, and the bear is silhouetted against pale kaleidoscope patterns of yellow and red and blue sunlight.

"You know, it's still not too late—" Odd Willie begins, but Soldier interrupts him.

"Not too late for *what*? You want to go to the hounds, instead? Or maybe you'd rather try to cut and run?"

"Well, to tell you the gods'-honest fucking truth, I *was* growing kind of fond of that motel room back in Massachusetts."

"We don't know," Soldier says and takes a long, deep breath. "We don't know that he set us up. Until we do, Willie, he's still calling the shots. He's a bastard and a son of a bitch, but he's never betrayed the hounds."

"Not that you know of," Odd Willie sighs. "Maybe those things Saben said last night, maybe she wasn't so far off the mark."

Emmie flinches at the mention of Saben White. She looks at Odd Willie and Soldier and then back to the taxidermied black bear towering over her. There's a Plexiglas barrier surrounding it, so no one can get too close. So no one can pull out its fur or try to snap off a tooth or a claw or something.

"She wanted us dead," Soldier says. "She sold me out to that cocksucker Joey Bittern, and then she sold us *both* out to Ballou. She'd have done or said anything to get to the kid. I *do* know that much."

"We could always head for Boston. Ask for sanctuary—"

"Right now, he can hear every single goddamn word we're saying. You think you'd even make it back to the car alive?"

"Killjoy," Odd Willie sighs and shakes his head.

Emmie places her hand flat against the Plexiglas, and it ripples like water. "Is it supposed to do that?" she asks Soldier, who nods her head and places her own hand against the clear plastic, creating a second set of ripples that spreads out and eclipses the ones that Emmie made. Where the ripples cross, there are gentle shimmers of light.

"You stay close to me," Soldier tells Emmie again. "Stay close and don't touch anything."

Soldier takes her hand, and for a second Emmie Silvey pretends she's any child at the museum, and maybe Soldier is only her big sister. Maybe they'll go to Ben & Jerry's after the museum. Maybe they'll go to Johnny Rockets and have chocolate milkshakes and chili-cheese fries. *Maybe,* she thinks, *I have green eyes, just like her. Maybe Deacon's waiting outside to take us both home.*

"The horse is dead," she says and squeezes Soldier's hand. "From here we walk."

"Anyone ever told you you're sort of a creepy kid?" Odd Willie asks.

"All the damn time," Emmie tells him. "I don't bother keeping count anymore."

"Just checking." Then Odd Willie brushes the Plexiglas with the fingertips of his left hand, and a third set of ripples spreads rapidly across the barrier. Emmie realizes that she can see *through* the bear now, through the bear *and* the stained-glass window behind it. There's some sort of hallway on the other side, past the museum wall, where the park should be, a long hallway dimly lit by bare lightbulbs screwed into sockets strung up along the ceiling.

"That's where the Bailiff is?" Emmie asks, but no one answers her. Soldier takes a step forward, and the rippling, shimmering Plexiglas and the stuffed bear and the wall of the museum parts for her like a theater curtain . . .

*   *   *

... and before Soldier went up the foldaway stairs, before she climbed into the attic of the yellow house and met the Daughter of the Four of Pentacles, but *after* the Bailiff lied and promised her that he was coming, too, that he'd be right behind her—in the fleeting moments in between, she almost told him the truth about her dream. She paused at the first step and looked at him and *almost* said, *In my dream, you didn't slit your own throat. I did that.*

But there was something slick and sharp and icy in his eyes, something like a snowy January night or the edge of one of Madam Terpsichore's scalpels, and Soldier had decided, even if he might be better off knowing, she'd be better off keeping that part to herself. *There are worse things than lies,* she thought (and it seemed like a very practical, grown-up thought), and then Soldier said her silent prayer to the Lady of the Abyssal Plains and started up the ladder.

"Oh, but he's in a *most* peculiar temperament," the rat who isn't Reepicheep, who probably isn't even a real rat at all, says nervously and scratches at a scabby spot behind its right ear.

Emmie looks back the way they've just come, at the bricked-up doorway where there ought to be a museum and a stuffed bear. Coming through, entering the hall, there was only a slight shiver and the faintest passing nausea, and she wonders if the bricks would ripple the way the Plexiglas did were she to walk back and touch them.

"Care to be just a little more specific?" Odd Willie asks the rat, and it frowns and glances towards the shadows at the far end of the hallway.

"Yeah, sure, whatever you say, Mr. Lothrop," the rat sneers. "If you wanted a goddamn turncoat, you should have tried pumping the fucking bear before you came across."

"The bear doesn't talk to changelings," Soldier says. "You know that."

Emmie starts to ask her why the bear won't talk to changelings, and how a stuffed bear can talk to anyone at all, but then she decides both questions are too ridiculous to bother with. She looks past the rat, at the hall, at the faraway place where it ends. The walls are made of doors set one against the other—black doors, crimson doors, weathered gray doors, and doors the color of butterscotch. None of them have knobs or handles, only empty black holes where doorknobs ought to be.

"Anyhow," the rat says and waves a paw in the air dismissively, "you'll see it all for yourselves plenty soon enough now. The Bailiff ain't shy with his little indiscretions, not down here. Follow me, and don't any of you say peep until—"

"We know the drill," Soldier tells the rat. "Let's just get this over with."

The rat shrugs and drops down onto all fours. It sniffs at Emmie's boots and scowls. "Just trying to keep the peace," it snorts. "What precious few crumbs are left of it." And then it turns and walks slowly down the long hall of doors, slipping through the yellow-white pools of light from the bare bulbs overhead and the dark patches dividing them.

"Fucking fleabag twat," Odd Willie mutters and follows the talking rat.

"I know," Emmie says to Soldier. "Stay close to you. Don't touch anything."

"If I hadn't killed her, you'd *both* be dead by now," Soldier replies, answering a question that Emmie hasn't asked in hours. "No reason you should take my word for it, but it's the truth. I'm not saying that's *why* I did it. I did it because I didn't have any choice."

"You said that already."

"Well, I thought maybe I should say it again."

"They're getting way ahead of us," Emmie says and points at Odd Willie and the rat. "We're gonna have to hurry to catch up."

"Take my hand," Soldier tells her, and Emmie does, squeezes it tight like she did before they walked through the bear into this place of doors and bare lightbulbs and missing doorknobs, and Soldier leads her down the hallway. Emmie tries to keep her mind off whatever's at the other end by silently counting the doors on her right, and she makes it as far as fifty-eight before they get to the spot where Odd Willie is waiting with the rat. The hallway ends in something that Emmie at first mistakes for a mirror, because she can see herself and Soldier and Odd Willie reflected there in its smooth, glassy surface, but then the rat steps through it and vanishes.

"You guys know what a cliché is?" Emmie asks.

"Hey, *I'm* not the prick that built this funhouse shithole," Odd Willie says, "so don't go complaining to me."

Emmie stares back at herself a moment, then glances up at Soldier. "We go *through* a mirror?"

"It's not a mirror," Soldier says. "And I don't have time to explain, so don't even ask."

Odd Willie coughs and smoothes his hair with both his hands. "Stand up straight," he says, and for a second Emmie thinks he's talking to her, so she stands up straight. "Chew with your fucking mouth shut," he continues. "Mind your Ps and Qs, Master Lothrop." And then he steps through the mirror that isn't a mirror and is gone.

"The Bailiff built this place?" Emmie asks.

"No. He's just renting it. A demon built it."

"There's no such thing as demons. I mean, I don't believe in them," Emmie says, even though she's starting to think that maybe she does, that perhaps she believes in lots of things that Deacon's told her are only fairy tales and horseshit. But mostly, she says it just to have something to say, just to buy a few more seconds before Soldier leads her through the looking glass.

"It really doesn't matter what you do and don't believe," Soldier tells her and then chews at her lower lip a moment. "But you'll figure that out, sooner or later."

"*If* I live that long."

"Yeah, Emmie. That's the way it always works. If you live that long," and then Soldier steps through her own reflection, and there's nothing Emmie can do but follow her.

The passage lasts only a glittering instant, but it fills Soldier's head with the cavernous, shattering, hopeless noise of storms, of waves pounding the shingles of rocky shorelines, of the unanswered prayers of dying men. An instant of the raw chaos and pain woven together centuries ago to fashion this place from the nothingness between worlds, and then she's standing with Odd Willie and Emmie, looking down at the great octagonal chamber, the Bailiff's hiding place, standing on a dais carved from obsidian and petrified cypress logs. It might easily double as the set of some silent-era Rudolph Valentino romance of Arabian horsemen and harem girls, this room, half-lost beneath the clutter of draperies and carpets and silk pillows, Moroccan antiques and Syrian hookahs. The air is warm and smells like blood, like hot wax and frankincense, opium and shisha tobaccos. And there are bodies everywhere. Soldier gags and covers her mouth; astral travel has always made her a little queasy, and the stink of the room isn't helping any.

"Well, well," the Bailiff says, and spreads his arms wide. He's wearing a shabby lime-green bathrobe thrown open to reveal that he's wearing nothing else. There's a kukri in his left hand, its broad blade glinting wetly in the candlelight. "Have a look at what the cat's dragged in." His voice booms, amplified by the countless imperfections and peculiarities of the room's geometry. "I was beginning to think you'd lost your way, Soldier girl. But here you are, safe and sound, almost pretty as a painted picture. Imagine my relief."

"I know you're gonna tell me it's none of my goddamn business," Odd Willie says and points at the corpses of the Bailiff's boy whores scattered about the chamber, and the room turns another trick, making his voice seem small and distant. "But why'd you do this? Why did you kill them?"

"Shall we tell him, do you think?" the Bailiff asks Soldier, and then he laughs and tugs hard at his beard, which is tangled and matted with drying blood and claret wine and slobber. "Do we dare? Shall we be bold and let him in on our little secret?"

"I've done what you asked, old man. I've brought you Saben's daughter," Soldier says, and then she pauses to cough and clear her throat; her mouth tastes like bile and incense. "Was it only so you could murder her, too?"

Emmie tightens her grip on Soldier's right hand, digging her nails into Soldier's palm, and takes a small step backwards.

The Bailiff stops tugging his beard and shakes his head in an unconvincing pantomime of disbelief. "Forgive me, dear, but that seems a most improbable and ironic word to hear from *your* lips."

"Second thought," Odd Willie says and glances anxiously at Soldier, "maybe you should both *keep* your secrets. Just pretend like I never asked, and I'll forget I ever saw any of this shit."

"I don't want to be here anymore," Emmie says, and tries to pull Soldier back towards the portal and the hallway of doors, back towards the stuffed black bear and the stolen Chevy waiting for them in the museum's parking lot.

"*Be still,*" Soldier tells her, almost growling the words, not taking her eyes off the Bailiff in his lime-green bathrobe, his fat, hairy belly smeared with the dead boys' blood, the huge knife in his hand.

"He killed them," Emmie says. "Now he's going to kill me, too."

"I'm gonna do it *for* him," Soldier tells her, "if you don't shut up and stand still."

The Bailiff grins and scratches at his crotch. "It's quite all right, Master Lothrop," he laughs. "Some secrets go sour if you let them sit too long. They go rancid and lose their potency, that dreadful spark that made them secrets in the first place."

"Odd Willie did everything he was told," Soldier says, walking to the edge of the dais. "Whatever quarrel you might have with me and the girl, it doesn't have anything to do with him."

The Bailiff stops scratching at his balls and lets the kukri slip from his fingers and fall to the floor. Then he bows once and claps his pudgy hands together, applause made loud as thunder and sledge-hammers on steel rails by the room's deceiving acoustics.

"*Brava,*" he says and bows his bald head again. "You've grown into a fine and gallant woman, Soldier girl, a veritable fucking Hotspur. But Master Lothrop has his role to play, and we mustn't deprive him of his rightful part in this exquisite comedy of ours. That would be exceedingly unfair. Never rob a man of his place in history."

"He's going to kill us *all,*" Emmie says and tugs on Soldier's arm again.

The Bailiff comes nearer, steps over the body of one of the slaughtered boys, and slips in a pool of blood. For a moment, Soldier thinks he's going to fall, that he's about to land in a heap atop the gore and silk damask and spilled absinthe. But then he finds his balance again and steps gingerly over the remains of a broken sitar and another corpse, neatly decapitated, gutted, its intestines wound tightly about its pale legs.

You're afraid of him, Soldier thinks for the second time that morning, hating herself more than ever, hating her fear and all the years she's allowed her fear of him to steer her life. *He knows it. He fucking banks on it.* She draws the pawnshop 9mm and aims it at the fat man.

Odd Willie makes a sudden strangled noise, part confusion, part dumbfounded surprise, and turns from the Bailiff to Soldier. "What the hell are you *doing*?" he asks her. "Come on, now. You know the score. *I'm* the fucking lunatic with a thinly veiled death wish. You, you're just the sullen drunk with a bad temper."

"Shut up, Odd Willie," Soldier replies. "Take the kid and get the hell out of here. Go to Master Danaüs. Tell him everything."

The Bailiff stops stepping over cushions and dead boys and applauds again.

"Sublime," he says and tugs at his beard. "I did not even dare to *hope* that you'd ever find the courage to stand up to me, little Soldier girl. What a wondrous, sublime turn of events, here, before the end."

"Soldier," Odd Willie says, and she wants to look him in the eye, wants to make him see that she means what she's said, but she doesn't dare take her eyes off the Bailiff.

"Just fucking *do* it. Get her the hell out of here."

"You know I can't do that. The Cuckoo—"

"Oh, yes you can," Soldier says and thumbs off the Smith & Wesson's safety. "Yes, you fucking can, Willie, because this doesn't have jack shit to do with the Cuckoo. This is old business between me and the Bailiff, and that's *all* there is to this."

The Bailiff leans over and lifts a severed head from its place on a large plum-colored pillow, his fingers tangling in ash-blond hair, its blue eyes open and staring forward. He holds it up so the dead boy is facing him. His grin is so broad now that Soldier thinks it's a wonder his skull doesn't split open.

"The question at hand," the Bailiff says, speaking to the severed head, "is whether or not she has also found the courage to pull the trigger. It seems most unlikely, but I can't entirely rule it out, of course, the weight of these particular secrets being what they are."

"Talk to *me*, old man," Soldier says, tightening her grip on the trigger. "Stop playing games and fucking talk to me."

The Bailiff presses his lips to the left ear of the head and whispers something, then pretends that the dead boy whispers something back to him.

"Only her bless'd girlhood," the Bailiff says and licks blood from the dead boy's chin. "All in all," he says, "it actually wasn't such a very terrible loss. She's overreacting. Some vague hysteria arising from her uterus, most likely. A crying shame she wasn't born with a dick. Then, my lad, perhaps she could have lived up to her name."

"I said talk to *me*, you fat son of a bitch!" Soldier shouts, and the Bailiff acts startled and drops the head. He puts one hand over his heart, and his mouth is hanging open wide in a perfect, astounded O. The dead boy's blood stains his lips like a smudge of rouge, and Soldier notices that he has an erection.

"She's mad!" the Bailiff wails and rolls his eyes. "Master Lothrop, you are a Child of the Cuckoo, and, as such, you *must* do your sworn duty."

"Last chance," Soldier says, almost whispering, speaking just loudly enough that she's sure Odd Willie will hear. "Get *out of here.*"

"*Now,* Master Lothrop!" the Bailiff screams, and the walls shudder and dust sifts down from between the struts of the domed ceiling. "You were delivered unto the Hounds of Cain and have passed through the trials of fire and swords and laid your hands upon the tongue of the dragon. You *know* your obligation."

Odd Willie draws his own pistol and cocks it, hesitates a moment, and then points it at Soldier's head. "Don't you make me fucking do this," he says. "Not after all that shit in Woonsocket, don't you make me fucking have to pull this trigger."

"He dies, either way," Soldier tells him. "You're not that fast, Odd Willie."

Emmie lets go of Soldier's hand, and the Bailiff takes another step towards the dais. "Don't worry about the girl," he says to Odd Willie. "The girl's a trifling thing. She can be dealt with anytime, at our convenience."

"I don't know what to do," Emmie says, close to tears. "Please, Soldier. Please tell me what I'm supposed to do now."

"Yes," the Bailiff says, and then he sits down on the floor amid the pillows and hookahs and corpses. "Do please tell her. Tell her what you told me the day I took you to meet the alchemist's daughter. Tell her—"

"I'm not afraid of you anymore, old man."

"Don't make me do this," Odd Willie says again. "Just put the fucking gun down, and we'll sort this shit out."

"No," the Bailiff says, speaking to Odd Willie now. "She won't do that. Not *our* Soldier girl." Then he pauses and surveys the carnage strewn about the octagonal chamber, the naked bodies and broken glass, feathers and torn cloth, the blood splashed across walls and portieres. "My, but I have managed to make quite the mess, haven't I? Have I killed them *all*?" he asks no one in particular.

"We were both supposed to die in Woonsocket," Soldier says. "Saben made a deal with Ballou, to get her daughter back, but she made a deal with you, too, didn't she?"

The Bailiff shrugs and then lies down beside one of the dead boys. "It hardly matters now, does it? We both know what happens next, dear. We *both* know . . ." He trails off and buries his face in the dead boy's long black hair.

Odd Willie presses the barrel of his gun to Soldier's temple. "*What* do we both know?" he asks her. "What's he talking about?"

"I know a trick," Soldier says. "I was born knowing a trick. When I was a child I had dreams that came true, and I know this fucking trick. And that's what happens next. That's what he *thinks* happens next."

The Bailiff rolls over on his back again, gazing up at the high ceiling. "She misleads you with eloquent understatement, Master Lothrop. This one here, our pretty little Soldier girl, she knows something more than any mere *trick*. She knows *time,* Master Lothrop, and she bends it to her will as easily as you might turn back the hands of a clock. She's poor Professor Einstein's darkest nightmare, a veritable imp of Kronos. Even so, she only half comprehends these things she does—that slick getaway out at Quaker Jameson's, for example."

"You meant for us to die in Woonsocket," Soldier says. "You and Saben White. Just let me hear you say it, old man. Say it so Odd Willie at least knows the truth before he puts a bullet in my brain."

"A man tries as best he can to elude his fate," the Bailiff sighs, all the gleeful fury drained from him now, and he sits up and leans towards them, crouched there on the floor like some obscene Buddha. "Three and half years ago, Soldier, you *showed* me my fate. You told me about drops of blood sealed in a beautiful china-blue bottle. You told me about a lead box and my path down to the Mother and the Father."

Soldier shakes her head, denial the only thing like sanity she has left, and Odd Willie tells her not to move.

"It was only a dream," she says to the Bailiff. "It was only a dream, and I was only five years old."

"Where *does* the time go?" the Bailiff laughs and tugs his beard. "See, that's what she's been asking herself, Master Lothrop, even though she was never *quite* aware of the question."

"I think you've both lost your goddamn marbles," Odd Willie says. "Soldier, put down the motherfucking gun. I've had enough, and I'm not going to tell you again," and he jams the barrel of his pistol against her left cheekbone hard enough to tear the dental-floss stitches and reopen the wound there.

The Bailiff makes a gun with his thumb and index finger and puts it to his own temple. "What was it that I'm supposed to say when the hounds have gone?" he asks Soldier. "Ah, yes. How could I ever forget *those* words—We have fallen on hard times. Our lords and ladies have all deserted us, and our purpose lies in ruin. A masque which has endured down untold ages is ended here this night, and now we are castaways in our own land. Did I get it right?"

"I don't know," Soldier replies, her voice trembling almost as badly as her hands and the 9mm. "That was a long time ago. I was only a child."

"Oh, but it's such an awful shame to forget such poetry. Even Shakespeare and Blake would have envied such perfect lines as those. Wouldn't you agree, Master Lothrop?"

"I've never cared much for poetry," Odd Willie says.

The Bailiff shrugs, and the green bathrobe slips off his right shoulder. "Soldier, surely you can't blame a man for trying to outwit destiny. Do you honestly believe I could have acted otherwise?"

Soldier slowly lowers her gun, easing back on the trigger, and turns her face away from the bore of Odd Willie's .45. Then she glances down at Emmie Silvey, who's still standing there beside her on the dais. "You asked me," she says to the Bailiff, "and I told you my dream, and then you took me up to the attic."

The Bailiff laughs, his laughter made painfully loud by the demon's architecture. "Finish it, Soldier," he says. "I am a foolish old bastard, and my clumsy schemes and machinations have only made my fate more terrible. Our purpose lies in ruin. The Cuckoo is undone. A masque which has endured down untold ages is ended here. *All* my world is ended here."

"Take me home," Emmie says, and there are tears streaking her cheeks. "Please, Soldier. Take me home now."

"Close your eyes," Soldier tells Emmie, and she thinks about that stormy night in Ipswich, and she thinks, too, about the cemetery in Woonsocket, the shrill voices of imagined birds singing on a misplaced summer day—*All lost, lost, lost now.* And, as easy as blinking an eye, Soldier does her trick for Emmie . . .

. . . and they're sitting in the car outside the Museum of Natural History in Roger Williams Park, and Soldier asks Emmie if she knows where the stuffed black bear is.

"No. I don't remember a black bear," Emmie tells her.

And then Soldier remembers the Bailiff and his dead boys, the cold muzzle of Odd Willie's gun against her skin, and the words she spoke three and half years ago, when she was only five years old.

"If there's a bear in there somewhere, then I never saw it. I think I wouldn't forget a whole damn bear."

"Never mind," Soldier says, and to Odd Willie, "Something's wrong. We have to go to Benefit Street instead." And he has questions, but only one or two, and it's easy to fake the answers she doesn't know. She tells him what he needs to hear, and then Odd Willie turns the key in the ignition and starts the car again and pulls out of the museum parking lot.

TEN

The Yellow House

Soldier can't remember the first time she saw the yellow house on Benefit Street, not the first time that she saw it from the *outside*. It seems she might have been a grown woman before she ever looked at it the way that other people do, those unsuspecting people of the sunlight who have not been raised in the deep and rotten places of the world, who have never walked the silent halls of the house or climbed the narrow stairs leading into and out of its vast basement. If Soldier had ever paused to consider this juxtaposition—that she knew the terrible heart of the yellow house before she ever glimpsed its concealing face—she might have thought it odd.

There has never been a less haunted house, nor a house more filled with bad memories and restless spirits.

It has a reputation, of course, but then many old houses in this city suffer from unpleasant reputations; too many houses that have stood far too long to escape insanity and murder, suicide and all the less mundane improprieties of men and women. But the "haunted Providence" tours never stop in front of the yellow house, and no medium or investigator of the "paranormal" has ever held a séance in its front parlor or attempted EMF readings in its upstairs bedrooms.

388 CAITLÍN R. KIERNAN

There are occasionally sensitive minds who feel a sudden unease whenever they pass by, and some will even cross to the western side of the street to put more distance between themselves and the house. But these people are few, and they rarely spare the house more than a quick, anxious glance.

Mr. H. P. Lovecraft (1890–1937), who made the yellow house the subject of one of his stories, wrote: "Originally a farm or semi-farm building, it followed the average New England colonial lines of the middle eighteenth century—the prosperous peaked-roof sort, with two stories and dormerless attic, and with the Georgian doorway and interior panelling dictated by the progress of taste at that time. It faced south, with one gable end buried to the lower windows in the eastward rising hill, and the other exposed to the foundations toward the street." He also noted, "The general fact is, that the house was never regarded by the solid part of the community as in any real sense 'haunted.' There were no widespread tales of rattling chains, cold currents of air, extinguished lights, or faces at the window. Extremists sometimes said the house was 'unlucky,' but that is as far as even they went." And, fortunately for him and innumerable others, even Lovecraft's excitable and prying imagination never guessed more than a misleading fraction of the truth.

Since its appearance in 1764 (in no conventional sense was it constructed), the great yellow house at 135 Benefit Street has kept its secrets to itself, ever faithful to the iron wills of its architects, just as Soldier and Odd Willie Lothrop and the other changelings have kept their covenants with the Bailiff and the Cuckoo and the Hounds of Cain. The sum of improbable geometries and Cape Ann granite, nails and fallen trees and dim words whispered in forgotten tongues, the house knows its purpose well, as do all those who dwell within its walls and all those who might ever have cause to enter its doors or windows or come slipping up its drainpipes.

"Do you think they're expecting us?" Odd Willie asks, and Soldier shrugs and drops the butt of her cigarette. She grinds it out with the toe of her cowboy boot.

"I'm not sure it much matters," she says. The three of them— Odd Willie, Soldier, and Emmie Silvey—are standing together across the street from the house, standing there on the icy blacktop beside the stolen Chevy Malibu, and Emmie keeps sneezing. Soldier watches the house and knows that it's watching her, in turn, that the silver-eyed ladies and gentlemen inside are waiting for them to cross Benefit and come up the steps to the front door. She knows that somewhere below the yellow house, Madam Terpsichore and Master Danaüs and the other *ghul* are whispering among themselves, that Madam Mnemosyne sits in her burrow, hunched over her scrying glass, watching the black water for the moments Soldier hasn't yet caught up with. And in the attic, the alchemist's daughter is waiting, too.

"I *know* this house," Emmie says and sneezes again.

"*Gesundheit,*" Odd Willie mutters and jingles the car keys in one hand.

"I've had dreams about this house," Emmie says and wipes her nose. "I dreamed it isn't really a house at all."

Soldier looks nervously back up Benefit Street. They'd picked up a tail shortly after leaving the museum parking lot, Kennedy and Seagrave and that dyke bitch Amasa Sprague in the same black hearse that Soldier and Sheldon Vale had used for the long drive up to Ipswich. She knows that Odd Willie saw it, too, but neither of them has said anything about the hearse.

"I used to know the difference between my dreams and being awake," Emmie says. "Now I don't think I ever will again."

"Soldier, we can't just fucking stand here all day," Odd Willie says. "If we're going in, let's please just get it the hell over with."

"Maybe you better hang back," Soldier tells him. "Stay here with the car. I don't think this is about you."

Odd Willie shakes his head and rubs his freezing hands together. "Fuck that. You got me into this shit—you and the Bailiff and Saben and that kid," and he stops talking long enough to point at Emmie. "And now I'm *in* it, right, and it's too damned late for valiant fucking gestures, and you know that just as well as I do."

"*I* was just trying to go home," Emmie says. "I'd go home right now, if she'd let me," and she sneezes, then wipes her nose on the sleeve of her coat and glares at Soldier.

"You had a chance to run," Soldier says, "both of you. You could have left me to die back in Woonsocket, or you could have left me in that motel room in Uxbridge."

"Well," Odd Willie sighs, "we can't stand here all goddamn day long waiting for you to take your thumb out of your ass and finally make up your mind. I swear, I think I'm getting fucking hypothermia."

Soldier shuts her eyes, and she's back in Miss Josephine's dining room, sitting across the wide mahogany table from Sheldon's corpse, and he looks sad and smug and angry and very dead, all at the same time.

"You already know what comes next," he says. "All you have to do is cross the street. It's all been arranged. They're waiting for you inside."

And the clock on the mantel, the tall clock with a girl's tattooed face, begins to chime the hour.

Soldier gasps and opens her eyes, and the yellow house is still there, gazing indifferently down at her. An awful, bottomless box of secrets hidden in broad daylight for the past two hundred and forty-six years, and Soldier takes Emmie's hand and crosses the slushy street. A moment later, Odd Willie whispers a well-worn prayer to Mother Hydra and follows her.

*   *   *

Standing in the anteroom of the yellow house, Emmie tries to be polite and not stare at the woman who opened the door, the woman whom Soldier calls Miss Josephine, but she's never known that anyone could be so beautiful *and* so completely hideous. The woman, who is very tall and dressed as though she's just returned from a funeral in an Edward Gorey book—Miss Underfold in *The Other Statue,* perhaps—has skin like an antique wax doll. Emmie thinks that if she pressed a finger too roughly against that pale skin, she'd leave an impression behind. But the hardest part about not staring is the woman's shimmering silver eyes, eyes that remind Emmie of an experiment with liquid mercury that she did in science class just before winter break. *And mercury is poisonous,* she reminds herself and stares at her feet.

"I didn't think anyone would be awake," Soldier says, but Emmie can tell that she's lying. She suspects the silver-eyed woman knows Soldier's lying, too.

"We've all been very concerned," the woman says, and something about her voice makes Emmie flinch. "The household is not quite itself today. There have been the most extraordinary rumors, and sleep has eluded most of us. The Bailiff—"

"Yeah, he said that I should meet him here," Soldier says. "He said that I should go to the attic and wait for him there."

The woman nods her wax-doll head and leans close to Soldier, sniffing the air around her. Then she smiles, and Emmie's sorry that she isn't still staring at her feet and minding her own business, because she knows she won't ever be able to forget that smile, not if she lives to be a hundred and twenty. Like the dead starling, the bird she killed when she was only six, and Deacon said, "Just try not thinking of a white elephant sometime."

"This unfortunate affair," the woman says, her voice all honey and ice and broken bottles, "it is not truly any of my concern. This affair, it's between you and the ones *downstairs.* We mind our business, and the hounds kindly mind theirs. But the Bailiff, and the attic . . ." and the woman pauses and sniffs at Soldier again. "You've hurt yourself, my dear," she says and touches one index finger gently to the cut on Soldier's cheek. "You should be more careful."

Odd Willie glances apprehensively at Soldier and shifts from foot to foot. Emmie wonders if he's about to take out his gun and shoot the silver-eyed woman; she wonders if it would make any difference.

"Stop your fidgeting, Master Lothrop," Miss Josephine says and looks directly at him. "If the Bailiff said the two of you should meet him in the attic, then meet him in the attic you shall. As I have said already, this is no proper concern of ours. You and Master Lothrop answer to the Bailiff and to the hounds, not to me nor mine."

"Thank you," Soldier says, and Emmie isn't sure if she sounds relieved or only frightened in another way.

"This one here," Miss Josephine says and turns towards Emmie. "She is also a Child of the Cuckoo, is she not?"

"My name's Emmie Silvey," Emmie says, and the woman nods her head.

"Then I have a message for you."

"She's with us," Soldier says quickly, and the silver-eyed woman flashes her another of those smiles, a smile like a shark only pretending to be a woman, and Soldier takes a step backwards, bumping into Odd Willie.

"Indeed," says Miss Josephine. "Nonetheless, this is an urgent message that I have promised to deliver, and I am ever bound to keep my promises. Unless, dear Soldier, you should object. Unless you believe, possibly, that I am overstepping my rightful boundaries." And Emmie wants to shut her eyes, wants to turn away from that monstrous smile, but she seems to have forgotten how to move.

"Of course not," Soldier says, almost whispering. "I didn't mean to imply that."

"Then be about your business, changeling, and I will be about mine," and she waves her left hand, dismissing Soldier and Odd Willie. Then, before Soldier can protest or Emmie can cry out or Odd Willie can even go back to fidgeting, the smiling, silver-eyed woman places her right thumb firmly against Emmie's forehead. There's sudden cold, an ice age spilling out of the woman and into Emmie, and then a brief electric jolt, and the anteroom dissolves into dusk and the sound of a dry desert wind . . .

. . . and the twilight air smells like the dust between grains of sand and, more faintly, the musky sweat of the black-skinned woman.

"I didn't think I was ever going to see you again," Emmie says. "I thought that part of the story was over."

"You ought never second-guess a story," the black-skinned woman says. She's crouched only a few yards down the dune face from Emmie. She's almost completely naked, wearing only a ragged sort of leather breechcloth strung about her waist and a few pieces of jewelry that shine faintly in the glow of the rising moon. Her white dreadlocks are tied back away from her face.

"Not even a story I'm in?"

"Not even then," she replies. "*Especially* not a story that you're inside."

"It's a very bad place, isn't it?"

"That old house?" the woman asks and begins tracing something in the sand between them. "Dangerous would be a better way of describing it. Think of it as you would think of a nest of hornets. The nest itself is neither good nor evil, not as men reckon such things, but it *can* hurt you, because of the things that live inside."

"Like that horrible woman."

"Like her. And the others of her kind. And things you haven't seen yet. And things I hope you never will."

The black-skinned woman draws a circle in the sand, then draws a smaller circle inside it, then an even smaller circle at the center of the other two.

"So why am I here again?" Emmie asks, trying to figure out what the image in the sand is meant to be. "She said that she had a message for me, but then she sent me here to you. Why'd she do that?"

"Because she owed me a debt, an ages-old debt that she could never truly repay, and I offered to dismiss it if she would be sure you found your way back here."

Emmie frowns and scoops a small hole in the sand, working the fingers of her right hand in like the spade-shaped snout of some furtive desert creature. Only an inch or two below the surface, the sand is still warm.

"They won't take me home," she says. "I did what you asked, but they won't take me back to Deacon. It's been days and days. He must think I'm dead by now. By now, he must have given up."

The woman stops drawing in the sand and looked at Emmie, shadows hiding her golden eyes. "This path you're on is a roundabout sort of thing, fraught with many twists and turns. But I believe, Emmie, that it will lead you home very soon."

"You *believe*?" Emmie balks and digs her fingers deeper into the sun-warm sand.

"I'm sorry, but on this path nothing is ever certain. Even when the story seems to be finished, and the book is closed, even then, it may not truly be done."

"We went into the museum, didn't we?" Emmie asks, quick, before she loses her nerve. "We went in, but then she did something so it never happened."

"You're a very observant girl," the black-skinned woman says and goes back to tracing her patterns in the sand. "You're beginning to catch on, which is more than could ever be said for most."

"I thought so," Emmie says, and looks up at the moon and all the stars winking on above the dunes. "It was sort of like having déjà vu, almost. We were about to get out of the car and go into the museum, and then Soldier changed her mind, and, all of a sudden, I had memories of things that hadn't happened."

"It was passed down in her mother's blood, that particular gift, that curse. It's kept her alive many times now, even without Soldier knowing what she was doing, but it could still destroy her . . . and others."

"It scares me, almost more than anything else," and Emmie gives up trying to find the Big Dipper, because there's something not quite right about these stars, something just unfamiliar enough to be disorienting. "I keep wondering if Soldier's changed things I *don't* remember. I keep wondering if that first time I saw her, when I gave her Pearl's snow globe, if maybe it wasn't only two days ago, because she keeps changing what happens to make it come out different, and so we keep doing the same things over and over again."

"She's trying to find something, Emmie," the woman says, and draws a crooked triangle to enclose the circles within circles within circles. "Something that was stolen from her. When she finds it, I think the story will end, and you can go home. *If* she finds it."

"Is that what I'm supposed to do? Help her find what she's looking for?"

"That's a part of it. But there are other things, as well."

"Building bridges," Emmie says very softly. "Building bridges for the ghouls and Pearl."

"You have grievous choices ahead of you, Emmie Silvey, and I do not envy you."

"You know, half the time, I have no idea what you're talking about."

The black-skinned woman laughs softly to herself and stands up, wiping sand from her thighs and legs. "You are a wonder, child. I'd keep you here with me, if I thought the world would ever permit such a thing."

"But I don't *want* to stay here with you," Emmie tells her, even though part of her does, the part that doesn't really want to know how the story's going to end, the part that's more afraid than home-sick. "I want to go home. I want to go home and be with Deacon."

"Then you must watch your steps, and you must make these choices with great care. You must decide if you will help Soldier again, and if you'll build the bridges the hounds desire of you."

"I keep saying that I don't *know* how to build a damn bridge," Emmie tells her and pulls her hand free of the sand.

The black-skinned woman is silent for a moment. She stands silhouetted against the evening sky, the moon like a bright coin hung above her head. She seems to be admiring whatever it is that she's drawn in the sand, the complex arrangement of lines and curves and curlicues that Emmie can only just make out in the moonlight.

"There was a great war here once," the woman says. "You know that, don't you, Emmie?"

Emmie nods her head. A yellow scorpion as long as her middle finger has crawled out of the sand where her hand was buried only a moment before, and she watches it skitter towards the edge of the shapes drawn on the dune.

"I was dreaming, and Pearl showed me. Or I thought I was dreaming. She said it was a war to drive the ghouls out of the wastelands."

"It was that, and other things. In a sense, it has never actually ended. In a sense, it never will."

The scorpion pauses at the edge of the outermost line the woman has traced in the sand and stirs at the night air with its pincers.

"The warriors still battle in the sky, Emmie. You've seen them, too. Sea and sand, waves washing against the edges of this place, and two demons tearing at one another, two demons perched upon the edges of two maelstroms, one always in flame and the other always in shadow."

"Yeah," Emmie says, still watching the scorpion and starting to feel sleepy. "I saw them. She showed me."

Light has begun to leak from the sand, streaming up from the designs traced into the dune, brilliant, blazing ribbons of crimson and turquoise, amber and tangerine, the deepest, purest blues Emmie's ever seen. The ribbons swirl and dip and swiftly rise, each color racing all the others, twining tightly together, then breaking free again. The scorpion has stopped waving its pincers about, and it vanishes beneath the sand.

"Forgive me," the woman says, stepping into the light. "I have grown too weary of my own secrets. I cannot carry these things forever." And the colors wash over and *through* her, and Emmie realizes that the ribbons aren't merely light and color, but music, too. Each hue a different voice, and together they form a vast and clamorous symphony, a drowning roar of harmony and discord that rushes forward only to shatter against some shore she can't quite see. The woman holds her arms up, and the ribbons of color and sound wrap themselves about her, playing her ebony flesh like the strings of a thousand guitars and violins and cellos.

"Close your eyes," she says; Emmie can hear her very clearly above the music, can hear her as clearly as if there were no music at all. "Quickly. There's only a little time left."

And Emmie doesn't ask what the woman means about time. She shuts her eyes, but the colors are still there, the colors and the music and the woman standing like a lightning rod planted at the center of it all. The night has disappeared, as have the stars and the moon and the sky, the desert and the dry, dusty smell. *If I open my eyes,* Emmie thinks, *will the world come back, or has she taken it away forever?* But then the ribbons of light are moving even faster than before, the music become a perfect cacophony; the black-skinned woman holds out a hand, and Emmie only hesitates a moment or two before she accepts it.

"The hounds tell a story about me," the black-skinned woman says. "They teach it to all the changelings, to keep them close, to keep them slaves, to make them afraid to even wish for what the Cuckoo has taken from them."

And then Emmie is standing somewhere else, somewhere just beyond the high Arabian dunes, the cracked and wind-scoured bed of a lake or inland sea dried up a thousand or a million years ago. There's a dead tree nearby, its charred trunk jutting from the heart of a roaring fire, and the body of a young girl hangs from its lowest limb, a noose pulled tight about her broken neck. Three naked women dance around the fire, and they aren't alone; there are other things dancing with them, feral, loping things with canine faces and bristling fur. The fire licks at the dead girl's feet and legs, and Emmie understands without having to be told—the girl hanging from the tree is the black-skinned woman, and it wasn't the desert sun that burned her dark as pitch. Then the three women become crows and fly away, but the ghouls continue dancing around the burning tree and the body of the girl. Their howls and coarse laughter fill the night.

"They call me a traitor," the woman says from somewhere behind Emmie. "They know it's not that simple, but find half a truth more useful than the whole."

"I'm sorry," Emmie says, not wanting to see any more of it, not wanting to hear the hounds or the wind or the hungry, crackling sound of the flames gnawing the girl's corpse. She would cover her eyes, but she knows this isn't something that she's watching with her eyes and so it wouldn't do any good.

"Look closer, Emmie Silvey, and see through the myth the hounds have fashioned here. Look deep and see *all* there is to see."

And she's about to say that she has already, and that she's seen more than enough of it, thank you very much, when the night ripples like a stone dropped into still water, breaking some subtle masquerade, an illusion Emmie hadn't even guessed at. There is not one tree. There are dozens of trees studding the floor of the dead sea, each strung with its own body, each rooted in flames. There are hundreds or thousands of dancers, and the sky is filled with crows.

"Oh," Emmie says, a very small sound coughed out like the breath being knocked from her lungs. "Oh."

"I *was* a traitor," the woman says, "but it was never the hounds that I betrayed."

Overhead, the murder of crows has begun to sing, cawing triumph in their brash crow voices.

"In those days, the *ghul* were growing weak, their powers diminished by the long war with the *djinniyeh,* and the Children of the Cuckoo had plotted together and appointed an hour when they would finally rise up, as one, against the hounds."

"But you," Emmie whispers, "you told the ghouls it was going to happen. You *told* them."

"I *loved* them," the woman says. "They were all I knew and all that I could comprehend. For all I understood, freedom was nothing more than another wild beast waiting to devour me, no different in my eyes from the jackals and the leopards. So, yes, I went to my mistress, and I warned her."

The air stinks of woodsmoke and searing flesh, and the wings of the crows batter the air until Emmie thinks even the sky will begin to bleed.

"But they killed you, too," Emmie says. "They killed all of you, just to be safe, didn't they? Just to be sure."

"Yes," the black-skinned woman replies, "all of us. Just to be sure. They had to be absolutely certain that they'd found out all the renegades. And then they rewarded my loyalty by naming me the sole conspirator, only me, one foolish girl child who'd defied them because she was selfish and weak and wanted what other children had. They feared what might happen if the truth survived that night, if their slaves knew that once upon a time all the children had turned against the Cuckoo. If changelings knew such a thing were even possible, it might happen again."

Emmie turns away, because there's nothing else she needs to see. "Why are you still here?" she asks.

"They wanted the alchemist to capture *this* moment, what they'd *made* of this moment, so that they wouldn't have to rely on mere words and imagination, so that the Children of the Cuckoo could each and every one watch my death again and again and *again* and all fear the same fate or worse. But time's slippery, Emmie, even for wizards. Even for those who can spin hours and days like spider silk. And I have long guarded this night against them. They will not have it, ever."

"Please send me back now," Emmie whispers, close to tears, and the shade named Esmeribetheda grips her hand and drags her free of the night of fire and crows and dancing ghouls. They stand together at the center of the drawing in the sand, their feet smudging and rearranging the countless grains into something new and necessary. Esmeribetheda holds Emmie close as the ribbons of color and music weave a bright lattice around them.

"What's coming," Esmeribetheda says, "it's a choice that you must make for yourself and for your own reasons and no one else's. But I needed you to see. I needed you to know this."

Emmie, bound in light and trilling crystalline notes, in the horror and sorrow of what she has seen and what the black-skinned woman has told her, feels the cold sinking into her again. The same cold she felt when Miss Josephine touched her forehead, and she knows what's coming and braces herself for the jolt. Esmeribetheda wipes the tears from Emmie's face and then pushes her all the way back to the yellow house on Benefit Street.

*   *   *

Soldier stands on the topmost of the foldaway stairs leading into the attic, and Hester, the brown girl, the Daughter of the Four of Pentacles, is sitting on her milking stool, exactly where Soldier first saw her. *And just how long ago was that?* Soldier thinks, the last thing she wants to ask herself, but asking it anyway, it and all the questions that come tumbling after it: *Was that a long time ago, when I was a child? Was I a child a long time ago? Was it only three years ago, when I was a child?*

The girl's holding an antique gold pocket watch, and its ticking seems very, very loud in the stillness of the attic. When the alchemist's daughter sees Soldier, she looks surprised, surprised and perhaps a little disappointed, but not alarmed.

"Oh," she says. "It's only *you* again. I thought perhaps it was someone else. I thought perhaps you'd died in Woonsocket."

"You were there, weren't you?" Soldier asks her. "You were there, and you helped me. You untied us. How—"

"Did I?" the brown girl smiles. "Well, then, that's my own business, isn't it? I had my reasons. Besides, you haven't even said thank-you."

Odd Willie mumbles something impatient from the stairs behind Soldier, and so she climbs the rest of the way into the attic. He follows, and she sees that he's drawn his gun.

"I really don't think you're going to need that," Soldier tells him and points at the .45.

"Yeah, well. Chance favors the prepared," he replies. "Isn't that what you said back at the museum?"

"Whatever," Soldier says and wonders if there's a way to pull the stairs up after them.

"How did you escape?" the brown girl asks. "I mean, how'd you get out past George Ballou?"

"I killed him. I think maybe I killed them all."

The Daughter of the Four of Pentacles nods her head and asks another question. "Did they catch her?"

"Did they catch who?"

The girl frowns and rolls her eyes, then slips the watch into a pocket of her black dress. "Emma Jean Silvey. Did they catch Emma Jean in the railroad tunnel? She has something that belongs to my father, and I would very much like to get it back."

"The kid's with us," Odd Willie says, staring up at the massive pine beams supporting the roof of the yellow house, half-hidden in the shadows far above their heads. "You know, it's a whole hell of a lot bigger up here than it ought to be."

"Well, I don't *see* her," the brown girl says.

"Miss Josephine wanted to talk to her," Soldier replies. "You *remember* me?"

"Of course I remember you. You're Soldier. You're the one the Bailiff brought to see me. The nasty little brat who dropped the wildebeest."

"That happened? That really happened?"

"Unfortunately, yes. That Noah's ark is my responsibility. I'm supposed to keep it safe. It was made in Italy by Signior Anastagio Baldassario Moratti in 1888."

"Is there any way to pull these stairs up from here?" Soldier asks her, and the Daughter of the Four of Pentacles sighs and stands up.

"What possible difference does it make?" she asks, straightening her dress. "Is someone chasing you, too?"

"Jesus goddamn bloody Christ," Odd Willie says and glances back down the stairs. "This kid's even more annoying than the other one."

"Can we *shut* the trapdoor?" Soldier asks again, starting to think maybe guns aren't such a bad idea after all.

"There's a crank over there, mounted on the wall. But don't turn it too fast or it gets stuck. And don't let go until you feel it catch."

"Thank you very fucking much." Odd Willie snorts, and Soldier squints into the attic gloom until she spots the hand crank.

"If we close it, how's Emmie supposed to find us?" Odd Willie asks her, and Soldier shrugs.

"Maybe it's better if she doesn't. Better for her, anyway."

Odd Willie shakes his head and runs his fingers through his hair, slicking it down flat against his scalp. "I swear to fuck, Soldier, I hope you're planning on telling me what the hell's going on someday real soon. 'Cause I'm getting awfully damned tired of trying to figure it all out for myself."

"Who are you, anyway?" the Daughter of the Four of Pentacles asks Odd Willie, and he snickers nervously and wipes at his nose.

The hand crank squeals and groans and pops, dry-rotted rope and rust and neglect, and Soldier half expects it to come apart at any moment, sending the stairs and the trapdoor crashing to the hallway below. The stairs are still half-extended, and now she's having to strain to turn the crank. "Odd Willie," she says between gritted teeth. "This is Hester—"

"Pearl," the alchemist's daughter corrects her.

"—*Hester,*" Soldier grunts, "this is Odd Willie Lothrop."

"I see," the brown girl says. "I've heard stories about you from Barnaby."

"I never fucked a dead cat," Odd Willie tells her. "If Barnaby said that, he was lying."

"He said it was a live chicken. Either way—"

"—it's a goddamn lie. Soldier, if you shut that all the way, it's going to get awfully damn dark up here."

"You should have brought a lantern," the brown girl says. "Usually they bring lanterns when they come. It was silly of you to have forgotten."

"It was a whole lot sillier, girlie, that we didn't bring a ball gag and a pair of handcuffs," Odd Willie says and goes to help Soldier with the crank.

"Crap. It's locking up on me," she tells him. "The damned thing probably hasn't seen a drop of oil in at least a hundred years."

"Oh, not quite as long as all that," says the brown girl. "My father used it all the time, and I used it, too. He always kept it in good repair."

And Soldier thinks how much easier it would be to give up and let the winch start turning counterclockwise, letting the old rope unspool, and when the stairs were down again, she could go back to Miss Josephine, could go all the way down to the basement and the tunnels and the ghouls. Then *they* could figure out what to do with Emmie Silvey, and Soldier would never have to face whatever's waiting for her in the attic. She could find a pint of cheap whiskey and save the truth for people who don't have to go looking for courage and resolve in a goddamn bottle. She could accept her fate and wash her hands of the whole mess, turn Emmie over to Madam Terpsichore and Master Danaüs. She belongs to them, anyway.

Just like me, she thinks. *Just like Odd Willie.* Then there's a dull crack and a fainter thump from somewhere inside the winch, and it stops turning altogether, leaving the attic stairs suspended halfway between up and down.

"Now you've gone and *broken* it," the Daughter of the Four of Pentacles says indignantly. "Do you break things everywhere you go, or only when you come up here?"

"Everywhere I go," Soldier replies and takes her hands off the crank handle; her palms are red and tingling. *Well,* she thinks, *I guess that fucking well settles that.*

"Piece of shit," Odd Willie says. "It was probably broken to start with."

"It most certainly was *not,*" the brown girl snaps at him. "It worked just fine. It was right as rain, as long as you knew how to handle it."

"Soldier, I'm gonna fucking shoot her if she keeps this up much longer."

Soldier stops staring at her palms and glances at Odd Willie. "You can't. At least not until later on. She's the reason we're stuck up here. She's—"

"—had quite enough of the *both* of you," the brown girl says. "You're ungrateful and rude, and I don't think you even have permission to be up here. I don't think the hounds even know."

Odd Willie laughs and spits at the foldaway stairs. "Look, kid, I don't care what she says; either shut up or get shot."

The Daughter of the Four of Pentacles glares at him silently for a moment, her mouth hanging half-open in dismay. Then she narrows her eyes and crosses her arms. "You can't shoot me, changeling. *No one* can hurt me. *Ever.* There are *rules* here, Mr. Lothrop."

Odd Willie flips the safety off his gun, then flips it back on again. "Lately," he says, "I've noticed that the rules don't seem to mean a whole hell of a lot."

Soldier looks at the stairs, one last, exasperated glance before she gives up and turns to the alchemist's daughter. "Pearl," she says, "no one's going to shoot you. No one's going to fucking *hurt* you. But you need to try to be just a little more helpful. The more you cooperate, the sooner you'll be rid of us."

"I don't even know what you want."

"I want you to tell me what happened when I was here before, when the Bailiff sent me up here."

The Daughter of the Four of Pentacles uncrosses her arms and smiles a hard smile that's really more of a smirk. "Maybe I was going to tell you. But now I've changed my mind. Anyway, that's a secret," she says to Soldier. "That's a very important secret that I've promised never to tell anyone—especially not *you*—because there are rules."

"Then we have a problem," Soldier tells her. "Because me and Mr. Lothrop here are already standing in shit up to our fucking eyeballs, and if you can't—or *won't*—help me, Pearl, then I might as well let him put a bullet in your face and be done with it."

The brown girl stops smirking and sits back down on her milking stool. "You're even more unpleasant as a grown woman than you were as a child," she says to Soldier.

"Now, I'll buy that," Odd Willie snickers, and then he puts his gun away.

"How old am I?" Soldier asks the girl. "In Woonsocket, you said it wasn't time for that question, that it would come later. And here we are, later. So tell me, how *old* am I?" But the alchemist's daughter only shrugs and makes a show of twiddling her thumbs.

"That's not a simple question," she says.

"Answer it anyway. We've got the time."

"There's more than one answer."

"But I think you know the one I'm after," Soldier says, gazing into the shadows behind and above the brown girl, the immense attic of the yellow house stretching out before her like a half-remembered nightmare. "The last time I was here, you led me somewhere. I want you to take me there again. On the way, we can talk about what you were doing in Woonsocket."

The brown girl watches her for a moment, then smiles again, and something about that smile makes Soldier want to hit her, something precious and cold and calculated.

"Soldier, haven't you ever learned that you catch more flies with honey than with vinegar?" the girl asks. "Didn't the Bailiff teach you that? You should try using 'please' sometime."

"Fine," Soldier says. "*Please*, Pearl, will you take me wherever the hell you took me before?"

"Him, too?" And the Daughter of the Four of Pentacles points at Odd Willie.

"Yes, please, him fucking too."

"I don't like guns, Soldier. And I don't like being threatened with them, particularly not by men whose lives I've helped to save. I really don't like being around men like that."

Soldier turns and punches Odd Willie in the stomach as hard as she can. He yelps and doubles over, then sinks to his knees.

"There," she says. "He's very sorry that he pointed a gun at you. He's learned his lesson and promises he'll never do it again."

"You should know, I wasn't trying to help you," the brown girl says. "I was trying to help Emma Jean, and—"

"I don't need an explanation. I just need you to stop fucking around and do what I've asked you to do."

"I thought I should be clear, that's all," and then the alchemist's daughter gets up from her stool again and walks away into the darkness.

"Don't be such a goddamn pussy," Soldier tells Odd Willie, and he gags and calls her a cunt and tells her to fuck off. But she helps him to his feet anyway, and they follow the girl deeper into the attic.

Open your eyes, Esmeribetheda says, and it takes Emmie a moment or two to remember exactly how one does that, opens her eyes, because she's had them closed for so long. Ages, it seems, long ages as she fell through the wrinkled time and space and vacuum cold and starfire that lies between the black-skinned woman's desert and the attic of the yellow house. And it takes her a moment more to realize that Esmeribetheda hasn't traveled with her, that she's come alone into this musty, disorienting place of half-light and shadows. She sits down on the floor, sits down before she falls, her legs weak and trembling, and tries to figure out where she is and what she's supposed to do next.

"Can you still hear me?" she asks Esmeribetheda, but no one answers, only her own echo bouncing back from the darkness. Emmie blinks, realizing that the dim shapes towering around her are pieces of furniture and high rows of shelving. She calls out again, louder than before.

"Can you still *hear* me?"

This time her echo is more distinct and clearly repeats at least seven times.

"You can't, can you?" Emmie sighs, gazing up at the shelves. There are faintly glinting objects on them that she thinks at first must be fishbowls, row upon row of goldfish bowls of different sizes, until she remembers Pearl's snow globe. A sun inside a crystal sphere, the thing that Soldier used as a weapon to drive away or destroy a demon or maybe something even worse than a demon. And here, here there are a *hundred* spheres—no, a thousand. At *least* a thousand.

That's one of my father's later experiments, and he's extremely proud of it. He was careful to take a star none of the astronomers had ever seen. . . .

Staring up at the shelves and all those glinting spheres, Emmie wonders just how many of them contain stars that Pearl's father decided no one would ever miss and what other things he might have trapped.

My father moved places and moments. . . .

There's a dry, fluttering sound then, somewhere overhead to her left, and Emmie squints into the dark, hoping there aren't bats in this place, but fairly certain there are probably lots of them. She gets to her feet again, her legs feeling a little stronger now, and she spots the nub of a candlestick on a nearby table, a long table that's really more like a workbench, crowded with odd mechanical contraptions and glass containers, books and hardened pools of candle wax. She goes to the table and finds a big box of kitchen matches sitting on top of a very ancient-looking book bound in brittle leather; Emmie shakes the box and is relieved to hear wooden matches rattling about inside. The candle stub makes only a small pool of warm yellow light, but it's a welcome thing in this place. She sets the matchbox down a safe distance from the candle's flame, and now she can see the title of the book, *Astronomicum Caesarium,* stamped into the cover in dingy gold. Emmie begins to open it, disturbing several large silverfish, but then she hears voices and footsteps and looks up to see Pearl and Soldier and Odd Willie appear from behind one of the tall shelves.

Pearl furrows her eyebrows and points an accusing finger at Emmie. "How did you get up here? What are you doing with my father's things?"

"I was just looking at a book," Emmie replies, closing it quickly and stepping quickly away from the table. "That's all. I didn't touch anything."

"Liar. You lit that candle there," Pearl says, "so you touched *that,* and that means you must have touched the matches, as well."

"Her bark's worse than her bite," Odd Willie says and rubs at his stomach like someone with a bellyache. "Problem is, she never fucking *stops* barking."

"Shit," Soldier says, stepping past Pearl and walking towards one of the shelves. "This is it. This is the place you brought me before, isn't it? I was here."

"Don't you touch *anything,*" Pearl warns her, instead of answering the question.

Odd Willie plops down on a moldering, threadbare settee, raising a thick cloud of dust, and something inside it cracks loudly.

"What was *that*?" Pearl says and turns away from Soldier to find Odd Willie coughing and fanning the dust away. "Be *careful,*" she groans. "That belonged to my mother."

"Are we in the attic now?" Emmie asks and watches Soldier examining the crystal spheres on the shelf. "We are, aren't we?"

"*We* had to take the goddamn stairs," Odd Willie wheezes. "You must have found a shortcut."

"There are *no* shortcuts," the brown girl says emphatically.

"Oh, hell, there are *always* shortcuts," Odd Willie croaks and then starts coughing again.

Emmie starts to tell them about Esmeribetheda and the desert, about the burning trees and the crows who were really women (or women who were really crows), but then she decides maybe it's best if she doesn't. Just because she needed to know the secret doesn't mean that everyone else needs to know it, too.

"Miss Josephine showed me the way," she says, and Pearl glares at her suspiciously.

"Where is my father's experiment?" she demands. "You had it when the ghouls came and I lost you in the tunnel. You have to give it back, right this minute."

"She doesn't have it anymore," Soldier says, bending close to a particularly large sphere, one almost as big around as a soccer ball. "She gave it to me. And I can't give it back, because I don't have it anymore, either."

"Why not? Where is it?"

"Hell, maybe. Or Niflheim or Sheol," Soldier tells her. "If you believe in such places." Then she brushes her fingers across the dusty surface of the large sphere, and it begins to glow very softly.

"I *told* you not to touch anything!" Pearl shouts at her. "The three of you have done enough damage as it is."

"*You* came looking for *me*," Emmie says and walks over to stand beside Soldier. "You started this, Pearl. I certainly never wanted to run off in a snowstorm and hide in a tunnel and get kidnapped and chased by monsters."

"There's an entire island in this one," Soldier says.

"It's *not* an island," Pearl protests. "It's a small continent. My father hardly bothered with islands. That's a place called Lemuria. It's *very* important, and you're not to touch it again."

"Why did we come here?" Emmie asks Soldier. "Why did you want to come to this attic instead of going to see the Bailiff?"

"Because I think maybe I left something here once," Soldier tells her.

"Do you know what it was, the thing you left?"

"I'm starting to figure it out," Soldier says, and then she turns away from the sphere containing a small, stolen continent, and faces the brown girl.

"Why *did* you help her?" Soldier asks and nods at Emmie. "And why'd you help me so that I'd wind up helping her, too?"

Pearl frowns and mutters something to herself and picks at a loose thread on her black dress. *Maybe she doesn't know,* Emmie thinks. *Maybe this is just another one of her father's experiments. Maybe we're all stuck inside one of those snow globes. Maybe we're sitting on a shelf somewhere, and her father is watching everything we do.*

"You'll have to speak a little louder than that, Hester," Odd Willie says. "Me and Soldier here, we're a little hard of hearing. That's what happens when you play with guns. Next thing you know, you're deaf as a stone."

"I *said* that I have my reasons."

"The first time I saw you," Emmie says, "you told me you needed me to build a bridge for you. That's why you were helping me, isn't it? Because if they killed me, I couldn't build your bridge."

"You make it sound much more selfish than it is," Pearl tells her, and she picks up something that looks like a clarinet grafted onto a ship's sextant. "I probably would have helped you anyway."

"And what you took from me," Soldier says, "where is it? Where did you put it? Is it here, on one of these shelves?"

Pearl shakes her head, but doesn't say anything.

Emmie feels dizzy and shuts her eyes. *This is where it finally ends, Deacon. This is where the story finishes, in the attic of this awful old house.*

"You can't do what they thought you could do," Pearl says to Soldier. "I knew it all along, of course, but I had to acquiesce. I had to do whatever the Bailiff and the hounds told me to do. I didn't have a choice. They have my father."

"Soldier's not the bridge builder," Emmie says and opens her eyes, but the dizziness doesn't pass. "I am. I'm the one the hounds need to go back home, but they thought it was Soldier, didn't they?"

"The quadroon daughter of Saben White," Pearl says and smiles and fiddles with a tarnished brass knob on the sextant-clarinet thing. "They made a mistake, a serious miscalculation. If my father had been here, if they hadn't sent him away to Weir and exile, *he* could have shown them the error of their reckoning. He could have shown them it was you, Emma Jean Silvey, and you'd not have been shuffled off to be raised by that drunkard who is not your father, and none of this would ever have happened."

"Where is it?" Soldier asks her again, and then she takes a step towards the Daughter of the Four of Pentacles.

"Really, what difference does it make?" Pearl asks her. "Surely you don't think you can ever have it *back*? The Bailiff would never permit me to do any such thing. And the hounds—"

"How about you let me worry about the Bailiff and the hounds. Show me where you've put it, Pearl. Show me now. I'm tired of asking."

Emmie looks back at the crystal spheres lined up neatly on the shelf, the dust and cobwebs, all those imprisoned places and times and lives. And then she looks up at Soldier again, and she knows that the changeling woman isn't bluffing, that she'll kill Pearl, just like she would have killed all those people at the Cumberland Farms, just like she killed Emmie's mother and the creatures below Woonsocket.

"You won't hurt me," Pearl tells Soldier, her dark eyes bright with smug confidence. "You *know* the rules. You were raised by them, and you won't cross the hounds. You wouldn't ever dare cross the Bailiff."

"I already have," Soldier says very softly, calmly, and draws her pistol from the waistband of her jeans. "So, I hope you appreciate how little I have left to lose."

"Pearl, she's not kidding," Emmie says and steps in between Soldier and the alchemist's daughter. "Just do what she wants, and we'll leave."

"No. It's out of the question. I most certainly will not. My father—"

"*Pearl,*" Emmie snarls, the same way she snarled at the fat kid who said her mother was a cat, snarling like the half-breed sire she's never met. "You want to go to your father. You want to be with him. That's why you saved me, because you believe that I can make the bridge you need to reach him."

Pearl stares back at Emmie and chews her lower lip, her smile faded and her eyes not so bright now. She slowly lays the sextant-clarinet contraption back down on the long table.

"Give her what she wants," Emmie says, "and I'll build a bridge for you so you can be with him again."

"Soldier, I can't let you do this," Odd Willie laughs, a flat laugh that Emmie can tell isn't really a laugh at all. He's still sitting on the old settee, but now his pistol's pointed at Soldier. "Whatever all this shit's about, I'm pretty goddamn sure you're right, and it's *not* about me, and I have to go on living with the ghouls and the Bailiff when it's over."

"Willie, you don't know—" Soldier begins, but Odd Willie cuts her off.

"Damn straight. And I don't fucking much care, either. I've stood by you this far, because I figured maybe I owed you something after Ballou and Saben and all that crazy shit. You probably saved my life. But, Jesus, this is the *wizard's daughter,* and I have a pretty goddamn good idea what'll happen to me if I just sit here and let you shoot her."

"You don't know," Soldier says again, not looking at him, her eyes still locked on Pearl, her finger on the trigger. "When I was five, that son of a bitch used to call me up from the tunnels and feed me sweets and ask me about my dreams. And I guess he didn't like what I told him, because one night he sent me up here and this . . . this self-important little *shit,* she took my childhood, stole it, just like her father used to steal bits and pieces of the universe and lock them up in all these *things,*" and she motions towards one of the shelves with the hand that isn't holding the gun.

"Well, boo-fucking-hoo." Odd Willie snorts, and then he giggles nervously and wipes his nose again. "Look, I'm sorry, okay? Soldier, I'm sorry as a motherfucker, but I'm still not going to let you kill her. So put the goddamn gun away, 'cause it *ain't gonna happen.*"

"Fuck you," she says, almost whispering now, and shoots Odd Willie in the throat. The attic is filled with thunder that swells and booms beneath the faraway ceiling, and Pearl screams. There's a spurt of blood from the soft spot below his larynx, and he looks surprised as the pistol slips from his hand and clatters to the floor.

"You're not that fast," Soldier says, and Odd Willie Lothrop slumps back against the settee.

Pearl is crouched on the floor, both hands clasped over her ears, and Emmie's head is ringing from the gunshot, the gunshot and the dizziness that's getting worse instead of better. She turns around, and Soldier's pointing the gun at Pearl again.

"If you kill her, you'll never find it," Emmie says, and the ringing's so bad that she can hardly hear herself. "You'll never get it back, not if she's *dead.*"

"Maybe not. But you never know. You never know anything for sure. I might get lucky."

Emmie shakes her head, but the ringing won't go away, and she wonders if it ever will. She glances over her shoulder at Odd Willie sprawled on the settee. "Soldier, he was your *friend*. You were dying, and he *carried* you out of that place and took care of you."

"She's a *changeling,*" Pearl sobs from the floor, her hands still covering her ears. "She's a liar and a murderer, a Child of the Cuckoo, and people like her don't *have* friends. She's a monster, Emma Jean, just like *you*."

"Pearl," Emmie says, and the room swings and tilts and she has to lean against the table to keep from falling. "Give her what she wants. Don't make her kill you."

Pearl crawls the rest of the way beneath the table, as though it might protect her, leaving little teardrop spatters of salt water and snot on the dusty floorboards.

"I'm only a little girl, Emma Jean. They've had me locked away up here forever and ever, locked up here alone without time or sunlight or anyone to talk to, but I'm *still* only a child, not an old woman, and *I'm afraid of them*! I'm afraid of what they'll *do* to me!"

"You really should listen to her, Hester," Soldier says and squats down so the gun's still aimed at Pearl. "I think maybe she's trying to save your miserable hide."

Pearl's crying so hard that Emmie can't make out whatever she says next, but apparently Soldier can, because she laughs and cocks the pistol again.

Maybe I'm dying, Emmie thinks, wishing that the room would stop rolling drunkenly about like the deck of a boat. *Maybe when Esmeribetheda sent me back, she did something wrong. Maybe she messed something up inside my head, and I'm dying.* And the thought doesn't frighten her like she's always imagined it should, because maybe when she's dead there will be no one and nothing at all, and she won't even have to bother trying to forget all the horrible, impossible things she's seen in the last six days.

"I'm going to ask you one last time," Soldier says, and that only makes Pearl cry that much louder.

"*Stop it,*" Emmie says, and for a second she wonders if she means the swaying attic or if she means Pearl and Soldier. *I'm going to puke,* she thinks, but then the nausea passes, and Soldier's looking at her instead of the alchemist's daughter.

"Pearl's right; we're just children," Emmie says, sitting down, holding tightly to one of the table's legs. "Just kids. That's all we are, all *three* of us. Sure, I'm too weird and too smart and my eyes are yellow, and Soldier's too old, and Pearl's not nearly old enough, but we're all *three* still just children."

Soldier glances at the gun in her hand, then back at Emmie. "If you have a point—"

"That *is* my point, Soldier. Can't you see? That *is* my goddamn point," and she rests her face against the leg of the table. The nausea's back again, worse than before, and she's trying to decide which of the two Soldiers she's seeing is the real one. "Pearl, please, if you still have it, give it back to her. It belongs to her. Give it to her, and I'll build your bridge for you."

"You don't understand," Pearl sobs. "They'll find me anyway. They'll come across the bridge, too, or the ghouls that live in Weir will kill us both, me *and* my father."

Soldier, both of her, sits down on the floor, halfway between Emmie and Pearl, and looks down at the pistol again.

"*Please,*" Emmie begs the two Pearls huddled under the table. "I'll tear the bridge down once you're across. No one will follow you, I promise. Cross my heart—"

"Hope to die?" Soldier asks, and then she laughs again and rubs at her forehead with the barrel of the gun.

"Yes," Emmie says. "Yes. Cross my heart and hope to die. Give it back to her, and then I'll build your bridge, and then, when you're across, I'll tear it down so *no one* can come after you or your father."

"They *made* me do it," Pearl whimpers. "They can make you do things, too, Emma Jean."

"No, they can't. I have a secret place to hide where even they can't follow." Emmie only half understands the things she's saying, but she says them anyway. "I can go there, if I have to. Give it to her, Pearl. Give Soldier what you took from her." And then there are no more words, nothing left to say, and she wants to shut her eyes because she's tired of the tilting and there being two of everything and everyone, but she doesn't because Deacon always said that closing your eyes only makes nausea worse. *And he ought to know,* she thinks and hangs onto the table leg.

"I'm sorry," Pearl says to Soldier, and she reaches into the pocket of her dress, the same pocket where she keeps the gold watch. She takes out a very small thing, round and smooth and glassy, something the color of buttermilk and no larger than a marble. "I knew how wrong it was, but I was so afraid." And she holds it out to Soldier.

"That's it?" Soldier asks, and Pearl puts the marble into her hand.

"There wasn't much," she says and wipes at her eyes. "You weren't yet even six years old."

Soldier stops rubbing at her forehead with the pistol and rolls the buttermilk marble back and forth in her palm. "What the hell am I supposed to do with it?"

"That's the easy part," Pearl tells her. "Just put it beneath your tongue."

"I think I'm going to pass out," Emmie says, but the words sound so strange, having been said, that she decides she's probably wrong. Anyway, neither Soldier nor Pearl seems to have heard her.

"Put it under my tongue?"

"Yeah," Pearl replies and makes a wet, sniffling noise. "Time will do the rest. My father used to say that time is always trying to repair itself, and that's why it's so hard to change the past."

"That doesn't make sense," Emmie says, trying to sit up straighter. "You just contradicted yourself."

"I'm only telling you what *he* said. I can't help it if you don't understand." And then Pearl starts weeping again.

"Try it," Emmie tells Soldier. "Put it under your tongue and see what happens."

"What the fuck," Soldier says, and stares at the marble a few seconds more before slipping it into her mouth.

"Emma Jean Silvey, you've *promised* me." The two Pearls sniffle and blink their four bloodshot eyes at Emmie. "You've promised to build a bridge for me. You've crossed your heart and hoped to die."

"As long as I don't pass out first," Emmie says and lets her head rest against the table leg again.

Soldier tries to say something, but the words come out all wrong because of the marble beneath her tongue.

"Don't swallow it," Pearl tells her. "If you swallow it, it'll only make things worse."

How could things possibly be worse? Emmie thinks, and then Soldier opens her mouth, as if she's about to cry out, and there's a brilliant burst of blue-white electricity, a lightning flash and the throaty rumble of thunder right behind it, *real* thunder this time, and it's nothing like the rumbling noise the gun made when Soldier shot Odd Willie. Emmie turns her face away, and Pearl screams again, and then Emmie can *feel* the time flowing around her, flowing from everywhere all at once towards Soldier—the smallest fractions of seconds and countless interminable hours and days that never seem to end.

"You promised me!" Pearl shouts above the din of the storm raging around and inside Soldier, the storm that Soldier has become. *I did,* Emmie thinks. *I did promise, and I have no idea how I'm supposed to build a bridge.* But then it comes to her, just the same way she realized that she'd always known how to play a piano, even though no one had ever taught her. The same way she sometimes knows the right answers before people even ask her the questions. It's just something that's *there,* buried deep inside her and wanting to escape, and Emmie doesn't try to stop it . . .

*   *   *

... and in his big empty house on Angell Street, the house that Sadie bought for him and Emmie after her first novel sold, Deacon Silvey feels something unpleasant in his sour, alcoholic's belly, something that isn't quite a chill, but isn't anything else he could ever name, either. He sets down the pint bottle of rye whiskey that he's been working on since just after noon and glances at the clock mounted above the kitchen sink. At first, he's not sure which way the black second hand is moving—forwards or backwards—and he tries to recall the last time he got so drunk that he hallucinated.

She's never coming back to me, he thinks. *Not after five days. After five days, even the fucking cops know she's never coming back.*

The clock ticks forward, and the February wind brushes roughly past the kitchen windows. He wants to cry, but there are no tears left in him. Everything cried out and nothing left inside but whiskey and helpless anger and sorrow and regret.

You're an old man now, Deacon Silvey, the wind mutters. *Too old to fight the monsters anymore and too old to find lost children. Too old to do much of anything but get drunk and wish it hadn't all turned out this way.*

There's no point arguing with the wind. Only madmen argue with the wind. So he takes the bottle of rye over to the kitchen table and sits down. He thinks about the open cardboard box in the bedroom, the box Emmie must have dragged out from under the bed, all its treasures scattered shamefully across the floor. He wouldn't let Sadie pack those things away again.

I'll call Sadie, he thinks, wishing she were still there with him, there to make him stop drinking, there to keep him from giving up, wishing she hadn't taken the train back to New York the night before. But she'd already given up herself. *And she's gone too. And she's not coming back, either.*

You're an old man, the wind laughs. *You're an old man, and now you're alone. Better start getting used to it.*

And Deacon pours himself another glass of whiskey and tries to ignore the cold and vacant feeling coiled in his stomach, the feeling that says the wind is always fucking right, any way you look at it, and he watches the clock eating up the day . . .

. . . and Madam Terpsichore pauses on the creaking wooden steps leading up from the great basement of the yellow house on Benefit Street. It's been at least a hundred years since she last climbed those stairs, a long red century since she had any cause to venture from the security of the burrows and tunnels and secret underground meeting places and enter the house itself. She sniffs anxiously at the air, flaring her nostrils, licking her mottled lips, and catches an unfamiliar scent slipped in amongst the comforting cellar smells. Merely a spicy, unexpected *hint* woven almost imperceptibly between mold and old rot and the pungent white mushrooms that grow in fleshy clumps beneath the stairs.

"Too late," she growls very softly and looks back down at Madam Melpomene, standing at the foot of the cellar stairs. "It's already begun. It's already finished."

Madam Melpomene bares her crooked yellow fangs and scratches furiously at the hard-packed earth with a long thumb claw. "Then we have failed," she says. "We should have killed the wizard's bitch long ago and been done with it. She would have been sweet, at least."

Madam Terpsichore grunts, neither agreeing nor disagreeing, and stares at the basement door, still another dozen steps away. She tries to push back the dim memories of that other world, that place of deep, wooded valleys and steep white mountains rising to scrape the undersides of flickering violet clouds. The towers of slate and granite built a million years before her birth, decaying beneath a dying and indifferent sun. The home her race fled millennia ago, scattering themselves between the stars, coming at last to Weir and Earth and a dozen other alien worlds.

"We've been betrayed," Madam Melpomene says and sighs and then goes back to scratching at the dirt floor.

And Madam Terpsichore, High Dame of the Providence warrens and the last of the *ghul* alive who even half remembers the passage from *that* world or the subsequent war with the *djinniyeh* in *this* world, slowly turns and begins making her way back down the noisy basement stairs . . .

. . . and in her bottom bunk in the warrens below College Hill, the changeling girl named Sparrow Spooner wakes from a dream of the father she'll never have. Mr. H. Elgin Higginson, late of 7 Thomas Street, the witch who lied to her and used her, who never really loved her, who only pretended that he would carry her far away from the Cuckoo and the hounds. The man who cost her two fingers before he was fed alive to Madam Terpsichore's students, before the ghoul snatched his escaping soul and devoured it. Sparrow Spooner lies still in the darkness, surrounded by all the other stolen children and the *ghul* pups sleeping all around her.

She's trying to find whatever it might have been that woke her, whatever interrupted the familiar, well-worn dream of Mr. Higginson buying her a Dell's lemonade and walking with her under a summer sun while he talked about all the strange and distant places they'd visit together, places like Hollywood and Miami Beach. There was *something*, a ripple, a wrinkle, the faintest stutter between one moment and the next. Something not quite déjà vu that almost anyone else would have missed, but not Sparrow Spooner, who was first in Discord and Continuity, after all, and she thinks it was not so very different from what she felt that rainy night three months ago when she stood trial and her masters and mistresses spared her life but took her fingers . . .

. . . and the Bailiff, who is not the god of men and churches or the Cuckoo or a demon or even much of a magician, who has never been anything more than the hounds needed him to be, sits with the cooling bodies of his murdered harem boys. He finishes wiping blood from the blade of the kukri onto one sleeve of his lime-green bathrobe, and glances up at the dais and the doorway connecting the octagonal chamber with the old museum in Roger Williams Park. It's been almost two hours since he last spoke with Soldier, since he appeared to her in a convenience store and she told him he looked like a circus clown. He was so, so sure that she would come, even after Woonsocket, that Soldier would bring him the child of Saben White, and when the girl was dead and crazy Willie Lothrop had taken care of Soldier, the hounds would never have been the wiser.

"Surely," he says, gazing into the dead blue eyes of one of the boys, "you cannot blame a man, not merely for trying to outwit his destiny."

The boy doesn't reply, though the Bailiff half expects him to.

"Would they spare me?" the Bailiff asks. "If I carved the lot of you up nice and neat as a butcher's window and delivered you ripe and raw, might they at least let me keep my eyes, my tongue, my hands? Might they at least spare my sorry life?"

A sudden breeze stirs the folds of silk and muslin strung from the ceiling, and the Bailiff shivers and pulls his bathrobe closed. He's unaccustomed to breezes in this place, sudden or otherwise. He glances at the dais again, an empty stage readied for players who will never now appear, and then, because time is precious, he begins the task of skinning and dressing the bodies . . .

*   *   *

. . . and in her apartment on St. Mark's Place, Sadie Jasper stands inside the sacred circle she's cast upon her bedroom floor. She holds the double-bladed athame in her good hand, her power hand, and strains to see a cleansing blue-white flame dancing about the tip of the dagger. She points the athame down and to the east, then begins walking clockwise, following the inner perimeter of the circle.

"I consecrate this circle to the Dark Mother," she says, her voice trembling, but she's sick of crying, sick of tears and blame and fear, and she takes another step. "To the Dark Mother and the Lord of the Hunt. Here may they manifest. . . ."

There's a noise from the hallway, then, a sound like wind chimes or the sea on a summer's day, and she takes a deep breath and draws a circle in the air with her dagger. "Here may they manifest," she says again, "and bless their child."

She's gone, a hard voice whispers behind her eyes. *He asked you to stay and watch her, but you were too afraid, too angry, too weak. You were weak, and you left her there alone, and now she's gone forever.*

"This is a time that is *not* a time," she says, "in a place that is *not* a place, on a day that is *not* a day. I stand here at the threshold between the worlds, before the veil. . . ."

From the hall, a sound like distant thunder.

And the voices of lost children.

And the careless, calculated shattering of one moment against the next.

Sadie takes another halting step, but now she's forgotten the protection ritual, the holy words that have never before felt so completely powerless to stand between her and all the real and imagined evils of the universe. Another step and she stumbles and breaks the unfinished circle, as the walls of her bedroom collapse and melt into steam and she finds herself standing on an immense bridge built from fire, a burning, writhing span above some chasm too vast and too deep to even comprehend.

Ahead of her, a young girl with black hair and almond skin is crossing the bridge alone, and she turns and looks back towards Sadie. *Pearl,* Sadie thinks. *Her father calls her Pearl.* And the girl's eyes sparkle in the light of the burning bridge. Sadie looks over her right shoulder, then, peering down the bridge into a dark place, a place of shadows and secrets and lies, and there's Emmie, and Sadie can see where the bridge begins.

Then, all of a moment there was a rending of the blue wall (like a curtain being torn) and a terrible white light from beyond the sky, and the feel of Aslan's mane and a Lion's kiss on their foreheads and then . . .

"They might take us to other places," Emmie said.

"Good places or bad places?" asked Sadie.

Emmie shrugged. "That remains to be seen," she said, as the bridge fades and Sadie finds herself in her bedroom on St. Mark's Place again, standing inside the ruined circle, the athame gripped tightly in her good hand. Out on the street a car horn blares, and Sadie sits down on the floor. When the tears come, she doesn't fight them . . .

. . . and when it's over, there's only a very small burn, hardly larger than a penny, perfectly centered between Emmie's yellow eyes, and the dizziness has gone and taken the nausea away with it. Pearl's gone, too, and the air in the attic of the yellow house smells like ozone and blood and dust.

"Is it done?" the little girl named Soldier asks, the child who chose her name from a headstone in Swan Point Cemetery. The gash on her cheek is gone, as are all the other scrapes and bruises, and her skin doesn't look sunburned anymore. Already, her memories of everything that's happened since the Bailiff led her up to the attic have begun to dissolve, coming apart like a cube of sugar in a cup of tea. "Was it that simple?"

Emmie gently touches the burn on her forehead, her mind still filled with the heat of the inferno and the ice of all the not-quite-empty space between worlds, with Pearl's joy and the surprise of seeing Sadie standing there on the bridge, looking back at her.

"Do you think she'll find her father?" Soldier asks. The clothes and boots that Odd Willie brought her from the Salvation Army store in Uxbridge are far too large for a girl who's not quite six years old, and she looks like she's been caught playing dress-up.

"I think she already has," Emmie says and stands up, holding on to the edge of the table, just in case the dizziness decides to come back. "I think he was waiting for her on the other side." She's not entirely sure if that's the truth, but it seems like the right thing to say, here at the end of the story, and even if it's not true, she doesn't think that it's a lie.

"What do we do now?" Soldier asks her and kicks off the ridiculous cowboy boots. "I don't think we should stay here."

"No, we definitely shouldn't stay here," Emmie replies and tries to imagine what comes next. "I have to go home," she says. "I have to go back to Deacon and Sadie."

"And I shall go back down to the hounds. Is that what I'll do, Emmie Silvey?"

"Will they hurt you?"

The child with Soldier's green eyes picks up the pistol lying on the floor, and Emmie immediately bends down and takes it away from her.

"No, I don't think they'll hurt me. I think it will take them a while to understand exactly what's happened, and then, then . . ." and Soldier trails off and stares at her hands, as if the pistol has left some stain behind that only she can see. "I won't tell them," she says to Emmie. "I won't ever tell them that you're the bridge builder."

"Thank you, Soldier. But do you think they'll *let* me leave?" Emmie asks her and lays the pistol down on the table beside the clarinet-sextant contraption. "Do you really think they'll let me go home now?"

"I don't know," Soldier says after a moment.

"Then I guess that's what happens next. I guess we find a way out of this place and see if they'll let me go home to Deacon."

"My father," Soldier says and frowns.

"He's my father, too," Emmie tells her and helps Soldier up off the dusty attic floor. When she stands, the too-big jeans slide right back down, and Soldier steps out of them. Fortunately, the sweater reaches all the way to her knees, and Emmie helps her roll up the sleeves so they don't flop down over her hands.

"Maybe I can meet him someday," Soldier says. "Maybe when I'm grown, maybe one day then."

"I think he'd like that," Emmie tells her, and she takes Soldier's left hand, and together they cross from the alchemist's workshop into the greater gloom of the attic, leaving behind the tall shelves of glass spheres filled with stolen places and Odd Willie's corpse and the pawnshop 9mm that killed him. They get lost only once, in a twisting, roundabout maze of dollhouses and dressmaker's dummies, before they reach the milking stool and trapdoor and the foldaway stairs. Miss Josephine and another silver-eyed woman, whose name is Adelaide, are waiting for them there, and at first Emmie's afraid of the pale, waxen women in their high collars and black mourning gowns. But then Miss Josephine smiles and tells her there's a taxi-cab waiting outside, a driver to take Emmie home to Angell Street, and the four of them go down the stairs, and Adelaide closes the trapdoor.

"I'll try not to forget you," Soldier tells Emmie, though she's already having trouble recalling exactly who the yellow-eyed girl is or when they met.

"A shame about Master Lothrop," Adelaide says. "I expect he'll be missed Below."

"Who?" Soldier asks and blinks up at the vampire.

"Never mind," Emmie says. "It doesn't matter anymore," and then she remembers the gold ring, the ring from the box beneath Deacon's bed, Soldier's mother's wedding ring, and takes it out of her pocket. "I want you to have this," she tells Soldier. "Maybe it'll help you remember me."

"It's pretty," Soldier says, and Emmie lays the ring in her palm.

"What's that?" Adelaide asks, bending close for a better look. "It's rather plain," and then Miss Josephine tells her to be quiet.

"Maybe you'll look at it and dream about me sometime," Emmie says, and then the two women with mercury eyes lead them downstairs.

> *Except the smaller size, no Lives are round,*
> *These hurry to a sphere, and show, and end.*
> *The larger, slower grow, and later hang—*
> *The Summers of Hesperides are long.*

> —EMILY DICKINSON

EPILOGUE

April

Upstairs in Deacon Silvey's big gray house on Angell Street, Emmie lies in her bed, listening to the rain drumming hard against the roof and the bedroom window. She was dreaming of the desert again, the desert and the black-skinned woman, and then something woke her, probably the rain or a thunderclap. She isn't surprised to find that her father's sitting at the foot of the bed, watching her. He does that a lot these days.

"Were you having a bad dream?" he asks. "You were talking in your sleep."

"I was dreaming," she replies, "but it wasn't a bad dream."

Deacon scratches his chin and nods his head.

"Why aren't you asleep?" she asks him.

"I was, but then the storm woke me, and I thought maybe I should come up and look in on you."

"I'm not afraid of thunderstorms," she says, though he already knows that.

"Yeah, well . . . maybe I am. Anyway, no harm done."

"No harm done," Emmie says sleepily and rolls over to watch the spring rain streaking the window. The dream is still fresh, and she thinks about taking out the journal that Sadie bought her and writing down all of it she can remember. Sadie says her dreams are magick, the most powerful magick that Sadie's ever seen, and that one day they'll help her to become a very powerful witch, if that's what she wants. Deacon says they're only dreams and to ignore Sadie whenever she starts talking like that, but even he thought the dream journal was a good idea.

"Do you want me to go away?" Deacon asks.

"No," Emmie says. "Sit with me until I fall asleep again," and he says that he will.

I'm much too sleepy to write anything down, Emmie thinks, hoping that she'll still remember the dream in the morning. Climbing up and over the dunes with Esmeribetheda, guarding the memories of the dead, and finally they'd come to a rocky place looking down on the sea.

"They have their suspicions," Esmeribetheda said, and Emmie knew that she meant the ghouls. "They are watching you, always, Emmie. One day, when you're older, they may come for you."

"I won't help them. I already made that decision," Emmie told her and sat down in the shade of a huge red rock. There was a lizard beneath the rock, and it winked at her and then crawled quickly away.

"You may have to make it again."

"That doesn't seem fair," Emmie told her.

"No," the black-skinned woman said. "It doesn't seem fair at all."

And then Emmie woke up to the storm and Deacon at the foot of her bed.

"I should leave," he says. "And you should get back to sleep, kiddo. Tomorrow's a school day."

"It's already tomorrow, Deacon."

"My point exactly," he says. Before he goes, Deacon kisses her on the forehead, presses his rough lips to the small pink scar between her eyes. His breath doesn't smell like beer or whiskey; it hasn't for a long time, now.

"You want me to turn Doris Day back on?"

"No," Emmie says. "That's okay. I think I just want to hear the rain for a while."

"Yeah, the rain's good," Deacon Silvey says, and then he leaves her, and Emmie watches the storm at the window until she finds her way back down to sleep and unfinished dreams.

About the Author

Caitlín R. Kiernan has written seven novels, including *Threshold, Low Red Moon,* and *Daughter of Hounds,* and her short fiction has been collected in four volumes—*Tales of Pain and Wonder; From Weird and Distant Shores; To Charles Fort, With Love;* and *Alabaster.* Trained as a vertebrate paleontologist, she lives in Atlanta, Georgia.

Web sites:

www.caitlinrkiernan.com

greygirlbeast.livejournal.com